SURVIVAL GAME

Gary Gibson

SURVIVAL GAME

TOR

First published 2016 by Tor
an imprint of Pan Macmillan
20 New Wharf Road, London N1 9RR
Associated companies throughout the world
www.panmacmillan.com

ISBN 978-0-230-77277-9

1 3 5 7 9 8 6 4 2

A CIP catalogue record for this book is available from the British Library.

Typeset by Ellipsis Digital Limited, Glasgow
Printed and bound by CPI Group (UK) Ltd, Croydon, CR0 4YY

Acknowledgements

I owe a debt of gratitude to my editor Bella Pagan for her enormous input into multiple drafts of this book. Thanks also go to my agent John Jarrold. Also appreciated is input from Jim Campbell regarding weaponry, and from Jamie Scott regarding acts of sabotage. Thanks also go to my wife, Emma, for her continued suport and encouragement.

SURVIVAL GAME

PROLOGUE

Takhterum Old Quarter, Alternate Two-Seven-Six
A Long Time Ago

Exhaustion nearly overwhelms Lars Ulven before he can ascend to the top of the university's tower. He stumbles, hands clutching at the topmost steps, so that he almost has to crawl the final distance to the stone balustrade. He leans on it heavily, breathing hard, almost shaking from the effort, but filled with a need to look at the streets below and see if there is anyone, anywhere, still alive.

The skies of this alternate, at least, are empty of the invaders: no dark forbidding shapes falling out of the sky and destroying whatever they touch. Lars looks out across the still green waters of the Bosphorus towards the city's Public Transfer Facility, a vast pyramid rising from its artificial island at the mouth of the river. Closer to hand lies the city's Old Quarter, dominated by ancient domes and minarets that glisten beneath the afternoon sun. But instead of the bustle of street markets and music, and the dance of holographic displays, there are only deserted avenues, abandoned vehicles and a terrible, unending silence.

Lars makes his way back down to the university's transfer facility and crosses to Alternate One-Nine-Four. Takhterum becomes Kushta: once again, Lars seeks out the version of the tower that exists in this universe, and counts the steps as he climbs to the top. There are two hundred and fifty-six. There are always two hundred and fifty-six.

Once again, he sees only empty streets and hears only the thin wail of the wind.

The Syllogikos is a single culture spread across hundreds of parallel Earths, linked one to the other by transfer gates. Within the Syllogikos are two hundred and seventy-three iterations of this city on the Bosphorus, nearly all of which contain, in turn, some version of this university. In some alternates the streets are spread wide, while in others they are squeezed close together. In some, the tallest buildings rise no more than five or six storeys, while in others vaulting towers of steel and glass reach all the way to the clouds.

Since the invasion from the Deeps began, Lars has visited barely more than a dozen of the alternate universes that make up the Syllogikos. And yet everywhere he goes, he finds only the silence and stillness of death.

He comes very close to climbing onto the balustrade and throwing himself to his death. Then he thinks of his daughter, and somehow he finds the willpower to make his way back down into the bowels of Kushta's university.

Lars sleeps that night in an office picked at random. He dreams of his wife, her hand slipping from his grasp, of the surging, panicked crowd around the transfer stage, of the great dark shapes of the invaders floating down to swallow terrified refugees in their thousands. He sits up, gasping like a drowning man, and searches through his rucksack for the tiny carved box he has carried through universe after universe. He opens it and picks out the string of memory beads, shuffling them through his fingers one after the other and sinking briefly into the memories with which each one is encoded. His favourite is of his daughter when she was still a little girl, running in the field by the house when he was only just starting his career in the sciences.

If there is even the slimmest chance his daughter Erika is still alive, he cannot allow himself to give up.

His hunt goes on. Kushta becomes Fu-Lin; Fu-Lin becomes Istambol, then Constantinople, then Chalcedon, and on and on, the name of the city morphing and shifting in line with the buildings and streets as he travels from alternate to alternate.

Often, on arriving at an alternate, he finds the control console for the transfer stage has been wrecked, in the misguided belief that this could halt the spread of the destruction. On such occasions, he is forced to hunt through supply cupboards and break into equipment bays in order to locate the portable stage he needs to continue on to the next universe.

It is not long before he comes to the conclusion that his search is hopeless, that there cannot be a single unaffected alternate the length and breadth of the Syllogikos. If there is anyone left alive, they must be located in those alternate universes that are *not* part of the Syllogikos – those of interest solely to the scientific and research community.

And that, at least, is a community Lars knows better than any other.

Lars travels back home to Alternate Seventeen. From here, as head of research, he has led numerous expeditions to dozens of unexplored parallel Earths – some populated, some not, and some with such wildly divergent histories that they might as well have been alien worlds.

Once there, he quickly locates a list of all the alternates currently under investigation by the Eschatologists, the group of which his daughter is a member. Unsurprisingly, every last one of the alternate universes on the list is a post-extinction reality. In Lars' eyes, the Eschatologists are little more than a death cult, religious fanatics obsessed with the apocalyptic end of worlds.

He visits nearly a dozen of these in quick succession, searching the forward bases established on each by the Eschatologists. Despite his efforts, he finds no clue as to where Erika and her husband might have gone.

On one, in an abandoned laboratory, he stumbles across an uncalibrated Hypersphere – one of the devices responsible for the destruction of the Syllogikos. He uses a chunk of rebar to smash it over and over until it crumples on one side and turns forever dark.

Then, at last, the miracle.

This time, when he steps off a transfer stage and out through the wide doors of a hangar, he finds himself on a semi-tropical island with a deserted town nearby. The Eschatologists have, as elsewhere, vandalized all of their equipment, although the transfer stages remain functional. He remembers visiting this alternate years before, when Erika had only just joined the Eschatologists and they were still – just – on speaking terms.

He discovers amidst a pile of discarded luggage a purse containing more memory beads, much like the ones he carries in a carved wooden box. He shuffles these new beads through his fingers, and they throw up a plethora of images and memories that clearly belong to his daughter. He catches glimpses of her husband, as well as some of their fellow Eschatologists. One bead records her memories of a statue that gazes out across a desolate cavern, its bearded face full of anguished sorrow.

Once, Erika told him of this statue, and the post-apocalyptic alternate of which it is part, and of how she and her husband hoped to set up a religious retreat there one day.

A getaway for fanatics, he had said dismissively. Even so, it is the first real clue he has found to her whereabouts, and he still has the coordinates for that alternate. She is all that is left of his former life, and he knows he cannot rest until he knows she is safe.

He quickly gathers what he needs, then climbs onto one of the island's two stages, his heart full of desperate hope as the light transports him to yet another universe.

When he materializes at his destination, Lars finds himself immersed in a darkness so profound it is almost physically tangible. He drops to his knees, fumbling through the heavy canvas bag he has brought with him, until he finds a torch. He shines it around, seeing he is at the centre of a portable transfer stage set amidst ruins. Perhaps he was wrong and his daughter is not here. Worse, perhaps she has been taken by the invaders, as uncountable millions already have, and his search is in vain. Even so he shouts her name into still air that smells of mould and damp earth, unpleasantly reminiscent of a graveyard.

It is only when he is on the verge of giving up that he finally hears voices, coming closer.

There are six survivors, all bedraggled, dirty and tired-looking by the light of their own torches. His daughter Erika is amongst them, her husband Brent by her side. Suddenly she is in Lars' arms, crying so hard she can hardly speak. When Lars looks past her, however, he sees only disapproval on Brent's face.

'Lars,' says Brent, fixing a smile on his face as he shakes his father-in-law's hand, 'how did you find us?'

'With difficulty,' Lars replies and looks around the others. 'How many more of you are there?'

'This is all of us that's left,' says Brent, his voice clipped. Lars senses he is far from welcome, even amidst disaster. 'You shouldn't have come here, Lars.'

'Is there anyone else left out there?' a brown-skinned girl with large, frightened eyes asks him.

Lars shakes his head. 'You're the first living people I've seen in nearly two weeks.' He starts to elaborate, but the words choke in his throat. 'There's something all of you need to see,' he says finally.

Brent's face settles into an unreadable mask. 'We have a camp,' he says, nodding back the way they came. 'Come and eat first, then we can talk.'

'Here,' says Lars, once he has shared some of their meagre rations, taking out the carved wooden box and passing it to Erika.

They are huddled around a campfire amidst the ancient ruins. Light glows softly from within tents. She opens the box, seeing the string of beads within. She lifts them out carefully, laying the beads across the back of her hand so they do not come into prolonged contact with her fingertips or palms.

'Memory beads?' she asks.

He nods. 'Everything you need to know is in them.' He looks around the rest of the survivors. 'They prove the Hyperspheres are the cause of the invasion.'

Erika frowns. 'But . . . how is that even possible? They're just transportation devices.'

'No, our transfer stages are "just" transportation devices. The Hyperspheres are much, much more than that.'

'But how could they . . . ?'

'I don't know the exact mechanism,' Lars explains. 'Given time, I could work it out.' He gestures towards the beads. 'Please. I spent a long time gathering the evidence. It's all there.'

The beads glint dully in the firelight as Erika shuffles them through her fingers, one after the other. Her pupils dilate, and almost a full minute passes before she takes a sudden, sharp inward breath and drops the beads back into the box.

'Oh God,' she says faintly. 'It was like reliving it all over again, seeing them falling out of the sky . . .'

'You see that the invaders originate from the Deeps – from universes with different physics from ours, universes that cannot support life as we know or understand it.' But life of a kind is there, nonetheless: he knows this now.

She nods uncertainly and Lars frowns. How could she doubt the evidence, presented so clearly? But then he looks at Brent, his mouth set in a thin, angry line, his shoulders and neck rigid with tension.

The box is passed around the fire until all have taken their turn with the beads – all except Brent. He darts an angry look at Lars, then finally shuffles them through his own fingers.

'Now you see?' says Lars, when his son-in-law drops them back into the wooden box. 'If I'd known then what I know now, we might have been able to prevent this disaster from ever happening.'

Brent stands, then, every muscle in his body trembling, his face a mask of furious rage. The rest watch him with terrified, silent eyes. Lars is appalled by their submissiveness, and he understands for the first time that they look to Brent as their leader.

'There may be other survivors out there, on other, equally remote alternates,' Lars continues, hoping to calm the man down. 'We have to try and find them, but we need to work together if we're going to survive.' He gestures to the shadows all around. 'Skulking in some hellish tomb isn't going to help us survive and rebuild, Brent.'

Erika stands and tries to take her husband's hand, but he shakes her off, storming away into the darkness.

Lars sleeps fitfully that night, the box of memories close by his side. He dreams of feet shuffling around him, of whispers in the darkness. When finally he wakes and reaches out to the box, he finds it is no longer there.

He sits up quickly, searching frantically all around. His bag is gone as well – along with the portable stage he had packed inside it.

For a terrible heart-rending moment, he fears the memory beads have been thrown into the campfire. But then Brent steps into view, the box held tightly in one hand. Erika is by his side, but she does not meet his eyes.

Lars turns, seeing that the rest of the group are awake as well, standing in a half-circle on the far side of the campfire, watching him with fearful expressions.

'These,' says Brent, raising the box in his hand, 'are lies.' He throws the box far into the shadows, spilling its contents amidst the ruins. 'God chose us to inherit the coming world, not you.'

Lars sits frozen. 'I don't understand.'

'I've dedicated my life to sifting through the ruins of endless extinct alternates, looking for the evidence of holy judgement,' says Brent. He pounds his chest with a fist, eyes bright with madness. 'Then I realized my hubris. By looking for God, I had doubted Him. He requires faith, not evidence. It took the invasion for me to understand that it was our turn to await judgement.'

Erika finally meets her father's gaze. She looks pale, but determined, and he realizes that the little girl he remembers running through a field is long gone. Brent is right: he should never have come here.

For the first time, he notices the sledgehammer gripped in one of his son-in-law's hands. Brent's chest is heaving, as if he has just exerted a great deal of effort.

Lars stands, filled with a terrible chill. 'What have you done?' he demands, his voice hoarse.

'God guided us here,' says Brent. 'And here we stay.'

Lars snatches up his torch and flees into the darkness, soon finding his way back to the transfer stage that first brought him to this dreadful place. When he sees the kicked-over field-pillars and smashed control unit, his throat constricts with horror, the high ceiling of the cavern seeming to press down on him until the air is choked from his lungs. Next to it lies his canvas bag, and the smashed remains of the portable stage.

Lars falls to his knees in the dust and the blackness. Without being entirely aware of it, his hand reaches down to grasp a chunk of loose masonry. He stares off into the dark until he hears footsteps approach.

He turns to see Erika looking down at him, Brent by her side. The others are there, too, hanging back in the darkness.

'You've murdered us all,' says Lars, choking the words out as he stands. 'And murdered my daughter, damn you!'

Brent looks back at him. 'You don't understand now, but you will. Give yourself to God, Lars. Pray with us, and you'll find peace.'

And with that, Lars lets out a roar, swinging the heavy lump of stone against Brent's skull with every ounce of strength he can muster. Brent staggers and falls, the blood pouring down the side of his face.

Erika's screams echo far through the empty air for a long time. But eventually there is only darkness, and silence.

ONE

West African Principality,
Twelfth Republic of the Novo-Rossiyskaya Imperiya
Now

From the moment I saw their broad, Slavic faces and long dark coats, I knew they were agents of the Tsar. The two men stood together at the far end of the swaying train carriage, questioning the water merchant who had set up pitch there.

I wondered how they had found us so quickly. Our last stop had been at N'Djamena, barely a few minutes before; they must have got on board then. It was just by luck that I had spotted them on my way to buy water.

I retreated into the compartment and slid the door shut. Tomas looked around from the carriage window. He had spent most of our journey staring moodily at the lush green hills in the distance.

'They've found us,' I said, unable to hide my terror. 'Imperial agents. Herr Frank must have sent them.'

His face grew pale. 'Are you sure?'

I nodded sharply. 'Very sure, yes.'

He swallowed and licked his lips, fingers gripping his thighs. 'Then we have no choice but to turn back.'

'Tomas, we can't, not after coming all this way.'

'Katya, it's our only choice! If they know we're here, we have to get off this train and . . . and trek back to N'Djamena. At least then we'd be able to try and find some other way north!'

I pointed out of the window at the scrubby terrain whipping by. 'You can't be serious,' I said. 'Look how fast the train is going! Not to mention it's the middle of nowhere and over forty degrees out there. We can't just—'

'There's no time,' he said, pushing past me and sliding the compartment door back open. He peered cautiously left and right along the corridor. 'I don't see them. They must have gone into one of the other compartments.' He reached back in and grabbed my hand. 'Now *come on*.'

He led me out into the corridor. We were in the last carriage, and we hurried to the end, Tomas slamming open the door. Raw heat baked through my clothes in an instant, drenching my skin in sweat. I looked down, seeing the rails and patchy clumps of grass whip by in a blur. The rattle and thunder of the wheels was deafening.

'Are you insane?' I shouted over the noise. 'We'll be killed!'

He pulled me close and kissed me. 'We have no choice,' he shouted back.

Before I could raise any further objections, he had swept one arm around my waist and lifted us both up and over the safety rail. I screamed as we fell, rolling and tumbling down an embankment, the force of the impact driving the air from my lungs.

Once I had come to a stop, I pulled myself into a crouch with my face pressed against the hard black soil, tasting sand and grit in my mouth. My ribs ached more than I would have believed possible. It was a miracle I hadn't broken my neck.

I looked up, and saw that the train had already receded far into the distance.

I dragged myself upright and looked around until I saw Tomas lying sprawled on his side in the dust several metres away. When I stumbled over to him, I saw he had both hands wrapped around one thigh, his teeth bared in a snarl.

But at least he was alive.

I dropped onto my knees beside him. 'I might have broken something,' he gasped.

'Can you stand?'

He shook his head tightly. 'I don't know.'

I hooked an arm around his shoulder and managed to ease him upright. He leaned on me heavily. I kept expecting the train to grind to a slow halt, and the two agents to jump down and come running back for us with their guns drawn. Instead it continued into the far distance and out of sight.

The heat already made it hard to think clearly. I thought longingly of the water merchant, his steel insulated trolley loaded with ice-cold jugs of water. Just another few hours on the train, and we would have reached the rebel-held territories . . .

It wasn't worth thinking about. With a little bit of effort, Tomas was able to take first one step, then another, and then another.

After a while, Tomas found the going a little easier, though he still had to lean on me most of the way. It took several hours more than it should have to walk back to N'Djamena, but by the time the sun began to drop towards the horizon we had reached the city's outskirts. I was soon able to locate a store, where I bought water and other supplies.

'N'Djamena isn't Free Africa,' said Tomas, once he'd had something to eat, 'but it's close. If we can find the right people, someone might be able to help us get the rest of the way.'

13

'And if they're the wrong people?'

Tomas didn't reply at first, and I immediately regretted my words. If not for him, we might never have got even this far.

'They won't be,' he said at last. 'And even if they are, we still have this.' He patted the bulge in his jacket where a pistol was concealed.

I resisted the urge to say that since he had never shot anyone in his life, I doubted whether he had it in him to do so now.

The streets were still busy even at this late hour. N'Djamena, on this alternate at least, was a frontier town. Mosques and churches stood side by side with bars, tobacco shops and trading posts. From time to time a few people approached us from out of the gloom, looking for easy pickings, but Tomas warded them off by showing them his pistol. Instead of jeering at us and snatching his weapon from his grasp, as I half-expected them to do, they vanished back into the shadows.

'Wait,' Tomas croaked, still leaning on me heavily. With a nod of his head, he indicated a blocky whitewashed building with smoky dark windows and a twisted neon sign above the door. 'We can try in there. It's as good as anywhere else we've seen.'

Despite my trepidation, I helped him inside the bar and into a booth. There were perhaps three or four customers at most, but I felt the eyes of every one of them following us as we entered. A broken screen above the bar ghosted fuzzy holographic images: a news report about General Yakov leading the Tsar's imperial forces against the rebels on this alternate.

The bartender was a gangly Sudanese with tribal scars on his cheeks. I bought something to drink and asked him how I might go about buying a vehicle, without specifying exactly how far I intended to go and in what direction. As I did so, I drew out the small metal token I had been given by a contact at the Khartoum inter-parallel transfer facility: an imperial coin, with the symbol of the revolution stamped over the Tsar's face.

The bartender gave me a knowing look, and I listened to the thudding of my heart, unsure how he might react. But then he directed me in halting Russian to speak to a man sitting in a shadowed corner, and twenty minutes later, at the cost of all our remaining money, I had somehow managed to negotiate the purchase of an all-terrain vehicle that had once, apparently, belonged to a goat-herder.

I excused myself briefly and went back over to Tomas. 'He'll know we're on the run,' he said. 'You didn't tell him where we were going, did you?'

'We're two white people speaking Russian on the edge of Free North Africa, who just wandered out of the desert and bought transport in cash from a random stranger in a bar,' I said. 'Where the hell else would we be going but north? The only reason anyone comes here any more at all is because they're headed that way.'

'You know, he could probably make a lot more money by selling us to Yakov. We're obviously on the run.'

'You said yourself we had no choice,' I snapped in irritation. I glanced around the bar, in time to see multiple pairs of eyes suddenly look the other way. 'He has no idea who we are, anyway.'

The man I had spoken to walked past us and headed for the door. He glanced back at me, then pushed the door open and stepped outside.

'I think he wants us to go with him,' I said, helping Tomas stand.

'Here,' he said, turning away from the rest of the bar and

pressing his pistol into my hands. 'I can barely stand, let alone shoot. Just in case he tries anything funny. There's no law here, Katya, unless you count General Yakov.'

Outside, the wind blew grit in my eyes. The man led us several blocks before presenting us with a battered, open-top all-terrain that was clearly worth a tiny fraction of what we were paying for it. Even so, I gave him the last of our money and we soon left N'Djamena behind, racing along beneath a wind-battered moon. I drove while Tomas slumped beside me.

We had been underway for a couple of hours when Tomas glanced up at the night sky. 'Do you hear something?'

'No,' I said. I could hear hardly anything over the rattle and thump of the engine.

He frowned. 'I can hear *something*.'

Then, at last, my ear picked it out of the noise of the engine and the wind: a thin, high-pitched whine that seemed to come from somewhere directly above us. I looked up, but could see nothing in the darkness.

I glanced at him uneasily. 'It's probably just some surveillance drone that wandered off-course. We can't be that far from the fighting.'

Tomas kept his attention fixed overhead. 'I swear, I think it's coming closer.'

I listened again. It *did* sound louder than it had a moment before . . .

Tomas reached out, grabbing hold of the wheel and twisting it so that we slewed off the road.

'Tomas!' I shouted, 'what are you—?'

'Just keep your feet on the pedals!'

The whine faded – then grew stronger once more, finding its way back above us.

'Is it tracking us?' I asked, when he let me have the wheel back again.

'Of course it's tracking us,' he said. 'I think we're going to have to—'

Suddenly, the desert all around lit up as bright as day. I glanced up, seeing the outline of an unmanned drone against moonlit clouds.

Something slammed into the desert floor directly in front of us, kicking up a great fountain of dust and dirt. The transport crashed to a sudden halt as its front wheels fell into a hole that hadn't been there a moment before.

I swallowed and coughed on the choking dust billowing through the shattered windscreen. My vision was blurred, but I could hear a rumble of car engines, coming closer.

'Tomas?' I felt for him next to me. 'Are you all right?'

'It's too late, Katya,' he mumbled, his speech slurred. 'They've found us.'

I blinked and looked out through the windscreen. A troop-carrier rolled to a halt before us, disgorging half a dozen troops with imperial insignia on their uniforms. Moments later, a black limousine pulled up next to it.

The troops came forward and hauled us out of the transport. One pushed a gun against my head. I watched as Herr Frank, wearing a long dark overcoat despite the dusty heat, emerged from the limousine, followed by the two imperial agents and the man who had sold us the transport. The man looked dazed, his face covered in cuts and bruises.

'Very good work,' said Herr Frank. He nodded at the man from the bar. 'We don't need him any more.'

'Sir,' said one of the agents, drawing a gun and shooting the man in the head.

I watched in horror as he crumpled, lifeless, to the ground.

I barely had the strength to protest when one of the soldiers pulled a black hood over my head.

TWO

Department of Okhrana Special Operations,
St Petersburg,
First Republic of the Novo-Rossiyskaya Imperiya
Two Days Later

'Gospodin Borodin?'

The man whom Herr Frank had addressed turned from the window at which he stood. He had deep-set eyes and thinning dark hair, and hollow cheeks that gave him a consumptive appearance. His gaze briefly passed over Tomas and me, taking in our bruised faces and plastic cuffs, then moved on to Herr Frank, standing beside us at the door, along with two guards.

'Thank you, Herr Frank,' said Borodin. 'You can remove their cuffs. It won't be necessary for you to be present.'

Herr Frank blinked. 'These two are my responsibility. I should be there throughout their interrog—'

'You can wait downstairs until I'm finished,' said Borodin. 'That is final.'

I risked a glance at Herr Frank and saw a muscle twitch in his bony cheek. 'Gospodin Borodin, I must insist that—'

'Do as I ask,' Borodin interrupted him, 'or you can explain to the Tsar in person how you let these two escape in the first place.'

Herr Frank grew pale, but spun on his heel and spat orders at the two guards. They removed our cuffs and then departed with Herr Frank, pulling the heavy double doors shut behind them.

'Well,' said Borodin, turning to us and gesturing towards two chairs placed side by side at the centre of the room. 'Sit. We have a lot to talk about.'

I glanced at Tomas, his face as full of indecision and fear as my own, then sat carefully, massaging my sore wrists. After a moment, Tomas did the same.

Apart from an antique-looking desk standing in one corner, the room was bare of furnishings or personal effects of any kind. A pistol lay on the desk, next to several dark green folders and a heavy lighter set in a block of onyx. Borodin pulled a drawer open and removed a slim steel case, from which he tapped out a single cigarette. He touched it with the lighter, then breathed blue smoke into the air. Bare-branched trees swayed in a late autumn breeze through the tall windows behind him.

'My name is Mikhail Borodin,' said the man, 'and yours are Katya Orlova and Tomas Szandor. I gather you're a native of the Twelfth Republic, Mr Szandor – I suppose that helped you get as far as you did.'

Tomas nodded warily.

Borodin sat on the edge of the desk and touched a finger to one of the green folders by him. 'I've been studying your records. Both of you were separately found guilty of seditious activities some years ago. You, Miss Orlova, were sentenced at the same time as your father and a number of his colleagues.' He took another drag on his cigarette, and smoke jetted from his nostrils. 'Instead of execution, the Tsar decreed that you should all be permitted to continue your work in exile at

Herr Frank's research facility at the Crag. Can you tell me why that is?'

'It was felt that we could best repay our disloyalty by further-ing the greater glory of the Novo-Rossiyskaya Imperiya,' I said, repeating words that had been drilled into me almost from the moment I had arrived at the Crag.

'And what,' asked Borodin, 'has been the primary focus of your work over the last ten years?'

I hesitated. 'Don't those folders tell you?'

Borodin regarded me critically. 'I am not a scientist, Miss Orlova. There are things I would wish you to explain to me in terms I might clearly understand. So far, the primary focus of your collective research has been the Hypersphere. Am I correct?'

I nodded.

'Explain to me what it is, if you will, Miss Orlova,' he said. 'In layman's terms.'

'A technological artefact recovered from an abandoned Syllogikos base,' I replied, 'designed for the purpose of estab-lishing stable traversable links to alternate universes.'

'What makes the Hypersphere different from, say, the trans-fer stages the Empire already uses to achieve that same end?'

'It can take months – more often, years – to identify even a single viable alternate using our current methods. These methods further necessitate the use of exotic forms of matter, which are enormously difficult to refine and store even in trace amounts.' I spoke with growing confidence: this was a subject I knew well, after all. 'By contrast, the Hypersphere – at least according to the historians of the Syllogikos, before they dis-appeared – can establish a link with *any* imaginable alternate – instantaneously – merely by holding it in one's hands.'

'Then why did the people of the Syllogikos bother with

transfer stages, if they were capable of creating such wondrous devices?'

I shook my head. 'They didn't create it. All the evidence points to it having been created by some other, presumably older and certainly more advanced, civilization whose ruins they probably encountered in the course of their own explorations.'

'And they just *stumbled* across it?'

I nodded. 'Much the same as an Imperial survey expedition "stumbled" across an abandoned Syllogikos transfer stage on our own First Republic, yes. Or at least,' I added, 'that is our primary conjecture.'

'And it can take one to *any* imaginable destination? What if I were to ask the Hypersphere to take me to Heaven, or even Hell?'

'Nothing, Gospodin Borodin. Those are abstract and supernatural concepts only. But even then, the multiverse allows for a near-infinite range of possibilities—'

'Yes, yes,' said Borodin, sounding impatient. 'I take your point. Now – will one of you tell me why it is, after all these years of study, and despite your collective scientific acumen, none of you has managed even once to make the Hypersphere function in the way it was supposedly intended to?'

I felt a sudden, sharp spike of terror. 'There are still avenues of research to be explored,' I replied in a babble. 'The algorithms that control the Hypersphere's internal systems have not been mapped out in their entirety. It might be possible that with sufficient time—'

Borodin sighed and put a hand up to stop me. 'I assume you are afraid to tell me the truth, because you fear punishment for your collective failure.'

I said nothing.

He picked up one of the green folders again and held it high. 'Herr Frank, as part of his administrative duties at the Crag, provides the Tsar's security services with regular detailed reports about your work – and every one of them, I assure you, is a masterpiece of obfuscation.' He dropped the folder back down with a slap. 'His reports are designed not so much to inform, as to prolong the period of time that he remains in charge of the Crag and the Hypersphere research project. The longer you take to achieve any real results, the more comfort-able he becomes in his sinecure. However, matters have recently come to something of a head.'

Borodin reached across the desk and picked up the pistol, then held it loosely in his lap without pointing it directly at either of us.

I heard Tomas swear quietly under his breath.

'Let me rephrase my question,' said Borodin. '*Can* the Hypersphere you've been picking apart all these years ever be made to do what the Syllogikos said it could?'

My heart beat so wildly I found it difficult to speak. 'When . . . when it was found, it turned out to have been severely damaged, Gospodin Borodin. The only reason we know as much as we do about it is because some of the Syllogikos' records survived the vandalism its own people appear to have inflicted on every one of their bases we've found.'

'Would it be reasonable to suggest,' asked Borodin, 'that contrary to Herr Frank's reports, the artefact is in fact so badly damaged that it is unlikely to *ever* function?'

'Reasonable?' Tomas sneered at Borodin. 'Is locking us all up in some remote fucking prison just so we can find a way to make the Tsar young again *reasonable*? As if conquering entire alternates and enslaving their populations wasn't bad enough!'

'Ah. You speak at last, Mr Szandor. You came very close to

stealing away one of our most brilliant minds and handing her over to our enemies.'

'Maybe you should ask Herr Frank why it was so damn easy for me to hack into the Crag's computer network,' Tomas snarled, his hands gripping the sides of his chair. 'It was all there – the truth behind why we wasted so many years locked up in that Godforsaken shit-hole, just so that drooling cretin you call a Tsar could grab himself a few more years on the throne. As far as I'm concerned, you and him and all the rest of them can go fuck yoursel—'

Borodin raised the pistol from his lap and shot Tomas three times in the chest in rapid succession. The force of the impact threw him backwards. He landed in a sprawl on the floor and lay unmoving.

I stared at his corpse, a keening sound fighting its way up from my throat before I managed to find the words to speak.

'Why . . . why did you . . . ?'

'Mr Szandor was not essential,' said Borodin. He pressed a button set into one corner of the desk. I heard a faint buzzing from somewhere outside the double doors. 'You, unfortunately, are. Now, if you could answer my question?'

'I'm sorry?'

'Is the Hypersphere too badly damaged for it to ever function again?'

I swallowed hard and nodded, my eyes fixed on the weapon once again resting on Borodin's lap. 'Yes. Yes, it is.'

'Thank you,' Borodin said drily. 'That's actually more of a straight answer than I've heard from Herr Frank in nearly ten years. I gather much of what we've learned about the Hypersphere is thanks to you, Miss Orlova.'

The doors swung open, and the same two guards stepped into the room. 'Clean this up,' said Borodin. They saluted, then grabbed hold of Tomas by a leg and arm and unceremoniously dragged his body back out through the doors, pulling them shut as they went. A trail of smeared blood marked his passage.

'Now, Katya,' said Borodin, 'I want you to focus. Look at me.'

By an effort of will, I turned back from the doors and looked at Borodin. I felt sure I would never leave that room alive.

'Herr Frank,' said Borodin, 'was recently given orders that, should the Hypersphere programme fail to produce conclusive results within the next six months, all of the research personnel under his supervision are to be executed. That means you, your father, and all the rest of the exiles held in the Crag. However, there has been a new development, one that even Herr Frank is not yet aware of: we have learned of the existence of a second Hypersphere – and an undamaged one at that.'

'A . . . second Hypersphere . . . ?'

Borodin placed his pistol back on the desk beside him. 'What I'm about to tell you is a state secret, Katya, so listen very carefully. For a few years now, we have known of the existence of another civilization that, like our own, is in possession of transfer stage technology. And like us, they are engaged in exploring Earths parallel to their own.'

'You mean . . . the Syllogikos? But they disappeared long ago.'

Borodin shook his head. 'No. Not the Syllogikos.'

He handed me a folder – a blue one, its cover stamped with warnings. My hands were shaking so badly that I had some difficulty opening it. I gazed blankly at the pages within. After witnessing Tomas' murder, the words might as well have been in Swahili.

'As you'll see,' said Borodin, as I stared down, 'this other civilization refers to the Syllogikos as "Stage Builders".' He moved to stand beside me and slid a photograph out of the back of the folder in my hands, placing it on top of the pages. It showed several men and women, all standing grinning in front of a number of huge metal shelves piled high with an assortment of unidentifiable machinery of all shapes and sizes. Just barely visible in the shadows behind them was a Hypersphere, mounted in a cradle.

The shock of seeing an intact Hypersphere was almost enough to make me forget what had just happened. 'Do they know what it is? Or what it can do?'

'Not at all. Their understanding of Syllogikos science is, so far as my spies can ascertain, extremely limited.'

'Then . . . why are you telling me all this?'

'Your insight regarding the Hypersphere makes you well-suited to a very specific task I require of you. Consider it recompense for your escape attempt. You will identify on which specific alternate this Hypersphere is located, and then travel there to assess whether it is indeed operational. If it is, you will aid one of our agents in its retrieval. Because this will initially require infiltrating this other civilization, you will undergo a period of training specific to your mission, before being embedded amongst them with a cover identity sufficient to allow you to pass as one of them.'

I struggled to take all of this in. 'Gospodin Borodin,' I said, 'I am no spy.'

'You and Tomas managed to subvert the Crag's security systems and escape from a secure penal facility in one alternate, before escaping to another. I think you're entirely qualified. If you manage this, then you, your father and all of your colleagues will, I assure you, remain alive. But from this point on you take orders only from me, and you will not see your father or anyone else until this task is completed. Is this understood?'

I licked suddenly dry lips, my head full of a deep bass thrumming. I knew to refuse would mean a bullet in the head. 'Yes.'

'Good.' He pressed the buzzer again and stepped back towards the window, studying the view. Footsteps approached and the double doors again swung open to admit Herr Frank, his face a mask of fury.

Borodin turned from the window. 'Herr Frank, Miss Orlova will remain with me until further notice. I trust the details of our . . . arrangement remain satisfactory to you.'

Herr Frank regarded the other man with hard, flat eyes. 'Please wait outside a moment, Miss Orlova. I wish to discuss something.'

I hesitated, then Borodin gave me a small nod. 'Wait in the outer office, Miss Orlova.'

I made my way through the double doors and sat in the chair that was the only furniture in the room beyond. Herr Frank slammed the doors shut, leaving me alone. I stared dully at the streaks of blood on the tiles. No tears came, no grief. At least, not yet.

I looked around. Another set of doors leading back into the corridor were also closed. I got up and tentatively tried the handle, but they were locked.

I stepped back over to the chair, then paused. I could hear muffled shouting coming through the doors leading into Borodin's office: the two men were arguing loudly.

I glanced up, seeing a narrow transom window situated above the office doors. Most of what I could hear was coming through it.

A sudden, powerful impulse gripped me. The chair was upholstered and set into a heavy wooden frame. It could easily take my weight. I pushed it up next to one of the doors, then clambered on top of it, kicking off a shoe for ease of balance before placing my bare foot on top of its backrest. I hauled myself up, catching hold of the lip of the upper door frame beneath the transom window by my fingertips.

The chair teetered dangerously beneath me, and for one panicked moment I thought I might be sent tumbling to the floor. But then I managed to steady myself enough that I could lean in close to the transom and hear what they were saying:

'. . . The Tsar is unsatisfied with your progress, Herr Frank, but this is the last straw. We cannot – *cannot* – afford to be discovered. If Dmitri's agents had got to those two before you did, I doubt even the Tsar could save our necks.'

'Prince Dmitri will find out nothing,' Herr Frank replied, his voice cold and angry. 'Nor are you in any position to make demands, not since your demot—'

I heard a sharp intake of breath. 'Let go of me,' I heard Herr Frank say, his voice full of outrage. 'Damn you, *let*—'

'Listen to me,' said Borodin, so quietly that I had to strain to hear. 'Just because Dmitri handed my department to some puppet of his doesn't make a difference. All that matters is that the Tsar has at most a few months to live, perhaps less. And I am not the only one with close ties to him, *Herr Frank*. We have no choice but to help each other, because if we fail, the instant Dmitri takes the throne he'll eliminate anyone loyal to his father – and you and I will find ourselves kneeling over a ditch with a gun against the back of our heads. Do you understand me?'

'I understand perfectly,' said Herr Frank.

'Remember – this must remain between the two of us, and no one else.'

'Of course.' Herr Frank's voice sounded distant, terse.

'I am not so lacking in resources as you seem to think. The girl will undergo training. And you still command the Crag.'

'So long as Dmitri doesn't find out what we're up to,' said Herr Frank. 'There are rumours his network of spies rivals your own.'

'Then you had better get back there,' said Borodin, 'and make sure he doesn't. Is that understood?'

I listened for more, but heard nothing. Then came the sound of footsteps approaching the doors. I dropped back down in a panic, the chair briefly wobbling beneath me before I managed to drag it back to where it had been.

I had just managed to sit back down when the doors swung open and Herr Frank emerged, his mouth a rigid line of anger.

His gaze dropped to regard my feet. 'Your shoe,' he said.

I glanced down. My shoe still lay on the floor. I picked it up and quickly tugged it back on.

'It's very tight,' I said feebly.

He stared at me for what felt like an eternity. Then he stalked past me without another word and into the busy corridor beyond.

THREE

**Easter Island Forward Base,
Alternate Alpha Zero, under Authority Jurisdiction**
Six Months Later

For a barely measurable instant, I hung in a grey void, caught between one universe and the next. Then I found myself standing on a transfer stage in a broad hangar, while brilliant sunlight poured unfettered through wide open doors directly before me.

I put up a hand to shield my eyes. Even so, the sunshine felt wonderful after long months of freezing rain and unbroken wintry skies. Even the air, when I next drew breath, made me dizzy with its extraordinary richness.

I was not alone. Four others stood next to me on the stage, and it was clear that the transfer process had proven particularly wrenching for at least one of them. I watched as Elena Kovitch stumbled down the broad ramp and past several bemused American soldiers, before vomiting her breakfast against a wall.

Like the others on the stage around me, I wore a uniform, which we had all come to detest – a modified jumpsuit with a hammer and sickle over the breast. Each had a carefully stitched label reading *Soviet Science Detachment*, in case our hosts somehow forgot who we were. Beneath it was stitched my name:

Katya Orlova. That much of my old identity Borodin had allowed me to retain. Everything else was a carefully constructed lie.

Nina Gregoryeva and Vissarion Chakviani, meanwhile, simply stared with stunned expressions, as if until that moment they had been unable to believe that the means existed to travel from one universe to another. Boris Yedov, the Georgian, just stood quietly with eyes half-closed, reciting some Orthodox litany under his breath while fingering the tiny crucifix he habitually wore.

The day before, we had been flown from Moscow to Washington onboard a specially chartered Aeroflot passenger jet, amidst conditions of absolute secrecy. We had barely touched down before we were bundled onto yet another plane and flown to an unnamed military camp somewhere in the American Midwest. Finally, and without delay, we were bussed directly to a windowless concrete bunker that proved to contain a transfer stage.

And now I was here, on a post-apocalyptic alternate that functioned as the Authority's primary foothold in the multiverse – or the 'Provisional American Civil Authority for the Emergency', to give it its full name.

While the others were occupied, I took a moment to observe my surroundings. Americans with accents that sounded strange and vulgar to my ears yelled to each other as they hauled crates containing our equipment and personal effects down from a second transfer stage adjacent to our own. Although most wore military uniforms, a few others in dark suits were clearly civilians. From the way they directed the soldiers it was equally clear they were in charge. One of the suited men regarded us with barely concealed distaste.

I stepped down from the stage and went out through the

open hangar doors to savour the sunshine more fully. I looked up into a pale blue sky dotted with seagulls riding high on a thermal. They dipped out of sight behind a rocky bluff, from the far side of which I could hear the boom and hiss of waves. I could feel the watchful eyes of the soldiers on me as I bathed beneath the porcelain sky, but I did not care.

'Katya?'

I turned when Elena called my name. She had accepted a handkerchief from one of the two men in suits and was wiping her mouth and apologizing profusely for her loss of control.

'Come back inside, Yekaterina,' she called to me again. 'We must keep together.'

I took a last longing look at the sky and went back inside the hangar.

Vissarion and Nina had by now recovered sufficiently from the shock of transferral to make their way down the ramp to join us, closely trailed by Boris. Elena stared pointedly at the crucifix still grasped in Boris' hand, the chain around his neck drawn taut, until he blinked and finally tucked it back out of sight.

'I understand all of you speak English,' said a uniformed man who stepped up beside the two men in suits. We nodded – fluency in English was a requirement for membership of the expedition, and even before I first set foot in his office Borodin had known that I spoke the language. 'My name is Major Howes,' the soldier continued, before turning to the two civilians beside him. 'I want to welcome you to Alternate Alpha Zero, though you'll find most people tend to refer to it as just "the island". Easter Island, to be specific.' He gestured to the nearest of the two civilians. 'This is Art Blodel, our new director of operations. And this is Kip Mayer, assistant director.'

Blodel was broad and muscular, spine ramrod straight as he

surveyed us. His expression was flat and hard, his mouth set in a thin line, his hair a wiry grey brush standing straight up from his scalp. Mayer, by contrast, was small and wiry, almost delicate in appearance, although there was a sharp intelligence in the eyes of both men.

'Just so you know,' Kip Mayer said to Elena, 'I puked my guts up the first time I used a transfer stage. It gets easier after the first time.'

'Thank you,' Elena replied gratefully. 'May I ask – where are the other members of our team? My understanding was that they arrived before us.'

Blodel nodded stiffly, and I sensed he was less than comfortable in our presence. 'The Russian engineering team got here a few days ahead of you, yes. We're putting you up in neighbouring houses – one for them, the other for you . . . theoretical types. You'll get to meet them later this afternoon.'

The Soviet engineers had arrived in advance of us, in order to be more thoroughly briefed regarding what little the Authority had so far learned about how their transfer stages worked. I knew nothing about the engineers beyond their names and specialities, although I had heard that Wasikowska, the expedition's political officer, had been replaced at the last minute.

'We'll let you settle into your new digs first and save any further briefings until later,' said Mayer. 'But tomorrow we're dropping you in the deep end. You're going to visit a couple of other alternates of particular interest to us. Then we're going to have a little meet and greet so you can get to say hello to our Pathfinders.'

Vissarion frowned. 'What is Pathfinder?' he asked, in heavily accented English.

Blodel looked around us with evident irritation, realizing

that none of us knew what a Pathfinder was. 'Whenever we open up a new alternate, the Pathfinders are the first people to go in and explore it. As you can imagine, they're a pretty hardy bunch. They're also going to be responsible for escorting all of you through some alternates we're currently exploring.' He frowned. 'Weren't you briefed about all this already?'

Elena and the others shook their heads, clearly mystified.

'Are you joking?' spat Vissarion. 'Nobody back home tell us one damn thing, because you Americans refuse to tell us anything outside of barest facts. *Chert vozni*, I never even knew such places existed until was told I would be sent here two weeks ago. Parallel universes! Transfer stages! Alternate Earths struck by meteors or destroyed by plagues!' He swore under his breath. 'When they hauled me into the Kremlin and started telling me all this, I nearly accused them of being drunk.'

'I apologize for my colleague's language,' said Elena, darting Vissarion a hard look. 'He was a late addition to our team.'

Blodel muttered something under his breath that sounded a lot like *fucking Russkies*, and Mayer shot him an angry look. Major Howes, beside him, closed his eyes for a moment.

'I'm sorry, Director Blodel,' said Elena, smiling sweetly as if she hadn't just thrown up against the hangar wall. 'I didn't quite catch that?'

'I was just saying,' said Blodel, smiling thinly back, 'that we look forward to having you here as our guests. It must be nice to have your first taste of visiting a free country.'

'I wasn't aware this was a *country*,' drawled Boris. 'I thought we were on some deserted parallel Earth. And speaking of free countries, just how many years has it been since the war ended, and you Americans still haven't had a free election?'

Blodel's face coloured, and Mayer stepped quickly forward, clapping his hands to get our attention. 'Okay!' he exclaimed brightly, 'I think it's about time to get you all settled in, don't you?'

A few minutes later, we were guided into the back of an open-top truck with benches mounted on its rear bed. We drove away from the hangar, passing through a wire cordon and then onto a dusty road edged with weeds. I looked back to catch a last glimpse of Meyer and Blodel shouting at each other just outside the hangar, pugnacious expressions on both their faces.

The road ran parallel to an air strip that looked disused, and I saw the roofs of buildings just a mile or two ahead. There was no sign of any of the *moai*, the megalithic structures unique to Easter Island: only bare scrubby land segmented here and there by low stone dykes.

We soon arrived at the outskirts of a settlement that appeared to be long abandoned, judging by the number of shattered windows and collapsed roofs. But as we drove down a long avenue, I saw that some had been repaired and refurbished and showed signs of being occupied. We came to a stop outside a two-storey wood-and-brick house, its garden as overgrown as those of the neighbouring properties, although all its windows and those of the house next door were intact. Two more men in dark suits were waiting by the gate, and Elena muttered something to the effect that they were probably members of the Authority's intelligence agency.

We were led inside. The house smelled faintly of mildew and rot, but it was obvious a lot of repair work had been recently undertaken. I could see where rotted floorboards had been re-placed, but even though most of the rooms looked to have been replastered, dark stains still showed through the wallpaper here and there. In the kitchen, several bags of groceries –

mostly tinned fruit and other non-perishables – had been left along with a stack of what one of the Americans described as 'orientation manuals' written in both Russian and English. There were also laptops for each of us to work on for the duration of our stay.

Kip Mayer, we were told, would arrive that afternoon to carry out our first briefing.

I flicked through one of the manuals, which appeared to summarize everything the Authority had so far learned regarding the Syllogikos – or the Stage-Builders, as they called them. They had done well enough at deciphering the Syllogikos language, which shared many of the same roots as Greek and other Hellenic tongues. Beyond that, however, nearly all of their conclusions concerning the Syllogikos seemed to be almost wilfully wrong. That was hardly surprising, given that they lacked access to the comparative wealth of data that had long been available to the Crag's exiled scientists.

Elena went upstairs to take a look at the three bedrooms, while the rest of us explored the downstairs, followed by the agents. 'I'll take the last room on the right for myself,' Elena announced crisply on her return. 'Vissarion, Boris, you can share the middle bedroom. Nina, you and Katya can share the remaining room.'

Nina looked delighted by this news and went upstairs immediately to take a look at our room. I gazed sourly at Elena, who smiled humourlessly back. Clearly I wasn't the only one who found Nina deeply irritating.

I went upstairs, to find Nina peering out of the corner window of our room. 'Isn't this going to be fun?' she said, grinning merrily as I entered. 'And what a lovely house!'

I stared at her, struggling to believe she could find a half-derelict ruin 'lovely'. I watched as she bounced around the room, pulling out drawers and talking to herself, with all the apparent joy of a child presented with a doll's house.

'There's only one bed,' I noted.

'But it's huge!' Nina exclaimed. 'Plenty of room for both of us.'

I mentally cursed Elena. To add insult to injury, Boris and Vissarion's room, which I had passed at the top of the stairs, contained two large and entirely separate beds.

There was little I could do, so I dropped my rucksack next to a dust-laden dresser and filled a drawer with my meagre luggage: a book of nineteenth-century Georgian poetry by Soselo, some underwear and a few changes of clothes. Nina wittered on about her life in Sebastopol (*her* Sebastopol, I had to remind myself), while she pulled drawers open and shut, wrinkling her nose at the bedsheets before finally flinging a window open to let in the light.

Later that morning we congregated in the kitchen to eat and talk about the contents of the orientation manuals. Everyone had changed out of the ridiculous jumpsuits.

While little in the manuals constituted a revelation for me, this was certainly not the case for the Soviets. Vissarion would occasionally snort with derision as he flicked through his copy, as if suddenly remembering afresh that he was now in an alternate universe, while Boris gazed unblinking out of the window at the perfectly clear sky, his meal half-forgotten.

Then, at Elena's instruction, we gathered for our first full briefing in the dining room, which contained only half a dozen plastic chairs and a table. Five of the chairs were arranged on one side, the sixth on the other. Kip Mayer arrived shortly afterwards, in the company of the two agents.

'Isn't Director Blodel joining us?' asked Vissarion.

'He's otherwise engaged,' said Mayer, smiling stiffly. He took a seat in the chair across from the rest of us. 'Can I assume you've all read the orientation manuals?'

We all nodded.

'Good. But let's go over the basic details again to make sure we're all on the same page.' He clasped his hands before him on the table. 'It's been twenty years since the Third World War, and we all know what came after: nuclear winter, radioactive dust in the atmosphere and a global mean temperature drop that we know now for certain has triggered the start of a new Ice Age. That's more than enough to make civilization unsustainable in the long term on our own alternate.'

During my training and embedding in the Soviet team I had learned that, in the alternate from which the Authority and the Soviets came, America and Russia had been locked in a mutual stand-off for decades that finally resolved into nuclear conflict; whereas back in my home alternate of the Novaya Empire's First Republic, America had never been more than a land of farmers and small impoverished settlements.

'That means,' he continued, 'we need to find a viable, safe alternate suitable for a mass evacuation for *all* our people. It's going to require a unified, global effort lasting years, if not decades. Helping us figure out how to find the right alternate is the problem you're all here to help us solve. And that's going to mean putting all our past differences behind us, regardless of which side of the war we were on.'

Boris cleared his throat and tapped one finger on the table. 'For the record, Mr Mayer, the manual contains statements regarding the effects of nuclear winter that are not the considered opinion of the Soviet Union. There are many papers published within the Soviet Union that show this process is most likely far from irreversible.'

I glanced at Elena and saw the muscles of her jaw grow rigid.

'I'm not aware of that research,' Mayer said lightly. 'But that is *not*, I assure you, the private opinion of the Soviet leadership, based on my direct personal knowledge. Their views are in line with our own.'

Boris leaned forward, eyes bulging and jaw thrust out. 'If not for an act of American aggression that triggered the war in the first place, none of this would ever have been—'

'Boris.' Elena spoke softly, but with sufficient steel in her voice that even I felt a flash of tension, as if I were the subject of her ire. Boris glared at her reproachfully, but nonetheless fell immediately silent.

'Okay.' Mayer nodded. His smile had not faltered once. 'Now, the transfer stages are clearly the product of a much more advanced civilization than our own. We believe these Stage-Builders visited literally thousands of parallel universes, including this one. But as to who they were or why they disappeared so suddenly, we have no idea.'

'Excuse me.' Nina raised a faltering hand. 'Please, I was wondering – why can we not colonize *this* parallel universe?'

'Apart from this island, the whole of this alternate is uninhabitable,' Mayer explained. 'We're just very lucky that this island escaped the worst effects, because out of all the alternates we've found so far, this is the only one that's remotely hospitable.'

'About these transfer stages,' asked Boris, 'these miraculous devices that allow you to travel between one universe and another. It is my understanding that you first learned of their existence after your army found one abandoned in a jungle in Bolivia.'

'That's right. It was discovered by a routine military patrol during the war. We—'

'That transfer stage,' interrupted Boris, growing red-faced, 'by rights belongs to the people of Bolivia, who were allies of the Soviet Union at the time you wilfully invaded their—'

'*Boris!*' Elena's voice cut him off. She twisted in her chair to glare at him, gripping the back of her seat with one hand, and I pictured her wielding it like a club and bringing it down on his head. 'One more act of deliberate provocation and I will arrange for you to be returned home *immediately*. Do you understand?'

Behind Mayer, the two agents watched Boris with unwavering focus.

Boris, seemingly oblivious to their attention, gazed sullenly back at Elena. After a moment, his eyes dipped down towards the table. 'Yes, I understand,' he mumbled.

'Mr Mayer,' said Elena, a look of deep weariness in her gaze, 'I apologize for the interruption. Please continue.'

Mayer blinked, then smiled again, albeit somewhat fixedly. 'Okay,' he said. 'Well, just like this alternate we're on right now, every single universe we've so far visited has undergone some form of apocalyptic event that renders it uninhabitable either in the short or long term. That's unfortunate, to say the least, and I'm going to be frank with you – we've made very little progress in understanding how the stages even work. It should be possible to program them to find alternates that are safe to inhabit, but we still don't know how.'

'But you did say you visit other alternates,' Vissarion pointed out. 'How can you do that, if you don't know how to operate the stages?'

'They found a list of pre-programmable destinations here on

this island,' said Elena. 'It was in the orientation manual, Vissarion.'

'We can travel to alternates that are on that list,' added Mayer. 'Travelling to alternates for which we *don't* already have the coordinates is what we're trying to work out.'

'How could these Stage-Builders simply disappear?' asked Boris.

'We don't know,' said Mayer. 'The Bolivia transfer stage brought us to this alternate, and it was obvious they'd abandoned the place in a hurry.'

'Then . . . are we safe here?' asked Boris.

'It's the same wherever we find one of their bases,' Mayer explained with a shrug, 'on alternate after alternate. They were all abandoned more or less overnight.'

Nina shivered. 'It's almost like a ghost story.'

'Mr Mayer,' asked Elena, 'is there a chance these Stage-Builders might . . . come back?'

'The only certainty we have,' said Mayer, 'is that if we don't manage to make some kind of breakthrough in the next couple of years, we are in deep shit.'

There was silence after that.

'But there's always hope,' said Mayer, after letting that sink in. 'We sometimes find artefacts – machines – that might turn out to be useful, assuming we can work out what they're for. We're hoping some of you geniuses can figure out if they can do anything useful for us, particularly if it proves relevant to our mission. For all we know, some of them are futuristic juicers, but others could help us find out how to program the stages – or even build our own stages. In fact, your engineers have already had a chance to take a look at some of these artefacts.'

'Where are the engineers just now?' asked Nina.

'They just got back after spending the day with our own science staff,' Mayer replied. 'They're waiting for you next door. Soon as we're finished here, you can all go and say hello.' He glanced around us, then stood. 'I want to wish you luck while you're here with us.'

I watched him leave and Vissarion looked around the rest of us. 'Well, what do we do now?'

'Just what he suggested,' said Elena, standing and moving towards the door. 'Go and say hello to our fellow scientists.'

Boris stood, brushing invisible dust from his shirt. 'I hope to hell they've got something to drink, because I'm going to need it.'

Damian Kuzakov, who built containment systems for high-energy particle experiments as well as being the overall leader of the expedition, greeted us heartily when we arrived next door. A glass of champagne was pushed into my hand as I entered the vestibule of the house. Illyenna Iremashvilli and Aleksi Chulkov appeared from out of what I assumed was the living room, welcoming us with smiles and handshakes and questions. I could hear music coming through the door behind them, and wondered where Wasikowska's replacement had got to.

Damian led us all back into the living room, which turned out to be contiguous with the kitchen, and big enough to take up most of the ground floor. There he clapped his hand on the shoulder of Wasikowska's replacement, who had been playing with the settings on a portable stereo.

That was when I realized that Wasikowska's replacement was Mikhail Borodin himself.

*

That Mikhail Borodin, the man who had brutally murdered Tomas in cold blood before me, could be here seemed impossible. Yet there he was, grinning and chatting and shaking the hands of my fellow scientists and introducing himself.

The shock of seeing him felt like a physical blow, driving the breath out of my lungs. My discomfort was evident enough to draw one or two curious glances from the Soviets around me. But after a few moments I managed to recover sufficiently that I could gulp down the fizzy wine in my hand, then force myself to breathe evenly and slowly until I felt more in control. I forced a smile onto my face, and greeted each of the engineers in turn – all except Borodin himself.

For the moment, Borodin was happy to ignore me in his own turn, not even looking in my direction after that first glance. All of the Soviets were busy availing themselves of the Authority's generous hospitality, which came in the form of numerous bottles of Scotch, vodka and orange juice – incredible luxuries on their home alternate. I made small talk with Illyenna about my impressions of the island and the people we had so far met, while my heart thudded and my head pounded and my whole body screamed to run, to hide . . . to be anywhere but there.

I saw Elena lead Damian into a corner, leaning into him as she spoke. Someone turned the music up. Borodin, when I allowed myself a quick glance, appeared utterly at ease, as if unaware how much his presence had affected me.

He saw me looking and stepped towards me. 'You must be Yekaterina Iosifovna,' he said loudly, making a small bow. *Play along*, his expression said.

'Nice to meet you,' I stammered for the sake of the others around me. 'I-I . . .'

The words died in my throat. He touched my elbow, guiding

me away from the others. Another glass of wine materialized in my hand without my being quite aware how it got there.

'They should have trained you better,' he hissed under his breath. 'Drink up. You look like you need it.'

'What are you doing here?' I whispered all too loudly. 'I mean . . . how?'

'The same way as you,' he said quietly. 'By assuming a false identity that would allow me to live incognito amongst the Soviets. I had been waiting for an opportunity to insert myself into this research team, and one came up. Or did you think I was above getting my hands dirty?'

'I thought it would be someone else,' I said faintly.

'No,' he corrected me, his voice cold. 'You *assumed* it would be.'

I felt his hand brush mine, pushing something against my fingers. I glanced down, seeing a small black object, shaped like a comma, in the palm of my hand. A headset originally designed to interface with the Crag's captive Hypersphere.

I quickly palmed it, sliding it inside a pocket. 'How did you manage to smuggle it here?' I whispered.

'I hid the separate parts inside a watch casing.' He glanced casually across the room: no one was looking our way. 'It might help us to find the exact location of the undamaged Hypersphere.'

I had my doubts, but said nothing. 'So it's here on the island?'

He shook his head. 'They're taking us on a tour of some alternates tomorrow morning – including, I believe, the one where they found the Hypersphere.'

'How did you manage to work that out?'

He gave me a sharp look that said *Don't ask questions.* 'From the same source as the photograph,' he snapped, taking a quick glance around to make sure no one was listening. 'Now, the photograph itself shows the Hypersphere is stored along with other artefacts in some kind of central repository. Since they apparently want us to carry out assessments of these artefacts, it's possible they'll take us directly there. In which case . . .'

He paused, looking past me with a smile. I turned to see Elena Kovitch approach us from across the room.

'Why, you must be Mikhail,' said Elena with a smile. 'Wasikowska's replacement. I heard about his accident. Any word on how he's doing?'

'Recovering well, I hear,' Borodin replied. 'A hit and run, I believe. Most likely they will never find the culprit.'

'Well, I can promise that you won't have any trouble with us theorists,' said Elena. She smiled at me in a way that showed too many teeth. 'Have you two already met? I swear, as soon as you set eyes on each other it was like you didn't know the rest of us were even here.'

I forced a smile. 'I'm afraid we've only just made each other's acquaintance.'

'Well,' said Elena, 'it's good to meet our new *zampolit*, Mikhail. I have many questions to ask you – if you would excuse us, Katya?'

'Of course,' I said.

'Miss Orlova,' said Borodin with a tight nod. 'I'm sure we'll have the opportunity to speak again soon.'

My breath constricted in my lungs. 'I should mingle,' I said. 'Talk to the rest of the engineering team.'

'Indeed you should,' said Elena. 'Keeping Mikhail all to yourself – what would people think?'

I blinked at her like a fish, then turned away, wondering what it was about the woman's gaze that I found so unsettling.

FOUR

'First of all, welcome to Alternate Sigma Seventy-Three. I want everyone to stay together at all times. If you see something interesting or something you think we need to know about, tell us – *don't* go wandering off on your own to investigate. And if it turns out to be important, or even better if you've discovered something new, well . . . we'll make sure you get full credit. You all got that?'

There was a chorus of *yes* and *da* and nodding heads from me and the rest of the Soviets, our voices carrying far in the still air of the caverns. Even our whispers echoed back to us like the plaintive cries of ghosts.

It was the next morning, and our hosts had, as promised, brought us to one of the many post-extinction alternates they were engaged in exploring. Wherever the Hypersphere was, however, I felt sure it was not to be found here. Perhaps Borodin had got his information wrong.

Borodin himself was there, of course. I still hadn't quite got over the shock of encountering him the previous evening. Fortunately, he had ignored me since arriving at the island's transfer hangar that morning.

The man addressing us stood on top of a broad flat boulder pushing out of the floor of the cavern, a large rucksack resting by his foot. He and two women, who stood near the transfer stage on which we had materialized just minutes before, had been waiting for us on our arrival.

We were all dressed in heavy boots, hard hats and thick layers of waterproof clothing. Our breath frosted in air that smelled of damp and mould. A string of lights, supported on poles that stretched off into the distance, made it clear just how enormous the caverns were; past a bridge over a chasm, I could just make out shadowy ruins beneath a high, curving ceiling. They looked as if they'd been abandoned for centuries.

Suddenly, the man on the rock seemed to snap into focus and I realized where I had seen him and the two women before: in the photograph, standing in a line with several others, the undamaged Hypersphere visible behind them.

'Before we get moving,' the man continued, 'just a reminder – we've only mapped a tiny fraction of these caverns, so if you *do* wander off or somehow get lost, that's going to make it that little bit harder to find you.' He took out a whistle and held it up. 'You all got one of these?'

We held up our whistles, handily secured to our jackets by pieces of nylon cord.

'Great. Anything happens and you get separated, just blow on that. And watch your step – there's a lot of slippery moss and fungi growing basically everywhere, like on our friend back there. We've already had a few broken legs from people taking a tumble, so try not to add your neck to the list.'

As he said this, he jerked a thumb at the enormous statue of Christ behind him that rose almost to the roof of the cavern. Part of its face and a chunk of one shoulder were missing, and much of the body was hidden beneath a dense overcoat of moss.

'Most of your work,' he continued, 'is going to involve analysing recovered technology and data, but one of our biggest discoveries in recent years is right here in these caverns, and it just might go a long way towards helping us figure out why the Stage-Builders disappeared so suddenly. That's a big part of why we brought you here today – to see some of our current research. It's just possible something you see here or in some of the other places we'll be visiting later might help you form a connection or put things together in a way we haven't thought of – and it's just as important for you to have a solid idea of exactly what it is we're up against every time we open up a new alternate for exploration. It's not like we can just press a button and open up a door to some place we can all go and live in safely; if it was, we wouldn't need to be here today.'

'I don't see anything here,' said Damian Kuzakov, 'apart from shadows and statues.'

'We've got a little bit of a walk ahead of us first,' said the man. He nodded towards a broad paved road that wound between the ruins on the far side of the chasm. 'But it shouldn't take more than twenty minutes. Sorry we couldn't put you down any closer to where we're going, but this is one of the few places in these caverns that's got enough clear space for a stage.'

'Excuse me,' asked Damian, raising his hand. 'What is your name, please?'

The man blinked. 'Uh, sorry – I should have said. My name's Jerry Beche.'

'And you are a Pathfinder?' asked Illyenna.

Beche dropped down from the boulder and began to hand out torches to each of us from his rucksack. 'Guilty as charged.' He glanced around, seeing the perplexed looks of some of the Soviets. 'You *did* all read the orientation manuals, didn't you?'

'The manuals said that you are . . . last man on Earth?' Illyenna sounded as if she was struggling to get the words out.

Beche laughed uneasily. 'Well . . . the last man on one *particular* alternate Earth,' he said. 'Until the Authority rescued me.'

'And the other Pathfinders?' asked Vissarion, chipping in.

'The same,' said Beche. 'All of us were rescued by the Authority from various post-apocalyptic alternates.'

'I just thought . . .' Illyenna's voice trailed off.

That it was all some elaborate joke, I suspected she had been about to say.

'And you?' asked Vissarion, turning around to look at the two women accompanying Beche. 'This is true of you too?'

'Yep,' said the dark-skinned woman. 'Although I'm obviously not the last *man*. I'm Rozalia, by the way.'

'I'm Chloe,' said the second woman. 'And ditto what both of them said.'

Beche looked back at Vissarion. 'This *was* all in the manual, Mr Chakviani,' he said.

Vissarion just stared around at the three Pathfinders as if he'd swallowed a live frog. Clearly, some of the Soviets were still struggling to come to terms with the reality of living in a multiverse. I, by contrast, had grown up with the concept as a daily reality.

'Well, anyway,' Jerry said into the uneasy silence that followed, 'there's a lot to see, so we'd better get going!'

I could hardly take my eyes from the statue as we skirted past it: in any populated alternate, it would surely have ranked as one of the greatest works of art ever made, yet it presided over an abyssal graveyard, with no one left to witness its lonely vigil but visitors from another universe. It must have been at least thirteen metres in height, and to my admittedly untrained eye appeared to have been carved from a single piece of unbroken stone. Skulls in their thousands had been piled all around its feet, rising in great mounds to its shins – and all, Pathfinder Chloe informed us as we traipsed past, quite real.

'Quite a sight, huh?' asked Jerry, coming abreast of me and nodding back at the statue.

I nodded. 'But haunting, yes? To think of it lost down here in the darkness for so many centuries . . .' I shivered, and not merely because it was so very cold.

'Still, heck of a story how this place came about.'

I looked blankly at him, as did one or two of the others.

'Okay,' he said, 'I know for a *fact* they briefed you this morning before you transferred here.'

I winced. 'I . . . was feeling a little under the weather. Perhaps I did not pay as much attention as I should have.'

He gave me a knowing look as we moved on, following the string of lights deeper into the caves. 'Partied too hard last night?'

I didn't quite understand his choice of words. 'Excuse me?'

We had drifted to the rear of the group. He angled his head closer to mine as if sharing a confidence. 'Looked to me from up on that boulder like some of your colleagues were nursing major hangovers.'

I had not failed to notice this myself, although in my own case my inattentiveness had more to do with a lack of sleep following my unexpected encounter with Borodin. Elena had decided the engineers should join us for breakfast that same morning, and Illyenna had bolted from the kitchen the moment a plate of sausage and eggs was placed before her. Boris and Aleksi had sniggered like schoolboys at the sound of her retching.

I gave the Pathfinder a faint smile. 'Yes – a little too much indulging. So what did happen here?'

'The sun expanded, starting sometime in the early twelfth century, and by the time the seventeenth rolled around, most of the surface was a baked and lifeless desert. The few people still alive had spent nearly half a millennia digging way, way down – either starting with existing underground complexes, like this one, or constructing brand new warrens.'

'But they didn't survive, did they?'

He shook his head. 'Nope. They were just delaying the inevitable. I—'

We came to a halt as a faint tremor rolled through the ground beneath our feet. It lasted for several seconds, then faded away.

'Nothing to worry about,' Rozalia called back. 'Tremors aren't unknown here. Everyone just keep moving.'

Chloe came to a stop until Jerry and I caught up with her. 'Try not to get left behind,' she said, flashing me a taut smile. 'This is a *group* expedition, remember?'

'We're fine, Chloe,' said Jerry, with an edge to his voice. 'I've been here like a hundred times.'

'Sure.' She nodded and regarded him with narrowed eyes before stalking ahead to walk with Rozalia.

Jerry looked at me and shrugged amiably. 'C'mon. Don't want to set a bad example.'

We came to a Bailey bridge the Authority had constructed over the chasm, beyond which lay the long-abandoned ruins of a subterranean city. I glanced over the side of the bridge and saw the tumbled remains of what must have been the original stone bridge, far below.

We picked up our pace and for the next few minutes we walked in silence. Something made me think Jerry Beche and

Chloe might be more than merely colleagues – not that this was any of my concern.

By now, the statue had slipped into the shadows behind us, but there was no lack of fresh wonders to catch our attention. The Pathfinders directed us to look upwards, and I saw vast murals painted across the cavern ceiling, barely visible by the string of lights that marked our route through the city: angels, armed with swords and with capes flowing around their shoulders, battled demons all across a curving expanse of stone that stretched far off into the darkness. I saw images of demons casting men and women into vast pits of sand littered with the wrecks of ships. Jerry became talkative once more, explaining that the oceans on the surface above had by now largely evaporated.

'I knew I'd seen something like this before,' exclaimed Aleksi Chulkov at one point. 'I once visited the salt mines at Wieliczka. They had something like this there too.'

'That's just about where we are right now,' Rozalia informed him, sounding pleased. 'They dug cathedrals and halls out of the rock salt hundreds of years ago. Except here, they went further. A *lot* further.'

'How many people did they manage to get in here?' asked Damian.

'Up to half a million when things got really bad,' said Rozalia.

'But how did they eat?' Damian persisted. 'And what about water?'

The Pathfinder smiled tautly. 'You'll see.'

We passed clusters of houses – hovels, really, and wretched ones at that – apparently constructed from clay and, if my eyes did not deceive me, bone. There was no apparent order to their construction, and as we passed I took a glance inside one, seeing small pits dug into the floor where once, presumably, cooking fires would have burned.

The cavern broadened the farther we went, and our guides directed our attention to balconies carved into the nearest walls, reaching all the way to the ceiling. I also saw the rusting skeletons of iron chandeliers hanging far above, appearing blood-red in the dim light.

Then the ground began to rise, and we ascended a slope.

At first, when I looked down the other side, I thought we had stumbled across the edge of some abyssal void – reaching, perhaps, all the way to the Earth's core: the string of lights that had guided us this far came to a halt at the very edge of the void. But as I looked closer my perspective shifted, and I realized I was in fact looking at the shore of a subterranean lake, its waters as still and perfectly smooth as a black mirror. Farther out, beyond the point where our lights reached, bioluminescent fungus clinging to parts of the ceiling revealed the outlines of enormous stone pillars rising out of the waters.

We fell quiet, staring around us. It was an astonishing sight.

'Just remember,' said Jerry, breaking the silence, 'pretty much everything you see they dug out of the rock with their bare hands. That lake down there is artificial. As for what they ate . . . well, you have to remember these people were living in the Middle Ages when the surface got too hot to inhabit. There's no way to sustain crops and livestock down here in the dark, even with access to underground springs. They really didn't know a damn thing about staying alive in a place like this. Once farming on the surface finally became impossible, things down here got very bad, very quickly.'

'So they . . .' Elena began.

'They ate each other, yes,' Rozalia finished for her.

'All right,' said Chloe, 'this way, folks.' She beckoned us to follow her along a narrow, winding alley that snaked between buildings that looked to my eyes to be on the verge of collapse. '*This* is what you're here to see.'

We followed her down the alley. It broadened at its far end, then angled suddenly to the right. We turned a corner to find ourselves in a cul-de-sac, most of which was occupied by a white rectangular tent with translucent walls and a zippered opening, brightly lit from within.

Chloe unzipped the tent door and beckoned us to enter. 'But don't touch *anything* inside, hear? Spread out around the walls once you go in.'

We filed in, one by one, and I saw the tent housed a ring of Syllogikos field-pillars – the main components of a portable transfer stage, identical to the one by which we had arrived on this alternate. Several of the pillars had been kicked over, however. A control unit lay next to one, smashed beyond repair.

In one corner of the tent stood a pair of metal tables supporting a centrifuge, microscope and several racks of chemicals. Once we were all packed in, it began to feel very crowded. Jerry and Rozalia stepped carefully into the centre of the stage, then squatted by a mound of bones and rags on the ground.

'So what is this?' asked Damian.

'This,' said Jerry, 'is the body of a Stage-Builder. One who got away.'

'Got away from what?' asked Elena.

'From whatever made the rest of the Stage-Builders disappear,' he said. 'Not that it seems to have done him much good. Until we came to this alternate, we'd never managed to find even so much as a single body, so finding this was a really big deal.'

Elena stared at the forlorn little pile of bones. 'But how can you know he's a Stage-Builder? I saw plenty of bones on the way here.'

'For a start,' said Rozalia, pointing at the skull by her feet, 'a forensics analysis showed that this guy died centuries after the people who dug out these caves all starved to death.'

'Not to mention,' said Chloe, 'we found him lying in the middle of a transfer stage, which is a pretty big clue all in itself.'

'But that's not all,' said Rozalia, pulling a small torch out of one pocket and shining it directly on the skull. 'Look closer.'

The bone glittered, giving off a faint sheen of rainbow colours.

'See that?' she asked, looking around at us. 'Like a very fine metal filigree, fused with the bone of the skull.'

'What is it?' asked Aleksi, gaping in wonder.

'We think it's some kind of bionic computer implant,' said Jerry. 'And there are other bodies nearby, all with implant technology that's far too advanced to be native to this alternate.'

Nina stepped closer and peered down. 'The skull has a deep indentation in it. Perhaps that was the cause of death?'

Rozalia nodded, turning her torch on a dark grey chunk of masonry lying nearby. 'And that, we think, is the murder weapon.'

'Murder?' I echoed.

'Sure looks like it,' said Chloe, standing by one of the tables. 'That rock has blood on it. After we analysed everything we put it back where we found it in case we could figure out what might have led one of them to murder another.'

'And did you?' asked Elena. 'Work out what happened?'

The Pathfinder shrugged her shoulders. 'Beats me.'

'My theory,' said Jerry, pointing at the ruined stage components, 'is that one of them decided to smash up the transfer stage, and another of them objected strenuously by bashing the first guy to death with a rock.'

'But why would anyone choose to deliberately strand themselves in such a dreadful place?' asked Boris, sounding appalled.

'All we have are questions,' said Jerry. 'And not much in the way of answers. But sometimes we've been able to pull co-ordinates even out of damaged equipment, and this time we got lucky. We discovered the last couple of alternates these people visited before they arrived here. One of those was the island back on Alternate Alpha Zero.' He grinned. 'And the other one we're taking you to later today. But we've got a couple of pit stops to make first.' He stood and brushed dirt from his knees. 'Trust me, we're saving the best for last.'

The full import of what I had learned was only just beginning to sink in. The Novaya Empire had never found so much as a single body belonging to the Syllogikos, yet these people had apparently found several. It was, indeed, a find of huge significance.

The ground once again trembled very slightly. I tensed with alarm, but the tremor passed quickly. I glanced around the tent, seeing anxious expressions, then heard a crack, echoing through the cavern. A few seconds later it was followed by a booming, rushing sound.

'What the hell was that?' demanded Boris.

'I don't think it's anything to worry about,' said Jerry with a tight grin.

'You don't *think*?' Boris spat, his voice rich with disbelief.

'It happens not infrequently,' said Jerry. 'Sometimes bits break off from the cavern roof and land in the lake. They built this place in a hurry, and it hasn't been maintained in centuries.'

'So it's dangerous?' Boris continued. 'Should we even be here?'

'Well, it's pretty much guaranteed to all come crashing down *sometime* in the next several years, we think, because it's just too geologically unstable to last more than—'

The air was filled with a chorus of frightened, angry voices as several of the Soviets all spoke at once.

'*Hey!*' Jerry shouted, hands raised in a placating gesture. 'There's no way we'd bring you all the way here if we really thought there was any kind of imminent danger, okay? Now let's just look at the other bodies, and then we can move on to our next stop. All right?'

The Soviets still muttered with discontent as we were led back outside. We exited the cul-de-sac and followed the three Pathfinders inside the ruins of a building, the roof of which had collapsed long ago. I saw an altar and dust-shrouded tabernacle, and realized we were inside a church. There were indeed more skeletons, scattered amidst the collapsed remains of tents and sleeping bags. There were also a small number of technological artefacts – something that might have been a wristwatch, save for its smooth blank face, and a translucent device within which clouds appeared to drift. All the skulls had the same fine metal filigree clinging to them.

'So we're not here just to help you figure out the transfer stages, are we?' asked Vissarion. 'You want us to help you work out what happened to these people, too?'

'We've been trying to analyse that metallic netting attached to the skulls on the assumption that if it really is some form of computer technology, it might have useful data hidden away in it. Anything and everything might hold the clues we need. But first, we should—'

Another tremor, considerably stronger than the last, rolled beneath our feet. It was followed by a rustling, whispering sound, like wind through trees, or several hundred tons of gravel and rock sliding down a hill.

'Ah, crap,' said Chloe, her eyes wide. 'We really picked a bad day, didn't we?'

'Let's get out of here,' said Jerry, 'before anything else—'

I heard a creaking sound and turned in time to see one wall of the church begin to lean over towards us. There were yells and shouts as people moved to try and get out of the way, and moments later bricks and ancient mortar came raining down, kicking up enormous clouds of blinding dust. I got some in my lungs and began to choke, squeezing my eyes shut as I tried to feel my way to safety.

A hand grabbed me by the shoulder, pulling me after them. I let whoever it was lead me as I stumbled over bits of debris while shouts echoed all around.

'We're out,' I heard Borodin say. 'Can you breathe?'

I shook my head. *No.* A moment later he shoved a piece of cloth into my hand. I used it to wipe the grit from my eyes, then blinked and coughed, looking around. Torchlight flickered through clouds of dust as people called to each other or blew their whistles. I realized Borodin had pulled me out of the building. Someone called out my name, and Borodin yelled back that we were both unharmed.

I looked around for somewhere to sit, and caught sight of something lying tumbled amidst the shattered bricks and powdery mortar: a tiny wooden box, small enough to fit inside the palm of my hand. I reached down automatically and picked it up, turning it over in my hands while I coughed and tried to clear my throat.

Borodin stepped away from me a moment and picked something up: a dropped torch. He flicked it on and shone it around.

'Here, give me that,' I said. He regarded me curiously for a moment, but gave me the torch. I shone it on the box and saw that the wood was intricately carved on its sides with swirling, abstract designs. The lid of the box opened easily on tiny silver hinges, but it was empty. I shone the torch around, but all I saw were clouds of dust, slowly settling back down.

Then I saw light reflecting from something half-hidden in the dust: I bent to look closer, and discovered numerous tiny beads, scattered all around. They were of all different colours, but each had an iridescent, slightly metallic sheen to it.

Without thinking about it, I pulled off a glove with my teeth, then reached down to pick up one that was coloured a pale grey.

And just like that, I was somewhere else.

The breath caught in my throat. The cavern, Borodin, the Pathfinders – all of it was gone.

I was standing in a green field, beneath a warm sun. My hands, when I looked at them, were not my own. The fingers were long and delicate, but clearly those of a man.

I turned and saw a stone-built cottage off in the near distance. A woman with dark skin and Mediterranean features stood by my side.

A little girl, no more than five or six, ran past me, her hair flowing around the shoulders of her red and green dress. Her mouth was wide open, and her laughter pealed like tiny bells.

She was past me in an instant. I whirled around to follow her, and saw her run towards the cottage, her long hair billowing.

As suddenly as the experience had begun, it was over. I was back in the caverns, still crouching over the rest of the scattered beads as if no time at all had passed. I rocked back on my haunches, my heart beating a rapid tattoo inside my chest. The grey bead I had picked up was still nestled in the palm of my hand.

I stared at the rest of the beads, wondering what I would see if I touched them too. They were clearly some form of highly advanced technology. I dropped the single grey bead inside the box with shaking hands, then pulled my glove back on before reaching for a second one. I didn't dare pick it up with my bare fingers until I had a better idea what I'd found, but with the thick gloves on I couldn't get hold of any of them.

'What the hell are you doing?' demanded Borodin, coughing hard as I finally managed to scoop up a second bead and drop it in the box along with the first.

I glanced up and saw Borodin had pulled out a handkerchief and pressed it to his mouth. When he took it away again, I saw in the light of the torch still grasped in my other hand that it was specked with blood.

'Are you all right?' I asked, nodding at the handkerchief.

'It's nothing,' he replied, quickly folding the handkerchief and putting it away. He looked at the box. 'What did you find?'

'Beads,' I said. 'Or at least they look like beads. I saw something when I touched one.'

He frowned. 'Saw what?'

'You didn't see anything?'

He shook his head, clearly mystified. Of course: I had touched the bead, so only I had seen the girl. The experience had been mine, and mine alone.

Jerry Beche strode into view before I could gather up any more of the beads or explain further.

'There you are!' he said, looking relieved. 'Thank God. You're both all right?'

Some instinct made me quickly tuck the box into a pocket before he could see it. 'You're both in one piece, right?' he asked again, looking between us. 'I'm really, really sorry about that. I think maybe it was a mistake not just moving the bodies back to the island before now, but we were worried about viruses and killer plagues and all the rest, and our decontamination facilities need some major upgrading.'

The rest of our party soon appeared as well, all equally dirty and dusty. 'Well, guess we owe you people a drink for putting you through all that,' said Rozalia. 'You know about the welcoming party the Pathfinders are throwing tonight?'

Elena nodded. 'Director Blodel mentioned it.'

I couldn't help but notice the pained look on Beche's face when he heard the Director's name. 'Well,' he said, blinking through a mask of dirt, 'I figure we can take some time to get cleaned up before we hit our next stop, don't you?'

FIVE

Altogether, we visited five alternate Earths that day, and after each visit, we returned to the island in order to collect whatever equipment or supplies we needed for our next destination – or, in the case of the caverns, to make use of shower rooms. We were given keys for lockers, and I took care to make sure no one was looking when I gently pushed the wooden box into the back of my own locker.

After the caverns we were next taken to an Earth orbiting a rogue black hole which had dragged it far from its sun; the atmosphere had frozen into a thin crust of snow covering the planet's entire surface. The next found us all standing together on the roof of a ruined skyscraper, watching fearfully as great saurian things rumbled and howled through the deserted city streets far below. The alternate after that was buried beneath glaciers that had spread to cover most of the Earth's surface; it was of particular interest, we were told, because the Authority's own alternate stood a good chance of meeting the same fate.

But it was the fifth, and last, alternate that proved the most interesting.

Before transferring over, we were given half-mask respirators. While we waited on the stage, I saw Jerry Beche go down the ramp to talk to the technician manning the stage's control rig.

The Pathfinder pulled a tattered notebook out of a pocket and showed something in it to the technician. I was close enough to them that I was able to catch a glimpse of long strings of numbers and letters written in the notebook's pages, and recognized them as transfer stage coordinates.

The technician nodded and got to work tapping at the control rig's keyboard. Jerry ran up on to the stage to join us and pulled on his own respirator before pushing the notebook back in a pocket.

'Problem?' Rozalia asked him.

'The rig crashed,' he said, and patted the pocket containing the notebook. 'Had to enter the coordinates manually.'

Then the hangar faded in a rush of light.

We materialized in another hangar, apparently identical to the one we'd just departed. In fact, the only hint we had gone anywhere at all was that the stage technician on duty was now a woman, and the sunlight coming through the open hangar doors behind her was of an entirely different hue.

I took a breath. Even through the respirator, the air smelled . . . strange.

The Pathfinders were the first down from the stage, and we followed them out through the hangar doors in a group.

Outside, I saw an unearthly blue and yellow forest spreading towards distant hills beneath a pink sky. Although when I say *forest*, these organisms bore at best a tangential relationship to any tree I had ever seen; instead of branches, they had long, whiplike fronds that spiralled up and around broad twisting trunks. There were also preposterous growths like huge sea anemones, swaying in the breeze.

All of this riotous, alien flora came to a precise halt at the edge of the paved area, as if it had been neatly trimmed back that very morning. For all I knew, it had.

I turned to look behind me and saw that the hangar was at one end of a huge paved expanse, perhaps a kilometre in length and half as wide, scattered across which were about a dozen gargantuan metal-walled sheds, huge compared even to the hangar.

A dandelion seed drifted past me, except that no dandelion seed I had ever seen moved in sudden, sweeping motions with hummingbird rapidity. I caught a brief glimpse, there and then gone, of a pale, grub-like body at the heart of a feathery cloud. In the next instant it had zipped away from me, almost too fast to follow.

Then I spied what at first appeared to be an enormous spider, several inches in diameter, wobbling on spindly legs in the shade of one of the anemone trees. A stalk extended upwards from its body, and it had something very like an eye on top. The creature rushed towards me, then fell back in a shower of sparks the moment it tried to cross onto the pavement.

I watched, stupefied, as it leaped back in amongst the anemone trees, screeching a flurry of bird-like notes as it fled out of sight. There must, I thought, be some kind of field separating the paved area from the surrounding forest.

The Soviets all had stunned expressions. Most likely I did too.

'Are we . . . are we still on Earth?' Boris asked plaintively. All that morning, his hand had constantly twitched towards his neck, until he finally had the good sense to take his crucifix off and simply carry it in one hand.

'Sure,' said Chloe. 'Just one where evolution took a very different path.' She spread her arms. 'Welcome to Site A, Alternate Delta Twenty-Five.'

'Site A?' asked Elena. 'So there's a Site B?'

'There surely is,' said Jerry, 'about eighty kilometres north-west of here.'

'At least the grass looks normal,' muttered Damian, staring past the invisible fence.

'Really?' Illyenna exclaimed tartly. 'Is there an abundance of blue and pink grass in Kursk?'

'Why do we have to wear these masks?' asked Elena.

'There's a risk of anaphylactic shock from coming into contact with the local bugs. To be honest, only one or two people ever had a problem, but we'd rather not take any unnecessary risks.'

'Could we live here long-term?' asked Damian.

'Not a chance,' Jerry replied.

'How can you be sure?'

'The organisms here have a different molecular chirality from our own – our bodily enzymes wouldn't be able to break them down for energy, and they couldn't get anything from eating us. It might as well be a barren wasteland for all its ability to support human life. But some people did have a reaction, so keep your masks on.'

'And according to what you found, those dead Stage-Builders back in those caverns had first spent time here?'

Jerry nodded. 'That's right.'

'But this isn't actually the alternate they originate from, then? They were human, like us?'

'Human *exactly* like us,' said Jerry, 'so, no, they didn't come from here. They were just visitors.'

'So what brought them here?' asked Boris.

Jerry nodded to the sheds scattered across the compound. 'Can't say for sure, but I'm guessing it had a lot to do with what's in some of these buildings.'

The sheds had clearly been intended as temporary structures. Their metal walls were rusting and their plastic roofs were in a state of near-collapse.

The Authority had pitched tents outside some of them, and as we made our way past I caught sight of workers, their faces hidden behind respirators, photographing or studying objects that might have been machines or weapons or even simply abstract sculptures of some kind.

'We've identified some very old ruins in the jungle out beyond this compound that make it clear this alternate was once home to an extremely advanced culture,' explained Chloe, taking the lead. 'They're long gone though, whoever or whatever they were. The Stage-Builders collected all these artefacts while exploring the ruins.'

'They weren't human?' I asked.

'Probably not, given that they must have come from a very different evolutionary history,' Chloe replied.

Nina shuddered. 'It feels more like an alien planet.'

Chloe nodded. 'I know. It's easy to forget, but we are actually on Earth.'

She led us inside a shed easily big enough to house a couple of passenger jets side by side. Broad metal shelves stretched into its depths and rose far above our heads, countless gantries and stairways threading through it all. Nearly every shelf was crammed with technological artefacts of every imaginable shape and design – enough to keep the Novaya Empire's scientists working around the clock for a century.

And somewhere in one of these sheds, I knew, was a pristine Hypersphere.

'Go on in,' said Chloe. 'Take a look. Wander around, but not too far. And for God's sake,' she added, 'don't *touch* anything.'

We moved farther in, staring slack-jawed at the wonders piled around us. A vehicle of some kind was parked beside a gantry, floating above the floor of the shed without visible support.

'It's going to take decades to figure out what even a fraction of this stuff is for,' said Chloe. 'You won't be the last people we bring in here by a long shot. We've got plans to bring in researchers from all over to work on figuring all this stuff out.'

Borodin came up next to me and nodded towards the shadowy depths to the rear of the shed. I looked around, seeing no one was paying either of us any particular attention. Moving quietly, I followed him into the shadows. We stood together, pretending we were studying the artefacts all around us.

'It's close by, Katya,' he said quietly. 'I can feel it.'

'I noticed something,' I said. 'When we were preparing to transfer here. One of the Pathfinders had a notebook with stage coordinates written in it.'

'Which one?'

'Jerry Beche.'

He glanced back over at the others. 'So there's more than one of them, then.'

'What do you mean?'

He smirked. 'A few of them seem to carry such notebooks. Perhaps all of them do. I saw another Pathfinder consulting a notebook when I first arrived at Alpha Zero with the engineers. He was more than happy to tell me what he used it for when I asked.' He looked back over at the rest of our party. 'See if you can use the headset to locate the Hypersphere. There's no better time.'

I fitted the device above one ear, where my hair would cover it. Immediately, the air around me filled with ghostly symbols that would have been easily visible to the citizens of the

Syllogikos, amongst whom neural implants were ubiquitous. I had helped my father design the interface in order to communicate with their computer systems.

I quickly identified a detailed virtual map of the complex, floating to one side of us, complete with an index of the contents of each shed. I studied it closely while Borodin kept an eye on the rest of our party.

'Well?' asked Borodin. 'Found anything yet?'

'I think I've got it. It's in the shed next to this one, in the south-west corner.'

Borodin nodded. 'Then let's go.'

'What about the others? They'll notice if we disappear.'

'Let's just find the damn thing first and worry about them later,' he muttered.

I led the way. To my surprise, no one appeared to notice our departure, so engrossed were they with the contents of the shelves. We threaded our way between shelves until we arrived at another exit from the shed we were in. I stepped outside, then hurried over to another shed just metres away, with Borodin close on my heels.

Almost as soon as we stepped through the entrance, I saw it: a Hypersphere, floating just millimetres above a three-legged cradle and identical in every respect to the one back in the Crag – except, of course, it was entirely unblemished.

Even without the headset, I could have picked it out immediately. It was half a metre in diameter, its surface a mottled patchwork of bronze, silver and gold that swirled and moved like a time-lapse film of clouds seen from space. I had never seen the surface of the damaged Hypersphere back in the Crag move in such a fashion: in fact, it was quite ethereally beautiful in a way that other one had never been.

No wonder the Pathfinders had picked it for a backdrop to

their group photograph, little suspecting the device could take them to any alternate they desired, instantly.

'Can you find out if it's working?' asked Borodin, sounding breathless.

'It's not that simple,' I said, stepping closer to the Hypersphere.

As soon as I did, virtual signposts in the language of the Syllogikos appeared all around the device, warning me not to come any closer to it without prior authorization: 'Keep Out' signs, in essence.

'Well?' Borodin demanded.

I ignored him, circling the artefact and studying it from all sides. Like the one back in the Crag, a Syllogikos-designed computer interface had been laid over the original, nearly incomprehensible, command system. It was indeed quite perfect, its skin flawless. But was it fully functional?

I stepped a little closer and another message appeared, flashing red. I selected it with a glance and it expanded to reveal a more detailed warning: native defence systems had been set to guard the device – with lethal measures, if necessary. Any attempt to interfere with the Hypersphere, in any way, carried the risk of triggering those measures.

But as to what those lethal measures might be, I had no idea. I hesitated to get any closer to it until I knew more.

'Hey!' a voice shouted, from the depths of the shed.

I quickly snatched the headset from above my ear and hid it in my fist. Rozalia came stamping towards us, her face twisted up in an angry scowl. 'Goddammit, what the hell are you people doing wandering off like that?'

Borodin tensed, his hand moving towards his rear pocket. I wondered if he had a knife or some other weapon hidden there.

'I'm sorry,' I said, moving quickly to stand between them.

'It's just that we couldn't resist taking more of a look around and . . .'

'And we got lost,' said Borodin, affecting a smile that even I found far from convincing. He let his empty hand flop to his side, and I realized I had been holding my breath. 'I must apologize. It was my fault, really.'

Rozalia just stared at us. 'Well, I don't know what the hell you were doing all the way over here, but I need you back with the rest of our group. Please don't *ever* do something like that again.' She looked past Borodin, at the Hypersphere. 'I see you found the Beachball, huh?'

I blinked, unsure what she meant. 'The what?'

'That thing,' she said, nodding at the Hypersphere, then let a small grin twist up one side of her face. 'Catches the eye, doesn't it?'

'Yes,' I said. 'Yes, it does.'

'This way,' said Rozalia, gesturing back into the shadows. She waited as we made our way past her before following behind – careful, I noticed, never to turn her back on us once.

SIX

After that, we returned to the island. I retrieved my jacket from the locker I had been assigned, along with the box of beads I had found, taking the utmost care to make sure no one saw me tuck it deep inside a pocket. Then I followed the Soviets outside, where they sat on the grass close by the hangar, talking animatedly about everything they had seen. I wandered past them, towards a raised mound of land from where I could see the ocean.

I heard footsteps come up after me. I didn't turn around: all I wanted to do was stare out at that wild blue nothingness and let my mind empty of all thoughts. Instead it was filled with visions of a little girl dancing through a field by a cottage.

'You've done well today,' Borodin said from behind me. 'We still have to find a way to retrieve the Hypersphere, of course, but one step at a time. First, however, we need to get hold of the coordinates for Delta Twenty-Five so we can return for the Hypersphere.'

'That shouldn't be hard for you,' I said, still gazing at the ocean. 'You got us this far, after all.'

'As you said yourself,' he said, 'it's not that simple.'

I turned at last to look at him. I could see the Soviets past his shoulder, sprawled on the grass. 'You do realize that the Authority may be on the verge of finding out what caused the Syllogikos to disappear? We never found so much as a hint, but they have those bodies. They're right to think they're close to an answer.'

'That,' he said, 'is not relevant to our mission. You still have the headset?'

I dropped the headset into his outstretched palm and shook my head with ill-concealed irritation. 'Did it *never* occur to you,' I asked, 'to wonder why they disappeared? It is the *single greatest mystery* surrounding them. Yet by the looks of it, those dead Syllogikos deliberately stranded themselves in a place where they had zero chance of surviving.'

'So?'

'So maybe if we can find out what caused them to disappear,' I continued, stunned by his obstinacy, 'we might be able to prevent the same thing happening to the Novaya Empire. Those bodies might be the proof we need that the Syllogikos were overwhelmed by some kind of outside force. What if we were to run into that same force, while exploring new alternates? Shouldn't we be prepared for that eventuality?'

'Focus on your mission, and your mission alone,' he said. 'Nothing else should concern you. Is that understood?'

I nodded reluctantly.

'Now, about that Pathfinder,' he continued. 'Jerry Beche. You said he had the coordinates for Delta Twenty-Five in his notebook?'

I nodded again.

'For the moment I'll assume Beche is our best hope for acquiring them.' He gave me an arch look. 'I had the sense he was deliberately seeking out your company today. Would you say he was . . . interested in you?'

I looked at him sharply. 'What do you mean?'

'If he has some kind of romantic interest in you, we might

be able to exploit it. If you could get close enough to him to gain his confidence – seduce him, if necessary – you might be able to steal his notebook, or at least copy the necessary co-ordinates.'

I felt a sudden rush of loathing and had to struggle not to show my contempt. 'I had to watch as you murdered the only man I ever loved, and now you expect me to *whore* for you?'

'I expect you to do whatever I tell you to.'

'You're assuming he's even interested,' I said, fighting down my anger. 'He might just be keeping an eye on us. That woman Rozalia clearly didn't believe our story for one moment. Did you see how carefully she's been watching us ever since? She might have told the rest of them all about how she found us pawing over the Hypersphere.'

'That was a necessary risk. And if Beche isn't interested in you, then you'd better find a way to *make* him interested if it means you can get those coordinates. Remember, Katya, it's not only your life that's at stake. There's your father, not to mention your fellow exiles.'

I couldn't take any more and turned away from him. 'Please,' I hissed, 'go now, I beg you.'

I stared back out at the ocean, a blood-red tide of anger and hatred roiling in my veins. When I heard him finally move away, I let out a shuddering breath.

I had been holding myself so rigid that my ribs ached. I stayed where I was for another minute before I rejoined the Soviets, having waited until I felt sure they would not be able to see the anger and bitterness still burning within me.

When I walked back over, none of them paid me any particular attention, or gave any sign they were aware I might be upset.

All except Rozalia, who gave me a long, speculative look from where she stood chatting with a worker in overalls by the hangar entrance.

After that, we piled into several jeeps and went home. I ran to the bathroom and locked the door. I sat on the edge of the toilet seat before taking out the wooden box and balancing it on my knees. My hands trembled as I opened its lid. I took a long, deep breath and picked out the grey bead that had conjured such rich and powerful images when I first held it.

Once again, and through some unnamed man's eyes, I watched a little girl run through a field. Perhaps, I thought, he was her father, in which case the woman who stood watching by his side could well be the girl's mother. Perhaps they had lived in the stone cottage I could see at the edge of the field.

Something about the sight of her filled me with a terrible sadness. Once she faded, I let the tiny grey bead drop back into the box, then reached for the second, black bead – the only other one I had managed to snatch up from the dust before Jerry interrupted us.

There was nothing idyllic about what I next experienced.

Once again, I was in someone else's skin. I wore a long dark coat that flapped around my thighs as I ran, my feet echoing damply against stone. I hurtled down an arched passageway towards sunlight at the far end.

I emerged into the open to see I was surrounded by ancient stone buildings rising all around. Strange, futuristic-looking vehicles stood all along the street. Everywhere I looked, there were people standing pointing or staring upwards, all of them dressed in exotically weird clothes.

I – or rather, the person whose point of view I was sharing – glanced up to see a hole had somehow been ripped in the sky kilometres overhead. Beyond lay a starless void. From the way the clouds contorted as they passed before the hole, I guessed that a vacuum must lie beyond the hole, and that the atmosphere was rushing into it.

I noticed this only peripherally, however, given that most of my attention was instead taken up by the enormous *thing* at that moment passing out of this void and descending towards the ground. It was black and faceted, in shape not unlike an octahedral diamond. Dotted here and there on its hull – assuming it was indeed some form of craft – were hundreds of tiny points of brilliant light.

My viewpoint came back down to earth as whoever owned the eyes I was watching through ran towards a nearby vehicle with mirror-smooth skin. I caught a glimpse of a broad, bearded chin, the mouth wide open in panic . . .

. . . and there the memory, if that indeed was what it was, came to an end.

I dropped to my knees on the floor, turned, and vomited into the toilet. I had been able to *feel* the man's terror, somehow leaking through from the bead. I realized, then, that the sadness I had felt at the sight of the little girl was not my own – it had somehow been transmitted through the medium of the bead.

I flushed the toilet and washed my face, then quickly reached again for the wooden box, which had slipped from my fingers. The two grey and black beads had spilled out onto the floor. I hesitated at picking them up with my bare fingers, and grabbed a wad of toilet paper and used that instead. Once I had them secure, I sat on the edge of the bath and waited for my jangled nerves to settle.

Could they be real memories? If they were, what to make of that thing I had seen, tumbling through a hole apparently torn in reality . . . how could something like that have any kind of objective, solid existence?

But if it *was* real . . . then how did it connect to a desolate cavern filled with the bodies of people who had, to all appearances, deliberately starved themselves to death in the freezing dark? Was *that* what they had been fleeing?

Just thinking about the implications sent a terrible chill through me. However much I loathed him – indeed, however much I feared him – I had to tell Borodin about this as soon as possible. But he was in the next house eating with the engineers, and after that we were expected to join the Pathfinders in town for a social event.

It would not be easy, surrounded by so many others, but perhaps tonight I would have an opportunity to discuss my discovery with him. Despite his warning to focus on the mission, he would surely change his mind once he held the beads in his own hands.

I sat there for a long time, thinking of that little girl, and what might have become of her, until Vissarion angrily knocked at the door and told me to hurry up so he could use the toilet.

Later that evening I changed into dark slacks and a blouse and joined the rest of the Soviets on a short walk to the centre of town, where we were to meet with the rest of the Pathfinders. Rozalia, who had come to fetch us, led the way.

I caught Borodin's eye, and drew him aside while we walked.

'I discovered something important,' I told him. 'Those beads I found – they're much more than just beads. They're memory-encoding devices of considerable power and sophistication.'

I quickly outlined what had happened when I touched them.

'They must,' I reasoned, 'have belonged to one of the dead Syllogikos. There are more beads back there, but we were interrupted before I could grab up any more.'

He sighed. 'As fascinating as this undoubtedly is, Katya, you are once again failing to focus on our mission. Did my words fall on deaf ears?'

I felt a numbing pressure building in the back of my skull. 'I didn't forget what you said. But this is still *enormously* important. What if the rest of those beads back there contain information about the Hypersphere? If those people travelled to those caverns from Delta Twenty-Five then surely it stands to reason that they may have come into contact with the Hypersphere. All I ask is that you touch the beads I brought back. I am convinced they are hugely important.'

Up ahead, Elena glanced back at us. We were trailing behind the rest of the Soviets. Rozalia was walking by Elena's side, and the two of them had been deep in conversation. Borodin raised his hand in greeting to Elena and we made to catch up.

'Later tonight, perhaps,' he muttered, 'if there's an opportunity. But not before.'

Our destination turned out to be a whitewashed two-storey building close to the centre of the town, its exterior festooned with coloured lights that blinked in the dimming evening light. It was evidently a former hotel bar. I could see a pool area around the back, with seats and tables scattered around, although the water turned out to be filthy when I took a closer look. The bar itself, however, proved to be well-stocked with beer, wine and spirits – much of it home-made, judging by the still occupying a corner and the carefully hand-labelled plastic kegs lining the shelves behind the counter. The air was full of loud, abrasive, guitar-driven music that set my teeth on edge.

As promised, all the Pathfinders were present. I chatted briefly, glass in hand, with a ponytailed Asian American named Yuichi Ho, and he explained the circumstances by which he had come to be the last man alive on his Earth.

I then had essentially the same conversation with a woman named Winifred, as well as a slightly disreputable-looking pair named Randall and Oskar, the latter of whom had quite the most enormous hound curled up at his feet. All of their stories, I soon came to realize, shared essentially the same broad outlines: each had survived some catastrophic event that left them alone in a hostile world, before experiencing a miraculous rescue by the Authority.

I found myself drawn towards a series of framed photographs that hung together in a darkened corner. At first, they appeared to be identical pictures of a skyscraper, albeit taken from slightly different angles.

It was only when I began to study the pictures more closely that I perceived certain surprising differences. In one picture, the building had crumbled away on one side, while in another it was coated in dense vegetation. In the next picture, the entire upper half of the building had been demolished, as had much of the city behind it.

'I took one of these,' said a voice at my shoulder. I turned to see Jerry Beche standing by my side.

'Which one?'

'Here.' He tapped his glass against the last of the framed pictures. 'I also visited it once as a kid, back on my own alternate.'

'Visited what?'

'The Empire State Building.' He frowned at my lack of comprehension. 'In New York?'

'Oh.' The name was unfamiliar to me.

'See how bright and steady the stars are in the sky? We visited that alternate today – the one with no atmosphere.'

'I remember. You said when the air froze, it fell like snow.'

He nodded. 'There are other pictures taken from other alternates, but these ones are the best of the bunch, I think.'

'And do you do this every time you visit an alternate?' I asked. 'Take photographs of ruined cities?'

He grinned. 'Not every time, no. See that guy over there?' He indicated an Asiatic-looking fellow manning the bar. 'That's Tony Nuyakpuk. He helps run this place. He and his brother started taking the pictures, then the rest of us sort of got in on the action.'

'But why is it always alternates that underwent some form of extinction event?' I asked, thinking of holes torn in the sky, strange dark shapes plummeting towards the ground. 'Why were the Syll— the Stage-Builders so fascinated by them?'

I cursed inwardly at my near-slip; I had nearly said *Syllogikos.*

'Maybe they weren't,' Beche replied. 'The first time the Authority sent people through the first transfer gate they found, it brought them right here to this island. Apart from a couple more transfer stages, they found nothing but a bunch of smashed-up computers left behind by the Stage-Builders. Now, it's true we have a list of stage coordinates that runs into the high thousands – but that's just *one* tiny piece of data recovered from a single computer that wasn't quite as badly damaged as the rest. There's no reason to assume that list is remotely representative of *all* the alternate universes the Stage-Builders visited – it's just what we happened to find.'

'Well, now we're here,' I said, doing my best to play the part of an eager Soviet scientist, 'hopefully that will change.'

He shrugged, as if this were the least of his concerns. 'Sure. I guess that would be good.'

'You don't care?' I asked, unable to hide my genuine surprise.

'I didn't say that. Sure, I think with your help we'll figure out how to find a safe alternate eventually. But the thing is,' he continued, nodding around the bar, 'this is home to me now.'

'But they said the rest of this alternate is uninhabitable . . . ?'

'Sure.' He shrugged. 'Maybe what I really mean is that even if – *when* – you and all those other scientists manage to find some nice safe alternate to colonize, I'm not sure I'd be happy there.' His face cracked in a grin. 'I know it sounds crazy, but I hate the idea of always being stuck in just the one universe. I'd rather keep exploring, but on my own terms.'

'Do any of the other Pathfinders feel the same way?'

'Sure. Most of them, anyway.'

I realized that I had been standing talking with him for several minutes without taking advantage of it. 'I was wondering,' I asked him, 'how much freedom you have when it comes to visiting all these different alternates? Are you only allowed to use the transfer stages as part of your duties, or are you able to visit other alternates whenever you choose?'

'You mean . . . just for the hell of it?'

'I ask because we saw so much today, there was hardly a chance to take most of it in. I would jump at the chance to return to some of those alternates. Particularly,' I added, 'the last one, Delta Twenty-Five.'

'It *was* kind of a whirlwind tour,' he conceded.

I pushed away a mental image of Tomas lying dead on the floor of Borodin's office and made myself step a little closer to the Pathfinder. 'Then perhaps some time soon I could arrange to return there?'

'You could,' he said. 'But not without a guide. Those are the rules. Officially, there's a waiting list. A long one.'

I licked my lips. 'But *un*officially . . . ?'

His grin grew wider. 'You're asking me if I could take you there and skip the queue, is that what you mean?' He shook his head. 'I'd really love to, but I don't see how it'd be possible.'

'Ah well,' I said with a forced smile – although in truth, I found him easier to talk to than any of the Soviets. Perhaps, under different circumstances, I might have been interested in him . . .

I pushed the thought away immediately. Damn Borodin! The thought of seducing the Pathfinder merely because Borodin wanted me to made me feel physically sick. It was a vile, repugnant notion.

The conversation moved on, and my glass was refreshed, and I told him stories of my youth, carefully edited to avoid mentioning anything that might lead him to suspect I was anything other than the Soviet scientist he believed me to be. I tried again to see if there were some way to persuade him to take me back to Delta Twenty-Five, but I got the same polite decline. I drank more – too much, in truth. I asked him about his notebook, and he told me he had left it at home. I asked if I might see it, and he evaded me, making a joke and changing the subject.

I noticed then that Borodin was watching me from across the room with narrowed eyes. I was drinking too much, I knew; I was in no state to seduce anyone, let alone act like the spy he wanted me to be. When I next looked around for him, I saw he had left.

Much later, I weaved back through the empty streets along with several of the Soviets, singing some terrible pop song beloved of the Pathfinders. The rest had gone home, although when I got back to my room I found no sign of Nina.

Wherever she might be, I neither knew nor cared. I threw myself onto the bed and watched the room spin around me until, finally, I drifted into some semblance of sleep.

I did not hear Nina when she slipped back into the room an indeterminate amount of time later. I was too busy dreaming of the day they came for me and my father when I was still a little girl, hearing again the shouts of the Tsar's secret police as they beat down our door one winter's night.

And then I woke up and realized it wasn't a dream.

SEVEN

I could hear shouting, and the stamp of heavy boots on floor-boards, and Elena demanding in both Russian and English to know what the hell was going on.

I sat up straight and saw Nina was already awake beside me. Rain pattered against the window. She pressed the heel of one hand to her head before turning to me.

'Yekaterina?' she mumbled. 'What's going on?'

'I don't know.' I got out of bed and hurriedly pulled on some clothes. I opened the bedroom door in time to see two Authority troopers coming up the stairs to the landing, their carbines gripped in their hands.

'Get downstairs, now!' one of them barked at us. 'Boris Yedov and Vissarion Chakviani. Where are they?'

I shook my head, still blurry from too much drink. Nina came to stand by my side, wearing shorts and a T-shirt.

'Their room is next to ours,' I said, my tongue feeling thick and furry.

'Both of you go downstairs and wait there,' the soldier ordered. His companion stepped towards Boris and Vissarion's door and hammered on it. I watched him, too shell-shocked to move.

'*Now*,' the soldier bellowed.

His voice awoke some primal terror in me, as if I were once

again being hauled into a black van together with my father. I took Nina's arm and led her downstairs. Elena stood by the open front door in her night smock, looking as confused and tired as I felt. I saw a couple of jeeps parked outside by the gate, where Major Howes stood talking to several of his men.

I turned as Vissarion and Boris came clumping down the stairs in their bare feet, followed by the two soldiers who had roused us.

'Elena,' asked Vissarion, 'what the *fuck* is going on?'

'They think one of us is a spy,' Elena replied, looking around us all.

Her gaze landed on me, and I felt my heart clench, sure in that moment that Borodin and I had been discovered.

Boris and Vissarion muttered angrily. Vissarion's eyes were red and watery, while Boris stood with his head hunched low between his shoulders, squinting at the pale morning sky with sour distaste. To my surprise, Nina appeared relatively un-ruffled.

Major Howes came over, his face as joyful as a declaration of war. 'Miss Kovitch,' he said to Elena, 'we've already roused the engineers. Take your people over to their house and wait there with them until further notice. I need to speak to all of you together.'

It was very clearly an order rather than a request. We were led barefoot through the rain by two soldiers and into the house next door, where we found the rest of the Soviets wait-ing in the kitchen.

Borodin gave me a small nod from where he sat at a table, his grey eyes barely lifting from the coffee cup he gripped in both hands. Illyenna and Aleksi spoke to each other in low voices until Damian snapped at them to be quiet.

'Well?' Damian demanded in Russian, staring around at all of us. 'Which one of you fuckers is spying on the Americans?'

'This is just some bullshit attempt to—' Boris began to say.

'It's you, isn't it?' Damian shouted. 'I *thought* it was you all along, you miserable fucking toad.'

Boris stared back at him with a furious expression. 'What the hell are you talking about?'

'Elena told me all about how you've been winding the Americans up from the moment you got here,' Damian yelled back, 'starting with all that crap about whoever started the fucking war—'

'But they *did*!' Boris shouted back, with childlike petulance.

'Damian—' Elena stepped between the two of them, seeing they were about to come to blows, but it was too late. Damian pushed past her and took a swing at Boris, but Boris stepped quickly out of his reach.

'A fucking *spy*,' shouted Damian, pushing past Elena and following the other man around the kitchen. 'Which Kremlin shithead decided we should *spy* on these people – will you tell me that, Boris? Or should I—'

The kitchen door slammed open and Howes came in, followed by another two soldiers, their carbines levelled at us. 'I don't speak Russian,' he said, 'so you'd better all shut the hell up or talk in English.'

We shut up.

'Now listen,' said Howes, looking around us all, 'the whole point of you people being here is we're all in the same boat, and that boat is sinking. The key to survival, as you damn well ought to know by now, is cooperation.'

'Major,' said Elena, 'I want to reassure you that—'

'Shut the hell up,' Howes barked. Elena let out a gasp as if she had been slapped.

I felt numb, and feared I might collapse to the floor. Any moment now Howes would point me and Borodin out. His soldiers would come forward and take us prisoner. I would never see my father Josef or any part of the Novaya Empire again. Perhaps Borodin's spies within the Authority and also amongst their Soviet counterparts had been compromised; or perhaps they simply hadn't done a good enough job with our manufactured pasts.

Somehow, I could not imagine Borodin going quietly. I tensed, wondering what he would do.

Howes looked around us all before his gaze finally settled on me. 'We've been tracking someone amongst you since before you even left Russia,' he grated. 'The fact is, at least one of you has a story that just doesn't add up.'

'You mean you used your own spies to uncover one of ours?' asked Vissarion. 'How ironic.'

Howes shot him a look that would have melted steel. 'The next one of you who says a damn word goes straight the hell back where they came from,' he said quietly, then looked around us all. 'Got that?'

No one spoke. Not even Boris.

Major Howes' gaze returned to me, and he raised his hand and pointed. 'You.'

I felt my gorge rise. My heart pounded in my chest with such force I wondered if I might be about to suffer cardiac arrest. I covered my mouth with one hand, afraid I might be about to vomit.

Only then did I realize Howes was not pointing at me: he was pointing at little Nina Gregoryeva, standing behind me.

Howes looked down at a crumpled piece of paper that had appeared in his other hand. 'Nina Gregoryeva,' he said, looking back up. 'You are under arrest on charges of spying on the

Provisional Civil Authority of the United States on behalf of a hostile enemy power.'

I turned to stare at her. Nina glared back at Howes with a look of contempt. Gone was the gossipy little woman I had been forced to share a room with: she had been replaced by some stranger – a person whom I no longer recognized.

The soldiers brushed past me and grabbed hold of Nina by either arm. They dragged her past us and out through the kitchen door, Howes following in their wake. The rest of us listened in stunned silence as the jeeps started up, then roared off into the distance.

Damian muttered something under his breath, his face ashen as he sank onto a stool.

'So,' said Elena, haltingly. 'Did anyone suspect?'

'I did,' said Damian, nodding slowly. 'Just not her.'

Boris barked out a laugh. 'Is that the only apology I'm going to get for you trying to kill me, Kuzakov?'

'So what?' Damian snapped. 'You might not have been a spy, but you're still an asshole.'

Boris stepped towards him, his hands trembling at his sides.

'Damian.' Elena stared hard at the expedition commander. 'I think perhaps you should apologize to Boris, don't you?'

The muscles in Damian's jaw and hands flexed and moved as Elena stared him down. Finally his mouth curled up in a sour grimace and he looked over at Boris. 'I apologize for my actions,' he said, chewing the words as if they were rotten fruit. 'But I suppose it's not really any surprise one of us turned out to be . . . dually employed.'

'So what now?' asked Vissarion miserably. 'Will they send us all home?'

Aleksi shook his head. 'Unlikely. They genuinely need us, or we would never have been here in the first place.'

'As long as there aren't any more spies amongst us,' said Damian. The corner of his mouth twitched. 'Unless we're *all* spies.'

This got a few chuckles, even from me, though by that point it might well have been incipient hysteria.

'Fuck this,' said Boris, walking stiff-legged towards the kitchen door. 'What time is it – five in the fucking morning? I'm going back to bed.'

'We have work to do,' said Elena. 'It's not that long before we'd be getting up anyway.'

'Yes, I know,' Boris replied testily. 'But if those . . . bastards are going to drag me out of my bed at an hour like this, they can go fuck themselves before I lose my sleep.'

'Boris—'

'Not this time, Elena.' He stood with one hand on the door. 'I don't really care any more what you do. I'll see the rest of you whenever I manage to wake up.'

He left, and after a moment the rest moved to follow him, Elena vainly reminding them of their responsibilities as they trudged out into the dawn.

I turned to Borodin, still sitting at the kitchen table. He gave me the faintest of shrugs, then got up and walked out of the kitchen without a word.

Then it was just me and Elena. She gave me a look of contempt, then pushed past me and through the door, something in her look suggesting this had all, somehow, been my fault.

EIGHT

Despite his defiance, Boris managed to rise after a few hours for a late breakfast. We were driven to the military compound where the transfer hangar was located before being taken on a tour of various meeting rooms, computer facilities, labs and storerooms filled with both artefacts and biological samples from more unusual environments such as Delta Twenty-Five. Then we spent the afternoon in a wooden hut while a series of Authority scientists took turns explaining some of the more esoteric aspects of the transfer stages.

Even through my hangover, it was again obvious to me how pitifully limited their understanding of the stages was. Their theories amounted to little more than wild conjecture, almost entirely unsupported by anything in the way of experimental proof. All I could do was grit my teeth at their ignorance and keep quiet.

Borodin, while not exactly avoiding me, was rarely around. His official duties were political rather than scientific, after all, and while it was frustrating that I had still not been able to speak to him further regarding the memory beads, it was nonetheless a relief not to feel as if I were under his constant gaze.

Somehow, I managed to survive the rest of that first week with my sanity intact – but only just. I had to pay just enough attention to be able to take part in discussions and workgroups, and talk about their theories as if they weren't laughable in the extreme. I fantasized about how the Soviets and their Authority counterparts might react were I to tell them even a fraction of what I knew: to do so would no doubt revolutionize their understanding of both classical and quantum physics – as well as being very dangerous and extremely foolhardy.

Perhaps that is why towards the end of that first week, while taking part in a discussion of the role of exotic forms of matter in the transfer process, I made certain alterations to an equation while my thoughts were somewhere else entirely.

'That's interesting,' said Ivor Tilley. Tilley was a high-energy physicist, drafted into leading our discussion that afternoon. Rain drummed down on the tin roof of the shed in which we were gathered. 'What gave you the idea for that particular solution, Katya?'

I had sat back down with a yawn, a little girl running in circles through my thoughts. 'Excuse me?' I asked, looking back up.

'Your solution,' said Tilley, nodding at the whiteboard with a puzzled expression. 'I mean, that's a pretty radical way of solving the problem. How on Earth did you come up with it?'

I blinked at him, befuddled, then turned my attention back to the whiteboard on which I had scrawled my corrections. 'It's merely a standard deviation with respect to basic Heim theory. I thought everyone . . .'

I trailed off, suddenly much more awake than I had been a moment before. I noticed for the first time the strange way Tilley was looking at me.

'"Heim theory"?' Tilley repeated, then looked around the rest of the Soviets. 'I'm not familiar with that one. Anyone else?'

A thin sheen of sweat formed on my brow. Of course Tilley

wasn't familiar with Heim theory: Gerhard Heim had been a citizen of the Novo-Rossiyskaya Imperiya.

And the solution I had just written in front of them all was key to replicating the transfer process.

I forced a laugh. 'You're right. I made a silly mistake. I do apologize.' I got up quickly and snatched up an eraser, hurriedly wiping away my changes.

I could feel their eyes burrowing into me as I sat back down. Had any of them understood the implications of what I had written? They were, after all, each quite brilliant in their respective fields; it was why they had been chosen to come here.

Tilley gave me a searching look, then moved the conversation on to another subject. Even so, every now and then, I saw him glance my way and pause before continuing.

No one said anything to me afterwards, and I managed to convince myself I had got away with it.

As for the events stemming from that brief unfortunate moment of distraction, I have only myself to blame.

A little after midnight that evening, something struck my bedroom window hard enough to wake me up. I got up in time to see a second pebble bounce from the glass. I peered down into a garden half-reverted to jungle, then saw a tiny point of orange light move in the darkness. I squinted, then saw it was Borodin, smoking a cigarette.

I grabbed up the carved box with its memory beads and made my way downstairs to meet him.

'Is anyone else in your house?' he asked when I got there. 'The engineers have all disappeared from mine.'

'They all went off to look at the Easter Island statues.'

'Why didn't you go with them?'

'I said I was too tired. You?'

He blew smoke to one side. 'They didn't invite me.'

Clearly the Soviets had the measure of him. 'I need you to see something.'

He took a draw on his cigarette and sighed. 'These beads of yours?'

'Yes,' I said testily. 'I haven't seen you in a week. Where have you been?'

He gazed back at me calmly. 'Reconnoitring,' he replied. Something in the way he said it made me unwilling to ask for clarification.

I pulled on a pair of thin gloves, then opened the box, lifting out the grey bead and holding it in my palm before him.

'What is it, exactly?' he asked warily, peering down at it.

'Some form of highly immersive technology – perhaps the Syllogikos equivalent of a holiday snapshot. The experience is short, but powerful. Here,' I said, holding it out for him. 'It's quite safe, but takes effect the moment it comes into contact with skin. Frankly, there aren't the words to do the experience justice.'

He looked at it askance, but let me drop the bead into the cupped palm of his hand. I watched with interest: I had not yet had the opportunity to observe the effect the beads had on another person.

He stiffened immediately, his lips parting and his eyes becoming glazed. He remained quite still. Then, after barely more than a few moments, his shoulders relaxed and his gaze once again focused on me.

'The girl . . .' he managed to say. '. . . how? Who is she?'

'No idea,' I said, letting him drop the bead back in the box. 'Whoever she is, she was important to someone who died in those caverns.'

He nodded at the box. 'What about the other bead you've got there?'

'Not a holiday snapshot by any stretch,' I replied, offering it to him.

I waited and watched as he held it. When I myself had held either bead, the subjective experience had lasted perhaps a minute or two. But from watching Borodin, I realized that how-ever long the subjective experience might be, objectively it lasted no more than a few seconds.

By the time he dropped the bead back into its box, his skin had turned quite pale.

'Now you understand,' I said, 'why I wanted you to touch them.'

'Who else has seen these?' he asked, taking the box from me and studying the delicate carving on its sides.

'No one,' I said. 'Just you and me. Gospodin Borodin . . . based on that second bead alone, I urge you to consider making the retrieval of the rest of those beads as much a prior-ity of our mission as obtaining the Hypersphere.'

He snapped a look at me. 'Be careful what you say, Katya. I don't like having to repeat myself.'

'But think about that thing falling from the sky!' I tapped the lid of the box. 'It might be a memory of the very event that caused the Syllogikos to abandon every one of their bases that we found! Surely, if that is the case, we need to make finding out the nature of that threat a fundamental priority.'

'As academically interesting as such a goal might be, it's still far from relevant to our mission objective.'

My jaw nearly flopped open. 'How could it *not* be relevant? If these beads can give us clues as to what extinguished the Syllogikos, should we not focus all of our energies on avoiding the same fate? Someone carried those beads all the way to those caverns and died there. We only have these two beads, which means we're seeing only one tiny part of a much larger picture. The rest of them could contain information that proves equally devastating.'

'No,' he said with abrupt finality. 'Returning to the caverns as well as capturing the Hypersphere would significantly increase the risk of being caught – and it would cost both our lives, Katya, to return home without the Hypersphere.' He pushed the box back into my hands. 'Perhaps you should have left it where you found it.'

'For God's sake, Borodin!' I almost shouted, then dropped my voice again even though no one was around to hear me. 'This is as important, if not more important, than obtaining the Hypersphere. What use is it to the Tsar or anyone else, if there's nothing left of the Empire but ruins?'

Borodin stared calmly down into my face, then reached out without warning, taking a firm grasp of one of my hands. He dug his thumb deep into the inside of my wrist.

I gasped at the pain, and pushed my free hand against his chest as I tried to wriggle from his grasp. But for all my efforts, he might as well have been carved from stone.

'Do you know,' he said, digging his thumb ever deeper, so that the pain became nearly unbearable, 'that I wasn't sure until the very last moment whether or not I would let you live? Talented and resourceful you certainly are, but you are also wilful and unpredictable. The fact that you're as much of an expert on Hypersphere technology as your father is the only reason you're still alive, and the only thing I want to hear about from you. Stop questioning me, Katya, or I might decide I made a mistake in not shooting you as well.'

He stared hard into my eyes, listening as my breath came in short, sharp gasps. He finally let go of me, and I snatched my hand back, pressing my aching wrist close to my chest. Borodin started to cough, and pulled out a handkerchief, pressing it against his mouth as he hacked away for several seconds.

'I never want to hear about those beads again, do you hear me?' he rasped, pushing the rag away again. 'Now, concerning Jerry Beche – I saw you talking with him at the party a week ago.'

'I asked to see his notebook,' I said dully, still cradling my hand. 'I even asked if he would take me on a trip to Delta Twenty-Five and he flatly refused both requests.' I forced myself to meet his eyes. 'He's not interested. Surely even you can see that?'

'Then you might be interested to know that Beche is scheduled to return to Delta Twenty-Five tomorrow,' he said, 'and that he intends to invite you to join him.'

I stared at him. 'How could you possibly know that?'

'I listen carefully and ask the right questions,' he said. 'A skill I wish you shared.' He lit another cigarette with shaky hands and blew smoke into the air. 'But from what I understand from Damian, Mr Beche got talking to Elena Kovitch about you – one hopes out of romantic interest, rather than anything else. What else did you say to him, when the two of you were chatting?'

'Nothing of consequence,' I said. 'Mostly he told me about being the last man on Earth.'

'Ha.' Borodin grunted dismissively. 'They *all* tell the same story. Still, with any luck it means your effort is paying off.' He stepped closer to me and I ducked my head away from his, my cheeks burning like fire. 'Employ any means you can to get hold of those coordinates, Miss Orlova. *Any* means. And remember,' he added, in the moments before he disappeared back into the shadows, 'the lives of many people, not just your father, depend on it.'

The next morning when I made my way downstairs, I had to pretend to be surprised when I found Jerry Beche sitting at the kitchen table with Boris, Vissarion and Katya.

'Hey,' said Jerry, looking up at my approach. 'I was hoping I'd catch you.'

'What is it?' I asked, heading for the cupboard where the coffee was kept.

'I'm going back to Delta Twenty-Five this afternoon to take care of some routine stuff. You said a few nights back you wanted to take another look around, so if you feel like tagging along . . . ?'

'Thank you.' I nodded, fumbling the coffee jar and nearly dropping it. 'I would be delighted.'

Jerry stood. 'Great.' He clapped Vissarion on the shoulder. 'Thanks for the coffee. Can you be at the transfer hangar at two this afternoon, Miss Orlova?'

'Katya. Please.'

'Katya.' He nodded. 'Sure thing.'

'Perhaps he likes you,' said Boris once the Pathfinder had departed, as if announcing my execution. 'Maybe your boy-friend next door will be jealous,' he added, with a slight rise of his eyebrows.

I gave him a perplexed look as I poured hot water from the kettle into a mug. 'Who?'

'Borodin.'

'He is nothing of the kind!'

'Really?' asked Elena casually. 'The two of you do look terribly earnest when you're talking to each other. And always away from the rest of us! It's almost as if you knew each other before you came here.'

'Borodin is nothing to me,' I insisted, stirring my coffee a little too forcefully.

'Don't listen to her, Katya,' said Boris. 'No matter how hard you tried, you couldn't possibly be as big a slut as Nina was.'

'What are you talking about?'

'When we were at that bar with the Pathfinders, she disappeared with one of them for several hours,' explained Elena. 'The one named Randall Pimms? When I protested to Director Blodel about her arrest, he informed me she had also "compromised" one of his soldiers and stolen his keys for the main compound. All that, in less than a few days.'

'I fucked her too,' said Vissarion, flicking idly through his orientation manual. 'The night before we got here.'

'I hope you didn't tell her anything you might end up regretting,' Elena said darkly, her gaze fixed on me for some reason. 'I'll be coming along this afternoon, by the way.'

It took me a moment to realize what she was saying. 'To Delta Twenty-Five?'

She nodded, her gaze unblinking. 'I hope you don't mind that Jerry invited me as well. It'll be a wonderful opportunity for the two of us to get to know each other better. I'd love to ask you about your PhD work in St Petersburg,' she added. 'In fact, I think we might have mutual friends.'

And with that, I knew Elena had seen through the cracks in my disguise.

NINE

The rest of that morning passed quickly with a discussion led by one of the Authority's leading physicists. I ate a quick lunch, then walked the short distance across the compound to the transfer stage hangar, with Elena by my side.

Inevitably, she asked me questions I would have rather not answered, concerning when my studies had taken place and who my professors had been. I had been carefully coached on the details of my forged identity, but there are always gaps. For that reason I felt desperately grateful to see Jerry waiting for us by the hangar entrance, and for the opportunity to bring the conversation with Elena to an abrupt end.

We donned our respirators before climbing onto the transfer stage. The control rig was unmanned, and I saw Jerry walk over and sit down before it. He reached inside his jacket and slid out his battered leather notebook.

'What are you doing?' I called over.

'Technician's catching a smoke break,' he said. 'Might as well program it myself.'

I watched as he punched the coordinates for Delta Twenty-Five into the rig, and wondered how I might get my hands on the notebook.

*

We arrived on Delta Twenty-Five in early evening. I heard the regular, piercing cry of some animal or insect from far away. Elena's expression had become sour, and I made a point of avoiding her gaze whenever possible. I wondered if I had too obviously tried to dodge her questions.

There was no one around as we stepped down from the stage. Beyond the doors of the hangar, tall arc lights made silhouettes of the surrounding jungle. We traipsed outside, following Jerry towards an Excursion Vehicle parked near one of the sheds. These all-terrain trucks combined a mobile laboratory with living quarters and had a built-in airlock. Melancholic jazz drifted towards us from within the truck's open outer airlock door.

We passed some tents, lit from within but empty. I noticed a glass vial, shattered on the ground. We kept going until we were most of the way to the EV.

'Where is everyone?' asked Elena as we walked. 'Isn't someone always supposed to be on duty at the hangar? It was deserted when we arrived.'

Jerry's head bobbed. 'Supposed to be, yeah.' He came to a stop, gazing around the darkened perimeter, the shadowed buildings and huts and tents, then back at the hangar. 'There really *should* be someone here, except . . .'

'Jerry,' I said faintly, pointing at the paving stones underfoot. 'Is that . . . is that blood?'

He peered down near my feet at a dark red stain and his eyes grew wide.

'Jerry?' I asked again. 'What should we—'

'Get back to the hangar,' he said abruptly, turning to look every which way. 'I don't know what's going on, but I really don't like this.'

'Is that necessary?' asked Elena. 'Why don't we just look and see where everyone—'

'I *said*, get back to the hangar!' he roared, grabbing the other woman by the shoulder and pushing her back the way we had come. '*Run*,' he bellowed. 'You too,' he shouted at me. '*Now!*'

Elena's face was full of fright and confusion, but she did as she was told. As did I: something in Jerry's voice, not to mention the bloodstains, made it clear something was very, very wrong.

'Wait!' said Elena when we were only halfway back to the hangar. She stopped and put her hands on her knees, panting from the exertion. 'Look ahead. Can you see that?'

I looked towards the hangar. At first I saw nothing, and was about to open my mouth to say so, when I saw *something* slither through the shadows near the hangar entrance, as if moving to intercept us. It was more like a disturbance in the air than anything physical – a shadowy outline that almost revealed itself in my peripheral vision. When I looked straight towards where it should be, I saw nothing.

Almost, I thought, as if it were invisible.

'Do you see it?' Elena asked again, gasping for air.

'I see it,' I murmured. My eye caught more movement, this time up on the roof of the hangar – a liquid, flowing motion.

A breeze blew through the strange trees surrounding the paved compound, and in the swaying motion of their branches I imagined a thousand invisible monsters waiting to rend my flesh.

'I've changed my mind,' said Jerry, his voice thick with fear. 'Go back the other way. Head for that truck with the open door, and *run like hell.*'

We ran. Elena seemed to have caught her wind, and she

managed to keep up with both of us. It was a good hundred metres or so to the EV, and I was neck and neck with Jerry by the time we reached it. I never once looked back: I didn't want to know if any of those strange, undulating shadows were slithering towards us.

Jerry threw himself inside the truck's outer airlock door ahead of me. Soft jazz still played from somewhere inside. Somehow that made the whole episode even more frightening. I saw him hesitate before stepping through the inner airlock door and into the truck's main cabin, turning to look at me briefly as if there were something important he had to tell me. Then he stepped forward and out of sight just as I reached the truck myself.

Once inside, I glanced through the open inner airlock door at the truck's interior, most of which was taken up by a materials analysis lab. It looked as if someone had emptied the contents of a butcher's shop onto its floor. Jerry stood just inside the cabin, staring down at the shredded remains of what had once been a human being.

I turned back to see Elena pull herself inside the outer airlock door. 'Katya,' she gasped, 'help me get this door shut.'

I nodded, reaching past her and taking hold of a handle attached to the inside of the door. Before I could pull it shut, however, something slammed into the truck with such force that it rocked hard on its suspension.

I lost my grip on the door handle, and Elena stumbled backwards, falling out of the truck. She got to her feet quickly, and I grabbed her arm to help her back inside. But even as I did so, she let out a sudden, sharp gasp, the colour draining from her face.

To my unending horror, I saw what I can only describe as a monstrous outline trying to drag her away from the truck.

Whatever it was, it had hold of one of her legs. I could look right through the creature, as if it was made of living glass: the hangar was visible through its body.

Suddenly Jerry appeared at my side, reaching past me to grab hold of the outer airlock door's handle and slamming it repeatedly against whatever monstrous thing was trying to drag Elena away.

Suddenly the creature let go of her, and I fell backwards, Elena landing nearly on top of me. But at least she was inside with us, and not outside with that thing, whatever it was.

Jerry pulled the outer door shut and quickly locked it. I screamed as the creature again rammed the truck with such force that I feared the EV might tip over onto its side.

In the next moment, the air was filled with a high-pitched roar that drove sharp needles of terror deep into my flesh.

I climbed out from under Elena and saw an ugly gash torn down the length of her right leg. She was bleeding profusely through the tattered fabric of her trousers. I swallowed, feeling faint from nausea and stress.

'Jesus Christ,' said Jerry, over and over. 'What *was* that thing?'

I looked at him in disbelief. 'You don't know?'

'Of course I don't fucking know,' he snapped. 'We've never—'

There was a soft *thump*, and another, lighter tremor ran through the suspension. The truck rocked more gently this time, and I heard a sound like snuffling from just overhead.

Jerry looked up at the roof of the truck, then dashed past the ruined body in the main cabin and dropped into the front driver's seat. He hit a switch on the dashboard and the music finally cut off.

The truck rocked again, see-sawing from side to side. I

thought of a cat prowling around on top of a birdcage. Elena moaned and shifted beside me. I had to do something for her before she bled to death.

I looked around and saw a cupboard up high on one wall of the main lab section, marked with a red cross. I had to stand next to the gutted corpse in order to reach it, but I soon managed to find several long rolls of gauze, a bottle of iodine solution, a pair of scissors and a needle and thread.

The truck rocked yet again, and I heard more thumping from just above our heads.

'I think there might be two of them now,' I yelled at Jerry. 'Maybe even more.'

'I'm going to drive us back to the hangar,' he shouted, still leaning over the dashboard.

'How can we operate the stage from inside here?'

'I figure I can drive the truck all the way inside and try and block the entrance with it. It's at least worth a shot.'

The truck's engine rumbled into life and we began to roll forwards. I knelt next to Elena; her face was twisted up in pain. She glanced at the medical supplies gathered in my hands. 'I hope you know how to use all that,' she said, the breath hissing between her teeth.

I used the scissors to cut away her right trouser-leg, wincing at the bloody mess the creature had made of the limb. A gash extended from just above her knee all the way down one shin, but the bleeding wasn't nearly as bad as I'd thought it would be. She was lucky it hadn't severed an artery. I unscrewed the top from the iodine solution and gripped Elena's hand in my own.

'Hold on,' I said, leaning over her.

Her hand held mine like a vice. The muscles of her jaw grew rigid, and her mouth formed a rictus of pain as I poured the solution liberally along the length of her wound. This was no time for niceties, I knew, but she didn't scream. I then set to work with the needle and thread.

'Where did you learn to do all this?' Elena hissed between her teeth as she fought back a scream.

'I was in the Young Pioneers,' I said. 'Didn't you know?'

'Hah!'

I wasn't sure at first if she had laughed or let out a gasp of pain; perhaps both. 'You don't believe me.' I finished sewing up the wound as best I could. I would have made a terrible seamstress.

'You don't strike me as the Girl Scout type,' she said, her breath coming in quick, short pants.

How true. But the Crag was short on surgeons, and somehow the task of sewing up the occasional wound or salving the occasional burn had fallen to me entirely by virtue of my sex.

I glanced forward and saw through the windscreen that we were already nearly back at the hangar. I finished my crude stitchwork and cut off a long length of gauze, lifting Elena's leg onto my lap so I could more easily wrap the gauze all the way around.

Elena's skin had taken on a curious pallor. 'Those things,' she said. 'They can't be natural.'

'What are you talking about?'

'No animal could ever evolve invisibility,' she said, her voice strained, 'in this universe or any other. They are machines, I think. Biological or mechanical, it does not matter; they must be made things.'

'Remember that evolution took a very different path here,' I said, to keep her talking more than anything else. 'Besides . . . they're not entirely invisible. They're more transparent, than anything.'

She winced as I moved her leg slightly. 'Either way, they are manufactured, I tell you . . . perhaps by whatever creatures originally ruled this alternate. I . . . I don't feel so good,' she croaked, her voice falling away.

'You're in shock,' I said. 'You'll be fine once we have a chance to get your wound properly—'

'No,' she insisted, then closed her eyes for a moment and grimaced. 'There's a . . . a feeling. I don't know how else to describe it. A numbness. It's spreading up from my leg.'

Poison, I thought immediately. But how could any poison, designed to work on creatures radically different to us, have any effect? But then I remembered what we had been told – some had suffered anaphylactic shock after coming into unprotected contact with the local flora and fauna. I had no idea how to treat such a thing, if that was indeed what was happening to Elena.

'You'll be fine,' I said, knowing how transparently useless the words must sound. 'We'll get back to the island and the hospital there. It won't be long.'

Just as I finished, the truck ground to a sudden halt, rocking hard on its suspension. I grabbed hold of Elena to keep her from tumbling onto her side, and looked up front in time to see a blurry shape slide across the windscreen directly before Jerry.

For one brief instant, the fading sunlight, streaking red through nearby foliage, caught the creature in such a way that I was able to make out its shape more clearly than before. I had an impression of a long, powerful body with spikes rising from its back, and a tail that whipped rapidly back and forth.

Then came a loud crack, and Jerry twisted sideways in his seat as the windscreen starred, but held. He suddenly slammed the truck into reverse, and the hangar began to slip into the distance with increasing speed.

'What the hell are you doing?' I screamed. 'You're going the wrong way!'

'There are more of them!' he shouted. 'I swear to God they're trying to get between us and the hangar. We're going to have to think of something else!'

The truck lurched to a stop, and Jerry spun the wheel before driving forwards again, this time aiming for the jungle. I braced myself, holding onto Elena as best I could as he rammed the EV between two of the anemone trees. As soon as the truck came into contact with whatever invisible field surrounded the paved compound, a shower of sparks danced across the windscreen. The truck bounced hard as it hit uneven terrain, but I had read in the orientation manuals that the vehicles were built for rough and hilly conditions.

'I think I can get us to the other camp,' Jerry shouted over his shoulder. The engine changed pitch as he took the truck up a steep incline. 'You're going to have to navigate, Katya, at least until we've put some distance between us and those things back there.'

'Site B? How far is it?'

'About eighty kilometres. There's another transfer stage there.'

'We need to get Elena to a hospital as soon as we can,' I said. 'She's seriously hurt. We need to go back—'

'No,' I heard Elena say. She pulled free of me and pushed herself into a sitting position against the outer airlock door. She kept one hand pressed against the wall beside her to keep from being knocked around as the truck jerked and rolled its way up the incline. 'Jerry is right – going back to the hangar is suicide.

After coming face to face with that thing, believe me, I'd rather take my chances out here.'

I saw a plastic flip-down bench set into the wall next to the outer airlock door, with a safety belt attached to it. 'All right,' I said, 'but let's get you secured first. I don't think getting thrown around is going to help you any.'

I got the seat down and secured Elena in it, then scrambled past the gutted corpse and dropped into the front passenger seat next to Jerry.

'Strap in and keep an eye on this,' he said, pointing to a screen on the dashboard that displayed a contour map. Starred as the windscreen was, it was still possible to make out the way ahead with the aid of the headlights. 'See that flashing point in the upper left corner? That's Site B. We're the orange dot towards the centre.'

'You really think we couldn't have made it to the hangar?'

'Trust me, from what little I could make out it looked like there were a *lot* of them.'

'But what *are* they? And how come we couldn't see them, like they're . . .'

'Invisible?' He laughed harshly. 'It sounds crazy, I know.'

I peered through the side window at the forest as it slipped by, then studied the terrain map, seeing tight bunches of lines up ahead that suggested a steep valley or gorge.

'What if we get to Site B and there are . . . more of those creatures?'

He was silent for a moment. 'I'm sure there won't be,' he said, sounding far from convincing.

'But once they know something is wrong, surely the Authority will send people to look for us . . . ?'

He glanced at me, then back at the darkened forest. 'It depends.'

'On what?'

'Once they figure out something's up, the first thing they'll do is send in drones to bring back video so they can try and identify the threat. Every time we explore some new post-apocalyptic alternate, there's a risk that whatever killed everybody on that particular Earth might find its way back to the island and overwhelm the people there. Killer viruses, maybe, or genetically engineered insects, or something we've never encountered. We still don't know what killed off the dominant culture here. We've never had to abandon anyone so far, but the day might yet come – and when it comes down to it, we're all pretty much expendable.'

'Surely they won't strand us here!'

'Look, don't worry, okay? Once they see it's some kind of animal that attacked us, they'll put together a rescue team to come and secure one or both of the sites. Don't be too surprised if somebody's waiting for us by the time we get to Site B.' He glanced back at the corpse whose blood was splashed liberally across the truck's main cabin. 'My guess is those creatures struck no more than a few minutes before we transferred over. It's lousy timing, is all.'

I didn't know what else to say after that. Every now and then he asked me how close we were to the gorge, and I would do my best to tell him while he squinted through the cracked windscreen. He began to drive a little more slowly when the ground became rougher and increasingly difficult to traverse.

At least, so far, the creatures did not appear to be following us.

Jerry slowed to a halt as the forest finally fell away at the edge of a cliff. I could just make out the opposite side of the gorge in the fading light, and from far below came the unmistakable sound of a fast-flowing river.

Jerry reversed the truck, twisting the wheel until we were driving parallel to the edge of the gorge. I studied the map again and saw we were now headed west, and that the gorge ran in that direction for many kilometres. Unless we could find a way across, we'd be forced to take a very long detour before we could head north to Site B.

'It looks to me like the gorge gets much lower about five or six kilometres farther west,' I said, studying the map closely. 'If the river's not too deep at that point, maybe we'll be able to drive across.'

Jerry nodded and glanced at the map. 'I hope so, or it's going to be a fifty-kilometre detour.'

I went back through to the rear to check on Elena. She was still strapped into the plastic bench, her skin a worrying shade of grey. With my respirator mask pulled down below my chin so I could breathe the truck's filtered air, the stench from the body was nearly unbearable.

'Get back up here and strap in,' Jerry shouted back at me. 'It's going to get a little rougher from here.'

I went back up front and buckled in just as Jerry began to guide the truck down a long, shallow slope. Soon, the sound of rushing water became louder. I watched as he attempted to negotiate a narrow gap between a huge boulder and two tall, gnarled trees whose whip-like branches snapped across the damaged windscreen.

Suddenly the truck began to slide to the right, bumping into one of the trees. At first, I couldn't work out what was happening until I saw one of the trees tip over and then slide rapidly out of sight, its upturned roots scattering loose dirt and rock over the windscreen.

We were caught in a landslide.

Jerry shouted something, and turned the steering wheel in

vain. The vehicle opted to obey the law of gravity instead, sliding faster and faster towards the edge of the gorge until, suddenly, we were in free-fall.

I screamed.

Barely a moment later, the EV crashed hard into something, then tipped part of the way over on one side before coming to a sudden, jarring halt.

I listened to the sound of my own panicked breathing, and the patter and thump of pebbles and dirt as they came raining down onto the truck. I looked out through the windscreen, which by a miracle was still mostly intact, and saw a vertical wall of dirt and rock. A dense tangle of branches and thick, pale vine-like growths protruded outwards from the cliff, and I guessed they were the only thing keeping us from falling the rest of the way.

We were alive, but stuck halfway up a cliff, with invisible monsters hunting us through the night.

Jerry's hands were still locked in a death grip around the useless steering wheel. I could see him fighting to steady his breathing.

Finally, the rain of debris came to a halt, and the only sound I could hear was the rush and hiss of the river.

'I don't think we're going to fall any farther,' said Jerry, his voice cracking.

I unbuckled myself, then slowly climbed out of my seat, waiting to see if my movement unbalanced the truck in any way. It didn't help much that the floor was now leaning at a sharp angle.

I peered upwards through the windscreen, trying to see up to the top of the cliff. 'We slid quite a long way,' I said. 'Almost halfway down, I think.'

He nodded, then reached out to the dashboard and tapped

at a switch before falling back and cursing. 'Radio's out,' he said. 'I think we lost our transponder during the fall. That means search parties won't know where to look for us.' He turned to look at me with a deeply weary expression. 'I hate to tell you this, but I think we're going to have to go the rest of the way on foot.'

'No,' said Elena, from down the far end of the truck.

I turned to look back at her. She had pushed herself over on one side to compensate for the angle of the truck. 'I heard what you said,' she croaked. 'We can't go out there – not while those things are still prowling around. It would be suicide.'

'We've got no choice,' Jerry insisted, looking at me rather than at Elena. 'Nobody can help us if they don't know where to find us.'

'She's right that we don't know what's waiting for us out there,' I pointed out. 'At least we're safe in here for now.'

'Even so—'

'We don't need the radio,' Elena insisted. 'They'll be able to follow our tracks and figure out which way we drove.' Her voice trailed off slightly, as if the mere act of speaking took all of her energy. 'They have aerial drones. They'll search for us with those.'

'I agree with Elena,' I said to Jerry, pointing at the corpse. 'You've seen what those things can do – must have done to everyone back there. The only thing we can do in the circum-stances is stay right where we are and wait for rescue.'

'This is hardly secure,' Jerry protested, 'halfway up the face of a bloody cliff . . . ! And I don't think you realize just how hard it's going to be to find us. There's a hell of a lot more ground to cover than you imagine.'

'Still, better in here than out there with those things, yes?' said Elena, her voice slurring slightly.

'I'm telling you,' Jerry said heavily, 'staying here is a bad idea.'

'Do we have weapons with which we can defend ourselves?' I asked.

He looked away from me. 'No. No, we don't.'

'Your friends might be looking for us already,' I continued. 'What if they find the truck empty, with no idea where we've gone?'

Jerry cursed under his breath. 'Fine.' He nodded towards the corpse. 'But if we're stuck here, we're going to have to do something about that poor son of a bitch.'

It took a lot longer than it should have, with the truck tipped almost on one side, but with patience and a lot of effort we managed first to move Elena up to the front of the truck, then to get the outer airlock door back open. When it swung free, I found myself staring straight down at the churning river a dozen metres below.

Then came the rather less pleasant task of gathering up what remained of the nameless Authority staffer's body and moving him into position. Somehow, together with Jerry, I managed to do it without throwing up. By the time we had manoeuvred his remains onto the lip of the outer airlock door, we were both sweating profusely, and covered in sticky blood and gore.

We dropped the body into the river without ceremony. It hit the water with a splash, and was swept out of sight almost instantly.

'I feel as if we should have said something,' muttered Jerry. 'Jesus, we don't even know what the guy's name was.'

'What could you say?' I gasped, wishing more than anything for a level surface to sit on. '"I'm sorry an invisible monster ripped you apart?" We don't know just how long we have to stay here. As foul as it was, it could only have got much worse.'

He gave me a black look.

We found a tank of water stored in a cupboard, and took turns sponge-bathing ourselves as clean as we could manage. We should have saved it for drinking water, but even with our respirators on, the stench of blood and bodily fluids remained overpowering. It was dark by now, and Jerry put the lights on inside the EV so we could at least try to clean up the blood spattered all over the truck's middle section.

Finally we moved Elena back inside the airlock in case we needed to make a fast exit, and got her as comfortable as possible, given the circumstances. I slumped next to her for a while, and even though she was able to talk, I could see she was rapidly growing weaker. I put an arm around her shoulder and listened to her mumble incoherently.

I closed my eyes, just for a moment. When Jerry shook me awake what felt like an instant later, I could tell from the early-morning light coming through the windscreen that many hours had passed.

TEN

Jerry put a finger to his lips, then motioned to me to join him up front.

First, I touched the knuckles of one hand to Elena's cheek as she slept: her skin had taken on a terrible pallor and felt burning hot to the touch. I didn't know if she could survive without immediate medical attention.

I slipped out from beside her and followed Jerry.

'All right,' he said, turning to face me with one hand on the back of the driver's seat, 'I think it's time for some home truths, don't you?'

I looked at him in surprise. 'I don't know what you—'

He put up a hand to stop me. 'I don't know what our chances of getting out of this alive are, but what I *do* know is that the best way to get yourself killed in a dangerous situation is to not trust the people you're with – and right now, Katya, I don't trust *you*.'

'Why?'

'Because Elena knows you're not who you say you are.' He gave me a long, searching look. 'She told me she knows people who studied in the same places you supposedly did. She even got in touch with a couple of them through official channels.'

I blinked. 'From the island . . . ? How?'

'There are two mail deliveries every day,' he said. 'Official

114

communiqués, status reports – that kind of thing. Elena sent her letters back home in diplomatic bags.' He leaned in closer to me. 'Seems none of those people she knows ever heard of you. Borodin's story hangs together better, but only just.'

I swallowed. 'I see.'

'It took a lot of work to get the Authority to agree to let you Russians work with us,' he continued. 'That whole mess with Nina Gregoryeva came close to scuppering everything. But if Blodel even *suspects* you're another spy . . .' He shrugged. 'Then the whole deal with the Soviets is kaput.'

'Why would Elena tell you this?'

'Because she knows finding a safe alternate to evacuate to is a hell of a lot more important than stupid spy games, and from her perspective, the Pathfinders are the closest thing to a neutral third party. Where most of us come from, there wasn't a Soviet Union even by the time our worlds ended. Meaning we don't have a ball in either court.'

He leaned back, shifting his foothold. 'Now, Elena thinks Borodin might have some kind of hold over you, which is why she suggested bringing you here so we could talk to you without him around. So how about you start by telling me the truth?'

'Why should I say anything to you?'

'Because if you don't, soon as we're back on Alpha Zero I'll go straight to Blodel with everything she told me, and damn the consequences. Most likely you'll be arrested along with Borodin, and neither of you gets to see home again.'

I glanced back at Elena, who appeared to still be sleeping. 'It's . . .' I closed my eyes tight shut for a moment, fighting back despair. 'It's not what you think.'

'Then what is it?'

'I . . . I cannot tell you.'

'Why not?'

Because people will die and I will be responsible.

But before I could say anything, the truck shook around us as something enormous landed on top of it.

A terrible screech boomed through the air. I heard Elena stir, mumbling to herself.

'They've found us,' said Jerry, staring up. 'We need to get out of here.'

'No.' I shook my head violently. 'At least they can't get in. If we go out there—'

Perhaps one of the beasts heard me and took this as a challenge, for in the next moment something landed hard against the windscreen behind Jerry. The glass began to bow inwards, coming away from its seal on one side.

We both scrambled down the length of the truck and came to kneel by Elena, next to the airlock. 'No, Katya, we have to leave,' Jerry said urgently. 'It's our only chance!'

The very idea filled me with terror. *With those things waiting for us out there?* I thought of the body dropping into the river, the way it had been neatly sliced open by enormous claws . . .

Then came another shuddering impact; the windscreen bowed in even farther, and I saw that one of the beasts was trying to squeeze through the widening gap between the windscreen and the frame. The creature struggled to push its way through, then retreated, pulling its spiny head out before leaping back onto the roof. The truck shifted and creaked and moved: we all cried out at the sudden, jerking motion.

The truck became still again. I heard the creak and rustle of branches, as if the creature were making its way back up to the top of the cliff.

Perhaps it had given up and we were safe. But even as I thought it, I knew it wasn't true.

I heard Elena mutter something, and turned to look at her. 'I was wrong,' she said, her voice barely a whisper. 'We have to leave.'

'But which way?' I demanded, turning to Jerry. 'We can't climb back up the cliff, not with Elena in that condition – and we'd only find that fucking monster waiting for us.'

He nodded towards the airlock. 'Not up. Down, to the river. We jump. There's nowhere else we can go.'

I stared at him. 'Didn't you see how long that drop is? You have no idea if—'

'You want to stick around and wait for that thing to come back? Maybe it won't follow us across to the far shore. Maybe it'll lose our scent.'

'You can't know that.'

'Goddammit,' he shouted, 'it's at least worth a try!'

'That still doesn't tell me how we get Elena to safety,' I hissed.

'I'll manage,' said Elena from across the truck. 'I can walk if I have to.'

'I've been in worse jams than this before,' said Jerry. 'Trust me.'

I wondered how deep the river was. Most likely we would hit shallow rocks and bleed to death, or simply drown, swept away in the water.

I knew if I allowed myself to think clearly even for a moment about what Jerry was proposing, I would lose my nerve. I nodded sharply, which seemed answer enough for him. He made his way over next to Elena, unlatching the outer airlock door and letting it swing down.

The sound of rushing water filled my senses. It roared, I thought, like something alive. I joined them, even though I was almost numb with fear, and helped the Pathfinder unstrap

Elena from her seat before helping her into a sitting position on the rim of the airlock. Her skin still felt burning hot to the touch, but there was a look of determination about her.

Jerry sat down beside Elena, his feet hanging over the airlock's rim and nothing between him and the churning waters below but a dozen metres of air. He cradled Elena awkwardly in his arms like an oversized baby.

'We go first,' Jerry said to me, 'then you follow.'

I nodded, my heart hammering.

The truck shook with sudden violence. I looked back up front in time to see the windscreen shatter into a thousand glistening pieces.

'No more time,' Jerry shouted over the noise. 'Don't wait – just jump!'

And then he and Elena dropped out of sight, just as the creature finally forced its way inside.

I needed no further prompting. I pushed myself over the lip of the airlock and fell, screaming, towards the rushing water. I could see no sign of Jerry or Elena.

The water enveloped me like an icy coffin. I thrashed, still screaming, and somehow managed to fight my way to the surface. The water was deeper than I had dared hope, but now there was the risk of being carried away by the current and smashed against rocks farther downriver.

'Over here!' I heard Jerry yell when my head next broke the surface. I still couldn't see where he was.

The water was moving fast, and I flailed, searching for something – anything – I could grab hold of. My respirator mask had slid down past my chin, and I choked on water, feeling rocks scrape my shins as I kicked.

Somehow I managed to swim close enough to the shore that

I could feel the riverbed beneath my feet. I half-crawled onto a mossy bank next to a fallen tree, spluttering and gasping.

I looked up and saw the truck halfway up the cliff above the opposite bank of the river, entangled amongst huge ancient-looking growths. I was now on the far shore from the cliff. I looked up and up until finally I sighted the truck, entangled amongst huge ancient-looking growths. Its interior still glowed with artificial light.

I made my way past the fallen tree, shivering and soaked. Once again I heard Jerry shouting. Then I spotted him: he was farther downriver, with Elena collapsed on the shore next to him.

I ran over. Elena turned on her side and pushed her mask out of the way before vomiting up water. She looked more aware of her surroundings than she had in some time. Perhaps adrenalin and the shock of immersion had helped her shake off whatever strange fever had taken hold of her.

An animal shriek broke through the air and I looked over at the opposite shore of the river. A vague blur darted back and forth along the bank without venturing into the water. Then it leaped upwards, scrambling and climbing the steep cliff past the truck and all the way to the top.

'Perhaps we are safe for now,' Elena mumbled.

'Or maybe it's working up the nerve to swim across the river,' said Jerry. 'Come on, let's go.'

'Go where?' I asked. 'We don't have the truck. How do we even know how to get to Site B?'

'Trust me, I know,' said Jerry. 'I've got a compass, and I spent a lot of time looking at that contour map while you were conked out.' He patted a pocket. 'I even managed to draw a copy of the map while I was at it.'

We made our way alongside the river for several more kilometres, until the sun rose high above the gorge. The air roared
with the sound of strange insects as the afternoon wore on. The
cliffs gradually dropped lower on both sides of the gorge until
it finally merged with a valley of low hills. At last we were able
to make our way north and away from the river.

I soon developed a bad, itchy cough, and scared myself
wondering if some native bug had found a way to plant itself
in the rich, alien soil of my flesh.

It was clear Elena was growing weaker again – and we still
had perhaps another fifty or sixty kilometres left to cover. But
somehow she continued to stumble along, holding on to one
or the other of us. When I tried to speak to her, she responded
like a sleepwalker, her voice barely more than a mumble.

'We have to find water,' I said, when we stopped to rest sometime in the late afternoon. My feet ached, and my ankles were
bruised and scarred from banging into tree roots or scrambling
through thickets of wiry vegetation. 'For Elena's sake, if not for
us. This heat . . .'

Jerry nodded. 'Now that you mention it . . .'

He took a long blade out of a pocket and stepped towards a
tree, then spent several minutes digging a hole in its bark as I
watched, mystified. He grabbed up a rock and hammered the
knife deeper from different angles, then pulled it back out.
Then he retrieved a tiny silver tube from another pocket and
jammed it into the hole, angled downwards. He leaned into it,
screwing the tube deeper into the wood. Then he turned to
look at me with a satisfied expression.

'What on Earth are you doing?'

'You wanted water.' He nodded at the tree. 'If they're anything like the trees where I come from, we should get some before long.'

After another minute a few tiny, glistening drops of water emerged from the mouth of the hollow tube. Then it became a steady drip, then a thin stream. I stared at it as if I were witnessing a miracle.

Jerry pushed his mask down on its strap and let the stream pour into his cupped hands. He drank it down quickly, his throat working as he swallowed.

He grimaced. 'Tastes kind of funky, but what the hell. Your turn.' He stepped back out of the way.

'Is it . . . ?'

'Safe? Sure.' He shrugged. 'Probably. Hurry up before it stops flowing.'

I needed no further prompting. I bent before the tube, pushing my respirator out of the way and letting the water splash onto my tongue.

It tasted like the sweetest nectar imaginable. I stayed there, frozen with ecstasy, as it poured down my throat. Then the flow began to give out and I stepped back, and Jerry worked at tugging the tube back out, grimacing from the effort.

'Trees have capillaries,' he explained. 'Even weird-looking ones like these, to funnel water up to the top of their trunks. Now let's get some for Elena,' he said, walking over to another tree and pulling his knife back out.

'Why did you happen to bring that thing with you?' I asked as he pushed the blade deep into the trunk.

Jerry finished his work before replying, again screwing the thin metal tube into the flesh of the second tree. 'Habit,' he said, letting the water dribble into his cupped hands. 'I take it pretty much wherever I go. You just never know.'

'What else have you got hidden away?' I asked, helping Elena into a sitting position. She managed to push her own respirator out of the way so Jerry could feed her water from his cupped hands.

'Hunting knife, compass, matches and a mirror. Can't leave home without being prepared for the worst.'

I shook my head in amazement, and before long we were underway again.

The forest thinned out over the next several hours, giving way to more open grassland. We kept moving, even past the point where I felt sure I could not take one more step. Somehow, I stumbled along, losing all sense of time beyond the slow passage of the sun.

Finally we came to a halt as the sunlight dwindled. Jerry again found us drinking water, and we sat down against a tree, the last of the light cutting down through its spiral of branches and making strange patterns on the ground.

I helped Elena to sit down beside me, amazed she had managed to keep moving for so long. I tried not to think about the fact we could have easily made twice the distance without her, probably even more. Jerry took out his notebook, in which he had sketched out a map, and spread its pages flat on the ground to help it dry more quickly.

Elena's head nodded to one side, and her chest rose and fell in sleep as the sky turned a deeper shade of blue.

But I couldn't rest.

If anything, staying still was worse than constantly moving. The mind conjured a thousand invisible predators in the wind-blown motion of a leaf. A branch, sawing in the breeze, became an extended claw, or part of a monstrous spiny head, its jaws gaping.

'Hey. Wake up.'

I jerked awake from an awful dream full of teeth and black, invisible fury and found Jerry leaning over me. I licked lips that were again parched and dry. 'How long . . . ?'

'Not too long.' The moon had risen above the treetops. 'About an hour. We're not even halfway to Site B. I know you're tired, but we need to keep going until we get there.'

From somewhere far off, I heard a sound like razors down my spine: a long, sonorous howl, unearthly and terrifying.

'Was that . . . ?'

Jerry nodded. 'Heard it a couple of times in the last few minutes. Doesn't sound like it's getting any closer, but I don't want to hang around one more second.' He stooped next to Elena; her head was still tilted to one side. 'Now give me a hand with—'

He froze, and I turned to look at Elena beside me. She stared sightlessly past me back in the direction we had come, her mouth slack and lips slightly parted. I shuddered at the sight of her empty gaze, and touched her hand. The skin felt cool and waxy.

I stood, feeling numb as I looked down at her. I wondered how long she had been dead.

'I'm sorry,' said Jerry, his voice urgent. 'I truly am. But we need to go.'

I was surprised at how much I felt her loss. I realized then that regardless of her suspicions about me, I had come to res-pect her the most out of all the Soviets.

'I didn't have time to tell her,' I said dully.

'Tell her what?'

'That I'm really not what she thinks I am.'

He looked at me strangely. 'Then what the hell are you?'

I looked at him. 'As you said, we should get moving.'

He regarded me for a long moment. 'This conversation isn't over, Katya.'

'I know.' I knelt next to the dead woman one last time and carefully closed her eyes. 'Goodbye, Elena,' I said, then turned to follow Jerry out across the grasslands.

ELEVEN

We were headed towards a range of mountains, following Jerry's crudely sketched map: Site B, apparently, lay on this side of them, in the foothills. Eventually the ground dipped towards another river, which proved easy to ford, and we took the opportunity to drink as much of its water as we could.

After that the grassland gave way again to moonlit forest, albeit more sparse than that we had previously encountered. We moved at a steady pace and heard no more howling from behind. I started to wonder if I really had it in me to walk the whole way to Site B: I was sunburned, starved, and my feet were so blistered that every step felt like a punishment. I hated the taste of the air inside my respirator, and the way its rubber seals pressed against my skin. I had my doubts whether there was any point in keeping it on, given the amount of unfiltered air and water we'd taken in.

See if you can get him alone, Borodin had said. *Do whatever you have to, to get hold of those coordinates.*

Up ahead of me, I saw the bulge in the back of Jerry's cargo trousers where he carried his leather-bound notebook. Everything I needed to free my father and the rest of the exiles lay in those pages.

During our long hours of walking, I had not lacked for opportunities to brood on my dwindling range of options. The necessity of survival had kept Jerry from pressing me further for the truth, but I knew that if I refused to tell him who I really was, and we survived long enough to be rescued, he would reveal all to Director Blodel. My mission would be a failure and, as Borodin had promised, my father, along with everyone else in the Crag, would die.

But if I told the Pathfinder the truth, I could not imagine either myself or Borodin ever being allowed to return home with the Hypersphere – and the result would still be the same. I had tried to think of some convincing-sounding lie as we walked, but there was nothing I could come up with that did not end with people I cared about being murdered.

Unless, that is, there was a way to keep Jerry from ever telling what he knew. Elena, after all, was in no position to tell anyone of her suspicions.

And out here, lost in the wilderness, I had an unparalleled opportunity to steal the notebook from him.

We were making our way uphill now at a steady pace. The slope was scattered with rocks and loose gravel that made it hard to get a firm footing. For the past several hours Jerry had taken the lead; I could see him just a few paces ahead, his back turned to me.

I stooped, scooping up a rock in one hand and holding it tight in my fist. I moved faster to catch up with him, raising the rock in my hand, ready to strike at him—

A pebble skidded out from under my foot. He turned and reached out, grabbing hold of my outstretched hand and squeezing it hard. I cried out, and the rock fell from my grasp.

'You know,' he said, maintaining his grip as I struggled to be free, 'I've been wondering if you might try something.'

'I didn't do anything!'

'See,' he continued, as if I had said nothing, 'when you've

lived all alone in the world long enough, there's no one to tell you if a bear or a wild dog is trying to sneak up on you from behind. But after a while you get this kind of . . . sixth sense, I suppose you'd call it. Or I guess you could say a heightened awareness, like you can smell trouble in the air. Ask any of the other Pathfinders, and they'll all tell you the same.'

'Let go of me,' I hissed.

'Do you really think you've got it in you to kill me?'

'No. I wasn't going to kill you. I just—'

'What?' He bent quickly and scooped the rock back up with his free hand. 'Then what the hell *were* you going to do?'

Once again I tried to pull free, but to no avail. 'Please,' I begged. 'Let me go.'

To my surprise, he did – and then, to my even greater shock, handed me the rock.

'Try again,' he said.

I stared at the rock clutched in my hand, then up at him. 'I don't understand . . .'

He tapped the side of his head. 'Right here. Maybe if you're lucky you'll knock me out. Maybe even worse. What are you waiting for?'

My hand trembled as it gripped the rock. I stared into his eyes, then let the rock slip from my grasp.

'Fine,' I said dully. 'You've made your point.'

'You're no killer. You're not even much of a spy, or whatever the hell you are. What did you think you were going to do, even if you could somehow get all the way to Site B on your own? Which, by the way, I seriously doubt you could do.'

'I would . . . tell anyone I found there that you were attacked by the creatures stalking us.'

'And you're sure they'd believe you?'

I rubbed my sore wrist. 'Why wouldn't they?'

'Did you forget about Rozalia?'

I stared at him.

'She told me how she found you sneaking around those sheds back there and pawing over one of the artefacts. So after Elena talked to me, I went back to Rozalia and told her what Elena said about you and Borodin. If I don't make it back, the first thing Rozalia's going to do is find Blodel and spill the beans anyway. So, since we're on the subject, how about you start telling me the truth now?'

I walked over to a tree – in my mind, I had begun calling them whiplash trees – and sat down with my back against it. 'You'd never believe me,' I said dully.

'Well, how about you start with telling me what the big deal is about the Beachball?'

I remembered Rozalia had called the Hypersphere by that name. 'Nearly ten years ago,' I said, 'my father was arrested and sent into exile, where he was forced to carry out research on an identical artefact.'

'You're saying the Soviets already got hold of a Stage-Builder artefact? How?'

'Not the Soviets,' I said, and began to explain.

After a while, we started to walk again, and I continued with my story. I came from an alternate where Tsarist Russia had come to dominate the globe. Then, precisely as had happened with the Authority, an abandoned but functioning transfer stage was discovered that led to a parallel universe – and a Stage-Builder outpost considerably more intact than any yet found by the Authority. A group of scientists – including my father, Josef Orlov – were set to work deciphering the recovered technology. It took them twenty years, but eventually they learned both how to program the transfer stages to seek out new alternates, and even how to build their own.

At first I could see Jerry didn't believe me, and he peppered me with endless questions, testing my story for cracks. But after a while his disbelief shifted towards sombre respect.

'So why arrest your father, after he did all that for them?' he asked, as we made our way up a hill.

'He was horrified when the Tsar used his discoveries to conquer other alternates, and even enslave their populations. Officially, those conquered alternates are known as the Republics. Along with some of his colleagues, Josef made contact with anti-Tsarist elements, but they were discovered and arrested.' I shrugged. 'It worked out well for the Tsar, because once in exile, he could put my father and the rest of us to work on projects he'd rather never saw the light of day.'

'But why lock you up as well? Just because you're his daughter?'

'I know as much as my father does about how the stages function,' I told him with no small pride.

'So, to be clear – you know how to program a stage to find new alternates? Even build one?'

I nodded, and he came to a stop. 'Katya . . . that's the *whole reason* we're out here, so we can figure out how to do just that! It's the solution to *everything*.' He stared past my shoulder, thinking. 'So that artefact back there, the Beachball – where exactly does it come into all this?'

I glanced up, seeing creatures like fleshy boomerangs drifting on a thermal far overhead. 'We call it the Hypersphere.'

'Why not just "sphere"?' he asked as we got underway again. The hill grew steeper as we worked our way upward.

'It exists in many more than our three physical dimensions,' I explained. 'What we see as a sphere is in reality only one tiny aspect of the whole. But, like much else left behind by the Syllogikos, it was badly vandalized. We've been trying for years to restore it to full functionality, without success.'

'While that one back there is undamaged, right?'

I nodded. 'There's every reason to think it can do everything the one we had never could.'

'And what is that, exactly?'

I stopped to catch my breath. 'Imagine,' I said, 'being able to locate any alternate with a greater than zero probability of existence, instantaneously, just by thinking about it. Imagine finding a parallel Earth where you are its supreme ruler, or where you could find a weapon powerful enough to destroy a universe.' I raised my eyebrows at him. 'Or a way to restore yourself to youth, and cure yourself of any imaginable ill.'

'Is that what Borodin wants?' asked Jerry. 'To be young again?'

The sweat poured from me as we finally crested the hill. 'No – but it's what the *Tsar* wants. The Syllogikos record that they used the Hypersphere to travel between numerous alternates, including their own, based on their desires at the moment of operating it. One alternate they visited contained something they referred to as a "healing pool".'

'Which is?'

'Some form of rejuvenation technology. They describe wading into this pool and emerging restored to youth and perfect health.'

He laughed uneasily. 'That sounds ridiculous. The Tsar really believes this?'

'In an infinite multiverse, almost anything might be possible, so long as it doesn't contravene the local laws of physics. The Tsar is dying, Jerry. He has some disease of the nervous system that makes him very frail. His son, Prince Dmitri, wants him to abdicate.'

'So why doesn't he, if he's so ill?'

'Dmitri is a man given to violent passions. He is surrounded by stories of debauchery and murder, and Nicholas fears what would happen to the Empire were his son to take the throne.'

'Doesn't sound like there's a lot of love in that family,' said Jerry. 'Say you did take the Hypersphere back home. What happens then?'

'The Tsar ensures he remains on the throne for many more years, and as a reward my father and I and the other exiled scientists will be allowed to live out our lives in some remote and isolated corner of the Empire.'

'Why doesn't Borodin just come straight here, then? Why go to all this effort, if the Hypersphere is all he wants?'

'Because he first needs this alternate's coordinates.' I nodded at his hip pocket. 'Which I believe you have in that notebook of yours.'

He blinked, his hand automatically reaching for his rear pocket.

'Well,' he said, loose scree tumbling from beneath his boots as we walked down the hill's far slope. 'Shit.'

'Now that I've told you all this,' I said, 'tell me what you're going to do.'

He stopped again and turned to face me. 'Let's say you're on the up and up. Maybe there's some other way we can sort this mess out.'

I regarded him warily. 'How?'

'You said this place where Borodin's been keeping you all locked up is isolated, right?'

I nodded. 'The Crag is the only inhabited structure on its alternate.'

'How well defended is it?'

I frowned. 'There's nothing to defend against. As I said, the whole alternate is deserted. It's essentially a post-apocalyptic, like this one.'

'But there must be *some* kind of security there.'

'Primarily to monitor the exiles. Apart from a network of cameras, there are perhaps half a dozen guards.'

'Just six guards for the whole place?'

'There are only a dozen exiles, and none of them is young. Some are extremely old. They don't need much guarding, believe me.'

He nodded thoughtfully. 'Then maybe there's some way we could break your friends out of there.'

I stared at him, astonished by the suggestion. 'How . . . *why* would you do that?'

'You said the Hypersphere can take you anywhere, right?' A grin spread slowly across his face. 'Then maybe we could use it to transport us to the Crag and break them out. Like you said yourself, they're not exactly expecting visitors, are they?'

I blinked in amazement. 'It's not as simple as you think. The Hypersphere first needs to undergo a complex process of calibration, then—'

'But it *is* possible?'

'Yes. I mean – theoretically. I'm just not sure . . .'

'About what?'

I spread my hands. 'I don't have the resources to carry out the necessary calibration. I would need computers, power sources, a laboratory . . .'

'Anything in that list we couldn't scrounge up?'

'No,' I admitted. 'Perhaps not.'

'Well, there you go. Way I see it, with all the information you've got in your head, you're just as valuable to us as the

Hypersphere is to your Tsar. You help us figure out how to find some alternate the Authority can relocate to, and we'll help you in return.'

'You would really do such a thing?'

'Well, *I* would,' he said. 'And I'm pretty sure I could talk the other Pathfinders around. The Authority themselves might be another matter. But as problems go, I don't think it's necessarily insoluble.'

For the first time in a very long time, I felt something like hope. 'But Borodin . . . ?'

'Well, yeah, there's him. But I'm sure we can find some way to deal with him.'

'You won't tell all this to Director Blodel?'

He laughed. 'Not now you've told me all this, no. Look – the Authority haven't been a democracy for a long time, not since that nuclear war of theirs. It's their own damn fault they're bound for hell in a hand-bucket. Blodel's a rule-bound idiot who makes the guy who used to be in charge look like a saint by comparison. We had to fight tooth and nail to bring the Soviets in over his objections, even though we were desperate for the help.' He shook his head. 'If we went to him with everything you just told me, I wouldn't be the least damn bit surprised if he locked us all the hell up and screw the consequences. No, we'll keep him out of the picture . . . at least for now.'

I turned at the sound of a familiar distant shriek. Some kilometres back the way we had come, a flock of the boomerang-like creatures spiralled up into the pre-dawn sky.

'I don't know if I can keep going like this,' I said, my voice flat.

'We stay still, they'll find us,' said Jerry. 'Simple as that.'

I nodded, and he waited for me to walk ahead of him.

Despite his promises, he made a point of keeping me in sight at all times.

We climbed again, high enough that we could once more see the foothills that were our destination. The ground dipped, then rose again, becoming gradually steeper until we found ourselves confronted by a sheer rock wall ten metres high. A small waterfall gushed over its lip before joining a stream.

'There's got to be some way up there,' said Jerry, standing back and staring around. He pointed west, towards where part of the cliff had crumbled, creating a steep slope. A tree had fallen down on its side, its trunk forming a bridge to the top of the cliff.

'I see it,' I said, nodding. I took the lead, splashing across the stream and working my way closer. On either side of the muddy slope was a dense mat of flat-edged vines that looked razor-sharp.

Jerry came abreast of me and nodded upwards. 'Want to give it a shot?'

I shrugged. 'It's either that, or we spend a day trying to find another route. I don't think we can afford to.'

He nodded. 'Up it is.'

He went first, pulling himself up and onto the lowest part of the slippery-looking trunk, balancing carefully as he used its bare branches as handholds. I watched with trepidation as he worked his way higher. Then, positioning his feet with care, he reached down, extending a hand towards me.

'I think it can take both of us,' he said, moving his feet slightly. 'It feels pretty stable.'

I kept my reservations to myself and slowly climbed high

enough until I could take his hand. I was desperately aware of the blade-sharp vines waiting for us if we slipped.

'Follow my lead,' he said, breathing hard from his effort. 'Do exactly as I do. Think carefully every time you move. Slow and steady, okay?'

He climbed the rest of the way with careful precision, testing each foothold and pausing before every move. I followed his lead as exactly as I could, placing my feet and hands as near as I could see to where he had put his own. At one point the trunk shifted beneath us, and I let out a terrified moan.

The trunk settled. I waited for my heart to stop thudding and continued, but even more slowly than before. I thought of the distant, impossible luxury of my bed back on the island.

We ascended carefully until we came to the torn-out roots of the tree. One by one, we negotiated our way around them, then continued on up a slope that felt satisfyingly solid beneath my feet. Soon we arrived at a small copse of growths with skinny, straight trunks and blue-brown leaves at their apex. We collapsed onto the grass beneath them, breathing hard.

'I swear to God,' said Jerry, panting hard, 'when we get back home, I will never, ever say anything bad about Yuichi's home-made booze, ever again.'

I was puffing just as much. 'You Pathfinders,' I managed to say. 'You are all very strange people.'

He looked at me in utter astonishment, and began to laugh. I stared at him, then started to laugh too, even though at first I had no idea what might be funny.

I looked over at him once I managed to stop giggling. For a moment, I thought he might lean towards me, and I wondered if that was what I wanted.

He sucked at his lips, then looked around. 'We're well past the halfway mark by now.'

'We should rest,' I said. 'We've been getting slower and slower, Jerry.'

He stood and shook his head. 'No. We've got all of the rest of our lives to rest. We have to keep moving.'

I nodded wearily and let him help me up.

TWELVE

Later still, after the sun had passed the midway point in the sky:

'That girl, Chloe,' I asked. 'Were you ever . . . involved with each other?'

He chuckled and shook his head. 'You picked a hell of a time.'

'Humour me,' I said, as we trudged through an endless-seeming forest.

'First you try to kill me, now you want to know about my love life?'

'We could still die out here,' I said. 'We haven't seen any evidence that anyone is looking for us. Even if those beasts don't kill us, we'll starve to death for lack of anything we can eat. And while you know some things about me, I know very little about you.'

He took so long to answer that I began to think he never would.

'Sure,' he said at last. 'We were involved for a while.'

'What happened?'

'I . . .' He sighed. 'It's complicated.' We walked on a bit farther. 'She was involved with another Pathfinder before me.'

'Who? Yuichi? Randall? Or . . .'

He gave me a wry grin. 'Me.'

'I thought you said *another* Pathfinder?'

'I *said* it was complicated. Thing is, I'm not the first Jerry Beche to be rescued by the Authority – I'm the second. The first one died.'

I stared at him.

'I know,' he said. 'The multiverse, right? There's more than one of everything, including people. Anyway, after he got killed on a mission, they went and got me from a timeline closely parallel to his own.' He shrugged. 'That's the great thing about us Pathfinders – lose one, you can always get another.'

'That's . . . *appalling*. Are any of the other Pathfinders . . . replacements?'

'A few. Anyway, the point is that Chloe had already been in a relationship with that other Jerry, so I guess it's no surprise she got together with his replacement.'

'But it didn't last?'

'Nope.' He shook his head. 'Turns out her and Jerry One were arguing a lot before he died.' He grinned. 'Guess in the end me and him were just a bit *too* similar.'

He came up abreast of me. 'You know, at first everybody thought there was something going on between you and Borodin, the way you were always whispering together.'

I stared at him. 'There was nothing going on, I assure you. At least, not in the romantic sense.'

'Yeah, I get that *now*. But Rozalia and a couple of the others were just about convinced the pair of you were at it like rabbits.'

I felt the anger rise within me like some great kraken from the depths of a still ocean. Perhaps it was the stress of fleeing for our lives, or the horror of *anyone* thinking the man who had killed Tomas might be my lover.

'The very idea makes me want to vomit,' I shouted, my voice ringing far through the trees. 'He is *chertov ubludok*. A piece of . . . of *fucking shit*.'

I screamed my rage at the world around us, sliding from English to Russian, employing the foulest gutter language to describe a number of anatomical impossibilities, all of them featuring Borodin as the central motif. Jerry, clearly nonplussed, came to a halt, staring at me in shock.

'I don't understand anything you just said, but it didn't sound too nice.'

I pulled my respirator off and threw it onto the grass as I stepped towards him.

'Hey,' he said, 'what the hell are you . . . ?'

I yanked his respirator over the top of his head and threw it down next to mine, then grabbed him by the ears and kissed him.

Kiss is perhaps too civilized a word. It was perhaps bordering on assault, the way I pushed my tongue into his mouth. He struggled to say something, his words reduced to an incoherent mumble, his face full of shock and surprise.

When I let go of his ears, however, he did not pull away. I slid my hands down until they pressed against his chest. He took a breath, sucking down the rich, strange-tasting air.

'What is it with you crazy fucking Russians?' he shouted.

Then he slid both hands around the back of my head and kissed me back.

We fell against the slick trunk of a tree, mouths still pressed together. My heartbeat grew to fill the sky like distant, pounding thunder.

He pushed me away, staring hard over my shoulder. I had a moment of freezing terror at the thought the beasts had finally tracked us down. But then I turned and saw a single point of brilliant pink light falling across the sky in the direction of the mountains.

'They're still looking for us,' Jerry croaked. 'Goddam, they're still looking for us! That's a flare, Katya!'

'Where is it coming from?'

'The same way we're headed,' he said. He gripped my shoulders and for a moment, I thought he might kiss me again. Then I saw his expression change, and he took a step back, his face sobering.

I realized then that with the appearance of the flare, everything had changed. A moment ago, we had been far from sure if we would live. But now . . .

'We'd better keep moving,' he said abruptly, without meeting my eyes. 'At least we know where they are – although they still don't know where *we* are.'

I nodded. Then I reached down to pick up both our respirators from where they lay in the grass, and hesitated. 'Are these things really necessary? I'm covered in shit and mud and slime – surely if anything here is capable of infesting me, it's already feasting on my flesh.' I nodded at him, equally greasy with filth. 'And you're no better.'

He looked at me, then gave out a small laugh that somehow eased the sudden tension between us. 'I guess you've got a point.' He squinted at me, and I thought I saw more than a hint of regret there. 'Ready to move?'

'Of course,' I said.

After that, it was as if nothing had happened at all.

We picked up our pace and soon emerged into open country, sighting a herd of animals off in the distance. They had, Jerry assured me, been studied and found to be harmless.

As we grew nearer, I saw them more clearly. They looked comical, with huge eyes on either side of a piscine skull, and mouths that gaped permanently open. Their heads constantly swivelled from side to side beneath hunched shoulders, their bodies balanced by long and powerful-looking tails that swept the ground behind them. They were feasting, I saw, on the fronds of the whiplash trees.

There were other animals that looked like nothing more than toy balloons gone adrift from their owners, trailing their strings along the ground. Closer examination revealed rudder-like tails that flicked from side to side, allowing them to steer in the prevailing wind, and the string trailing from beneath their bellies proved instead to be a multitude of rope-like tentacles that dragged along the ground, occasionally curling back up and toward their bodies, presumably to carry some morsel into their mouths.

We entered more dense woodland, and it grew quickly dark beneath tall and spindly trees that reached far, far overhead, swaying slightly in the breeze. Then I looked down and saw we were walking on a smooth, hard surface, hidden beneath a dense overlay of growth. I bent down and brushed some of the vegetation away, revealing cut stone.

'Let me see that,' said Jerry. He grabbed up a fallen branch and used it to brush away more of the dense vegetable matter.

'It's a road,' he said at last. He dropped the branch and looked around.

We came across the first buildings half an hour later. The forest now formed a dense canopy far above our heads, and at first the buildings looked like nothing more than great mounds growing up out of the earth, cloaked in thick vines and weeds. It was only when I sighted stone steles erected here and there throughout the forest, their smooth sides indented with strange and inexplicable designs, that I realized they were the product of intelligent minds.

'You know,' Jerry muttered, 'I think we might just have found ourselves a lost city.'

'I thought you explored this whole area with drones,' I said. 'Ruins were mentioned.'

'That's true, but not in this direction.' He nodded up at the canopy. 'Mostly we did aerial mapping. The drones wouldn't have been able to see too well through all of that. And this is definitely bigger than anything else we've seen so far.'

My eyes picked out glints of metal and glass scattered all across the gloomy forest floor. We arrived at a wide glade illuminated by fading sunlight, streaming down through a hole in the canopy, and found ourselves confronted by an enormous, metal-lined shaft, descending far into the earth at a steep angle.

I stared into its depths, speculating on what might be down there.

'I wonder what happened to them all,' said Jerry.

'It's getting dark,' I said. 'I really don't know how much longer I can keep going.'

Jerry stared down at something in his hand. 'That's not all. Something here's making my compass all screwy.'

'You mean you don't know where we're going?' I asked in alarm.

'Well, it's going to be hard, but as long as we keep aiming for those hills, we'll be fine.'

I sank to my knees, exhausted. 'But we can't even see them from in here!'

'Hang on,' he said. He stepped over to a tree and peered up its length, rubbing his hands together as if to keep warm.

'What are you doing?'

'I just had an idea, is all,' he said.

I watched as he reached up and took hold of a branch, pulling on it as if to test whether it could take his weight. Then he got a foot up on the trunk and started to climb.

The tree trembled and swayed as Jerry scrambled with remarkable agility from branch to branch. He climbed with care, but also with impressive speed, and before long he was almost at the roof of the canopy.

I could hardly bear to watch. I clutched my belly and moaned with fear as the top of the tree swayed from side to side as he scampered yet higher. I reminded myself that this was a man who had survived a global extinction event alone; he was undoubtedly of considerable resourcefulness.

I heard a shout from above and for one terrified moment feared he had lost his grip. Instead he waved to me, then worked his way back down over the next several minutes.

The tree had to be at least sixteen or seventeen metres tall, yet he had scaled it as if it were a fraction of that height. When his feet finally touched the ground, he collapsed onto the weedy soil, wheezing and gasping, his face gleaming with sweat.

'If we keep heading that way,' he said, pointing off into the darkness, 'we'll be fine. Except I saw something much, much better.'

'What?'

'Smoke. They're letting us know for sure exactly where to find them. Think I maybe even saw a couple of aerial drones, back the way we came. I tried to signal with my mirror, but I'm far from sure their cameras picked it up.' He grabbed my arm and chuckled. 'Even better, the smoke's coming from just a couple of kilometres from here. Which means we don't have to make it all the way to Site B! They might even have transport waiting for us to take us the rest of the way.'

'Then we keep going,' I said, grinning back at him.

He nodded with enthusiasm. 'We keep going.'

Soon the last of the light faded, and I caught occasional glimpses of unfamiliar constellations through breaks in the canopy. I started to feel as if I had been walking my whole life; that for the rest of eternity there would be nothing but escape, one foot in front of the other until the sun turned cold and dark, while screams echoed through the forest behind.

'Stop,' said Jerry.

I kept moving past him in a daze. He reached out and grabbed me by the arm.

I stumbled to a stop and blinked at him.

'Look,' he said, his voice hoarse. 'We're there. We nearly walked right past it.'

I looked around until I saw it: a campfire, just ahead in the next clearing.

We started to run.

I fell, exhausted, at the edge of the clearing. Flames rose from within a circle of carefully arranged stones. Damp heavy branches and leaves had been laid over the burning logs to maximize the smoke belching upwards.

And yet there was no one around. Jerry turned this way and that, calling out names. His voice echoed around the hills, with no reply.

I saw something near the fire and picked it up. A battered leather hat, with a wide, flat brim. I turned to show it to Jerry. His grin faded, and he stared at the hat as if it were a venomous snake.

Then I looked past him, seeing a shadow undulate down the length of a tree at the edge of the clearing. I opened my mouth to yell a warning, but he must have seen the look on my face, for he whirled around immediately.

The shadow leaped towards Jerry – and so did I. Without thinking, I flung myself at him, sending him crashing to the ground. He let out an *oof* as I rolled on top of him, and felt a rush of air as something passed directly over me.

The monster crashed headfirst into the fire, knocking away the leaves and branches and letting out a monstrous roar as the flames rushed up around it. In the next instant, it had jumped back up, trailing bright sparks as it sprinted for the trees on the opposite side of the clearing.

Jerry scrambled out from under me and ran towards the fire, grabbing hold of a thick branch, one end of which was ablaze. 'Grab another one,' he shouted.

I reached past the circle of stones and snatched up a burning branch. I turned my back to the fire and stared out at the surrounding darkness, Jerry by my side.

'Listen,' Jerry whispered. 'I think it's over there.' He nodded towards a puffy, mushroom-like growth. 'Can you hear it?'

I could; rocks and twigs crunched and snapped under its paws as it prowled unseen in the shadows. Then I heard a low growl from deep in its throat.

Then something extraordinary happened: streaks of bright fire slashed through the night, accompanied by a prolonged staccato thudding. The streaks moved from left to right, the trees shaking as something slammed into them again and again with tremendous force.

Then came a terrible, inhuman scream, and I momentarily caught sight of the creature, fleeing deeper into the woods. The streaks of bright fire followed it, then came to an end.

Wood crunched and snapped, and an engine roared. A huge armoured EV truck with caterpillar treads came crashing through the trees towards us. Its twin headlights nearly blinded me.

It ground to a halt next to the fire, and I saw its windscreen was also badly starred. Armoured or not, it had long jagged tears along one flank. A huge machine gun mounted on its roof swivelled this way and that, and I guessed it was under the control of someone inside.

The rear airlock door slammed open and an unfamiliar face leaned out, looking down at us where we still stood next to the fire with flaming sticks in our hands. I saw a tall, rangy-looking man with a beard and close-cropped hair, in his late forties or early fifties, his face partly obscured by his respirator. He wore a holster strapped to one thigh, gunslinger-style.

'So you managed to find your way here after all,' he yelled in a pronounced Australian accent. 'Now hurry the fuck up and get in before that bastard comes back with all his mates in tow. And – hey, you must be Jerry, Jerry Beche, right?'

Jerry stared, apparently speechless, at our saviour.

'And you're Katya, right?' asked the man, next turning to me.

'Yes,' I said. 'I am.'

'Well . . . be a good girl and bring my hat back over here, will you?' he said, nodding at the hat where I had dropped it. 'I knew I'd left it some damn place.'

Jerry didn't move: instead he continued to gape open-mouthed at the stranger, as if he had entirely forgotten how much danger we were still in.

I took hold of his arm and tugged him towards the truck. 'Come on,' I said, wondering why he was behaving so strangely. 'Time to get out of here.'

Inside the truck, I found two Authority soldiers in combat armour and comms helmets, seated before a brightly lit dashboard. Yuichi, the Japanese–American Pathfinder I had met briefly some days before, sat in the rear next to a small, compact-looking woman with short dark hair and fine crow's feet at the corners of her eyes.

'This is Katya,' Yuichi said to the other woman as Jerry and I sat across from them. 'One of the Russians.'

The woman looked at me and nodded curtly. 'Nadia Mirkowsky. Saw you at the meet 'n' greet, though I don't think we spoke.'

I nodded back. 'You're a Pathfinder too?'

She nodded again, then glared with contempt at the Australian as he climbed aboard, slamming the airlock door shut behind him before turning to look at both myself and Jerry.

'I meant to ask,' he said. 'What happened to your respirators?'

'We threw them away,' I said.

He frowned, then brightened. 'Knew the damn things were a waste of time,' he said, pulling his own respirator off and tossing it into a corner. He took a deep breath. 'Of course, if I wake up with a mushroom growing out of my head, it'll be my own damn fault.'

Jerry turned to the two other Pathfinders and gave them both a long, searching look. 'How . . . ?'

'He was already here when we arrived,' said Nadia, her expression funereal.

Our rescuer either failed to notice the tension caused by his presence, or chose not to acknowledge it. The throb of the engine grew, and I grabbed a handhold as the vehicle suddenly lurched forwards.

'Think we can outrun them this time?' the Australian asked the driver.

'We can definitely outrun them.' The soldier shook his head. 'Still can't believe how much damage that thing did to our armour.'

'Resilient fuckers, no doubt about that,' the Australian replied, then turned back to me. 'Sorry, I didn't have the chance back there to introduce myself properly.'

I handed him the hat and he pulled it on, touching one finger to the brim in mocking deference.

'Casey Vishnevsky at your service,' he said, with a toothy grin.

THIRTEEN

Site B, once we reached it, turned out to be the wreck of an enormous aircraft. Weeds and trees grew up through its torn carapace, much of which was in an advanced state of decay. Scattered all around its ruined hull were numerous artefacts that must have spilled out of its hold upon impact. I watched through the windscreen as we drove past several supply tents, then straight up the ramp of a transfer stage erected in the shadow of the derelict.

We materialized back in the island's main hangar and found ourselves surrounded by chaos. I followed Nadia, Jerry and Yuichi down the ramp and past several dozen people either shouting orders and directions at each other or standing in tight clusters while deep in conversation. Vishnevsky walked behind us.

Winifred Quaker, one of the Pathfinders, came to a dead halt when she saw Vishnevsky and stared open-mouthed at him.

The noise of conversation dropped noticeably and I looked around, seeing more and more eyes turn to regard the Australian.

Art Blodel came charging in through the hangar entrance, salmoning his way past a gaggle of technicians headed in the opposite direction. Kip Mayer followed close in his wake.

Blodel grasped one of Vishnevsky's hands in his own and

shook it. 'Looks like you got everyone back safe,' he said. 'Thank you.'

'Don't mention it,' said Vishnevsky. 'I, uh, had the chance to meet some of the Pathfinders.' He nodded at Yuichi, Nadia and Jerry, and they all stared stonily back.

'I don't understand what's going on,' I said into the sudden silence. I was tired and hungry and exhausted and lucky to be alive, and I was in no mood for guessing games. 'Why are you all behaving so strangely?'

'Goddammit,' yelled Nadia, her pale cheeks flowering red as she stepped up to Blodel, 'you *brought him back*, you son of a bitch!'

Blodel's expression became flat and hard. 'Maybe we should take this somewhere else, without making a scene.'

'A scene?' Nadia bellowed. '*That's* what you're worried about?'

'Nadia,' said Yuichi, stepping up beside her. '*Nadia*.'

She ignored Yuichi and kept her eyes fixed on Blodel. 'Do you *know* what that cocksucker did to me, before you turned up?' she said, pointing one trembling finger at Vishnevsky. 'He – he fucking *murdered* me! And not just me, but Rozalia, Jerry, and—'

'Nadia!' Yuichi grabbed hold of her shoulder and she spun around with a snarl, one hand raised and bunched into a fist. 'Look at him.' He nodded at Vishnevsky, who looked as if he would rather be in some alternate a long, long way away. 'He's dead too, Nads. *He's dead too.*'

If, at this point, a large white rabbit wearing a pocket watch had run by, I don't think I could have been any more confused or surprised than I already was.

'Let me be clear about this,' said Blodel, his face like thunder. 'I've had to mollycoddle you assholes enough as it is. The fact of the matter is, we needed every hand available to help deal with what was happening on Delta Twenty-Five, so we sprung Casey on you a little sooner than we intended. But do *not* think we haven't thought this through, or that I'm unaware of events prior to my taking over as director.'

'How long, exactly, since you retrieved him?' asked Yuichi.

Blodel gave him a furious look. 'It's not your business to—'

'We do your dirty work,' Yuichi snapped. 'You can damn well talk to us straight.'

Blodel's jaw worked. 'Twelve weeks.'

Nadia let out a long groan, and then they all started arguing again. I stepped past them and went outside to sit on the grass. After a while I let my head sink down onto my knees, closed my eyes, and tried not to think of anything at all.

It wasn't long before a couple of Major Howes' men came looking for me and Jerry, and they escorted us to the compound's medical facility. I spent six hours undergoing tests to see whether or not I would, as Vishnevsky put it, grow a mushroom out of my head. If I'd known I would have had to go through such an ordeal before they let me go home, I would have kept my damn respirator on.

While I was in there, I asked questions, and learned some more about Casey Vishnevsky. I discovered that, like Jerry, Vishnevsky had been a Pathfinder, who died – and was then brought back from the dead. Or, to be more precise, the man who had rescued Jerry and me from Delta Twenty-Five was *another* Casey Vishnevsky, retrieved from a post-apocalyptic alternate indistinguishable from that on which the *first* Casey Vishnevsky had been found.

As used to the idea of alternate realities as I was, contemplating such things tended to produce unpleasant stabbing sensations in the space behind my eyes. I also learned the original Casey had been responsible for the deaths of several other Pathfinders, who had since, in turn, also been replaced by their doppelgängers from identical alternates . . . and then I stopped thinking about it, because the stabbing pains were growing into a terrible headache.

When they finally let me go, I found Jerry waiting for me outside. He had dark bruises under his eyes that matched my own.

'Stop,' I said, when he started to open his mouth. 'Before you tell me anything else, I want to know – how can you be sure you can trust this man Vishnevsky, if he's the man who . . .'

'Who murdered me?'

'Yes,' I said.

'Honestly, I don't know whether we can. But then again, he's not the *same* Casey, so . . .' He shrugged his shoulders in apparent defeat. 'I don't know. All I can do is play it by ear. Maybe this Casey is different.'

He looked around, as if to make sure we were alone. 'Look . . . I'm going to talk to the others about everything you told me back there, when we were lost on Delta Twenty-Five. That's my priority right now. Can you handle Borodin in the meantime?'

I nodded. 'I'll do my best.'

'Just stay low for the next couple of days. And Katya,' he added, when I made to turn away, 'I hope for your sake you were telling me the truth.'

'I was,' I said wearily, then walked over to a row of jeeps parked nearby.

*

It was late when I finally pulled up outside the Soviets' house. Nobody else was around. I showered quickly, then crawled into bed and fell into a dreamless sleep. The next day soldiers fetched me back to the compound, where an interrogator examined me on every detail of my ordeal, a digital recorder by his elbow. I lied when necessary – quite skilfully, I thought. I signed a document and was told to take a few days off work to recover.

I still had not seen Borodin since my return. At some point, I knew, I would have to, and I dreaded the prospect; so much had changed, after all, and in so very little time.

That evening I joined the rest of the Soviets for dinner. Damian gave me a hug, as did Illyenna. They were eager to hear about my experiences, of course, and a glass of wine was soon pushed into my hand. Vissarion turned out to have a hidden talent: he had made fresh knish – fried potato dumplings, with blini pancakes and borscht. The meal was quite wonderful, and they did their best to make me feel welcome after a terrible ordeal. There was much talk of Elena, and the evening soon turned into an unofficial wake.

Borodin was there, of course, chatting with Aleksi; he nodded to me on my arrival but otherwise paid me no attention.

But for all their kindness, the gathering was haunted by Elena's absence. Once I had finished telling them all my carefully edited story of what had happened, the conversation rapidly dwindled, and they each made their excuses before finally departing. Damian announced he would wash the dishes just as soon as he had finished some paperwork – meaning, I already knew, that it would end up falling to either myself or Illyenna.

Then, at last, I was alone with Borodin, a sea of dirty plates and dishes scattered across the table between us.

He couldn't know how thoroughly I had betrayed him, of course. It would be impossible for him to know. And yet I felt sure he could read the truth in every line of my face, in the set of my lips.

'So,' he asked, 'did you get the coordinates?'

Sudden anger flared deep inside me. 'Weren't you listening?' I shouted. 'I was too busy being chased by invisible fucking monsters that wanted to tear me apart!'

He tapped his fingers on the table and studied me, unperturbed. 'But something *did* happen between you and the Pathfinder, didn't it? I can tell.'

I felt a muscle jump in one cheek.

He leaned back, nodding to himself in a self-satisfied way. 'A man, a woman, fleeing danger with no hope of rescue – surely under such circumstances nature could only follow its course, and what better way to gain his trust?'

'Nothing of the kind happened,' I said levelly, pushing my anger back down. 'He kept his distance. Even when he slept, he kept the notebook next to his fucking heart. There was no way I could get it without . . .'

'Without killing him?'

I swallowed and looked away from him.

His expression became hard. 'I was right. It *was* a mistake bringing you here. I thought I could use your scientific expertise and rely on your loyalty to your father. I'm guessing you had numerous opportunities to kill or incapacitate Beche and get the coordinates – and yet here you are, still empty-handed.'

He got up and stepped around the table until he stood by

my side. I felt my body grow rigid, my hands trembling where they pressed down on the table.

He placed the fingers of one hand under my chin, tipping my head back until I was forced to look up at him. 'Do you remember everything we've discussed since we got here?'

I fought to keep my voice steady and swallowed. 'I have not forgotten.'

He slammed a fist on the table and I jumped. 'Then why do you not understand what will happen if we *do not get those coordinates*!'

'And even if I got hold of them, then what?' I stammered in haste. 'Would you have us return to Delta Twenty-Five? Borodin, we were *attacked*. By *invisible monsters*. They tore everyone apart, and I am very, *very* lucky to be alive. I saw one of those creatures shot at with a roof-mounted machine gun, and I don't think it was even wounded. Going back would be suicide for both of us, I promise you.'

'I would say our odds of survival are better or at least equal to those faced by many soldiers on the battlefield,' Borodin replied, letting go of me. 'The Authority has been present on Delta Twenty-Five for quite some time, Katya, and the creatures never attacked until now. There is no reason to think they will again. In fact,' he continued, a note of satisfaction creeping into his voice, 'all this might be to our advantage. With the Authority having all but abandoned Delta Twenty-Five for the present, we could go and take what we need without their interference. But only if we act soon.'

'You know Jerry can't be the only one with those coordinates,' I said. 'Why haven't you—'

Before I could finish, he reached inside a pocket and pulled out a notebook with a faded leather binding, dropping it on the table before me. 'But I have,' he replied. 'This notebook

155

belongs to Yuichi Ho. He *thinks* he lost it. I broke into his house one afternoon while you were gone, and stole it. I had no way of knowing if you would ever return, after all.'

'And it doesn't have the coordinates we need?'

He shook his head. 'No. Beche, I have learned, is tasked with overseeing the retrieval and transport of artefacts from Delta Twenty-Five. He has a *reason* to keep a copy of those coordinates on him at all times. Ho, by contrast, rarely visits that alternate.'

'Then perhaps one of the other Pathfinders . . . ?'

He shook his head. 'They're all either a lot more careful than Mr Ho, or aren't currently on this island. We will focus on Mr Beche because we know for certain he has what we need.' He leaned down close to me, until I could feel his warm breath on my cheek. 'So get those fucking coordinates from him, Miss Orlova, and get them soon, or *I* will.'

I let out a shuddering breath as he stepped back around the table and towards the door. 'What do you mean?'

'I know how to get people to talk,' he said, pulling the door open, 'even if you don't. One way or another, be ready to return to Delta Twenty-Five in no more than a few days from now.'

'Borodin,' I asked him, as he turned to exit, 'why is it just the two of us?'

He stared at me, his gaze hard and flinty. 'What?'

'You are part of the Imperial Security Services. You must have thousands of men at your disposal. So why are you here and not one of them?'

'One more word,' he said, 'and I will not be responsible for what I do.'

Just for a moment, I thought I saw a flicker of something like fear in his eyes.

I sat staring at the table after he left. The very idea of returning to Delta Twenty-Five filled me with absolute terror. That, alone, would be sufficient motivation for me to betray him to the Pathfinders.

But first, I knew, I had to find Jerry and warn him of Borodin's threat. And the more I thought about my situation, the more I felt as if I were caught within an enormous steel vice, and it was growing ever tighter.

FOURTEEN

To my irritation, Illyenna unexpectedly returned before I could set out to try and find Jerry, offering to wash the many dishes still scattered across the dining-room table. It was the least she could do, she said.

I wanted only to be rid of her, but she was, unfortunately, quite adamant about cleaning up. Any opportunity to sneak away and warn Jerry entirely evaporated once the real reason for Illyenna's insistence became clear: she wanted to talk to me about Vissarion, with whom, it appeared, she had entered into a physical relationship. That Vissarion had a wife and two children back home seemed to make little difference to her, and I wondered how someone so vastly intelligent in the field of theoretical physics could simultaneously be so very dim in matters of the heart.

By the time I finally chased her out, it was long after midnight, and I barely made it to my bed before passing out fully clothed. I woke the next afternoon and, for the first time in many days, thought of the memory beads.

I sat up with a lurch. I threw myself off the bed and quickly dug the wooden box out from the back of the drawer where I had hidden it.

Perhaps Borodin had little interest in the beads, but Jerry, surely, would immediately recognize their importance. And since I had no work to do, I would take them with me while I went looking for him.

Unfortunately, I had no idea about where to look apart from the main compound, nor did I know where he lived. I headed for the hotel bar, where I found Tony Nuyakpuk diligently scrubbing out the drained pool with a long-handled broom.

'He's probably at the transfer hangar,' said Tony. 'They're taking a look around Delta Twenty-Five to assess the damage.'

'He hasn't gone back there himself, has he?' I asked, alarmed.

He laughed. 'Hell, no. They've been sending drones over. He's helping with the logistics, I hear.'

'Maybe I should offer my help?' At least that might give me an opportunity to talk to him.

The man shook his head. 'If they need you, they'll let you know.'

'Maybe if I could catch him at home . . . ?'

He gave me an appraising look, and I blushed. 'No guarantees when he'll be back, though. They're crazy-busy over at the compound.' He stepped towards the edge of the pool and pointed. 'Go back down two blocks, turn left on Policarpo Toro, take the first fork on the left, and his place is at the end of Sebastian Englert Road. Easy to spot. It's got these fake pink Grecian pillars in the garden.'

'Thanks,' I said, turning away.

'Remember what I said!' he called after me. 'Crazy-busy.'

Jerry's home was easy to locate. Unlike most of the neighbouring houses, it wasn't on the verge of collapse. Unsurprisingly, he wasn't there.

I headed back down Pont Avenue and grabbed one of several parked jeeps available for the taking. Fifteen minutes later I pulled up inside the main compound, which was, as Tony put it, crazy-busy. The hangar doors were closed, and from within I heard the faint whoosh and rumble of a stage in operation. Several soldiers were busy unloading two enormous multi-legged drones from the back of a truck parked next to the hangar. Neither they nor the guards stationed outside the hangar doors would tell me anything about what was going on, let alone whether Jerry was inside or not.

I returned to Jerry's house that evening, once again to no avail. Nor, indeed, could I locate any of the other Pathfinders: when I enquired again at the hotel bar, Tony informed me drily that every last one of them was, to his knowledge, carrying out some duty or other on some alternate. This was, I gathered, a frequent occurrence.

When I returned home, I found Boris sitting in the kitchen. He sourly informed me that Vissarion had decided to shack up next door with Illyenna. With the effective population of our house thereby reduced to just myself and Boris, it felt even emptier than before.

At dinner, next door in the engineer's house, I learned that probes had been sent into the deep shafts I and Jerry had stumbled across on Delta Twenty-Five. Dozens more such shafts had since been located, all leading into a single vast underground complex. One of the Soviets pulled out his laptop and showed us a video shot from the point of view of one of the drones I had seen earlier as it explored the complex. The breath caught in my throat when I saw a long row of empty three-legged cradles, identical to the ones that supported the two known Hyperspheres.

I wondered if Borodin had seen this, and if he had come to the same, obvious, conclusion: there might be more Hyperspheres on Delta Twenty-Five, waiting to be found.

Borodin, however, was conspicuously absent. I carefully asked where he might be.

'We thought maybe *you'd* know where he was,' said Vissarion, sounding surprised. He sat shoulder to shoulder with Illyenna.

'Why would I know his movements?'

'I have no idea,' he said with a knowing smirk. 'Anyway, I haven't seen him since this morning. Perhaps you could go back next door and see if he's waiting for you in your room?'

Boris stifled a snicker. I finished my meal in angry silence and returned next door at the first opportunity. It had been two days since my return: how much longer, I wondered, would I have to wait to hear from Jerry?

As it turned out, not long at all.

I rose late the next morning, and came downstairs to find Damian chatting with Boris in the kitchen.

'I thought I should let you know,' said Damian, as I poured myself a coffee, 'that the Americans have been asking about you.'

I looked at him over my coffee, still fuzzy from lack of sleep. 'What kind of questions?'

There was a look on his face I couldn't quite decipher. Not hostile, but not entirely friendly either. 'It had something to do with a discussion we took part in, back before your unfortunate experience on Delta Twenty-Five. Some solution you wrote on a whiteboard apparently got their attention enough that they asked me really quite a lot of questions about it.'

The coffee cup froze at my lips. In an instant, I was transported back in time to the hut where, in a moment of inattention, I had scrawled Heim's proof on a whiteboard. I had erased it immediately, dismissing it as a mistake and hoping it would be forgotten.

Clearly, that had been too much to hope for.

'Specifically, Kip Mayer called me to his office this morning,' Damian continued. 'He didn't come right out and make any kind of accusation, but he seemed to think that the only way you could have come up with that solution was if you somehow had access to classified information.' He paused and took a sip of coffee, studying me over the rim of his mug. 'Information,' he added, 'for which we have not yet been granted clearance.'

Beside him, Boris had grown very still.

'That's ridiculous,' I said. 'He clearly doesn't know what he's talking about.'

'Well, the gentleman leading the discussion on the day in question apparently made a point of memorizing what you wrote on that whiteboard even after you had wiped it away. He showed it to me, Katya. I still can't make up my mind if it's wrong, or if you're some kind of supernaturally gifted genius.'

'Then maybe I'm just smarter than you,' I snapped.

'Maybe,' said Damian with a forthright stare. 'Or then again, maybe it's neither.'

'Are you accusing me of something?' I said, much more defensively than I intended.

He leaned forward. 'Our position here is precarious, Katya. Nina almost got us thrown right back where we came from. Your resourcefulness and bravery on Delta Twenty-Five helped a great deal to redress the balance, but this could tip it back all the other way if the Americans think you've been stealing secrets from them, or somehow know more than they do about how the stages work. Moscow says you're not any kind of spy, but it's going to take a great deal of work to convince our hosts otherwise. So let me ask you, Katya, as one scientist to another – is there anything the rest of us don't know about you that we should?'

'I don't care what you think,' I snapped, my voice husky. I immediately regretted the words. They sounded unpleasantly like an admission of guilt.

Damian nodded and stood. 'Let me be clear about this, Katya: you tried to save Elena's life on Delta Twenty-Five, and that's why I'm here talking to you instead of just waiting for the Americans to come here and arrest you.' He tapped a finger on the table. 'If this really is a misunderstanding, explain it to me. Show me how you came up with that proof, and I'll believe everything you say from now on. Or, if you prefer, I can take you to the transfer hangar straight away. I can pull strings that will make sure you're back home and on a plane to Moscow before midnight.'

'I-I thought the hangar was all locked up?'

'Not any more, no. They opened it back up early this morning. But whatever you decide, it's going to have to be fast.'

'Okay. If you'll excuse me . . . I would like to go upstairs and get some of my things first.'

'You want to go back to Moscow?'

I nodded. 'I think it's best.'

'I see.' He nodded stiffly, looking less than pleased. I had essentially just admitted to being a spy. 'I'll wait for you here, then, if you don't mind.'

I bobbed my head and gave Boris one last glance. He had

sat unmoving throughout this entire exchange, but when I tried to catch his eye, he looked away.

'One other thing,' Damian called after me, as I made for the stairs. 'Have you seen Borodin?'

I turned back at him. 'No, I haven't. Why?'

'There hasn't been sight or sound of him since yesterday morning,' he said.

I nodded, then hurried upstairs.

I grabbed hold of the wooden box, checked the beads were still inside, then threw it into my rucksack. Then I pulled on my jacket, stepped over to the window and looked outside. There was no one else in sight.

I carefully eased the window open and looked down. There was a drop of a couple of metres to the overgrown garden below. I lowered the rucksack down first, then climbed out onto the window ledge. The grass and weeds looked thick enough to cushion me; I took a deep breath, then pushed myself into the air.

I did my best to roll when I hit the ground, but the force of the impact still drove all the air from my lungs. I lay there for several seconds, winded and in pain, but it didn't feel as if I had broken anything.

I staggered upright and grabbed up my rucksack before climbing over a low wooden fence that separated the house from an adjacent property. I made my way around the side of another house that had mostly collapsed and then I started to run, soon picking up speed.

Just as I reached the street, I heard Damian shout my name from back the way I had come. I ducked around a corner and kept going.

At least now I knew where to find Jerry. All I could do was pray that this time, he was actually at home.

I almost cried with relief when I turned into his street ten minutes later and saw him standing at his kitchen window with his back to me. I went up to the door and rapped on it hard. A moment later he pulled it open and darted a look at the road behind me.

'Anybody see you come here?'

'No,' I said, puzzled.

'Good,' he said, and stepped to the side, taking another glance up the road. 'Get inside.'

He led me through to the kitchen, where I found Nadia leaning against a counter. She blinked in surprise when she saw me.

I gave Jerry a questioning look. 'Nadia knows everything you told me,' he said. 'You can trust her.'

Nadia nodded, her eyes fixed on me like a hawk. 'That's one heck of a story I heard about you. Can't say I'm having an easy time believing it.'

'I just found out that the Authority are asking questions about me,' I said, ignoring her. 'Damian warned me they're on the verge of arresting me on suspicion of being a spy. They know I'm not who I'm supposed to be. I . . . didn't know what else to do, so I came here.'

'And we've been looking for Borodin,' said Jerry. 'Did you know he's pulled a disappearing act?'

I blinked in surprise. 'No, no I didn't – although Damian did ask if I'd seen him. He said nobody's seen him at all since yesterday.'

'He's a slippery bastard, that's for sure,' said Nadia. 'Me and Rozalia have been keeping an eye on him ever since Jerry told me about your conversation back on Delta Twenty-Five. He vanished right after we discovered his little bomb factory.'

I thought I might have misheard her. 'His *what?*'

'Some chemical supplies went missing from the main compound a couple of days ago,' she explained. 'We spotted him sneaking around one night and decided to follow him to see where he went. Turns out he's got a regular little production line set up in the basement of one of the derelict houses.'

'Do you have any idea why he's been doing this?' Jerry asked me.

I shook my head. 'I swear, hand on heart, I don't know. I had no idea. I've asked him more than once what he's been up to since we got here, but he didn't mention anything about this.'

'Well,' said Jerry, 'he's got to be *somewhere* on this island. It's only so big.'

'But why would he disappear out of sight like that?'

'I figure we did something that tipped him off,' said Nadia. 'Maybe disturbed something when we went searching around that basement. There's a million ways he could figure out we were onto him.'

'It's lucky you came here when you did,' said Jerry.

I gave him a withering look. 'I've been trying to find you for *days.*'

He shrugged amiably. 'It couldn't be helped. But here's our plan: find Borodin, get him to give us the coordinates for this place your father is being held . . . ?'

'The Crag,' I reminded him.

He nodded. 'Right. In the meantime, we need some idea what to expect when we go there – what the place looks like, for a start, the layout . . .'

'Hang on,' said Nadia, looking alarmed. 'You're taking her

story at face value. How do you know you wouldn't be walking into some kind of a trap?'

'We can get access to a drone if we really need to, can't we?' he said. 'We can send it over first to scope the place out.'

Nadia gave me a sharp look. 'That's something, but I still feel that we need solid proof that anything she says is true.'

'All the proof you need,' I said levelly, 'is right there on Delta Twenty-Five, in one of those sheds. You can use one of your drones, perhaps, to retrieve it. If you bring my father and the others here, I swear to you that we will do everything – *everything* – in our power to help you find a safe alternate. Would that be enough?'

'So what do we do with her for now, anyway?' asked Nadia.

Jerry shrugged. 'She can stay here.'

Nadia shook her head. 'No. You heard what she said. Blodel knows there's something up with her. If he sends people out to look for her, especially now she's on the run like Borodin, you're not going to be able to stop him coming in here if he wants to. Same goes for anywhere else on this island.'

He rubbed his chin. 'That leaves us with just one other option.'

Nadia nodded slowly. 'Fishing trip?'

'What are you talking about?' I asked, but they ignored me.

'Go find out from Roz if she's heard anything new,' Jerry said to Nadia. 'I'll take Katya up north in one of the jeeps.'

Nadia stepped towards the kitchen door, then paused. 'Got a particular destination in mind?'

'I figure we can maybe rendezvous at Beta Two-One-Five Orange. It's relatively low-risk, and there won't be anyone around.'

'Wait,' I said, looking between them. 'Are you talking about taking me to some other alternate? Won't it be dangerous walking into the transfer hangar if they're looking for me?'

Jerry smiled. 'Just wait and see. It's like Nadia says – as long as you're here, on this alternate, Blodel can find you.' He pulled a drawer open and lifted out his notebook, pushing it into the back pocket of his jeans. 'And until we know just where Borodin is, we need to make very sure that he can't find you either.'

Jerry went in search of a jeep while Nadia headed home. I sat waiting in his kitchen for the longest fifteen minutes of my life until I heard the rumble of an engine from outside, then grabbed my rucksack and ran out to join him.

We drove north along the west coast, towards the truly uninhabited stretches of the island. The coast road ringed the whole island, but where was there to go, on this tiny smear of land, inhabited only by ghosts and ancient megaliths?

After a while, we reached the island's northernmost point. To my surprise, Jerry kept going, turning the wheel until we were driving back south along the east coast. Off in the distance I saw some of the *moai*, the island's ancient statues, looming over the land as they had done for centuries.

Then, all of a sudden, he guided the jeep off the road and over bumpy grass, parking it next to a copse of palms, where it was entirely hidden from view of the road.

'Come on,' he said, getting out. They were the first words he had said since we got in the jeep.

I followed him down a gravelly slope to the edge of the ocean. He stepped around a boulder the size of a small house, and when I followed, I saw a small rowing boat pulled up onto the pebbles, entirely hidden from the sight of anyone driving along the road. He grabbed hold of the boat's prow and, with a grunt, dragged it down towards the water.

I watched, utterly mystified as to what was going on.

Once the boat was in the water he climbed in, taking the oars and pushing the tips of their blades down into the seabed to keep the boat from floating away from shore.

'Get in,' he called over.

I nodded towards the ocean. 'What are you going to do, row us all the way to South America?'

He twisted on the rowing boat's wooden bench and pointed towards a stub of rock, easily the size of the island's transfer stage hangar, rising out of the water twenty or thirty metres from shore. 'Nope. Just to there.'

'I'm not sure I . . .'

'Katya,' he said impatiently, 'I swear I'll explain everything, but please hurry up and *get in the damn boat.*'

Despite my misgivings, I climbed into the boat and took a seat on a bench facing him. 'I do not greatly like water,' I muttered, as the boat rocked alarmingly beneath me.

'You and me both,' he said, pushing off from the shore with a grunt.

Several minutes later we rounded the islet. I saw to my surprise that its ocean-facing side was covered over with a large tarpaulin, held in place by steel cleats hammered into the rock. From the way the tarpaulin billowed in the stiff breeze, it was obvious that a hollow space lay behind it.

Jerry tied one end of a rope attached to the boat's prow to a spare cleat just above water level, then he leaned out, unhooking the bottom edge of the tarpaulin. He stood, balancing expertly, and climbed under the tarpaulin and out of sight. He reappeared a moment later, sticking his head out and reaching down to me with one hand. 'Your turn. Stand carefully, so you don't capsize the boat.'

I stood, feeling far from steady, and took his hand. His grip was strong, and with his help I managed to get a foothold before pulling myself forward and beneath the tarpaulin. I found myself standing inside a shallow cave no more than a few metres deep, and perhaps as many high. There was just enough room to accommodate a wooden platform erected on top of the uneven stone floor, on which rested a portable transfer stage.

I stared at it with amazement. 'Does Blodel know about this? And where did you get it?'

'Never you mind,' he said, stepping towards a laptop computer plugged into one of the field-pillars. 'And where it came from is a long story.' He opened the computer and the screen sprang to life, revealing a standard transfer control interface. 'Just consider yourself privileged even to know about it,' he added, before pulling out his notebook. 'Right. I should have the coordinates I need here . . .'

A sudden thought occurred to me. 'I wonder,' I asked him, 'if we could possibly visit another alternate first?'

FIFTEEN

A few minutes later, we arrived back on Sigma Seventy-Three – the caverns where I had first encountered the memory beads.

This time, there was an absolute absence of light. My heart fluttered with momentary panic and I gulped down air, feeling almost as if I were drowning in darkness. It was also freezing cold; we had come unprepared, straight from a semi-tropical island and without the heavy arctic-style gear worn on our previous visit.

I heard a click; light suddenly flared. I blinked and saw Jerry had a torch in one hand. Its beam passed over the field-pillars surrounding us in a ring.

'Hang on,' he grunted, stepping away from me. 'I'll get us something to wear before we freeze to death.'

I wrapped my arms around my shoulders and watched the light from his torch roving across crates and equipment piled near the stage. The huge statue of Jesus slowly revealed itself in silhouette as my eyes adjusted to the near-total darkness, outlined by the faint glow of bacteria clinging to the cavern ceiling.

'Got it,' Jerry muttered.

A generator grumbled into life, and I squeezed my eyes shut against a sudden flood of brilliance. When I next looked, the pole-mounted arc lights were back on, illuminating the cavern's depths.

'Hurry up,' I shouted.

'One second,' he yelled back. He rooted around inside a plastic silo before uttering a cry of triumph and pulling out items of clothing.

His own teeth were chattering hard as he handed me a heavy coat and thick, fur-lined gloves. I pulled them on quickly, burying my mouth and nose in the coat's thick collar and feeling some of the chill loosen its grip on me.

'I don't know why the hell I let you persuade me to come here,' he said, his own coat pulled tight around him, 'but it had better be *really* good. You know, this whole place is about to fall down.'

'You did mention that, the first time we came here.'

'Yeah, well, it's getting worse, you should know. They're sending in collection teams to make a final sortie of this place, and after that, we're not coming back. It's just too risky.'

'Well,' I said, 'I wouldn't insist on coming here without a very good reason.' I reached into my rucksack and pulled out the wooden box.

He looked at it sceptically. 'What the hell is that?'

I opened it so he could see the tiny beads inside. 'I found these,' I explained, 'the first time we were brought here.'

He looked at me suspiciously. 'And you didn't tell anyone? Why?'

'I'm telling you now,' I snapped. 'And . . . I guess I didn't quite realize their significance at first.'

He frowned. 'They just look like beads.'

'They *are* beads – until you touch them.'

He darted another doubtful look at me. 'You're not about to try and whack me over the head again, are you?'

'There were many more beads,' I explained patiently. 'Along with this box. I saw them lying in the dust around that building that nearly fell on us when we were last here. They could only have belonged to one of the Stage-Builders. Just pick up the grey one with your bare fingers and see what happens.'

He sucked at his lips, thinking, then pulled off a glove and reached into the box, folding his fingers around the grey bead. He cupped it in his hand and became quite still, his gaze unfocused in precisely the same way that Borodin's had been. And, as with Borodin, the objective experience lasted barely more than a few seconds.

He blinked and swallowed, staring down at the tiny bead in the palm of his hand. 'What the hell . . . ?'

'A way of recording one's memories, is my guess. What did you see?'

'A girl.'

I nodded. 'Now try the other one. But be warned – it's quite different.'

He put the first bead back and picked up the second. When he next became aware of his surroundings, his face was ashen.

'I don't know what the hell I just saw,' he muttered, 'but it frightened the fucking life out of me. What was that thing, falling out of the sky?'

'I have no idea,' I said. 'But maybe if we can find the rest of those beads, we can find out.'

We followed the arc lights past the statue and over the bridge. I hadn't quite understood just how much the rate of collapse had accelerated until we were most of the way to our destination; many of the buildings I saw, and which I felt sure had been intact on my first visit, had by now fallen in on themselves.

When the pillars supporting the roof of the artificial sea finally came back into view, I could see huge, gaping cracks in many of them I also felt quite sure hadn't been there on my last visit. To my dismay, much of the vast ceiling mural had also crumbled and fallen.

We passed the site where the first body had been found, but it was gone, along with the ancient transfer stage. It had all, Jerry explained, been transported back to the island at last.

We soon reached the crumbled remains of the building where I had found the beads. 'Here,' I said, looking all around as I shone Jerry's torch onto the dust-shrouded cobblestones. I felt a rising sense of panic when I couldn't see them. 'They were right here, I swear!'

'Take it easy,' said Jerry, putting a hand on my shoulder. 'They'll be around somewhere. If the retrieval teams had found those beads, sure as shit I'd have heard about it. We just need to take our time and look carefully.'

A distant boom rolled through the still air, and Jerry's hand stiffened on my shoulder. We waited, but heard nothing more.

Jerry shrugged. 'See what I mean? Sooner we get started, the sooner we can get out of here.'

We got down on hands and knees and began sifting through the dust with our gloves. After a while, we took turns holding the torch while the other sifted through the dirt. I was very nearly ready to give up when Jerry spotted something.

'Hey, is that . . . ?'

I held the torch higher as he squatted lower on his haunches. He pulled a glove off, then reached down, his fingers folding around something I couldn't see.

I opened my mouth to shout a warning, but it was too late.

He became quite still, his face turned towards the ground in such a way that I couldn't see his expression.

'Jerry?'

I moved closer to him.

He took a sudden, sharp breath, falling back onto the dusty cobbles and blinking hard.

'What?' I asked in alarm as he scrabbled upright once more. 'What did you see?'

He pressed a wrist to his eyes. 'I'm . . . I'm not sure. Look – there's more of them.'

I kneeled by his side, and saw nearly a dozen more beads scattered all around, dully reflecting the light of our torch. I took off a glove and used it to carefully sweep them all into the box.

'My turn,' I said, nodding at the bead Jerry still held in his hand.

He dropped it into my hand, and I was somewhere else.

His name (I knew somehow) was Lars Ulven, a Syllogikos scientist. He – *I* – was talking to a short, stocky man with thinning hair, and who wore heavy dark clothes of a type I had never seen before. They were standing together in some kind of vault. There was something terribly familiar about that vault, although I couldn't yet quite put my finger on it.

The two men were speaking, and I had the curious experience of seeing through another person's eyes as they spoke in a language I only barely understood and had never heard spoken aloud. Lars beckoned to his companion, then led him across the vault.

I suddenly realized with a deep thrill of shock just where they were: in the underground complex on Delta Twenty-Five. Lars was looking in the direction of the very same row of cradles I had seen on video shot by a drone – except this time, every one of the cradles was occupied by a Hypersphere.

And Lars Ulven, I again somehow knew, was the man who had first discovered them – right there on Delta Twenty-Five.

The memory faded at that point. I blinked and looked around until I saw Jerry.

'Those things,' he said. 'They're the same as the Beachball, right? The Hypersphere?'

I nodded, and Jerry chuckled and shook his head. 'You've made the find of the century, Katya. Of the goddam century!'

We took turns holding the rest of the beads in turn, while the other kept watch. And together, we gradually realized, they told the separate pieces of a complete story.

Every one of them contained recordings of the memories of a single individual – Lars Ulven. Beyond some basic biographical information, such as his name and the facts regarding certain of his discoveries, lay only a kind of fog that obscured any deeper memories. One bead showed several Hyperspheres being loaded onto the flying machine whose wreckage I had glimpsed at Site B.

Another bead showed me a Hypersphere linked up to a transfer stage, on which Lars stood with half a dozen others, all of them talking animatedly. He reached out and touched the artefact, and there was a blaze of light as he and his companions were transported to some alternate it had selected for them. He was explaining to them that the civilization on Delta Twenty-Five had not in fact created the Hyperspheres – that they, in their own turn, had acquired the artefacts from elsewhere.

But where, I wondered?

I found my answer soon enough, as I handled more of the

beads, and the story proved to be considerably darker and stranger than I could ever have suspected.

One bead let me see through Lars' eyes as he stood on a broad expanse of green grass. Kites flew overhead, enormous constructions of alabaster and gold that spun slowly at the ends of cables rooted to the ground. The kites were massive – the size of buildings. In fact, the bead by some means informed me, they *were* buildings. Higher still, I saw a vast moon, much closer to the Earth than on any alternate I had yet visited, and I was stunned to realize that cables extended towards it as well – a great tangled nest reaching up from somewhere beyond the horizon like an enormous umbilical.

I saw more of the black octahedral ships, falling through holes torn in that other sky. I could feel Lars' anguish as he stared up at them.

And then, through whatever uncanny means the beads employed, I knew that the strange black ships had come from the Deeps.

The Deeps: both the name, and the concept, were familiar to me from fragments and pieces of records recovered from abandoned Syllogikos bases. If one were to program randomly generated coordinates into a transfer stage at a rate of one every second, an alternate capable of supporting human life might be found once every fifteen million years. As for all the failed coordinates, no one knew where they led – if anywhere – because no one who had stepped onto a stage and attempted to use them had ever returned.

The assumption was that these failed coordinates led to universes with different physical constants, or with many more physical dimensions, or perhaps even universes not yet born. The only certainty was that they were places where human life – perhaps even physical matter as we knew it – simply could not exist. The Syllogikos had called these the Deeps, and thought of them as a bottomless and perhaps unknowable ocean, devoid of life or even the possibility of life, while the sum total of alternates that *could* support life amounted, by comparison, to little more than a cosmic tidal pool.

But Lars (the bead showed me) knew better. He had studied the ruins of the civilization on Delta Twenty-Five and discovered it had somehow made contact with intelligent life that originated from within the Deeps. That life, strange and incomprehensible though it might be, used the Hyperspheres to navigate between parallel realities.

Then, by some means, Delta Twenty-Five's inhabitants had got hold of some of those Hyperspheres. Indeed, Lars believed they had stolen them, for the civilization had been wiped out, perhaps in retaliation, leaving no more evidence of their passing than the ruins Jerry and I had stumbled across.

By now, my hands were trembling, but I managed to pick up another bead, afraid though I was of what I might learn.

This time, Lars was standing on an enormous transfer stage, crowded with hundreds of people, all of them tired, dirty and scared-looking. He stood close to the stage's ramp, a woman by his side – the same one that had been with him when he watched a little girl run across a field. The woman was older now, with flecks of grey in her hair.

The stage was ringed by armed guards, struggling to keep at bay a great crowd of many thousands more. The air was full of their frightened baying.

A section of the crowd surged forward, swarming past the armed men with ease. Lars reached out to take hold of the woman's hand and tried to fight his way closer to the centre of the stage. A great surge of humanity came rushing up the ramp. Lars lost hold of the woman's hand. Just before the memory faded, I saw her stumble and fall from the edge of the stage . . .

I picked up another bead, and experienced Lars' joy when he and a group of explorers first found the Hyperspheres, and his increasing excitement as they carried out their first, tentative experiments with the devices. He had subsequently returned to Delta Twenty-Five on numerous occasions to search for clues to what had caused that elder race to vanish, unaware that one day, his own people would meet the same fate.

When Lars had recorded these more recent memories, he had been determined to impress one overriding fact onto the beads: his absolute certainty that using the Hyperspheres had somehow doomed the Syllogikos, much as it had doomed that earlier civilization.

But there was, I learned, a small ray of hope: so long as a Hypersphere remained uncalibrated and unused, it also remained dormant – undetectable to the creatures that created them. But once activated and used, the invaders could track it anywhere in the multiverse.

I understood then that if Borodin took a Hypersphere back home to the Tsar, it would undoubtedly be used – and the Empire and all its Republics would be doomed.

And somehow, I had to stop him before he did.

I dropped the final bead into the box and sat back on my haunches, numb. Jerry stared in silence off into the darkness.

'So,' he asked eventually, 'what do you make of all that?'

I laughed bitterly. 'What is there I could say that the beads haven't said already?'

'Did you see how some of those people had strings of these beads around their necks?'

I nodded.

'But do you think it's really true?' he asked. 'That using the Hyperspheres is the reason the Stage-Builders disappeared?'

'Lars Ulven certainly seemed to believe so.' I pictured those same monstrous black ships, falling through the skies above my home in First Republic Moscow, and shuddered.

'So.' Jerry stood on unsteady legs. 'At least now we know never to go near the damn things. But how on Earth could just using them cause those . . . things to appear?'

'I have no idea,' I said, also standing.

But I was already thinking about the possible reasons even as we headed back to continue our original plan.

We were halfway back to the transfer stage when the lights went out.

'Well, shit,' said Jerry, coming to a halt. 'Damn generator's always acting up.' He flicked on his torch and shone it around, until it showed the nearest arc light on its pole. 'Ah, fuck.'

'What is it?'

He swung his torch around, and I saw its beam was slowly fading. 'Now this damn thing's running out of juice as well.'

'Then let's not waste any time,' I said. 'I'd rather not try and find our way back in the dark.'

'Yeah, agreed,' he muttered, and we started to move faster. 'But it's mostly a straight line back from here.'

Even so, we picked up our pace again, enough so that despite the freezing temperatures, I began to grow warm inside my heavy parka.

After several minutes the torch stuttered, faded, and finally went out entirely. We came to a halt again, both of us panting hard. We had been walking as fast as we could without breaking into a run.

'Nearly there,' he gasped. I felt his hand touch my arm. 'That is you, isn't it?' he asked with forced levity.

'How in God's name do you intend to program the stage, if you can't even see it?' I demanded.

'There'll be another torch in one of those supplies crates,' he said. 'It shouldn't take too—'

The ground shook beneath our feet, gently at first, and then with increasing violence. I heard a crack like distant thunder, and then another, and another, following one after the other like gunshots. I coughed as dust swirled up around us.

A distant rumble began to grow in volume.

'That,' said Jerry, 'does not sound good.'

I looked back over my shoulder, to where I could see faint patches of glowing bacteria clinging to the roof of the cavern above the lake. As I watched, I saw some of these patches dissolve, as if the cavern roof was coming apart.

Great, shuddering shocks ran through the ground beneath our feet, followed by even greater booms and crashes that made my heart falter.

'I don't know which way to go,' Jerry shouted.

We had become disoriented. I looked around wildly, then realized I could just make out the outline of the statue, thanks to the bioluminescent bacteria that also clung to the cavern roof above it.

'This way,' I yelled, grabbing hold of him. 'We need to get to the bridge.'

It started to rain dust and grit, and we broke into a panicked run. The air soon became so choked with dust I could hardly draw breath. Somehow, I managed to keep the silhouette of the statue in sight.

I stumbled as the ground slid out from beneath me without warning. I screamed, and would have fallen if Jerry hadn't taken a tight hold of my arm. I kicked my legs and felt a rush of terror when they touched nothing but air. To one side I felt a rough stone wall.

'It's the chasm,' Jerry grunted. I couldn't see his face, even though it must have been right next to mine. 'We missed the bridge in the dark.'

I reached up with my free hand until I found him. 'Can you take my weight?'

'Sure,' he said, sounding as if he was under immense strain. 'Just let's try and get you back up.'

I pressed the toes of my boots against the chasm wall until I found some small purchase. Jerry wrapped both arms around my shoulders in an embrace, hauling me the rest of the way upwards. His breath hissed between his teeth as he lifted.

I crawled back onto flat ground, my lungs working like pistons.

'Let's take it a little more carefully now,' he said. 'I think the worst of the tremors have passed.'

My heart was still thudding hard as I pushed myself upright. 'What about the bridge? Is it still there?'

'Yeah. I think so. I can see a little better now. I think we missed it by just a couple of metres.'

We held on to each other as we stumbled along the edge of the invisible precipice until we reached the Bailey bridge. It was still intact, and we quickly made our way across. Before long we had rounded the statue and were approaching the camp.

'Shit. Did you hear that?' whispered Jerry.

'Hear what?'

'Jesus. Almost thought I heard voices.' He laughed nervously. 'I'm letting the damn place get to me, is all.'

I heard something move to one side of me.

'Hey, Nadia – is that y—?'

His sentence ended in a grunt.

'Jerry?' I asked in a panic.

No answer came.

'Jerry?' I called out. '*Jerry!*'

A hand gripped my shoulder from behind, while another clamped itself over my mouth, bending my head backwards.

'Hello Katya,' said Borodin, his voice a harsh whisper in my ear.

SIXTEEN

He kept his hold on me, but took his hand away from my mouth. Several torches came on, nearly blinding me. Voices called to each other in Russian.

'What are you doing here?' I gasped.

'Looking for you, of course,' he said. 'After you and Beche rowed out to that rock, I followed and checked the controls to see where you'd gone.'

The generator suddenly roared back into life, and the arc lights flickered on. Jerry was kneeling on the ground, looking dazed, while two Novaya soldiers with night-vision goggles pushed up on top of their heads stood guard over him. Jerry had a free-flowing cut on his forehead where one of them must have struck him.

'You were *following* us?'

One of the soldiers handed Jerry's notebook to Borodin. Borodin grinned with evident satisfaction.

'On the contrary, I was watching Mr Beche's house, and waiting for an opportunity to take his notebook.' He smiled thinly. 'I was listening from just outside his window, Katya, the whole time you were talking with him and that other woman. I heard everything you said.'

I stared at him. 'Then you know they were looking for you too.'

'And not very successfully, I might add.'

He barked an order, and one of the soldiers removed a gun from his holster and passed it to Borodin. He pressed it against my ribs and marched me next to the transfer stage.

How long had we been hunting through the shadows for beads? Long enough, it seemed, for Borodin to make use of the Pathfinder's secret stage to travel back to the Crag to round up some of Herr Frank's men, all without fear of interference.

'Borodin,' I said, 'there's something very important I have to tell you. I—'

He swung the pistol back and slammed it, hard, across the side of my face. I felt my teeth click together, and tasted blood.

'Shut up and be grateful you're still alive!' he bellowed. 'You're going to help me retrieve the Hypersphere or, God help me, I will not be responsible for the consequences!'

He gestured to one of the soldiers, then pointed at Jerry. 'Take this prisoner back to the Crag now and place him in the interrogation block. Is that understood?'

The soldier nodded and helped Jerry to stand before putting a pair of cuffs over his wrists. I watched as he was marched up and onto the stage.

'He doesn't know anything of use to you!' I said.

Borodin merely smiled enigmatically, then turned to face Jerry.

'Mr Beche,' he said, while Jerry stared back at him with a stunned expression, 'you are now a prisoner of the Novo-Rossiyskaya Imperiya. We're going to be seeing a lot of each other.'

I watched as the stage filled with light. A moment later, both the soldier and Jerry had vanished.

Then I did something that surprised me just as much as it

did Borodin: I pressed one hand against his chest in a gesture that was almost intimate.

'You have to listen to me,' I said, with as much earnestness as I could muster, 'and listen very carefully. If we take the Hypersphere back to the Crag with us – worse, back to the Empire – it's going to destroy us.'

Borodin, looking more befuddled than angry at my behaviour, batted my hand away. 'What are you talking about?'

'I came here to find the rest of those beads. We handled them, Borodin: they're a warning, left by a Syllogikos scientist, not to use the Hypersphere. It's the reason they all vanished. Here . . .' I slid my rucksack off my shoulder and reached inside for the box, but Borodin snatched the rucksack out of my hands and pushed it at one of his men.

'Let me tell you something,' he snarled at me. 'I have access to Syllogikos records you do not. The people who died in these caverns were religious fanatics. They were outsiders, largely spurned by their civilization.'

'What are you talking about?'

'They were a fringe group, obsessed with post-apocalyptic alternates. They went in search of them specifically because they believed they would find evidence of God's direct intervention in their destruction. That list of coordinates the Authority uses even comes from them. If those beads belonged to one of them, they are almost certainly the product of a delusional mind. They cannot be trusted.'

'But that doesn't explain all those other wrecked Syllogikos bases – or why they tried to destroy the Hypersphere we've been working on all these years!'

'I'm sure there's a perfectly adequate explanation without having to indulge in wild conspiracy theories.' He pulled me towards the now vacant stage, and the remainder of his men followed in our wake. 'As for the rest of the Syllogikos,' he added contemptuously, 'why assume they disappeared? It's far more likely that once they had the Hypersphere, they had no need of bases on nearby alternates and so simply abandoned them. What use could they possibly be, when the Hypersphere could take them to wherever their heart desired?'

'But the beads—'

'Later, Katya. I'll have you gagged if you insist on talking.'

'Where are we going?' I asked, my voice full of defeat.

'To Delta Twenty-Five, of course. Where else?'

Borodin handed the notebook to one of his men, who programmed the coordinates into the stage. Seconds later, we arrived on Delta Twenty-Five.

The air felt baking hot after the gloomy chill of the caverns. Borodin's men hurried down from the stage, and I saw Herr Frank standing waiting with several more of his men within the hangar. Everything looked exactly the same as when I had last been here, with Elena and Jerry.

'You have *no idea* how much danger we're in,' I insisted as Borodin dragged me down the ramp and off the stage. 'Those creatures—'

'The Authority's drones have recorded no sign of activity since you were rescued,' said Borodin. 'I see no reason to believe that the creatures that attacked you will return.'

It was immediately obvious that the Hypersphere wasn't all Borodin was intent on retrieving. I watched the soldiers under Herr Frank's command lift crates crammed with artefacts down from the back of an open-bed truck, placing them with other crates to one side of the stage. Clearly, they were grabbing everything they could while they had the chance.

Herr Frank stepped towards Borodin. 'We found a few more of the Authority's drones and had no problem deactivating them. They'll never know what happened here.'

'Good,' said Borodin. 'And nobody's touched the Hyper-sphere?'

Herr Frank shook his head. 'As per your orders.'

'Good. Then I'll go to it immediately.'

'One thing,' said Herr Frank as Borodin turned away. 'It does appear that the Authority were about to ship the Hypersphere back to their own alternate at the time they were attacked.'

Borodin glared at him. 'I hope that it's undamaged?'

'Entirely undamaged, rest assured. We found it in a tent erected next to one of the sheds. I can only assume they were preparing to move it to this hangar.'

'I see.' Borodin nodded stiffly. 'Thank you, Herr Frank. Clearly there's no time to waste. Does one of your men know where I can find it?'

Herr Frank nodded and snapped his fingers at a soldier. 'You,' said Herr Frank. 'Take Gospodin Borodin to the Hyper-sphere.' He turned back to Borodin. 'I'll be leaving shortly to take charge of things back at the Crag. I assume you can keep an eye on things here?'

Borodin nodded and pulled me along by the arm as the soldier led us outside. Pink sunlight blazed down on us, the shadows slanting lengthways across the paving stones: the sun was most of the way across the sky. I saw a multi-legged Authority drone standing not far from the hangar, as silent and unmoving as a statue.

We made our way across the compound on foot, past some of the big storage sheds. Borodin kept his pistol pushed up hard against my side the whole way. Everywhere I looked, I thought I saw monsters lurking, waiting to attack. Every shadow seemed to contain within it the promise of death.

Just as Herr Frank had said, the Hypersphere was sitting inside a tent along with several other artefacts, next to the shed where we had originally found it. A second open-bed truck stood next to the tent, the grisly remains of some unlucky Authority staffer slumped halfway out of it.

'Get rid of that body,' Borodin ordered Herr Frank's man. 'See if that truck can still run.'

The soldier nodded and turned away. Borodin led me inside the tent, then turned to face me. 'Right now, I don't care whether you betrayed me or not,' he snapped. 'All I care about is the Hypersphere. Do you understand?'

I nodded.

'Good.' He dug around in a pocket and passed me the headset. 'Now use this to make sure it's not damaged in any way.'

'Borodin,' I said, my voice shaking, 'if you would just listen to me—'

Before I could finish, Borodin aimed the pistol at a point just inches in front of my feet and fired a single shot. I screamed and stumbled back as concrete spat up from the ground before me. He stepped closer and pressed the weapon against my ribs. 'Damn you, Orlova. When I tell you to—'

'Sir?'

Borodin whirled to face the soldier, who was holding up a walkie-talkie. I looked out past him and saw he had already dragged the body away from the truck.

'Sir,' said the soldier, 'it's Herr Frank.'

Borodin snatched the radio from the soldier then turned to look at me. 'You know what you have to do. Get on with it.' He turned to the soldier. 'Watch her closely, do you understand? If anything happens to that artefact, I'll have you skinned alive while the rest of the Crag watches.'

The soldier turned a little pale, but saluted. He turned to face me, his rifle gripped in both hands while Borodin stepped out of the tent.

I fitted the headset to my scalp, thinking furiously all the while. As soon as the headset was in place, virtual menus appeared all around the Hypersphere.

Except this time something was different: there was something new in the foreground, flashing red.

I reached out to touch it and a message appeared. It said there had been an unauthorized attempt to move the Hypersphere. In response, 'native defence systems' had been triggered.

I remembered the nearly identical warning I had seen on my first encounter with this particular Hypersphere, when it had still been inside the shed. Of course, I still had no idea what on Earth these 'native defence systems' might be . . .

I froze as a realization hit me like a lightning-bolt.

Almost as soon as the Hypersphere had been moved from the shed, half a dozen Authority staffers had come to horrible and grisly ends. They couldn't possibly have been aware of the virtual warnings all around the artefact, such messages being designed for the benefit of Syllogikos citizens with cybernetic technology embedded into their skulls.

Was it possible that simply by moving the Hypersphere the Authority had unwittingly triggered these defence systems, and *caused* the invisible monsters to attack?

Were *they* the native defence systems?

Working feverishly, I dug down through the menus until I found what I was looking for – an option for activating or deactivating the defence systems.

At the moment, they were deactivated. I could only assume

they had shut down again because the perceived threat had been eliminated.

Suddenly, I knew exactly what I had to do. It was imperative I prevented the Hypersphere from being taken back to the Novaya Empire, even if it cost me my life – and so I nudged the defence systems back into active status.

'Aren't you finished?'

I turned to see Borodin had re-entered the tent. 'It's intact and operational,' I said.

He nodded. 'Good.' He held out his hand, and I gave him back the headset. 'Now we can get it onto the truck.'

He spoke into his radio. I stared towards the hills, wondering when the attack would come – *if* it would come. Just minutes ago, the thought of ever coming face to face with those beasts again would have terrified me to the core. Yet now, to my astonishment, I was no longer afraid – not even to die.

After all, if I didn't die here, I would most surely meet my end along with the rest of the Empire if the Tsar ever got his hands on the Hypersphere.

The truck was joined by the one from the hangar a few minutes later, carrying several soldiers in its rear. It rolled to a halt, and two of the men climbed down, carrying between them a metal sphere formed from closely spaced bars. An identical cage also protected the first Hypersphere, back at the Crag.

One of the soldiers touched an electronic lock on the side of the cage. It hissed open, becoming two hemispheres connected by a hinge. Working carefully, they slid one hemisphere of the cage around the Hypersphere, then closed the other around it. The Hypersphere bobbed slightly above its cradle as the locking mechanism engaged.

'All right,' said Borodin, looking relieved. The artefact glowed faintly through its bars. 'Let's see what else we can find and then we can get out of here.'

Three of the soldiers raised the Hypersphere by taking hold of its cradle from beneath and lifting it. The Hypersphere bobbed again, but remained locked in place above the cradle. Then it was placed in the rear of one of the trucks and driven back to the hangar, where it was placed together with other recovered artefacts next to the stage.

I had been afraid Borodin would take us all back to the Crag before the invisible beasts had a chance to kill him and his soldiers, but clearly he was in no hurry to leave just yet. I asked him why.

'The Soviet engineers showed me video of rows of empty cradles,' he replied. 'That means there might well be more Hyperspheres hidden away in one of those other sheds. We won't return home until we're certain this is the only one.'

'Take your time,' I said, and he looked at me strangely.

And off we went again, leaving two men guarding the hangar. Borodin sent both trucks careering around the sheds, the soldiers grabbing whatever else they could.

Despite Borodin's certainty that we would be safe, he ordered several of his men to keep a watchful eye on the surrounding forest. And yet, no attack came.

Hours passed, and doubt began to creep uninvited into my thoughts. Perhaps I had made a mistake. Perhaps I had misinterpreted the Hypersphere's warnings; or perhaps they had meant something other than the invisible beasts.

And the more time passed, the more my doubts grew.

Then, at last, just as night began to creep over the forests and hills, a scream full of terrible anguish echoed from far off across the compound.

Everyone came to a standstill. I looked up from where I sat hunched on the flatbed rear of one of the trucks, until that moment stewing in regret and misery.

Borodin, nearby, lifted a walkie-talkie to his mouth. 'Sergeant? Report in. Is the hangar secure?'

I pulled my knees close to my chin and hugged them.

'Answer me, damn you!' he shouted.

Gunfire came from the direction of the hangar. I looked the other way and saw a brief shower of sparks where the pavement met the jungle, as if something were forcing its way through the barrier surrounding the sheds.

'Get in the trucks,' Borodin shouted at the soldiers, who had been in the process of crating artefacts. 'Shoot anything that moves!'

Several of the men scrambled onto the back of the truck next to me. The rest got on board the second truck. They left the artefacts where they were. Borodin climbed into the front cabin of my own vehicle; its engine coughed into life.

We picked up speed. I peered into the window set in the back of the cabin and through the windscreen, in the direction of the hangar. A blur rushed towards us with impossible speed. Borodin's driver swerved, but too late: the creature had leaped onto the roof of the cabin, rearing over everyone in the back. I had a brief impression of fangs like shards of sharpened glass before the man next to me was lifted into the air, his legs kicking wildly.

The beast shot away from the truck with its prize gripped in its jaws. I heard frantic shouting and twisted around in time to see the other truck go crashing onto its side, spilling men everywhere.

Shadowy, liquid shapes slithered down the wall of the shed nearest them. Gunfire mixed with the sound of their screams as our own truck accelerated away. It veered again, and one of the men beside me lost his balance, falling out. We did not slow down.

Then, suddenly, we were back at the hangar. The truck slammed straight through the entrance before screeching to a halt.

Inside was a charnel house. Bits and pieces of the two men Borodin had left in charge of the stage were scattered everywhere. Bright streaks of blood smeared the Hypersphere's cage.

'Get the hangar doors closed!' Borodin screamed as he jumped down from the front cabin. 'Don't let those things get in here!'

Only three of the soldiers had survived. I climbed down from the truck as two of them rushed over to the hangar entrance, hauling the heavy doors shut.

'Who was in charge of explosives?' shouted Borodin.

'I am, sir,' said one of the men, coming over to him.

Borodin closed his eyes for a moment in silent thanks. 'Good. Your name?'

'Kuznetsov, sir.'

'Then you know what you have to do. Get to it.'

I saw my rucksack, discarded in a corner where one of the soldiers must have thrown it. I ran over and picked it up. The box fell out, spilling its beads across the floor of the hangar. I reached down to pick them back up, then remembered I wasn't wearing gloves. I pulled the sleeve of my jacket down around my fingertips and managed to grab up the grey one before a soldier pulled me away.

'Get her the hell up on the stage,' Borodin shouted.

I pushed the bead deep into a pocket as I was dragged up the ramp. Borodin and one of his men had already taken hold of the Hypersphere, lifting it together with its cradle onto the stage. They ignored the rest of the artefacts gathered around us.

I watched as Kuznetsov pressed something that looked like grey putty against the underside of the stage's control rig before tapping at its keyboard. The field-pillars hummed into life. Kuznetsov next pressed a small metal rod into the putty, then stood.

I looked up as light began to form between the stage's pillars. Then I looked higher still, seeing the vague outline of one of the beasts clinging to the steel support struts just below the hangar ceiling. It dropped onto the hangar floor, just behind Kuznetsov as he made to join us.

He let out a high-pitched gasp, then stared down at the fountain of blood erupting from his chest. His feet kicked as he was lifted screaming into the air.

The light grew towards maximum intensity. The creature tossed Kuznetsov's body to one side, then emitted a primordial roar fit to inspire a thousand nightmares.

I closed my eyes and waited to die. Instead the light faded, and when I next opened my eyes we were back in the Crag.

SEVENTEEN

The Crag's main transfer stage was housed in a space that resembled nothing so much as the dungeon of some ancient Carpathian fortress. A stone ceiling vaulted overhead, while a framework of steel girders of more recent vintage, criss-crossing beneath it, supported a heavy iron pulley. Chains dangled from the pulley nearly to the floor, which was almost completely hidden beneath great mounds and piles of crates.

Men came running onto the stage, taking hold of the Hypersphere and carrying it down the ramp. I watched as the artefact and its cradle were placed on a steel trolley that was rapidly wheeled through a narrow doorway and out of sight.

'There you are,' said Herr Frank, coming towards us as we descended the ramp. He frowned at the two soldiers making their way down beside us. 'Where are the rest of my men?'

'They're dead,' said Borodin. 'Killed by whatever attacked the Authority.'

Herr Frank blinked rapidly, looking fit to explode. Borodin stepped towards him and pulled him out of earshot. Even so, it was clear they were arguing violently.

When they came back over, Herr Frank was stony-faced and tight-lipped. He gestured to a guard, who came trotting over. 'Take her to the office assigned to Gospodin Borodin,' he said, pointing at me. 'Building Five, Office Seventeen. And keep an eye on her until further orders. Understood?'

The guard saluted, then unslung his rifle before turning to me and nodding towards a tall archway. 'This way,' he said.

'Don't worry,' I said. 'I know the way.'

Even so, I let him lead me through an archway and out into a broad courtyard paved with cobblestones, enclosed on all sides by a low wall beyond which only sky was visible. The air felt chilly and damp, the sun little more than a bright disc filtered through low grey clouds. We were on the very highest terrace of an ancient fortress that spilled down the slopes of a mountain.

We crossed the courtyard and entered an elevator contained within a framework of girders bolted to a steep stone wall. The elevator rattled and shook as we descended, and I got a good look at the Crag for the first time in many months. Our prison was built around a series of broad paved terraces, like a tide of granite and cut stone spilling downwards from a snowy peak. Ancient keeps, storehouses and granaries mingled with research facilities of much more recent construction. Each terrace was connected to those above and below by vertiginous stairways as well as more elevators, bolted either to the outside of walls or to the sheer rock of the mountain itself.

When I had first arrived years before, however, my attention had been drawn far more towards the titanic structures that dominated the horizon, some achieving such heights that clouds often gathered around their upper reaches. Their foundations were believed to reach deep into the Earth's crust, perhaps in order to draw on geothermal heat – but what purpose they had once served for whatever race had once called this alternate home, we would probably never know.

At last, the elevator clanged to a halt on the next lowest

terrace. I was led across another courtyard and inside a sand-
stone building. It was one of several administrative blocks with
unadorned whitewashed walls and concrete floors. The soldier
unlocked a door and I stepped into an office just as spartan as
the one in which I had first met Borodin: a desk, two chairs,
and a window.

And there I remained for some hours, rocking back and
forth on one of those chairs while the guard waited outside the
open door. I wondered how Jerry was coping, and felt a rush
of guilt and shame. I was the reason he was here, after all.

After a while, I dug around in a pocket until I found the
single grey bead I had managed to rescue during our escape
from Delta Twenty-Five. I had become strangely attached to it.

I held the bead tightly, watching the little girl run laughing
through tall grass, feeling as if I had found a secret window into
Heaven.

I don't know how long I had to wait before Borodin appeared,
but it felt like many hours.

He entered in the company of one of the Crag's guards, who
carried in his hand an electronic bracelet of a type with which
I was intimately familiar.

'Put it on her,' said Borodin.

The guard nodded and bent on one knee next to where I
sat. I watched, unmoving, as he locked the bracelet around my
right ankle. After my escape, it had been my fervent hope never
to see its like again.

'I assume,' said Borodin, 'you want to see Josef.' My father.

'I'm guessing that's conditional,' I said.

He nodded. 'Conditional on you helping him calibrate the

new Hypersphere, yes. A process I understand should take only days, given that it's undamaged.'

'In theory only,' I said. 'I already warned you, if we use the Hypersphere—'

'Shut up about the damn beads!' he shouted. 'Did you hear nothing I said about the people they belonged to? Now give me your answer – will you cooperate?'

'You must need me very badly,' I mumbled, 'to still be asking for my help.'

His hands twitched at his sides, as if he were contemplating throttling me, and I knew it was true.

'We have need of your expertise, yes,' he said. 'But even without your cooperation, the work will go on regardless. Do you understand me?'

I swallowed. 'And if I don't cooperate?'

'Then I will be forced to inform your father that you died while resisting arrest by Tsarist forces on the Twelfth Republic.'

All through those long, lonely hours, sitting in that office, I had mulled over what Borodin told me about the people who had died in those caverns, of their religious fanaticism and their obsession with the end of the world. Perhaps that was true: but when I held those beads in my hands, as Borodin had not, I had sensed enough of Lars Ulven's mind to know that he had not been one of them. He had sought evidence of a kind that had little to do with faith.

If I failed to act – failed to find some way to prevent the Hypersphere from being activated – I would sentence billions back in the Novaya Empire to an uncertain fate. The only course of action left, then, was to find some way to destroy the Hypersphere.

Unless I appeared willing to continue my work here, I would never get the chance to do that.

'Katya, I'm waiting.'

'Fine,' I said, choking the word out. I forced myself to meet his eyes. 'I'll cooperate.'

He studied me closely. 'Do you mean that, Katya? Will there be any more trouble from you?'

'I want to see my father,' I said, surprised at how much my voice trembled when I said it.

I looked back down at the floor and waited. I could almost feel his gaze drilling into me, searching for the lie in my words.

He took a step back towards the door. 'You will be watched,' he said, 'more closely than ever before. Do you understand?'

I nodded. 'I do.'

'Bring her,' he said to the guard, and I let the soldier pull me up by my arm.

It was dark by the time they led me back outside. The guard took the lead, Borodin following behind. We made our way down to the Crag's lowest terraces, where the Artefact Retrieval Division's exiled researchers lived and worked, and where I had spent the better part of ten years of my life. We exited an elevator and crossed a courtyard, passing enormous oak gates set into a crumbling and ancient defensive wall. Beyond lay a forest I had only occasionally glimpsed from the top of the Crag's battlements, since none of us was ever allowed outside the fortress.

We came to a door set in a plain concrete block. Herr Frank stood waiting outside, along with two more guards and the Hypersphere on its trolley. Herr Frank snapped an order. A guard opened the door and the trolley was wheeled inside.

We followed them down a short corridor to a service elevator that served as the main entrance to the Primary Experimental

Transfer Laboratory, which lay beneath our feet inside a vast cellar.

We boarded the elevator car, an iron cage contained within a shaft constructed from latticed girders. As we dropped, I looked down at the floor of the laboratory, which had changed little since I had last seen it.

Much of the laboratory was taken up by a transfer stage stripped of most of its non-essential components. Tables, work-stations, computers and other equipment surrounded it amidst a sea of cables. Arranged against the walls were industrial-sized lathes, machine-parts printers and magnetic containment systems.

The original Hypersphere sat at one end of a metal platform next to the stage. It was barely visible beneath a mass of sensor arrays and cables that trailed down over the edge of the platform and across the floor.

I looked around, seeing nearly all of the exiles – a dozen men and women – were present. None was younger than late middle age, and a few were considerably older. And, of course, they all wore electronic anklets that tracked their every move. Judging by the expressions on their upturned faces, our arrival was something of a surprise.

Then, at last, I caught sight of my father, staring open-mouthed, as the elevator clanged to a halt. A ring-binder slipped from his hand, and he pushed past a cluster of old men gathered by a lathe in his hurry to reach me.

Herr Frank pushed the elevator door open and I stepped out. I was shocked at how much my father had aged, even in the relatively short time since I'd fled the Crag. There were white streaks in his hair that hadn't been there before, and there was a certain stiffness in his movements I didn't recall either.

Sometime during my absence, my father had become an old man. Pierre Agerstrand came tottering up behind him, as always leaning heavily on his stick.

But all this faded from my thoughts as my father folded me into his arms. I pressed my face to his shoulder, sobs ratcheting their way up my throat.

A hand patted my shoulder, and I glanced to the side to see it belonged to Pierre. He, along with my father, had helped engineer my escape.

'Katya, little Katya,' my father crooned. I felt his tears dampen my shoulder. 'I thought I'd never see you again.'

'I'm sorry,' was all I managed to say through my own sobs. 'There's so much I have to tell you. I—'

Somehow he pulled himself free. He held me at arm's length and gave me a look I knew well: *Be careful what you say.*

'And Tomas?' Pierre asked querulously from beside us. 'Where is he?'

I tried to tell him, but the words wouldn't come. All I could do was shake my head.

My father's brow furrowed, and he darted an angry look at Herr Frank. His throat worked as if he were struggling to hold back words of anger.

'You can tell me what happened later,' he said, then squeezed my shoulders. 'But I'm glad to see you, Katya, whatever the circumstances.'

'I have something to show you,' said Borodin. He motioned with one hand to the two guards, and they wheeled the trolley forward.

Josef let go of me and watched as Herr Frank, holding a slip of blue paper in one hand, typed a code into an electronic lock attached to the Hypersphere's cage. It swung open with a faint hiss of hydraulics, revealing the artefact within.

I heard a murmur of astonished voices, and the rest of the exiles crowded closer.

'Where did this come from?' Pierre demanded, leaning heavily on his stick.

'That doesn't concern you,' said Borodin. 'All that matters is that it's entirely intact and quite undamaged.'

My father stepped closer to the Hypersphere, pulling out a pair of spectacles and peering through them at it. A guard prevented him from getting too close.

He looked around at Borodin. 'I believe we haven't been introduced?'

'My name is Mikhail Borodin, Gospodin Orlov. It is an honour to meet you. From now on, I will be supervising the Hypersphere Project in conjunction with Herr Frank.'

My father regarded him with suspicion, but I could see he was fighting not to give the Hypersphere his full attention. 'Is this the only one?' he asked guardedly, nodding at it.

'So far,' said Borodin. 'Although there may well be others.'

'Others?' Pierre Agerstrand hobbled closer. Advanced in years he might have been, but his eyes were bright and fiery. 'Are you seriously saying there are more of these?'

'The evidence suggests so, yes,' said Borodin. 'And with luck, we'll find them soon enough.'

I stared at Borodin. Did he mean he was going to go *back* to Delta Twenty-Five?

My father looked around at his fellow exiles. 'Well, let's take a look at the damn thing,' he called out. 'Pierre, if you could supervise swapping the other Hypersphere out for this one?'

Pierre nodded. Herr Frank again closed the cage, then ordered his men to wheel the artefact over to the platform. Up above, several guards watched from a walkway that ran around all four walls of the laboratory, just below the ceiling.

'You understand what this means?' Borodin said to my father. 'You'll be able to finish your work here sooner than expected. I think a week would be enough to carry out the necessary calibrations: after that, I expect to supervise the first test transfers.' He looked around the rest of the exiles. 'You'll have earned your freedom. All of you.'

'A week? I can't make any such guarantees,' said Josef. 'All we've ever had to work with before was a damaged artefact. We've got no idea how this one might respond. For all we know, it's structured completely differently.'

'You've had the best part of a decade to familiarize yourself with the technology,' Herr Frank berated him. 'After all that time, I damn well think you'd know how to deal with one that works!'

My father stared resolutely back. 'We've had conversations like this before,' he said, 'and I haven't been wrong yet.'

Herr Frank met his gaze, his mouth set in a thin line.

'*Two* weeks, then,' said Borodin. 'And no longer. You'll be seeing a lot of me, Gospodin Orlov, until it's operational.'

Borodin didn't wait for any further comment, turning and stalking back towards the elevator. Herr Frank stepped towards Pierre, watching as the old Hypersphere was replaced with the new.

The rest of the exiles gathered around me then, asking me how I was and what I had seen during my brief sojourn in the outside world – but word must have got around already, because none of them mentioned Tomas. Joanne Bertillon, tiny and frail and wrinkled, took hold of me by the arms and told me how glad she was to see me alive and well.

Finally my father managed to draw me away. 'Help Pierre get the sensor arrays up and running,' he said to a man named Vanya. 'And then we can all take a good look at just what we have, eh? Right now, though, Katya and I have some catching up to do.'

As he said this, he deliberately glanced up at one of the many security cameras dotted around the laboratory, then back at me.

I nodded. 'We do,' I said. 'A lot of catching up.'

'Come on,' he said, leading me across the laboratory. 'Let's take a walk in the gardens.'

EIGHTEEN

I followed him down a narrow corridor, then out into the open. A few metres away stood a low wall, just visible in the moonlight, beyond which a cliff dropped several hundred metres to the forest below. We were standing on a wide ledge protruding from the side of the mountain and accessible only through the laboratory.

Most of this ledge was taken up by a broad strip of cultivated land, filled with crops grown by the exiles to supplement our meagre rations. Carrots and small stunted apple trees grew in narrow, rectangular allotments, along with cabbages and turnips. More exotic-looking plants grew beneath plastic sheets stretched tight over wire and wood frames.

'Look,' said my father. 'Sevigny's finally managed to get his coffee beans growing.' He took an edge of plastic sheeting that had blown loose and re-secured it as I followed behind.

'It feels strange to be back here,' I said. 'I never thought . . .'

He nodded surreptitiously at another camera, mounted above the door behind us, and angled in such a way that nearly the whole of the gardens could be captured in its lens. He kept his eyes on me as he reached inside a pocket and took out a tiny, crude-looking device which he kept cradled in the palm of one hand. I watched as he thumbed the device before putting it away again.

I took a quick glance at the camera. 'How long do we have?'

'Twenty minutes. Maybe a little more. They still haven't tracked down every last one of our network exploits, but we shouldn't risk talking much longer than that or they might notice that one of their cameras keeps running the same footage over and over again.'

'Borodin warned me I would be under particular surveillance until the project is completed,' I said. 'We need to assume they're watching my every move.'

He leaned towards me. 'What went wrong, Katya? Pierre and I planned everything so carefully, I had hoped . . .'

'We badly underestimated Herr Frank,' I said. 'It only took him a few days to track us down. I was afraid they might have found out that you helped us.'

Josef grinned ruefully. 'Well, they couldn't find or prove anything. In some ways, we did our job almost *too* well.' He reached out and touched my hand. 'Now tell me – where did they take you to all this time? And what do you have to do with that other Hypersphere, and that man Borodin?'

I explained as briefly as I could about the Authority, and how Borodin had planned to steal the Hypersphere from them. We made our way past rows of broccoli, their broad leaves touched with frost.

'I see,' he said at last, looking grim. 'And what happened to Tomas, exactly?'

'He . . .' I fought to find the words. 'That man Borodin shot him right before me.'

He sighed heavily. 'And what is this man Borodin's background, exactly? What do you know about him?'

'He's close to the Tsar, or so I've managed to gather. He's well-connected within the state security services – and high up, I suspect, given the way he orders Herr Frank around.'

'Really?'

I nodded. 'Trust me when I say Borodin's the one in charge, not Herr Frank. But they're both terrified of Prince Dmitri. They're convinced that if the Tsar dies, Dmitri will have both their heads the moment he takes the throne.'

Josef chuckled and looked at me with respect. 'How did you find all this out?'

'I overheard them arguing. They're on their own, Papa – just the two of them. But that's not all.' I explained about the memory beads.

'And you still have these beads?'

I pulled my sleeve around my fingers and gingerly lifted the single bead I still had from my pocket. 'This is the only one I was able to save. Hold it in your open palm for just a few seconds.'

He sat on a wooden bench at the end of a row of crops while I squatted down next to him, peering towards the camera as I dropped the bead into his hand. He sat quite still for several seconds, then shook himself, letting out a gasp.

'This is . . . *incredible*,' he exclaimed.

I nodded. 'It feels like you're actually there, seeing through someone else's eyes, doesn't it?'

He nodded, looking dazed. I took the bead back from him in a wad of tissue. 'There were a lot more of these back where I came from – and believe me when I say they change everything. The memories belong to the Syllogikos scientist who first discovered the Hyperspheres. But he also discovered that even *that* culture didn't create them: they come from somewhere in the Deeps.'

He blinked. 'But that's inconceivable! No life can exist in such alternates – the differing physical constants would make it impossible.'

'Not impossible,' I said. 'Nobody really knows that life couldn't find some way to evolve, even in universes with radically different laws of physics – maybe even intelligent life.'

'And you're saying that something living in the Deeps actually created the Hyperspheres? You saw this, in these beads?'

I nodded, quickly summarizing the rest of Lars Ulven's discoveries.

Josef's jaw dropped open. 'You can't be serious. Are you saying all this really happened?'

'Lars Ulven discovered the truth too late to save his own people, but it's not too late for us: the Hypersphere is safe so long as it's dormant, but once it's been activated and used, the invaders will know where it is – and come looking for it.'

He squinted at me. 'And you're absolutely certain of all this?'

I nodded. 'I swear, as crazy as it sounds, it's all there in the other beads. If the Tsar takes that thing back to the Empire and uses it, that's it. It's the end of everything.'

Josef stood, looking appalled. 'And what about Borodin – did he use these beads? Or Herr Frank?'

'I tried to get Borodin to use them, but he would only use the first two I found, not all the others. He wouldn't even listen when I tried to tell him what they showed.' I shook my head. 'It's madness. Why would he do such a thing?'

'Some people only see what they want to,' said Josef, his voice grim, 'even when their world is falling apart around them. Especially if their necks are on the chopping block and they think they can save themselves.'

'But *you* believe me,' I said. 'If anyone understands just how much danger we're in, it's you! We can't allow the Tsar to lay his hands on the Hypersphere, or it could be the end of us.'

He stared out at the great machines far off towards the

horizon, his tongue pushed into one corner of his mouth in a way that I knew meant he was thinking hard.

He turned to me at last and shook his head. 'Katya . . . there's nothing we can do to stop any of this.'

At first, I thought perhaps I had misheard him. 'You can't seriously be suggesting we do *nothing*?'

'Do you remember why we were put to work on this project all those years ago? Because the one Hypersphere we had didn't work – and, to be frank, I always suspected it never would. A working Hypersphere, however, is quite a different matter.'

'So that's it?' I exclaimed, scandalized. 'We should do nothing? And all those people back in the Republics – don't you even care about what might happen to them?'

He gave me a look of exasperation. 'And just what do you think will happen if we refuse to work on it? We'd delay progress by a few weeks, no more. The Syllogikos' own records make it abundantly clear that an undamaged Hypersphere is child's play to use, once calibrated.' He nodded up at the fortress looming above us. 'Not to mention that non-cooperation would put the families of many of the exiles at terrible risk. I'm truly sorry about what happened to Tomas, but he had no family for Herr Frank to kidnap and murder in retaliation for running away. And Pierre's wife died in prison long ago, so even if they'd worked out his involvement, they couldn't have used her to get to him. And they'll never really hurt you as long as they think they need me.'

I decided not to tell him about Borodin's carefully worded threat to the contrary. 'But if they use the Hypersphere,' I insisted, 'their families are dead anyway!'

'Herr Frank has guns and trained soldiers and all of the Crag's resources.' He spread his hands. 'What do we have? Nothing.' He came closer, clasping me by the shoulders. 'The fact is, Katya . . . we tried, and they won.' He leaned towards me, putting heavy emphasis on the words. '*They won.* And there's nothing we can do to stop the inevitable, however much we might wish otherwise.'

I shook his hands from me, my whole body trembling. 'All those years of planning,' I said, 'all so we could warn people what was going on here. And now you're telling me we were just . . . *wasting our time?*'

'I suppose in a sense we were,' he said, as mildly as if he were commenting on the weather. 'As unfortunate as that is.'

I tasted something acrid at the back of my throat. I could not stand to stay there and listen to one more word. I turned and walked away quickly.

'Katya!' he called after me. 'Wait! Where are you going?'

I came to a halt, but did not turn to face him. 'Borodin sent a prisoner back here. I need to find out what he wants with him.'

'My advice is to forget about this man, whoever he is. There's nothing you can do for him or anyone else, not any-more.'

It was too much. I broke into a run, past the green plants in their hydroponics and into the stone passageway leading back into the laboratory.

'Katya,' he shouted after me. 'Katya!'

I ran across the laboratory and boarded the elevator, ignoring the perplexed stares of Sevigny and Agerstrand and the rest of the exiles. None made a move to stop me, not even the guards, who watched idly as I dashed past.

I found my way back to the tiny cell-like room that had been my home for all the years of my exile and collapsed, weeping, beneath its single narrow window. And there I remained, undisturbed, until the morning.

I was awoken by a light tingle in my right leg. I reached down and grasped the security anklet and tried to rip it free, but of course it was firmly locked in place.

I curled up into a ball and tried to ignore it. After another few minutes, the tingling grew to a persistent ache that I knew from bitter experience would only grow far worse if I delayed too long.

I got up and pulled my wardrobe open and found all my old clothes still there. The view out of the window was as bleak and depressing as I remembered. It was like nothing had changed . . . except, of course, that Tomas was no longer alive.

Perhaps my father had been right. Perhaps he was more of a realist than I gave him credit for. The idea that a bunch of old men and women, some barely able to walk more than a few feet without assistance, could take on armed guards and security cameras was ridiculous.

By the time I was dressed, the tingling was close to agony. Only once I had made my way out into the grey dawn light did it abate. I crossed a courtyard towards the main refectory, where I quickly became the centre of attention; the exiles gathered around me, demanding news about the outside world, although I still had little to tell them. My father wasn't there; most mornings, he was the first into the laboratory.

I drank my thin coffee and ate my pancakes and listened and talked and found out what had happened after I had escaped. Several of them had spent weeks in the interrogation block, half-starved and frozen, before being released. They had known nothing, of course. My father and Pierre had been very careful to keep the escape attempt to themselves. And besides, Herr Frank needed them too badly to risk damaging them too much.

I told them about the Authority and the people I had met there, and most especially about the Pathfinders. I wanted more than anything to tell them about the memory beads – but as my father had reminded me, Herr Frank's cameras were everywhere, and I dared not risk Borodin's wrath.

When I arrived at the laboratory with the rest of the exiles, I found my father and Pierre fawning over the new Hypersphere as if it was a newborn baby.

Over the next several days, the laboratory became a frenzy of activity as the new Hypersphere underwent a series of pre-calibration tests.

I determined to avoid my father at all costs and kept my distance. And there was work to be done, whether I liked it or not. I soon realized that I had forgotten the sheer ubiquity of Herr Frank's security: even getting near the Hypersphere was going to be extraordinarily difficult, should I make the attempt. Not only was it locked in a steel cage with bars too narrowly spaced for so much as a finger to squeeze past, it had a minimum of two guards standing by it at all times. Cameras watched the laboratory constantly, as did the guards permanently stationed on the walkway high above the floor.

Herr Frank's men made no secret of the fact they were paying particular attention to me. Worse, reinforcements soon arrived to bolster their numbers, along with several of the Tsar's own imperial guards, wearing black and gold uniforms and sporting beards thick and long enough to cover their chests.

Whenever I closed my eyes to sleep, I found myself reliving the same nightmare over and over again, of standing in the centre of First Republic Moscow, watching as death fell from the skies.

*

A week later, I had my first glimmer of hope.

'What about the sensor array?'

'It needs to be physically realigned,' Sevigny explained to me, as people bustled past us in the laboratory. Despite his shrunken frame and hairless scalp, Sevigny was easily the most energetic octogenarian I could ever hope to meet. 'It's too difficult to remap the sensors otherwise,' he continued. 'I'm telling you this because you'll have to do most of the calculations.'

'But they'll have to open the Hypersphere's cage first, won't they? The sensor arrays pass through the gaps in the cage, so . . .'

'Well, of course.' He gave me a weary look. 'And of course, security will be even tighter than it already is for that reason. Worse, we've been given only two minutes to carry out the realignment. Can you imagine? Your father protested, obviously, but Herr Frank was quite adamant. Two minutes: that's it. They won't trust us with any more time than that. You'd think, given the delicacy of such an intricate operation, they'd want to give us as much time as we need, but oh no . . .'

I nodded, no longer listening and letting my hair fan across my face as I leaned over a laboratory workstation. My throat felt dry, and my heart fluttered and shook in my chest like a trapped bird. For two whole minutes, the Hypersphere would be as vulnerable as it was ever going to be – if one disregarded the guards and cameras.

I asked Sevigny to repeat some of what he had said, and then began to work on the calculations, while my mind was somewhere far away. That same evening, and working with the utmost caution, I stole some materials from a supply cupboard and sneaked them, undetected, back to my room.

It had become rapidly clear, soon after my return, why Borodin was so keen to have me involved in the project once again, despite my betrayals. My father's work had apparently begun to slip badly during my absence. Even though I had largely avoided him since his refusal to help me, I could see nonetheless that he had occasional forgetful moments, and that his fellow exiles were doing their best to cover for him.

Two days after my conversation with Sevigny, and nearly a fortnight after my return, I found myself having my evening meal in the refectory, not far from where Josef sat chatting with some of our colleagues. My hands trembled from nervous exhaustion: apart from working all day, I had spent much of the previous night attempting to construct from stolen materials a crude device I hoped would help me sabotage the Hypersphere during those precious two minutes. I had worked in near-total darkness through the night, with only occasional moonlight to see by.

I chewed and swallowed my food mechanically, and found myself unconsciously tuning into what my father was saying.

'. . . see the resonance readings from that last test?' he said. 'I swear I've never seen anything of the kind.'

I took a quick glance over at him, pretending my attention was elsewhere. Leon Gulley, an English exile, sat across from him, looking tired and worn out; Borodin was pushing us hard to finish within the next few days.

'Why do you ask?' said Gulley.

'It's usually barely detectable,' Joanna Bertillon explained from beside him. 'But now we're seeing higher readings than ever before.'

'Phenomenal readings, actually,' said my father. 'Most times, trying to pick out a resonance signal from background noise is like trying to hear a feather falling from a mile away. But this . . .' He waved his spoon around.

'How high are these readings, exactly?' asked Gulley.

'Put it this way,' said Joanna, 'when the Tsar lays his hands on that thing, the readings are going to be less like a feather falling and more like God stamping on a mountain.'

I froze with a spoonful of borscht halfway to my mouth, my mind spurred into sudden action. Every time a transfer stage connected with another universe, it generated a ripple in the infinite void that contained all possible universes. The more energy used, the stronger the resonance – and the stronger the ripple.

I stood abruptly, sensing I was on the cusp of some revelation. In my haste, my hand brushed my bowl, and sent it clattering to the floor. Several people, including my father, glanced towards me at the sudden commotion.

'Excuse me,' I said, hurrying past them and out of the refectory in search of a spare whiteboard. I found one in an unoccupied office across from the main laboratory and quickly covered it in numbers and symbols.

N-spatial resonance: an energy burst, generated by the transfer process and spreading outwards at infinite speed through the medium containing all possible universes: something that could, theoretically, be traced back to its source – except that in most cases the burst was barely detectable.

In *most* cases.

I checked the figures again and again, but they came out the same: the first time the Hypersphere was used, it would generate a resonance signal powerful enough to be detectable to *any* alternate with the means to do so. It would be akin to a thunderclap in the void.

And what strange beasts might that bring up from out of the Deeps?

Even Lars Ulven had not been able to find the means by which the invaders detected the whereabouts of the Hyper-spheres. He had known only that to use one was to invite destruction. And, unlike him, it was not yet too late for me to act.

Back in my room, I worked feverishly at completing my sabotage device. It was simple, really: a junction box, made from heat-resistant plastic, normally used for splicing together cables as and when required. I had gutted it, replacing its insides with a pair of spring-loaded blades.

I got down on the floor and pulled up a brick beneath my bed, lifting out a packet of cigarettes Joanne had left, forgotten, in the refectory. I took one of the cigarettes out and carefully twisted the filter off.

Next, I opened the plastic case, and carefully – so carefully – inserted the cigarette between the two thin blades. The springs were not so strong, I hoped, that they would crush the cigarette held between them.

The cigarette held. I left the top off the device and placed it on the ledge of my window. Next, I took out a lighter, also stolen from the refectory, and lit the cigarette.

I watched as the crude timer burned down, and the two wires drew closer and closer to each other. I used my hands to waft the smoke out of my part-open window. I didn't want anyone wondering why my room smelled of cigarettes, when I didn't smoke.

As the cigarette burned down, the two spring-loaded blades came together . . .

. . . and touched.

I giggled with nervous exhaustion and pushed my balled

hand into my mouth to stifle myself. If I spliced together the right cables, when the cigarette burned down, the wires would cause a short-circuit. That, in turn, would trigger a breaker switch, plunging the laboratory into temporary darkness.

A few years ago I might also have had to worry about smoke alarms, but they had gone off with such frequency that Herr Frank had finally ordered their removal: safety had never been one of his priorities.

I tested it again with another cigarette, but it failed to burn down all the way. I drilled more holes in the plastic casing, fighting a growing sense of panic as I worked at the ridiculous little box with its spring-loaded wires. How could so much ride on so little?

When I tested it a third time, it worked. Just.

By then the room stank of cigarettes. If anyone noticed, I'd just have to lie and say I'd taken up the habit.

I carefully disassembled it all and hid it back beneath the loose brick, and slept an uneasy sleep.

NINETEEN

I woke, just an hour later, my heart palpitating. The nightmare was a familiar one: running under an endless grey sky from which vast black shapes tumbled.

Then I saw a figure standing over me in the dim pre-dawn light, and opened my mouth to scream.

A gloved hand clamped down over my mouth, pushing me back down against the mattress. I looked up into the face of one of Herr Frank's guards. A second guard stood by the open door of my quarters, and next to him stood Herr Frank himself, peering anxiously either way down the corridor outside my room.

'Don't waste time,' he hissed at the guard. 'And gag her, for God's sake, before she wakes anyone.'

The guard took away his hand just long enough to shove a thick, greasy rag smelling of oil and sweat between my jaws. Then both guards dragged me kicking and struggling out into the chill night.

Herr Frank led the way, casting furtive glances all around. I didn't want to imagine where we might be going, or why. They dragged me up steps and down echoing corridors, then aboard a clattering elevator that carried us upwards.

Their grip never loosened once. I was chilled to the bones by the time we reached the second-highest terrace, where the main transfer stage was housed.

I tried to scream around my gag, and kicked and struggled even harder when they took me into the interrogation block. Inside, one of the guards rapped on a door, then pushed me inside.

I found myself standing at one end of a long, darkened booth. One of the guards pulled the door shut, then ripped the gag from my mouth. I gasped for air, desperate to clear the awful taste of the rag from my mouth.

I saw that most of the booth was taken up by two rows of chairs facing a long window that took up one wall. Borodin sat alone in the front row, staring through the glass into a second room.

The ceiling, floor and walls of this other room were entirely covered in white tiles. It reminded me of a hospital operating room. A wheeled metal trolley stood in one corner next to a sink, while a cantilevered steel chair equipped with leather straps sat at the room's dead centre, its base bolted to the floor.

A man was strapped into this chair, his face so bruised and bloody it took me a moment to recognize him.

Jerry.

A thick rubber band had been looped around the chair's headrest and forced between his jaws: he could move his eyes, but not his head. The chair was turned sideways to the booth, meaning he couldn't see me or anyone else inside.

A door opened behind the chair, and a small, neat-looking man in a dark suit entered, turning to face the booth with a nod.

I lurched towards the window, banging my hands on the glass and shouting Jerry's name. He didn't react, or show any sign that he had heard me.

'He can't hear you,' said Borodin, shaking a cigarette loose from a packet.

I twisted around to stare at him. 'What is he doing here?'

He paused to light his cigarette before continuing. Herr Frank hovered near the door of the booth, looking as if he found the whole matter distasteful in the extreme.

'Answering questions,' said Borodin. 'What else?'

'About what?' I demanded.

'How much exactly,' asked Borodin, 'did you tell him about us? About the Novo-Rossiyskaya Imperiya?'

I shook my head. 'Nothing.'

'Really? Because I've had several long conversations with Mr Beche, and he appears to be surprisingly well-informed in that regard.' Borodin leaned forward in his seat, elbows on knees, and looked at me where I stood next to the glass. 'Under the tenets of imperial legislation, you've committed an act of treason. Do you realize that? People get thrown against a wall and shot for a lot less than that nowadays, Katya.'

'That's not how it was,' I said, fighting to keep my voice steady. 'He was onto us almost from the start. They *all* were. Your cover stories didn't fool Elena Kovitch for one moment. She'd already looked into our backgrounds. The reason they invited me to Delta Twenty-Five in the first place was so Elena could confront me away from the rest of the Soviets – and away from you. And Jerry made it abundantly clear I had to cooperate with him and the Authority, or he'd hand me over to Director Blodel the moment we got back to the island.'

Borodin looked past me, studying Jerry through a haze of smoke. 'So he *was* telling the truth.' He looked back at me. 'And he offered you what, exactly, in return for your cooperation?'

I swallowed hard. 'Nothing.'

Borodin dropped his cigarette into an ashtray on the seat

next to his, then leaned forward, pressing a button on a microphone just below the window.

'Monsieur Sauveterre,' he said into the microphone, 'I want you to cut off one of Mr Beche's fingers. Any one will do.'

I stepped forward and tried to grab hold of Borodin around the throat – but before I could get him in a chokehold, the guards had pulled me back, twisting my arms behind my shoulders and shoving me face-first against the floor. I lay with my cheek pressed against hard concrete, struggling to breathe.

I heard a click, and from the corner of my eye saw Borodin touch the microphone. 'Wait one moment, Monsieur Sauveterre.'

I was pulled upright, then shoved into the seat next to Borodin's. A guard made his way into the row of seats behind me, leaning over me and pinning me down so I couldn't move.

Through the glass, Monsieur Sauveterre stood attentively by Jerry's side, a gleaming scalpel in one hand. Jerry, who had seen it, struggled wildly be free.

'Are you going to tell me the truth now?' asked Borodin.

I nodded, my heart thudding. 'He offered me protection,' I said hoarsely, 'if I agreed to help the Authority with their transfer research programme.'

'They wanted you to help them build new stages and find new alternates they could colonize, I assume?'

'I had no choice! They were going to arrest you.'

Borodin let out a short, sharp laugh at this.

'They said you'd been making bombs.'

'I thought I'd have to take control of their hangar by force,' he told me, looking pleased with himself. 'Then you led me to that hidden stage and made everything so much easier.' He waved his cigarette at me. 'So, are you going to tell the truth from now on?'

'I swear,' I said, 'I'll answer anything you want.'

'Good. Now tell me – is your father deliberately delaying his work in any way? Or maybe even planning to sabotage it?'

He was so far off the mark I nearly burst out laughing. I had thought perhaps they had discovered my home-made device, and that was why I had been brought here. It appeared this was not the case.

'My *father*?' I said, utterly incredulous. 'You *destroyed* him, you son of a bitch. As if he could stand up to anyone or *any-thing* any more! He told me I should get used to life here again, that I should learn to . . . to *accept* it.'

Borodin sucked at his lower lip, studying my face, looking for evidence of a lie or a half-truth. I didn't need to fake my anger: it was entirely real.

'What, precisely, did he say?'

I let out an exasperated sigh: 'I took a walk with him after you brought me back,' I said, 'and he told me not to fight you. He told me to give up, that you'd won.' I glanced again at Jerry. 'Let him go, Mikhail, please. Anything I can tell you, I will. He's no use to you.'

Borodin kept his eyes locked on mine for several more seconds, then leaned back with a sigh. 'Very well then.'

'That's it?' I said, betraying my hopefulness. 'You'll let Jerry go?'

He pursed his lips. 'What I do isn't your concern—'

'Just tell her,' muttered Herr Frank from the back of the booth. 'You'll need to soon enough anyway.'

I stared between them. 'Tell me what?'

'As soon as the Tsar's health is restored,' said Herr Frank, 'we expect him to approve an expeditionary force against the Syllogikos bases currently occupied by the Authority. You, Miss Orlova, will have a role in that.'

I could hardly believe what I was hearing. 'Why? What the hell could the Authority have that you could possibly—?'

And then it hit me. 'The Hyperspheres,' I said heavily. 'You're going back there to try and find the rest of them.'

Borodin's mouth twisted up in irritation. 'We can't afford the risk of the Authority getting hold of even one.'

'You don't know there are any left on Delta Twenty-Five,' I said. 'The Syllogikos could have taken the rest away. Even if they didn't, you could search for years – all while being hunted by invisible monsters.'

'No matter,' snapped Borodin. 'Even a single Hypersphere could make the Authority as powerful as the Empire.'

'And given the sheer number of dead we left scattered all over one of their alternates,' added Herr Frank, staring hard at the back of Borodin's head, 'they must be aware of our existence by now. With a Hypersphere, they could gather weapons of unimaginable power to use against us. It's only logical that we must strike first – and you and that Pathfinder will be key to the invasion.'

'You'll drag us all down to hell with you, won't you?' I spat. 'You think I don't know what'll happen to you both if the Tsar dies? I overheard everything when you were arguing in that office, Borodin. Don't pretend any of this is for the Empire's sake: it's all to save your own worthless skins.'

Borodin's face coloured. 'Get her out of here!' he bellowed at Herr Frank.

Herr Frank nodded, and the guard behind me dragged me back out of my seat. I stared through the glass at Jerry. And when the guard shoved the gag back into my mouth, I did not struggle.

*

By the time I was returned to my room, the sky beyond the Crag's battlements had turned red from the approaching dawn.

As soon as the guard's footsteps had receded into the distance, I got down on my knees and dug out the home-made device from behind its brick, just to be sure it was still there. The sensor realignment was due to take place that afternoon.

I replaced the device in its hiding place and lay back on my bed. To my surprise, I slept soundly, until my anklet buzzed me awake just a few hours later.

That morning, the laboratory was busier than I had ever seen it. Two imperial guards, armed as always with machine guns, were stationed next to the platform supporting the Hypersphere.

I didn't let myself even think about how risky my plan was. Even a moment's doubt would be enough to stop me.

'Clear the room!' Leon Gulley shouted when the time came, clapping his hands until he had everyone's attention. 'Everyone out except for essential personnel. Josef?'

My father nodded as most of the exiles boarded the elevator and were lifted out of view. I remained since it was my duty to oversee the sensor array readings during the realignment.

I glanced up from my workstation to see my father conferring with Leon and Vanya. When I looked back down at my screen, I saw my own eyes reflected back at me. In contrast to my internal state, they looked quite calm. I expected to hear a shouted warning any second, before being knocked to the ground. Or perhaps Borodin would appear at the last minute and pull the sabotage device out of my pocket. Or perhaps . . .

Instead, nobody paid me much attention.

The elevator came back down again, this time disgorging

Herr Frank. 'Whenever you're ready to begin, Doctor Orlov,' he said to my father.

'This way, sir,' said Josef, guiding Herr Frank towards the platform. The two imperial guards moved apart as Herr Frank climbed the steps onto the platform and approached the Hypersphere, which was almost invisible within its profusion of cables. He consulted the same slip of blue paper I had seen him use before, then tapped at the cage's locking device.

The bars opened with a faint hiss, revealing the Hypersphere in all its exotic glory.

'Louis, Vanya,' said my father, 'you have two minutes.'

The two engineers stepped forward and began carefully rearranging the sensors that had been inserted through the slots of the Hypersphere's cage. They worked with machine guns aimed at their hearts. Their job was an intricate and complex one, but they were skilled men and worked quickly. I kept my eyes on the screen, seeing sensors go offline, then come online again.

Two minutes later Vanya gave my father a thumbs-up. Josef turned to me. 'Katya?'

I checked the screen again. My throat was so dry it hurt to swallow, my skin clammy with sweat.

'Everything looks good,' I called out. No one seemed to notice the quaver in my voice.

'First full calibration test in two minutes,' said Josef. 'Louis, Vanya, back to your workstations. Goggles, everyone.'

The two men climbed down from the platform, leaving the Hypersphere sitting in its half-open cage and, just for a few moments, vulnerable to attack.

I stepped away from my workstation and moved towards a wall-panel from which a myriad of coloured cables snaked down to the floor in an untidy tangle. I held my sabotage device close against my side, the blood pounding in my head like a war drum.

'Katya?' my father called out. 'Is everything all right?'

I stopped, stared at the panel, then swivelled around to face him. 'There's a slight fluctuation in the power feed,' I said. 'Probably just a loose connection, but I'd better check it.'

He nodded, and I resumed my journey. Each step felt like a thousand miles.

At last I kneeled before the panel. I had already picked out the cable I needed: I unplugged it, then, leaning over to hide what I was doing from the eyes of the guards and the lenses of the cameras, cracked open the plastic case in my hands.

The cigarette was already inside: it had slipped out from between the two spring-loaded wires, so I moved it back into place. I took out the lighter and hurriedly applied it to one end of the cigarette. I waited for a shout, for an alarm to sound, but it never came. Everyone's attention was on the Hypersphere.

I snapped the plastic case shut and hoped there were enough holes cut in it that the cigarette wouldn't run out of oxygen. Then I plugged it into the panel and pushed the cable into the device.

I nodded to my father, then pulled on my goggles just as he activated the link between the Hypersphere and the stage.

Light coalesced above the transfer stage adjacent to the Hypersphere. I gazed fixedly at the screen before me, too afraid to look up and see if anyone was staring in my direction.

'Not bad,' said Josef, who had hardly looked up from his own screen. 'Let's try configuration number two and see what we get.'

My hands grew clammy, a sick feeling gathering in my belly. Shouldn't the cigarette have burned down by now? When would somebody notice the smell of a cigarette coming from the wall-panel?

The cage was still open, the Hypersphere still exposed. The Crag's guards were handpicked for their loyalty to the Tsar: any one of them could have destroyed the artefact in an instant with a single bullet.

I waited, and still nothing happened. My crude, pathetic attempt at sabotage had failed, after all: I fought back a moan. It would be discovered, and they would soon work out I was responsible. I would either be executed, or sent to some place even worse than the Crag. I pressed my hand against the screen, dizzy with fear, my legs threatening to buckle . . .

. . . And then all the lights went out.

I did not allow myself to hesitate, even as voices shouted to one another. The only light in the laboratory came from the Hypersphere itself: the spring-loaded wires had touched, creating a short-circuit.

I kneeled quickly, ignoring the shouts and cries of the guards, and felt around for the heavy wrench I had secreted in the base of the workstation two days before. I could hear the clang of boots on the overhead walkway as Herr Frank's guards came running down the stairs.

I found the wrench and stood with it in one hand. It felt satisfyingly heavy in my hand. Even in the darkness, I could still clearly make out the exposed Hypersphere by its faint glow.

I ran forward, crossing the short distance to the platform. I could just make out one of the imperial guards moving to close the artefact's cage.

I threw myself up the steps and onto the platform and swung the wrench wildly at one of the imperial guards, hearing him cry with pain. I felt hands grab hold of me from behind, and swung the wrench back over my shoulder with furious, hysterical energy. I heard a grunt as the second imperial guard let go of me, falling back down the platform steps.

I climbed over his fallen compatriot, and stepped towards the Hypersphere, gripping the wrench with both hands as I lifted it high above the artefact.

But before I could bring it swinging down, hands again grabbed hold of me from behind, pulling me back towards the platform steps. I screamed as the wrench was suddenly torn from my grasp, and I was thrown bodily down the steps to sprawl on the floor of the laboratory.

I tried to stand, and felt someone's boot connect hard with my belly. I twisted into a ball, tasting iron and coughing wetly as the lights snapped back on. Someone must have found my sabotage device and removed it.

I looked up, gasping for breath, in time to see a bloodied imperial guard standing over me, his mouth set in a snarl. I put up a hand to shield myself, and watched, helpless, as he lifted his rifle high before bringing its butt down hard against my skull.

TWENTY

When I came to, I was sprawled on the floor of a windowless cell. A single light bulb contained within a wire cage hung from the ceiling. The floor was hard concrete, the walls unadorned brick.

I swallowed, again tasting blood. My body was wracked with aches and bruises. I reached around to the back of my head with trembling fingers and felt the huge, tender bruise there.

I let my head sink down again, until my forehead touched the cold concrete. I was surprised I was still alive. I did not expect to be for much longer.

Eventually I pushed myself upright against a wall and wondered which part of the Crag I was in: the interrogation block, most likely. The cell I was in certainly fitted some of the descriptions I had heard.

After a while, the cell door creaked open. Borodin stared down at me with a mixture of fury and contempt.

'Pick her up,' he said curtly to one of the two guards beside him.

They squeezed inside and pushed me upright against the wall. Borodin stepped up close, then drew back his fist and punched me hard in the belly.

I sagged, retching, between the two guards. He withdrew my sabotage device from his jacket, tossing it at my feet.

'Very clever, Katya,' Borodin said acidly. 'But not clever enough. I'm sure you'll be pleased to hear that all the calibrations have been completed and all the readings are optimal. The Hypersphere, according to your father, is now ready for the Tsar to use.' He smiled tightly. 'You'll notice we have not, so far, been invaded by monsters from another dimension.'

'If you're going to shoot me,' I croaked, 'get on with it.'

'You've wasted your life for nothing,' he snarled. 'Somehow, Katya, I managed to convince myself that once you were back at work on the Hypersphere, and able to exercise that remarkable intellect of yours, things would change. That, clearly, was an error of judgement on my part.' He pointed at me, his finger quivering. 'Your father has fulfilled his debt to the Tsar. So have the rest of them. But you . . .' He shook his head. 'You will be executed tomorrow morning. I'm afraid this really is goodbye, Katya.'

He gestured to the two guards, and they let me go. I slumped back to the floor and watched them slam the door shut. After their footsteps had faded into the distance, I curled into a ball on my side and wept.

I woke to the sound of hushed voices somewhere outside my cell, followed by a loud *shush*. After a moment the voices resumed at a slightly lower volume than before.

I sat up, suddenly tense. Whoever was out there, they clearly weren't Herr Frank's guards.

I heard the shuffle of footsteps just beyond the door of my cell and thought I recognized one of the voices as Sevigny's. There was a rattle of keys, and the door swung open to reveal my father, and half a dozen of the exiles crammed into the corridor behind him.

Sevigny slipped past my father and came to kneel beside me. 'Stay still for a moment,' he said, wrapping a crude-looking device around my anklet. It appeared to consist of little more than bare circuitry epoxied onto a rubber sheet.

To my astonishment, the electronic bracelet suddenly unlocked and fell from my ankle. I stared at it, open-mouthed, waiting for the alarm to sound. Yet nothing happened.

'How did you . . . ?' I paused, noticing for the first time that all the group were lacking their anklets. Indeed, I saw, to my growing shock, that a number of them were even carrying rifles – the same kind used by the guards. Others gripped long knives or short swords that looked as if they had been fashioned on one of the engineering lathes.

When I saw that some of the blades were stained with blood, I began to understand the import of what was happening.

I gaped at my father as he helped me to my feet. 'I lied when I told you there was no point in fighting,' he said, his voice fervent. 'Please forgive me, but I had to. The truth is, until you turned up with that second Hypersphere, I was quite convinced the programme would fail and we would all be killed. My only hope had been that by escaping, you and Tomas at least might have some chance at surviving.'

He shook his head. 'But when you showed me that bead, and told me your story – well, that changed everything. I knew you were right, and we had to prevent that new Hypersphere from being activated – which it will be, the moment the Tsar lays his hands on it. So I began making new plans.'

'You really threw us off,' said Joanne Bertillon, 'with your little stunt in the laboratory.' She held a knife in one frail hand.

'If you hadn't kept me in the dark all this time,' I nearly exploded, 'I wouldn't have had to!'

'But you see,' said my father, 'I was afraid to tell you. You said yourself they were watching you more than ever before – and Herr Frank knows he can use you as a lever to control me. If you'd had any idea I was planning anything at all, he would have found some way to get the information out of you. And Leon told me he saw you being bundled off by Herr Frank the other night. Did they ask you questions about me?'

'They did,' I said, amazed. 'But . . . what do we do now?'

A savage grin spread over my father's face, and for a moment it was like looking into the eyes of a stranger. 'I'll tell you as we go. The important thing is, working together, we have a much better chance at destroying the Hypersphere. But we need to move fast, while we still have the chance.'

'Where are the others?' I asked.

'Too old or infirm,' said Leon, pushing the door open and leading the way back into the corridor. 'They had the choice to join us, but elected to remain behind rather than slow the rest of us down.'

'Not even Pierre?' I asked, taken aback. 'I know he has trouble walking, but . . .'

I saw a look pass between Sevigny and my father. 'He chose to stay behind,' Josef said evenly. 'It was his decision.'

Leon eased open the door at the far end of the corridor. A cold gust of wind blew inside, and I looked out at a moonlit courtyard. My father leaned out to look along the side of the building. I looked up and saw a camera directly above the doorway in which we crouched. Its lens had been smashed.

'Where are we going?' I asked.

Josef slid Jerry's leather-bound notebook out of a pocket and held it up. I stared at it in astonishment.

'We had to kill two guards to get hold of this,' he said, put-ting the notebook away. 'We'll head for the lab and set the magnetic containment systems to override, then transfer over to the Authority before they blow. Once they do, they'll destroy everything inside the lab, including the Hypersphere. Now keep quiet, and stay low. We put most of the cameras out of action, but there are still plenty of guards around.'

'Wait,' I said. 'This is the interrogation block, isn't it?'

Josef nodded, and I grabbed hold of his arm. 'The Pathfinder that Borodin brought back, he's in here somewhere! We have to get him out too.'

Leon Gulley shook his head. 'We already looked. He's not in any of the other cells. Most likely he's being interrogated in some other part of the building.'

'But—'

'No, Katya,' said my father. 'It's risky enough as it is. We need to go before they raise the alarm. *Now*.'

I knew he was right. Of course I did. It did nothing to lessen my sense of shame as we made our way across the courtyard, running with heads low. I nearly stumbled over the body of a guard as we passed through a shadowed archway; I saw his throat had been cut. The sight of his body shocked me deeply. The exiles had always seemed such harmless old men and women: scientists, not fighters. It slowly dawned on me how thoroughly I had underestimated them – as, clearly, had Herr Frank.

'But what about the guards *inside* the laboratory?' I asked at the bottom of a stairway.

'There are never any more than three, after curfew,' said Sevigny. 'We'll take care of them the same way we took care of the others.'

We took one of the main elevators the rest of the way down, and it carried us to the lower terraces. I was afraid the evening patrol might find us, but in even this the exiles were already far ahead of me: they had obtained computer records that told them precisely where the patrol would be, and when.

Then, at last, we arrived at the lowest terrace. I saw more vandalized cameras as we disembarked from the elevator and hurried past the great wooden gates that guarded the entrance to the fortress.

The building that led into the laboratory was in our sights when sirens broke the silence. Powerful floodlights leaped into life all across the Crag.

'We're lost!' wailed Joanne Bertillon.

'No matter,' said my father, his voice full of grim determination. 'There's no turning back now.'

The sirens became deafening in their volume. I heard shouting from back the way we had come, and I turned to see a number of Herr Frank's men, as well as several of the Tsar's imperial guards, appear through a gate at the far end of the courtyard.

An amplified voice shouted at us to drop our weapons. A warning volley followed, bullets smacking into the cobble-stones before us and showering us with particles of stone. A vice of frozen steel closed around my chest, and I waited for the exiles to drop to their knees and surrender.

Instead, to my shock, Leon Gulley stepped past me and began to return fire. The rifle jerked in his hands with such force that I was amazed he could even hold on to it. As brave as he undoubtedly was, it would have taken extraordinary luck for him to hit anything at all.

The soldiers, rather than immediately shooting back, ducked back out of sight.

One of the exiles yelled in glee. 'Look at them run!' he shouted.

Something clinked against the cobbles close by my feet. I

stared down at a dull metal canister as it rolled past me, before coming to a halt next to Leon's foot. He glanced down at it with a puzzled expression.

Another canister landed, and another. Great clouds of gas erupted from them, stinging my eyes and burning my skin.

I pressed my hands against my eyes, desperate to be free of the burning. A hand grabbed hold of me and I squinted through the haze to see it was my father, his eyes streaming with tears. He nodded to the laboratory entrance and I followed him inside. On the way, he stooped to grab up a rifle one of the others had dropped.

Sevigny was the only other one who made it inside. He had wrapped a handkerchief around his mouth and nose. As soon as he entered, he swung the heavy doors shut with my father's help, before locking and bolting them shut. I meanwhile collapsed against a wall, hacking and coughing, my lungs and skin on fire.

'There are still the guards downstairs,' I rasped.

'I know,' said my father. He pulled me into an embrace. 'I suppose we might not get out of this, Katya.' His voice was ragged. 'But we've come too far to stop now, don't you think?'

The tears running down my cheeks were not entirely due to the tear gas. I nodded. 'If we can, we destroy the Hypersphere. That's all that matters.'

He nodded, then gently pushed me away before shouldering the rifle he had picked up.

I turned, startled, at the sound of something heavy ramming against the doors. There were muffled shouts from the other side.

'Perhaps we shouldn't delay,' said Sevigny, making for the elevator.

*

We ran into the service elevator, still coughing and gasping as it dropped down to the laboratory floor. Sevigny gazed down through the mesh surrounding the elevator cage and moaned with horror.

'The Hypersphere,' he shouted, pointing at the platform next to the stage with one wrinkled hand. 'It's gone!'

I hooked my fingers through the mesh and stared down at where the Hypersphere was normally mounted, willing him to be wrong. My heart flopped in my chest when I saw he was not.

'How?' Sevigny hissed between his teeth. '*How?*'

'The guards,' I said, staring around. 'Where are they?'

'They must have removed the Hypersphere to safety as soon as they knew something was up,' said Josef. 'It's the only explanation.' He grabbed hold of Sevigny's shoulder. 'Raymond, once we're down, secure the door leading to the gardens. Make sure they can't get in that way.' He turned to me. 'Find something to jam the elevator with so they can't call it back up. We need to delay them as long as possible.'

I didn't stop to ask him what he had in mind. I merely nodded, then looked around before heading for a nearby work table. I tipped it on its side, spilling equipment and half-dismantled electronics across the floor, then dragged it halfway inside the shaft that housed the elevator. As soon as anyone tried to call it back up, the table would jam against the shaft exit.

I turned to see my father tapping at a console mounted next to the containment systems. He made a final adjustment, then ran past me and over to the stage's control rig.

'But the Hypersphere . . . !'

He tapped a button, and the field-pillars hummed into life.

'Listen to me,' he shouted. 'There's nothing we can do about it if it's not here. If we stay, we die. Alive, we can still fight!'

'Josef!' shouted Sevigny, standing nearby. He pointed towards the top of the elevator shaft. 'They've broken through the doors!'

'Now, Katya!' Josef shouted, to the sound of boots hammering on steel. 'Get on the stage! You too, Sevigny!'

An alarm began to sound, abrasive and harsh. A message flashed up on a nearby screen, warning that the containment systems were close to critical failure.

Sevigny hurried towards my father's side. 'Josef! Your rifle!'

Josef threw the rifle to Sevigny. 'Now do what your father says,' said Sevigny, stepping back and aiming up at the walkway. 'Get onto the stage!'

I heard shouts from overhead, but the light forming above the stage was too bright for me to be able to make anything out. There was nothing for me to do but quickly climb the ramp.

Sevigny fired several shots upwards. I heard another sharp report, and Sevigny clutched at his chest, the rifle slipping from his grasp as he collapsed.

Josef was still crouched over the control rig, his hair plastered to his forehead by sweat. Jerry's notebook was open by his side.

'Please,' I shouted to him, 'you need to get up here!'

'No, Katya. I need to make sure you get across. Do what you can when you get to the other side.'

'Wait!' I shouted. 'Not y—'

In the very last instant before the laboratory disappeared from sight, I felt a savage rush of heat, accompanied by a terrible, deafening roar.

I screamed, sure in that moment I would die.

And then, miraculously, I found myself crouched low on a wooden platform at the centre of a portable transfer stage. To one side I saw the mouth of a cave covered by a tarpaulin, and heard the sound of ocean waves beating against rocks.

Standing open-mouthed next to a fallen deckchair, a yellowed paperback clutched in one hand, was Nadia.

TWENTY-ONE

I slumped forward, still in shock, and Nadia rushed immediately to my side. She said something, but all I could think about was that last glimpse of my father, and the awful roar of the explosion. Part of me refused to acknowledge the thought that he must surely be dead; perhaps, I thought, I had been mistaken. Perhaps . . .

But I knew how much damage a containment breach could cause.

'I said, where's Jerry, Katya? Where is he?'

I looked up at her, and somehow found the strength of will to answer. 'He's still there.'

'Still where?' She kneeled beside me, one hand on my shoulder.

I clutched my head, still disoriented. 'I have to go back.'

She shook her head, then glanced at the stage. 'Back where, exactly?'

The details came spilling out in a rush, the words all mixed together. I saw from her face that I wasn't making a great deal of sense. She shook her head again, picked up a walkie-talkie from beside the deckchair and thumbed it on. I saw a rifle leaning against the cave wall on the other side of the chair.

'Hey Randall, you awake, you asshole? Good. Listen up: I caught a fish – a *big* one, you get me? I want you to round up everyone else and tell them to meet me at the shack.' She glanced at me, then added: 'I think it's going to be a long night.'

She flicked the walkie-talkie off and dropped it down again. 'Just to be clear: you just came from whatever place you and Jerry disappeared to?'

I pulled myself to the side of the platform and let my legs dangle off the edge. My eyes were burning and I couldn't quite breathe properly – not to mention that I was still severely bruised.

'It's a long story,' I said.

'Yeah.' She raked a hand through her hair, looking perplexed as she studied me. 'No offence, but you look like hell.'

I nodded tiredly. She sucked at her lip, then picked up the rifle next to the deckchair and did something to it. She held it casually by her side, but I had no doubt she could bring it to bear on me in an instant.

'I don't mean to be lousy,' she said, 'but when you disappeared, you left a hell of a mess and no explanations.' She nodded at the stage. 'Anybody else likely to be joining us here? Like maybe Jerry?'

I shook my head. 'No one.'

'Okay.' She nodded at the deckchair. 'I want you to come over here and sit down.'

I hesitated, and she waggled the rifle towards the chair. 'Now, Katya. Nice and slow.'

I noticed for the first time the sheen of sweat on her forehead, but I did as I was told. I stepped past her, lowering myself into the chair.

'Good,' she said. She circled around me and knelt by a heavy rucksack next to the deckchair, angling herself so I was still in her sight. She rummaged around inside the bag and pulled out a pair of handcuffs.

She tossed them next to my feet. 'Put them on.'

I stared at them. 'Do you normally carry handcuffs around with you?'

'You'd be amazed the things I keep handy.'

I slowly reached down and picked them up. 'This really isn't necessary—'

'*I'll* decide what's necessary. Now put them on before anyone else materializes on that damn stage.'

I gave up arguing and reluctantly closed the cuffs around my wrists.

'There,' I said, holding my bound wrists up for her to see. 'Happy?'

She nodded. 'For now.'

She moved past me and knelt by the laptop controlling the stage. She tapped at it, taking the stage offline.

'It's been weeks since I left,' I reminded her. 'Have you been sitting there the whole time?'

'We take it in shifts.' She moved over to the tarpaulin covering the cave mouth and unpinned it. It fell away, revealing early evening sunlight sparkling from Pacific waves, as well as the rowing boat Jerry had used to bring me here the first time.

Nadia reached out and grabbed hold of a rope, tugging the boat closer. It made a hollow *thunk* when it banged against the rock.

She gestured to it. 'Get in.'

I held up my cuffed wrists. 'With these on?'

'Don't worry. I'll catch you if you slip.'

She scrambled into the rowing boat first and it rocked slightly. She dropped her rifle onto a bench and bent at the knees, lowering her centre of gravity until the boat stopped swaying. Then she gestured to me to come closer.

I sat down on the lip of rock, my cuffed wrists before me, and lowered first one leg and then the other over the boat while Nadia grabbed hold of a cleat to keep the boat steady. Then she reached up with one hand and held my shoulder as I half-dropped, half-fell into the boat beside her.

'Nadia,' I insisted, 'there's no need for such restraints. I am alone and unarmed!'

She wordlessly helped me settle onto one of two benches, and I realized I wasn't going to get an answer. I watched, resigned, as she untied the boat before slotting the oars through the row-locks.

She paused, the oars gripped in her hands, and looked at me from where she faced me on the opposite bench. 'I don't know what the hell's going on,' she said, 'or where the hell you're really from – the Soviet Union, or that Novaya-whatever-the-fuck-it-is Empire you told Jerry about. But what I *do* know is there's a bunch of dead guys nobody's seen before all over Delta Twenty-Five, and . . . and those fucking *beads*. Man.' She shook her head.

I started. 'The beads – you know about them?'

Her eyes narrowed. 'Hell, yeah. Me and a couple of the other Pathfinders were the first back on Delta Twenty-Five once they decided it was safe to take a look around. We found them scattered all around the transfer stage there.'

'I need your help,' I said, 'desperately. The information those beads contain—'

'Save it for when you talk to the others. The Pathfinders.'

I darted a look at her. 'What about Director Blodel?'

Her expression became dark. 'Just shut up already and let me row.'

I shut up. Nadia began to row hard, the muscles of her arms bulging under her shirt as she pulled and pushed at the oars. The rifle was behind her and out of my reach – not that I could have lunged for it even if I had wanted to.

No more than a few minutes later I found myself standing back on the island proper. It felt as if years had passed since I last stood there.

Nadia led me to a jeep parked behind the same copse of palms that Jerry had used as a hiding place. I climbed into the passenger seat, and moments later she guided us onto the road beneath a setting sun.

'What about the other Soviets?' I asked. 'What happened to them?'

'Sent home,' Nadia replied, 'just after you up and vanished.'

We headed south, along the east coast. After ten minutes she pulled up next to a small dilapidated jetty with a motorized dinghy moored to it. A low-roofed shack stood a little way inland, and was the only other sign of civilization I could see. She got out and I followed her, my wrists already chafing from the cuffs.

She nodded towards the shack. 'We'll meet the others here. Shouldn't be long, assuming Randall got his sorry ass in gear.'

She fished a ring of keys out of one pocket and unlocked the shack door. Inside I saw a cot, table, chairs and a wood-burning stove with a copper chimney poking through the roof. Nets and rods and fishing tackle hung from hooks. It looked surprisingly homely.

'Sit down,' said Nadia, nodding towards a table and chairs. She opened the door of the stove and threw in some wood, then got a fire started. She pushed the stove door shut, then looked around at me. 'You hungry? Want some coffee? Because I need to eat something bad.'

'Yes,' I said. In fact, I was starving. 'Thank you. If I can explain—'

'Just wait,' she grunted, putting a kettle onto the stove and spooning granules into two mugs before pulling a pan down from a hook.

Ten minutes later, she handed me a plate of beans and fried potato and I ate like a starved animal. I even managed to forget my wrists were chained together as I shovelled hot food down my throat. Nadia raised her eyebrows, but said nothing.

By the time I finished my coffee, the rest of the Pathfinders had arrived. Nadia went to the door, and I looked past her towards the road just as several jeeps pulled up. All of them had come – even Casey Vishnevsky. Perhaps they had decided to accept him – or perhaps they just preferred to keep him where they could see him.

'Why do they all have fishing rods?' I asked as they came walking towards us.

'Cover story,' said Nadia. 'If anyone asks, we were out on that dinghy.'

They crammed into the shack until there was barely room for them to stand. 'I think we can take those off,' said Rozalia, nodding at my cuffs, 'now we're all here.'

Nadia looked dubious, but produced a set of keys and released me. I briefly made eye contact with Chloe Wicks, who was staring hard at me with her arms tightly folded and her mouth set in a narrow line. I looked away again, guilt washing through me like a warm tide.

'So,' said Winifred Quaker, dropping into a chair across from me. 'How about you tell us where you've been all this time, Katya?'

I told them everything. By the time I had finished, the stars were visible through the single window. Winifred slumped back in her chair, looking exhausted.

'Well,' said Yuichi, 'that all pretty much ties in with everything the beads told us about the Portal-Monoliths.'

I looked at him, confused. '"Portal-Monoliths"?'

'The things Lars Ulven saw falling from the sky,' explained Rozalia. 'We had to call them something.'

'Then you know you must help me,' I said, with as much urgency as I could muster. 'Please, I beg you – help me stop Borodin before he destroys my entire civilization.'

'Before we do anything,' said Oskar, 'I just want to put something out there. If there really are more of those things out there somewhere – these Hyperspheres – aren't they at least worth studying, so long as we *don't* activate them?'

'No,' I said flatly.

'But forewarned is forearmed, right?' he insisted. 'Seems to me those Hyperspheres are the solution to *all* our problems, if they can find us any alternate we want just by thinking about it!' He looked around the rest of them. 'There's got to be at least a chance we can figure out how to use them without getting our fingers burned. I mean – that's got to be at least worth considering, hasn't it?'

I worked hard to push my temper down. 'They'd destroy you, the same way they destroyed the Syllogikos. Besides, you *don't need* a Hypersphere – not when you have *me*.' I pressed my hands against my chest. 'Give me time, and I can show you exactly how to construct your own transfer stages, and search for viable alternates – everything the Novaya Empire can do already. I am entirely willing to do this for you, and more, if you will just help me go back to the Crag and stop Borodin.'

'And what about Jerry?' asked Yuichi. 'How much danger is he in?'

'He's alive,' I said. 'That's as much as I can tell you.'

Nadia made a face. 'Well, we can't just leave him there. No Pathfinder left behind, and all that. That means we're going to have to go back there and get him.'

The rest of them nodded affirmatively.

'Wait a minute,' said Selwyn, a Pathfinder I hardly knew. 'I'm first in line to get one of our people out of a jam, but you're talking about storming a *fortress*.' He turned to me. 'Don't take it the wrong way, but for all we know you're still lying to us, and we'd be walking into some kind of a trap. How do we know Borodin didn't send you back himself?'

Yuichi chuckled and shook his head. 'Even for you, Selwyn, that's plumbing new and unexplored depths of paranoia. We're not giving up on Jerry.'

Selwyn shook his head, irritated. 'I'm not saying anything about giving up on anyone, but it still doesn't mean we go charging into a situation just on this girl's say-so!' This time, one or two of the other Pathfinders nodded. 'And even if she's telling us the unvarnished truth, we'd still be walking into a fortified castle guarded by a bunch of armed goons.'

'So what are you saying?' Chloe shouted. 'What if it was you, Selwyn – would you rather we left you there?'

'Wait!' Nadia shouted as the rest of them began to jump into the argument. '*Just shut up.* What we do is, we discuss this rationally and make a plan.' She turned to Rozalia. 'You're on pretty good terms with Barney, right?'

'Who the fuck is Barney?' said Oskar.

'One of Major Howes' men,' explained Rozalia. 'The guy in charge of the shed where they store the drones. He owes me a favour anyway. If I put it real nicely, he won't ask too many questions about me borrowing one.'

'There you go,' said Nadia. 'We send a drone over to scout out this Crag before we set one damn foot anywhere near it. Nobody's charging in there half-assed. You should know that, Selwyn.'

'But what about this invasion force she says Borodin's threatening to send our way?' asked Randall. 'Rescuing Jerry's one thing, but what do we do when some freaking army turns up?'

'He's got a point,' said Oskar. 'I know you all wanted to keep this between ourselves, but maybe we should be talking to Director Blodel after all.'

Rozalia barked out a laugh, and Oskar's face coloured. 'Will you use your brain? We'd have to tell him about the secret stage, you dingus. We wouldn't even draw breath before he had us all thrown in the clink.'

'But . . . surely he'd listen, given what's at stake?' I asked.

Rozalia shook her head sharply. 'Not a chance. Especially not after the mess on Delta Twenty-Five, and you and Borodin and Jerry all disappearing into thin air. First, he'd send you back to the Authority to be interrogated, and then he'd sit back and wait for Washington to tell him what to do because, unlike our previous director, he doesn't take a shit unless someone gives him an order first.'

'Rozalia's not kidding,' said Yuichi, before I could protest further. 'The Authority are a military dictatorship by any other name, and they're about as inflexible as they come. Blodel's job is to keep us in line, and that's it.'

'Yeah,' said Nadia, 'by which time your whole Empire's gone the way of the dodo – and taken Jerry with it.'

'Hey,' Chloe piped up, looking at me. 'I just thought of something. You said Borodin's intending to attack us *after* your Tsar's used the Hypersphere, right?'

I nodded.

'Look,' she continued, turning back to the rest of the Pathfinders, 'I don't mean to sound callous, but if they all end up getting killed by these Portal-Monoliths as a result, they're hardly going to be in a position to invade us, are they? I mean, doesn't that make it sound as if it'd be better for us *not* to save her people?'

I blinked, then tried to say something. Somehow the words stuck in my throat.

'Hey,' said Oskar brightly. 'Good point, Chloe.'

Around the tiny shack, heads nodded in agreement.

'That still leaves Jerry in the lurch, though,' said Winifred. They were all looking at each other as if I wasn't even there.

'What are you suggesting?' I asked with growing horror. 'Just *let* Borodin wipe out my entire civilization? You're talking about countless lives!'

'Do you have any idea how many full-on, world-ending apocalypses everyone in this room has seen with their own two eyes?' asked Chloe. 'Personally, I've lost count. If they're not frozen, or sucked into a black hole made in some lab, they're irradiated, or mutated, or whatever. Not to mention every one of us here had to watch the same damn thing happen to our *own* alternates.' She leaned towards me. 'Look, I'm sorry, but your Novaya Empire is just one more in an endless line of alternates that's doing its level best to wipe itself out of existence. By the looks of it you're going to be lucky – or unlucky – enough to be its sole survivor.' She spread her hands, as if to encompass everyone in the room. 'Congratulations, Katya.

You're about to join one of the most exclusive clubs in all of creation.'

'So that's it,' I said, clutching the table before me with a death grip. 'You won't help me.'

'Well,' Nadia said softly, 'we'll at least try to pull Jerry out of there, assuming it's possible. But as for the rest of it . . . You have to see our point of view, Katya. If we help you find and destroy that Hypersphere, we could easily find ourselves coming under retaliatory attack from your Tsar's forces. And it sounds as if your Empire's got the resources to roll right over the Authority – and us – without even blinking.'

I pushed my chair back and stood, panic gripping me. 'Please,' I said. 'You don't know what you're saying. Jerry's is just one life against billions.'

None of them would meet my eyes.

'So,' said Randall into the silence that followed, 'I guess we're all finally agreed.' He nodded at me. 'What do we do with her in the meantime?'

'If you're going back for Jerry,' I begged them, 'at least let me go back with you. Let me at least *try* and save my people.'

Winifred shook her head. 'Sorry, Katya. You told us yourself we can't risk losing you – not when you're the key to solving all our problems. That means you stay right here where you're safe. We'll have to tell Blodel about you eventually, but we'll deal with that after we've got Jerry back. With any luck, he'll take his head out of his ass long enough to see sense.' She stepped a little closer to me. 'I'd really rather it wasn't this way. You have to believe that. But if you can give us some idea in the meantime of how we could get Jerry out of that place, it'd be greatly appreciated.'

'No.' I shook my head violently. 'Not if you're going to stand by and just let this happen. I won't help you.'

I could take no more. I felt claustrophobic, as if my lungs had been stuffed full of cotton wool. I tried to push past the Pathfinders nearest me towards the door, but hands reached out, grabbing for me and pushing me back into my seat.

'We're going to have to put the cuffs back on her,' said Nadia. 'I knew we should have left them on.'

'Jesus, Nads,' said Yuichi, shaking his head, 'I'm starting to have my doubts. Have we really come to this?'

'It's a hell of a lot better than what they did to Jerry,' Nadia shot back. 'And a hell of a lot better than what they'll do to *us* if we give them half a chance!'

'Fact is, Yuichi, we're at war,' said Rozalia. 'Whether we like it or not.'

'So do we keep her here?' asked Randall.

'Can't take her back to town and risk her being seen,' Nadia replied. 'So yeah, we'll keep her here. Meanwhile, we'd better start getting everything together. We're going to need weapons as well as one of Barney's drones.'

'Agreed,' said Rozalia, stepping towards the door. 'We can talk over the details back in town.' She glanced at me. 'Anyone want to volunteer to keep an eye on our guest?'

Selwyn looked around. 'I guess I can take first shift,' he said, then looked at me. 'You okay with that, Katya?'

I looked away from him, trembling with fury.

Nadia shook her head and produced the cuffs once more. I spat furious insults at her and twisted away when she tried to snap them over my wrists. Randall and Oskar held me still until she managed to get them on.

'Think over what we've been saying, Katya,' said Winifred, standing on the threshold. 'I know you don't feel like it, but if you can see your way to it, we could really use your help.'

251

I snarled something foul in Russian, and she pursed her lips; the intent, if not the words, were clear.

'You'll be okay, Selwyn?' asked Rozalia. 'It's going to be a while before we get everything sorted out. You could be stuck here for some time.'

'I was all alone on my alternate for nearly twice as long as any of you,' he said, dropping into the chair Winifred had just vacated. 'If there's one thing I'm good at, it's passing the time.'

The rest of the Pathfinders shuffled back out into the night. Selwyn looked across at me, then took a rifle down from a hook beside the door and placed it next to the table. Then he reached over to a shelf and picked up a pack of cards, spreading them on the table.

'Fancy a game?' he asked, looking over. 'I know it won't be easy with your hands cuffed, but—'

'Fuck you,' I growled back.

'Sorry to hear that,' he said, and laid the deck out for Solitaire.

TWENTY-TWO

After a while, exhaustion took its toll on me. I persuaded Selwyn to let me try and sleep on the cot in the corner. He agreed, but kept a watchful eye on me as I lay back, twisting around until I could get as comfortable as the cuffs would allow. I fell asleep to the sight of him playing cards beneath a gas lamp hanging from a hook. His rifle lay within easy reach on the table.

When I awoke, it was to the sound of rain drumming loudly on the roof of the shack. It was light outside, the sky dense with rainclouds. Selwyn was still sitting in the same place, only now he was reading a paperback held folded-over in one hand.

I heard the sound of an approaching engine and Selwyn got up, stepping over to the door. I blinked and groaned then pushed myself upright just as Casey Vishnevsky came inside, rain dripping from his floppy leather hat.

He took his hat off and shook the worst of rain from it, then nodded to Selwyn with a cheery grin. 'Hey, Welshman.'

Selwyn smiled thinly back. Just before Casey stepped across the threshold, I had seen him glance towards his rifle.

'Casey,' said Selwyn, closing the door. The sound of rain became muffled once more. 'What are you doing here?'

Casey dropped a heavy bag next to the table. 'It's taking a lot longer than everyone expected to get stuff sorted out.

Nadia told me to take over and let you go home, get some rest.'

Selwyn yawned involuntarily, covering his mouth with the fanned pages of the paperback. 'And the two of us had so much more to talk about,' he said, nodding towards me.

Casey frowned. 'He's being sarcastic,' I said, leaning back on the cot.

'Oh.' Casey nodded, then pulled off his raincoat, dropping it on the back of a chair. 'Go on, Selwyn. Git.'

'Maybe I should radio Nadia first, check with her that everything's . . .'

'That everything's what?'

Selwyn opened his mouth and closed it again. 'Nothing,' he said, picking up his own coat and shrugging it on before stepping towards the door. He stared dubiously out at the rain, then hurried away with a final nod.

Casey pushed the door most, but not all, of the way shut. He kept his eye to the narrow gap, watching until the sound of Selwyn's jeep had faded into the distance.

He finally pushed the door all the way shut. 'Man. Son of a bitch came that close to calling my bluff.'

'What are you talking about?'

'I'm talking about getting you out of those cuffs, if you want,' he said.

I frowned, studying him. 'Is this some kind of trick?'

'No trick,' he said. 'I came here because I want to ask you something.' He sat at the table and nodded to the chair across from him. 'Look, at least come over here and sit down so we can talk face to face, will you?'

I hesitated for a moment, then got up and sat across from him. 'All right. I'm here.'

He tapped the table in a staccato rhythm for a moment,

studying me. 'Say I let you go,' he said at last. 'And say you made your way back to the Crag. What exactly are you going to do once you're back there?'

'What are you up to, Casey?' I asked. 'Did Nadia send you here to try and trick me into cooperating with you?'

He shook his head. 'I'm just here on my own. Humour me, Katya. I swear I'm here to help you.'

'If I could go back to the Crag,' I said carefully, 'I would do just what I said I would: destroy the Hypersphere before they have a chance to ship it back home to the Empire.'

'And if they already have? Shipped it back, I mean?'

'Then it's too late,' I said. 'But until I know otherwise, I still have to try.'

Casey leaned forward with his arms on the table. 'I've been thinking a lot since I handled those beads you left behind. Felt like I had chunks of somebody else's life upended into my skull . . . Anyway, seems to me there's a solution to your problem you mightn't have thought about.'

'Go on.'

'Lars Ulven worked out that the Portal-Monoliths detect a Hypersphere's whereabouts when someone first lays their hands on it, right?'

I nodded. 'If it's been calibrated, yes. After that, any physical contact will cause it to automatically seek out an alternate that best fits the user's thoughts and desires. Until that moment, it's essentially dormant.'

'And as long as it's dormant, the Portal-Monoliths don't know where to find it?'

I nodded again.

'But once it's been used for the first time,' Casey continued, 'they can find it wherever it happens to be in the multiverse – right so far?'

'Right so far.'

He grinned, looking pleased with himself. 'In other words, the danger isn't so much whether or not the Hypersphere's activated – it's where it goes. Now, this fortress they had you all locked up in – you said the alternate it's on is deserted?'

'There are guards in the Crag along with the prisoners, but there's nothing outside its walls but ancient ruins.'

'Okay.' Casey leaned back and spread his hands. 'Now, say the Hypersphere got activated for the first time while it's still in the Crag – boom, the Portal-Monoliths turn up. But since that whole alternate's unpopulated anyway, it's not really any great loss, is it?' He leaned forward again, a peculiar gleam creeping into his gaze. 'The *real* danger is if your Tsar takes it home to your Empire, or anyplace where there happens to be a lot of people.'

'What are you driving at, Casey?'

'Say someone else got hold of the Hypersphere first and, instead of taking it back to the Empire, or any place that's populated, headed for some entirely different alternate that's deserted. That way no one gets hurt, right?'

I studied him frankly. 'By "someone else", can I take it you mean you, Casey?'

One corner of his mouth twitched in a grin.

'You've only just been rescued by these people – when? A few months ago? – And now you're going to go behind their backs?'

The grin faded a little. 'You know why. Did you hear about the first Casey Vishnevsky they rescued?'

I nodded. 'He betrayed his friends too.' I had learned the full story shortly after my rescue from Delta Twenty-Five.

'They think I'm just the same. Well, maybe I *am* just the same. Did you see the way Selwyn looked at his rifle when I walked in, like he was thinking of reaching for it?' He shook his head. 'They'll never accept me – not any of them. They'll always be watching me with one eye, waiting for me to stab them in the back.'

'So you'll repay them for that,' I said, 'by actually stabbing them in the back.'

'No.' He shook his head tightly. 'This is a win-win situation.'

'I don't see how,' I said. 'Even if you did everything you've just said, and you got your hands on the Hypersphere, the fact is you'd be stuck all alone on some deserted alternate. How is that winning? The Portal-Monoliths will still come chasing after you. You'd have no choice but to keep using the Hypersphere to transfer from alternate to alternate – forever. Doesn't that strike you as a somewhat grim fate?'

'But you're not thinking far ahead enough,' he said, with no little fervour. 'Even with limited time and moving from alternate to alternate, I can still use the Hypersphere to find out the answer to every imaginable question. I could scavenge technology and weapons and know-how none of us could even conceive of – maybe even find something that could stop the Portal-Monoliths. We already know there's no lack of post-extinction alternates, but with the Hypersphere, I can find exactly what I want, anything I can dream up, each and every time. And all just by thinking about it!'

I looked at him with newfound respect. 'But what if you couldn't find a way to stop the Portal-Monoliths? You'd still have to keep moving.'

'No.' He shook his head abruptly. 'If it came to that, I'd find myself an abandoned alternate with a transfer stage and leave the Hypersphere there once I had everything I could possibly want. I'd transfer myself to some new alternate, where the Portal-Monoliths could never find me.'

I shook my head in amazement. The whole plan was completely insane, but I wasn't going to tell him that, not if it meant there was even a sliver of a chance he might free me. 'How long have you been thinking about all of this?'

'Ever since I held those beads,' he replied with manic fever. 'And especially since you turned up back here and told us all your story. Here's what I'm saying: I'll get you out of those cuffs, if you agree to take me back to the Crag with you. With me tagging along, your chances of getting back inside that place without being caught or killed go way, way up.'

'So, just to be absolutely clear,' I said, 'instead of destroying the Hypersphere, I let you steal it and take it far away from the Novaya Empire?'

'Sure,' he said. 'Why not? I get what I want, and you get rid of the biggest threat your entire civilization has ever faced.' He looked at me hopefully. 'Like I said, win-win.'

'As long as you realize that if you fail, I will do my utmost to destroy it.'

He nodded and stood. 'Then I guess it's a deal?'

I suddenly understood just why Casey Vishnevsky had the reputation he did. There was a dangerous, manic edge to him I hadn't perceived before – not, of course, that I'd spent much time in his company. But if he could really get me back into the Crag . . .

I swallowed hard. 'And if we get there, and the Hypersphere is gone?'

Casey smiled wanly. 'Like you said, still gotta try.'

'Then it's a deal,' I said.

'Great! Now put both hands on the table and I'll get you out of those cuffs.'

I did as he said. He unravelled a narrow strip of wire from his belt and carefully bent it at the tip, before inserting the wire into a hole in my cuffs. After several minutes of fidgeting and re-bending the wire, the cuffs finally came loose and fell to the floor.

'Before we go,' he said, pulling a notepad out of his bag, 'how well would you say you know the Crag's layout?'

'I was there for many years, Casey. There are few parts of it I haven't yet been to.'

'So you think you could draw or sketch it from memory?'

I thought for a moment. 'I'm pretty sure I could, yes.'

'Okay then,' he said, putting the pad and a pen in front of me. 'See if you can come up with a map to show where Jerry's locked up.'

I looked at him suspiciously. 'Why?'

'The least we can do,' he said, 'is leave something here for the others that'll help them find Jerry. With any luck, by the time they figure out what I've done, we'll both be long gone.'

I hesitated, wondering again if all of this might still be some convoluted trick to get around my refusal to cooperate. Then I looked at Casey and decided he'd be the last one they'd want to take into their confidence.

'Win-win, yes?' I said.

He nodded, a gleam in his eye. 'Win-win.'

I pulled the notepad towards me and began to sketch out as much as I could remember. I had decent drafting skills, since we had to build so many of our tools in the Crag from scratch. Even so, I had to start again several times when certain memories conflicted with each other. But eventually I had at least a dozen torn-out pages covered in detailed drawings.

Casey had gone to the door, peering up at the grey clouds as I worked. When I told him I was finished, he stepped back over and looked through the pages one after the other while I talked him through them.

'Okay. I guess that's enough.' He scribbled some additional notes on the pages, then dropped them back down. 'Ready?'

I nodded. 'Ready.'

We stepped towards the door, heads bent against the wind and rain as we ran for his jeep.

Half an hour later, we had rowed back out to the hidden stage and transferred over. I adjusted the coordinates so that we materialized deep within the forest that spread beneath the Crag.

Ancient trees loomed all around us. Frost clung to the hard ground, glowing red in the fading light of day. I shivered, once again woefully underdressed for the environment.

I didn't move until Casey had gathered up rocks that he arranged in a loose circle centred on my feet. Finally, he pulled a red handkerchief out of a pocket, and tied it to a branch where it flapped loosely in the freezing wind. We had set the hidden stage back at the island to automatically power up every twenty minutes, and bring back anyone or anything standing within this circle of stones. If Casey succeeded, and I managed to make my way back here, I would be able to return to the Authority's island.

I looked around, seeing a clear path through the forest. 'This way.'

He picked up his bag, following me. He came to a halt when the trees began to thin out, staring towards the machines that rose up high above the horizon.

'What the hell are those things?' he asked.

'I don't know.'

He looked at me askance. 'All this time you were living here, and you're telling me you don't know what they are?'

I shrugged. 'I'm not saying nobody tried to find out. I have no answer for you, Casey.'

He looked the other way, towards the Crag, rising high above the trees. This was the first time I had seen it from the outside; to say it appeared forbidding would have been an understatement. There were lights all across one of the upper terraces, and I thought I could hear faint noises drifting down towards us – an unusual amount of activity for the middle of the night.

I nodded at the holstered pistol strapped to his thigh. 'You said you were going to give me a gun once we got here. How about now?'

He squinted at me. 'Know how to use one?'

'Not really,' I admitted. 'But I still want one so I'm not completely defenceless.'

'You know,' he said, 'if it gets to shooting, we've pretty much lost. Just the noise alone is going to put the whole place on high alert. We need to avoid trouble.'

'Then why bring guns at all?'

'Because *they'll* have guns, and I'd rather take some of them with me if it comes to the worst.'

'Even so,' I said, reaching out a hand.

He gave me a look, then shook his head. 'Fine. But you're about to get the fastest lesson in how to use a firearm in history.' He reached around his back, pulled a small pistol out of his waistband and handed it to me.

I took it from him and regarded it uncertainly. 'It's a lot smaller than yours,' I complained.

'That,' he said, nodding at the gun in my hand, 'is a .38 Special. Anything bigger's too powerful for someone who's never had any practice. This,' he continued, patting his holster, 'is a nine-millimetre Glock semi-auto, and definitely not for beginners.' He nodded up at the Crag. 'What's our best route up there?'

'There's an old path leading up the side of the mountain,' I explained. 'Or at least, that's what I've seen from inside the Crag.'

'They don't ever let you out?'

I shook my head. 'You can see it from the lower battlements quite clearly. Assuming my memory serves me, it starts not too far from here.'

'Fine,' he said. 'I'll talk you through some of the basics on the way.'

We stopped several times so he could show me how to aim and squeeze the trigger, and how to hold the revolver in a two-handed stance. Then he had me repeat each action several times.

'Now pass it back here and I'll load it,' he said. 'Remember, we're not going to use these things unless we're absolutely forced to.'

Casey was a fast walker, and I hurried to keep up. My breath frosted white, hands and face prickling from the cold. Finally we came to the foot of the steep path that climbed one side of the mountain all the way to the Crag's gates. Now we were closer, I could more clearly hear the noise coming from the upper terraces. I thought I could make out occasional voices over the drilling and hammering.

He nodded upwards. 'What's going on up there, d'you think?'

'No idea,' I replied. 'There's usually a curfew by nightfall. I've never known there to be this much activity coming up to nightfall.'

Then, for a few brief moments, the underside of the clouds above the Crag lit up.

'What the hell was that?' breathed Casey.

'I think it was an outward-bound transfer,' I said, then frowned. 'That doesn't make sense. The Crag's main transfer stage is indoors, not outdoors.'

Casey nodded, then dropped his bag on the ground before rummaging around inside it. 'By the sounds of it, they're building something.' He pulled a pair of binoculars out of the bag and tipped his head back, scanning the lower battlements.

He passed the binoculars to me and I took a look. 'Doesn't look like anyone's guarding the place against intruders,' he said from beside me.

I handed him the binoculars back. 'This whole alternate is a prison, Casey. The only way in or out for anyone is by transfer stage. There's nothing out here for them to guard against, and as far as they know I'm dead.'

He used the binoculars again, tipping his head all the way back as he peered up at the upper terraces. 'I'd really like to know what they're doing up there.'

'Only one way to find out,' I said, and started to make my way up the path.

Casey muttered something under his breath, and moved to follow.

It was dark by the time we neared the Crag's entrance, my thighs were threatening to cramp up. The road was better suited to mountain goats than anything else. We scurried past tumbled boulders and half-frozen bushes towards the iron-strapped oak doors that, transfer stages aside, were the only way in or out of the fortress.

We dropped into a crouch by one of the oak doors where there was a gate just big enough to admit a single person. I peered through the iron bars of the gate at the darkened courtyard beyond, breathing hard from the long climb.

Casey reached through the bars and rattled a chain that held the door shut. 'Padlock's on the other side,' he muttered, dropping his bag to the ground. 'That's going to make things more difficult.'

'Do we have to find some other way inside?'

'I said difficult, not impossible.' Casey dug around inside his bag and produced a leather wrap of various spindly looking tools.

'Lock picks,' he said, when he saw me staring at them. He leaned forward, pressing his face against the gate as he reached through the bars with both hands.

I watched as he worked at what was clearly a very awkward angle. The long climb had warmed me up, but the cold was already seeping back into my bones.

After another minute the padlock came loose, and Casey sat back with it in his hands. 'Now tell me,' he said, holding it up with a grin, 'could you have got this far without me?'

'I take your point.' I watched as he put his tools away. 'What else do you have in that bag?' I asked, remembering Jerry's steel tube and Nadia's handcuffs.

He paused, thinking. 'Hacksaw, miniature crowbar, extra ammunition, a knife, can-opener, two two-way radios, six feet of ultra-light nylon rope, painkillers, a roll of bandage, antiseptic, needle and thread and . . . I forget what else.' He sucked his lip. 'A box of safety matches.' He put a hand on the gate, then paused. 'What's on the other side of this door?'

'A courtyard. The laboratory is to the right. There are stairs leading up to the next terrace past the building on the left.'

'You said there's usually a patrol at night?'

'Cameras, too, but they're out of action – my father and his friends took care of that.'

'I remember you said. No guarantees they're still out of action, though. We should keep to the shadows in any case.' He took a firm grip on the gate. 'Ready?'

I swallowed drily. 'As much as I'll ever be.'

'Okay.' He took a deep breath, and pulled his gun out of its holster. 'On a count of three. One.' He leaned towards the door. 'Two. And . . .'

He pushed the gate open, then dropped to one knee just inside the courtyard, panning his gun around.

Three, I thought to myself.

The courtyard was deserted. From far above came the clatter of machinery.

He pushed the gate shut behind us. 'So where do we look first?'

'I want to see the laboratory.'

'Why? It's been blown apart, right?'

'It'll only take a moment. I . . . need to see it.'

He looked disgruntled, and for a moment I thought he might argue. 'Just don't take long,' he muttered.

The air inside the courtyard smelled of smouldering wood and plastic. I motioned to Casey, and we followed the stink towards the burned-out entrance to the laboratory. Piled onto the cobblestones around it were several huge mounds of blackened junk. I picked through some of it and saw that it was mostly the remains of lab equipment.

I glanced up, listening to the noise from above. 'If the Hypersphere's still on this alternate,' I said, 'I think we'll find it somewhere up there.'

He looked up, then back at me. 'You sure?'

'I'm not sure about anything,' I said. 'But that's where the transfer stage is, and sooner or later, that's where the Hyper-sphere's going to be.'

He waved a hand. 'Lead the way.'

TWENTY-THREE

We passed through an archway, climbing the steps to the next highest terrace. Casey saw the elevators dotted here and there about the fortress, but we decided they were too risky to use.

The next highest terrace proved to be just as deserted as the one we had just passed through. We came across the remains of a bonfire of desks and chairs, as well as immense amounts of paperwork. I tentatively picked out a few stray sheets that had escaped the flames and glanced through them.

'It's all administrative stuff,' I said, throwing them back. 'They're burning everything. Why?'

'Looks to me like they're covering their tracks before they clear out of here for good.'

I glanced at a security camera, deeply relieved to see that its lens was still broken, and its status light still dark. 'I guess you're right.'

He nodded upwards. 'We should keep going.'

We climbed more stairs, still keeping to the shadows and listening out for voices or the sound of approaching boots. The third terrace was just as silent: if not for all the noise and light from above, I'd have thought the fortress had already been abandoned.

I led Casey down a narrow cobbled alley to the prisoners' quarters, then left him waiting outside while I slipped inside. It was deserted; there was no sign of any of the exiles, not even those who had played no part in the breakout.

I made my way to my old room and grabbed a coat and scarf, feeling the chill loosen its hold on my bones as I pulled them on. I took one last look around, then returned to find Casey crouching in the doorway.

'Can you hear that?' he asked, nodding towards the far end of the alley. 'Sounds like music.'

I listened, hearing unaccompanied voices singing in unison; a medieval madrigal, mournful and solemn.

'That's Pierre Agerstrand,' I said, gripped by a sudden excitement. I took hold of Casey's arm and led him farther down the alley. 'He was my father's closest friend.'

'How can you be sure?'

'It's what he listens to all the time. He says it helps him concentrate.'

I led him around a corner and saw light coming from an open window, three storeys up: Pierre's old workroom. I could hear the music more clearly now.

A shape moved in the window, momentarily blocking the light. I saw the outline of a man look out over the rooftops before moving back out of sight.

A low hum came from the higher terraces, followed by a brief flare of light.

'That was another transfer,' said Casey, unnecessarily.

'If anyone can tell us what's going on up there,' I said, 'or where to find the Hypersphere, it's Pierre.'

'You're sure?' Casey sounded dubious.

'I guarantee it. Come on.'

I didn't wait for his reply. I scuttled over to the entrance of the building and slipped inside. Casey hurried over a moment later, mumbling and cursing under his breath.

*

Stairs led upwards on our left, while a door on the right led into a storeroom. I climbed the steps as quietly and quickly as I could, Casey following close behind.

I came to the third-floor landing and stepped towards the door of Pierre's workroom, peering through a glass pane set at head height. I saw the back of Pierre's head. I pressed my face closer to the glass and saw that he was leaning heavily on his stick, his attention focused on a computer before him. A framed photograph of Pierre's long-dead wife sat on a shelf to one side.

The music came to an end. Pierre glanced to one side, looking down the far end of the workroom where I couldn't see, then returned his attention to the computer.

I glanced at Casey beside me. *He's alone*, I mouthed, then eased the door open.

Pierre turned, blinking in shock when he saw me enter.

I stepped farther into the room. 'Pierre, I—'

The old man stared at me with a look of blank terror, then again turned to look down the far end of the room.

I turned as well, and saw Herr Frank staring back at me from next to the open window. He gaped at me in open-mouthed disbelief, then put both hands on the windowsill and began to shout for help.

Somehow I couldn't move. I stood there, frozen, the fingers of my right hand still locked around the door handle.

Casey shoved me aside, barging past me and into the room. Herr Frank whirled back around to stare at him, and in that moment something flew out of Casey's hand, flashing across the intervening space between them.

Herr Frank stared down in disbelief at the knife protruding from his chest. He opened his mouth as if to say something, then staggered back against the windowsill before tumbling backwards and out of sight.

From outside I heard a *thump*, followed by silence.

'Sorry,' said Casey, turning to look at me. 'I couldn't think what else to do. Didn't want him bringing the whole place down on us.'

I walked over to the open window, my legs numb from shock. I leaned out and saw Herr Frank sprawled on the cobblestones three floors down, a dark stain spreading from beneath his head.

Casey stepped up beside me and peered down. 'I really hope nobody heard any of that.' He moved back from the window and turned to Pierre, at the same time taking out his gun and levelling it at the old man. 'Katya, ask him if anyone else is on their way here.'

'No one else is coming,' said Pierre, in heavily accented English. 'It's unlikely anyone heard him. They're all on the upper terraces.' He looked at me as if he couldn't quite believe his eyes. 'You're alive,' he said in a half-whisper.

I sank down onto the floor beneath the window. Casey glanced back at me and shook his head in pity. 'I really hope this is your friend here, and not whoever I just killed.'

I nodded shakily. 'This is Pierre, yes. The man you killed is Herr Frank. He's in charge of the Crag.'

Casey's eyes grew wide. 'No shit, huh?' He put his gun away and stepped towards the door. 'Then do me a favour and keep an eye on your buddy for a minute.'

I stood back up. 'Where are you going?' I asked in alarm.

'Gotta get that body out of sight. I'll be right back.'

'Wait!' I said, and he glanced back at me. 'The last time I saw him, he had a slip of blue paper on him. It has a code we need to open a cage they keep the Hypersphere in. He might not still have it, but . . .'

He gave me an approving look. 'Good to know,' he said, then hurried out of sight.

I turned to Pierre. For a moment, neither of us said anything. Then he collapsed slowly into the seat by the computer. 'I thought you were dead,' he muttered in Russian.

'We need your help, Pierre,' I said, also in Russian.

'Help for what?' He glanced towards the door. 'That man . . . who is he?'

'He's a Pathfinder,' I said. 'One of the people we stole the new Hypersphere from. What were you and Herr Frank doing here?'

'I needed to run some final checks, so he brought me here so I could use my own equipment. They won't let me out of their sight.' He nodded towards the window. 'The Tsar is on his way here.'

I gaped at him. 'Here? You mean he's coming to the Crag?'

He nodded. 'I was surprised myself. I thought they would simply ship the Hypersphere back to the First Republic, but evidently not. Instead, Tsar Nicholas apparently intends to test the artefact here.'

I shook my head in amazement. Maybe Borodin *had* been listening to me.

'Your father,' he asked me. 'Did both of you survive, or just . . . ?'

I shook my head. 'He set the containment systems to blow, but he insisted on staying at the controls until I was gone. I tried to get him to come with me, but . . .'

'Ah.' Pierre nodded, crestfallen. 'A terrible, terrible pity.' Then: 'Why did you come back, Katya?'

'To keep the Tsar from activating the Hypersphere. Why else?'

I heard the sound of footsteps climbing the stairs and tensed. Casey stepped through the door, looking flushed and breathing heavily. 'I shoved the body in that storeroom downstairs. There's still blood everywhere, but it's dark enough that anyone looking for him might miss it.'

'The slip of paper,' I asked him, switching back to English. 'Did he have it?'

He patted a breast pocket. 'Got it. How long before someone wonders where he's got to?'

'Not long,' Pierre replied, also in English. 'You're a Pathfinder, I gather?'

Casey nodded.

'How fascinating,' said Pierre. 'There are so many questions I could ask you.'

'Where are the rest of the exiles?' I asked.

'All sent away,' said Pierre, 'to some distant penal colony. They're only keeping me around because they need at least one person with the necessary technical expertise. They have what they want, after all – a functional, calibrated Hypersphere.'

I stepped closer to him. 'We need to finish what Josef started, Pierre. Will you help us?'

'I don't know how I could,' he said, looking bewildered.

'First of all, tell me what all the activity on the upper terraces is. They're building something, aren't they? We could hear the noise from all the way down in the forest.'

'The hall housing the Crag's main transfer stage is too small for their needs,' Pierre explained. 'They're reconstructing it outside, in the courtyard across from the interrogation block. They've been shipping in new equipment non-stop to replace everything destroyed in the explosion.'

'The interrogation block?' Casey looked at me. 'Isn't that where you said they were keeping Jerry?'

I nodded. 'I'm afraid so.'

Casey scowled. 'It's going to make it a lot tougher for the others to bust him out with all that activity going on right next to it.'

'I'm glad you survived,' Pierre said to me, 'but . . . you really shouldn't have come back, Katya.'

I turned back to him. 'Why do they need a transfer stage? The Hypersphere can take the Tsar anywhere he wants. He doesn't *need* a stage.'

'My understanding is he's bringing a considerable entourage with him,' explained Pierre. 'I'm also given to understand he's in no fit state to travel unaccompanied to some unknown alternate. When he first lays hands on the Hypersphere, we'll extract the coordinates it generates, then shut it down again before it can transport him there. Then we'll feed the coordinates into the transfer stage. That way, his medical support team can go with him.'

I nodded. That, at least, explained why they were keeping Pierre around. 'And the Hypersphere is where?' I asked.

'They've moved it outdoors, next to the new stage,' said Pierre.

'What about him?' asked Casey, nodding at the old man. 'We can't just leave him here.'

'If we can trust anyone,' I said, 'we can trust him.'

'Yeah, but what's he going to say when they come looking for Herr Frank and he's nowhere to be found? Or worse, if they find his body?'

'I can stall for time,' said Pierre. 'I'll tell them he left me here and never came back.'

'Sounds good to me,' I said. 'Casey?'

Casey looked unsure. 'Maybe we should take him with us,' he said.

'I'm afraid I would only slow you down,' said Pierre, indicating his walking stick.

'He can hardly walk as it is,' I said. 'Come on, Casey. Let's go. We're wasting time.'

Casey's hand twitched next to his holster, and for a moment I feared he was thinking of killing the old man. But then he shook his head irritably and nodded towards the door. 'Fine then. Let's go.'

'You'll be all right?' I asked Pierre, as I made to follow Casey.

'As much as I can be,' he replied with a sad smile.

I caught the scent of blood once we were back outside, and I felt the gorge rise up the back of my throat. I leaned against a wall until the nausea passed.

'Sorry,' I said, pushing away from the wall. 'I just . . .'

'You don't need to explain,' said Casey.

I nodded upwards, letting Casey take the lead this time.

A few minutes later, we crouched at the base of a stairway. There were voices coming from just above us, speaking Russian. Herr Frank's guards, most likely.

'Is there any way around them?' whispered Casey.

We ducked back as another transfer lit the air above the Crag. 'There's a second path running up the side of the Crag all the way to the top from here,' I said, pointing down a nearby alley. 'But I'm warning you, it was pretty derelict the last time I saw it.'

'Lead the way,' he said.

We detoured between two ramshackle old granaries until we came to the far end of the terrace we were on, and a gate that was more rust than iron. It was unlocked, but swung open with a shriek of protest that set my nerves on edge.

From what little I could see in the dim light emanating from the upper terraces, the path was in even worse shape than I remembered from the one time I had dared try to explore it, many years before. The steps were vertiginously steep, and here and there dense gorse blocked the path. And to make things even more difficult, a brick wall on the left of the path had entirely crumbled away in many places, exposing us to a straight drop down the side of the mountain. It would take only a single misplaced step in the dark to send one or both of us plummeting hundreds of metres to our doom.

Casey visibly baulked. 'Are you *sure* we can get up there this way?'

'At least we won't get seen,' I pointed out.

Casey shook his head, then took out the knife he had used to kill Herr Frank and began to hack a path through the gorse. We ended up covered in scratches regardless as we fought our way upwards, step by step. The stone underfoot was slick with moss, and as we struggled to ascend I wondered if coming this way had been a mistake after all. But we moved with care, and took our time, and after what felt like an eternity we passed a second gate on our right.

'Not long to go,' I gasped, stopping to rest. 'Listen – there are some buildings on the terrace we're headed for that haven't been used in a long time. I think we should be able to get a clear view of the whole courtyard from inside them.'

Casey nodded, his face bleeding here and there from the gorse. 'Sounds good,' he said and began to make his way upwards once more. I forced myself to follow him, despite the terrible ache in my limbs.

*

We came to the end of the path, and a gate so badly rusted we had to climb over it and drop into the narrow alley on the other side. I caught sight of the transfer stage beyond the alley's far end. I wondered if Nadia and the rest of the Pathfinders had discovered our absence yet.

We crouched in the shadows by the gate, watching as soldiers and workers moved around the stage. The air was filled with the sounds of industry. The buildings on either side of us appeared to be as empty as I remembered: their windows were barred, and the nearest door on our right, facing into the alley, was padlocked. Another door slightly farther along the alley, however, did not appear to be locked. I moved towards it, keeping low, and tested it. It swung open easily.

Casey followed me inside. It proved to be devoid of any furniture. The air was filled with the distinctive aroma of bat guano. Something fluttered past my face, making me jump.

'Jesus!' Casey hissed, ducking slightly as a bat flew past us and out the open door. 'First sign of an empty coffin, and I'm out of here.'

We made our way over to a stone staircase set against the far wall, and ascended to the second floor. We found it crammed full of junked furniture and unused metal shelving units. A single window, however, gave us an excellent view across the brightly lit courtyard below. Casey dropped down with his back against the wall on one side of the window while I risked a look outside, keeping myself low.

The transfer stage was bigger than I'd expected. It had to be at least five metres across, and surrounded by powerful flood-lights that shone down on it. I saw the spark of a welding-torch; they still hadn't quite finished constructing it.

As I watched, a sudden pulse of light filled the stage. When it cleared, there was an open-bed truck there, with an industrial-sized generator mounted on its rear. The arm of a mobile crane swung out over the stage while men in overalls hurried to hook the generator up to the crane. They shouted to each other as the generator was lifted up from the truck before being gently lowered onto the cobblestones by the side of the stage.

I finally caught sight of the Hypersphere, mounted on a low platform around the far side of the stage. Two imperial guards armed with machine guns stood on either side of it, while a technician sat at a control rig a few metres to one side. Closer to hand I saw a couple of multi-legged reconnaissance drones standing on the cobbles.

Casey raised himself up to take a quick look. 'There's got to be some way to get those two guys out of the way,' he said, nodding to the imperial guards.

'I don't see how.' It struck me then just how daunting our task was. The whole area was not only brightly lit, but well-guarded. I couldn't see any way for us to get near the Hypersphere without the alarm being immediately raised.

'Well, we've got to think of something,' he said, turning to peer at me with a curious intensity. 'Maybe what we need is some kind of a distraction.'

I didn't like the way he was looking at me. 'Such as?'

He licked his lips. 'Well . . . judging by what I can see out there, I could probably circle around to the far side of the courtyard by sneaking through the rest of these buildings, assuming they're all as unoccupied as this one is. That way I could work my way around until I was behind those two guys.'

'That would get you closer to the Hypersphere,' I agreed, 'but it still won't be enough. The Tsar's imperial guards are fanatics, Casey. They'll defend that thing to the death. You'd never get near it.'

'But if you could draw their attention for long enough, I might have a chance to do just that.'

I stared at him. 'Didn't you hear what I just said?' I hissed. 'Those two guards aren't just going to abandon the damn thing! And it's still locked in its cage. Do you really think you'd have time to enter the code and unlock it before every single guard in the Crag descended on you?'

'None of them,' he said with a malicious grin, 'is expecting *me*. Trust me, I know how to take these guys out. But it would help a lot if you could distract them somehow.'

I understood for the first time that it wasn't Casey's plan that was insane – it was Casey. 'How, exactly?' I asked, a leaden weight filling my gut.

He looked around. 'There's plenty of stuff you could throw out of the window to get their attention. Maybe shout and wave your hands – but not until I've circled all the way round.'

'You want me to be your . . . your *decoy*?'

He gave me a frank look. 'Sure, why not? We still both get what we want – I get the Hypersphere, and you get rid of it forever, right?'

'I'm beginning to understand,' I said in a level voice, 'why the Pathfinders all hate you.'

'You don't stay alive by winning popularity contests,' he grunted.

I closed my eyes and took a deep breath. 'I think your proposal is the single stupidest, most idiotic plan I have ever heard.'

'But at least it's a plan,' he said. 'Which is more than you had.'

'No. We need to stay right here. We have a direct line of sight to the Hypersphere, and we have guns that can hit it from here. Anything else isn't going to work.'

Anger flared in Casey's eyes. 'We *had an agreement*,' he hissed.

'Made under duress,' I pointed out. 'I was in handcuffs. What the hell else did you think I'd say?'

'I didn't come here to shoot the damn thing,' he said, 'and our guns aren't powerful enough to penetrate steel, particularly not at this range, given it's still, as you say, locked inside a fucking *cage*.'

'So you say,' I said, aiming my pistol squarely at his head. 'It's still a better chance than *your* miserable plan. The deal's off, Casey. You don't give a shit about me, or the people I'm trying to save, or anything except your own worthless skin. I was a fool to imagine otherwise. Now either you shoot the Hypersphere – or I shoot you.'

He gave me a nasty smile. 'You couldn't kill Herr Frank. What makes you think you've got the cojones to kill me?'

I wrapped both hands around the grip of the pistol in the manner he had demonstrated. 'Let's find out,' I said.

Casey stared back at me, hands by his sides and eyes fixed on mine.

There was another flare of light from the direction of the stage, and I automatically glanced towards the window.

It was all the distraction Casey needed. He threw himself on top of me, clamping his fingers around the wrist of my hand that still held the revolver. It slid from my grasp and clattered to the ground. I twisted around and managed to knee him in the belly, more by accident than plan.

He grunted with pain and shuffled back. I scooped the revolver back up and placed my elbows on the windowsill. Then I exhaled, aimed, and pulled the trigger.

Nothing happened.

I swore and pulled the trigger again. The gun clicked use-lessly.

I heard a movement from beside me and turned to see Casey standing facing me, one hand to his belly and the other aiming his own gun at me.

I cursed at him in Russian. 'You tricked me, you son of a bitch.'

'Sorry,' said Casey, sounding anything but. 'Now we're going to play it my w—'

He fell silent and I saw his eyes look past me, growing wide.

I turned to see Borodin standing at the top of the steps, three of the Crag's guards standing beside him in a line, their rifles levelled at us.

Borodin had much the same look on his face as Pierre had when he first saw me. 'You're . . . ?'

Still alive, I knew he meant to say.

'Don't move,' he said, recovering from his shock. 'Either of you.'

I dropped the useless pistol. Casey muttered something foul, then moved to do the same with his own gun.

I didn't allow myself to think. I snatched the gun from Casey's hand before he could drop it, then turned to the window, aimed towards the Hypersphere, and squeezed the trigger.

TWENTY-FOUR

Something punched hard against my shoulder. My shot went wild, echoing into the night.

My legs gave out beneath me and I slid to the floor, gasping. I felt as if I'd been hit with an iron bar. I reached up with one shaking hand to my shoulder and it came away red.

Borodin snapped an order at his men. They ran forward, grabbing hold of us. The gun slipped from my grasp and I screamed as my arms were wrenched behind my back; the pain was beyond description. They searched us both, taking Casey's knife and bag and the slip of blue paper he'd taken from Herr Frank's body.

'Put them in the interrogation block for now,' said Borodin.

I screamed again as we were dragged and pushed all the way down to the ground floor. As we emerged into the alley, I saw Pierre standing waiting outside, his eyes full of shame and guilt.

'I'm sorry, Katya,' he said in English. 'Truly sorry.'

'You led them to us, didn't you, you son of a bitch!' Casey shouted.

'There's no time for this, Pierre,' snapped Borodin.

'No, please,' the old man begged. 'I just want to explain.' He looked at me and Casey in turn. 'My wife, you see. All these years they told me she was dead, but . . .' He glanced at Borodin, then back at us.

'But she's not,' I said. 'Is that it?'

Pierre nodded, his face twisted up in anguish. 'There was a price for ever seeing her again, you see. I . . .' He swallowed, leaning on his stick. 'I know this must be hard for either of you to understand.'

Casey swore from beside me.

'I don't want to hear any more,' I said.

'Get them both out of here,' ordered Borodin. 'Pierre, I need you back at the stage. *Immediately.*'

The guards were not gentle as they dragged us past the transfer stage and across the courtyard. I struggled to stay on my feet. The numbness in my shoulder quickly grew into a dull ache that frightened me more than the pain.

'Looks like they only winged you,' Casey said as we were led inside the interrogation block. 'Shoulder wounds like yours aren't usually fatal. Still, you're going to have to do something about that bleeding.'

'Like you give a damn,' I said. The words emerged slurred.

'Those rifles of theirs look like shitty heaps of junk. I've used higher-calibre hardware hunting possums. Even so, I figure the bullet passed clean through.'

'I'd rather be dead,' I mumbled, 'than have to listen to you.'

The door swung open and we were pushed inside a corridor. 'If we'd just steered clear of that old fucker,' he continued, 'we could have avoided this whole me—'

I tried to hurl myself at Casey, and screamed again as something inside my shoulder gave. The guards dragged us apart, pushing me ahead.

One of them pulled open a heavy iron door before shoving

us both inside a cell. I sprawled on the floor, Casey shouting abuse at the guards as they locked us in.

Then I looked around and realized we weren't alone.

'Well, fuck me,' said Casey, staring into the corner. 'It's Jerry.'

Jerry was curled up on a bench suspended from a wall by two chains, his knees pulled close to his chest. He was either asleep or unconscious, with one arm thrown over his eyes.

'Hey, Jerry,' said Casey, pushing the other man's shoulder. 'Are you awake?'

Jerry groaned and coughed and lifted his arm. His face, I saw, was a mass of bruises. He squinted into the light, peering up at Casey through bloodshot eyes.

'Jerry,' Casey said again. 'Jesus, what did they do to you?'

Jerry's eyes focused on Casey, then grew wide with terror.

'Easy there,' said Casey.

Jerry sat up and threw a weak punch that Casey easily dodged. 'You!' he screamed, 'you son of a bitch, you killed them all! I'll—'

'Jerry!' I tried to shout, my voice coming out as a half-croak. 'It's not the same Casey. Don't you remember?'

Jerry twisted around to look at me, then back at Casey. His breathing grew less frantic, and he licked his lips, looking confused.

'This is the *other* Casey,' I reminded him. 'The one they retrieved a couple of months back. Remember? The old one is dead.'

Jerry nodded. 'Yeah. Okay. I . . . sorry.' He swallowed hard and slumped back on the bench. 'What are you doing here? And—' He blinked. 'Wait a minute. What about the others? Are they here? Where are they?'

'On their way,' said Casey. 'Right now, it's just me and Katya.'

'Just . . .' Jerry's voice trailed off. 'What the hell is going on?'

'Save it for later,' said Casey, then turned to me. 'Right now, Katya needs help.'

Only then did Jerry appear to realize I had been shot. He crouched beside me, probing my injured shoulder and snatching his hand back again when I yelped in pain.

'Don't they have any doctors around here?' asked Casey. 'What's Russian for doctor, anyway?'

I shook my head. 'There aren't any doctors here, believe me.'

'Then I guess we'd better do something ourselves,' said Casey, pulling off his jacket and then his shirt, tearing one sleeve of the latter into strips.

'How long since she was hit?' asked Jerry.

'Couple minutes, maybe.' Casey nodded at my jacket. 'We're going to have to get that off,' he said.

'Fuck you,' I hissed, shivering from the cold sweat that clung to my skin. 'Five minutes ago you were happy to let me get myself killed just so you could get your hands on the damn Hypersphere.'

Jerry's eyes grew wide. 'He did what?'

'That was then,' Casey grated. 'This is now.' He waggled his fingers at me. 'C'mon. Jacket off. Need to dress that wound.'

I swore at him again, but did as he asked, working first one arm and then the other out of the heavy jacket. The pain was so bad I thought I might pass out. Once it was off, I felt the chill of the air even more deeply. I sank back, feeling light-headed as he carefully tore my shirt open around the wound.

'At least the bleeding's stopped,' he murmured. He moved

in close and began wrapping his makeshift bandages around my shoulder. I pressed my lips together and breathed rapidly through my nose to try and keep from screaming again.

'You can still move your fingers, right?' asked Casey.

I flexed the fingers of my injured arm. 'They're fine.'

'Now you're done,' said Jerry, 'maybe someone can tell me what's going on?'

Casey did the talking, and I let my head sink back against the bricks, listening to him.

'So you were going to take the Hypersphere, huh?' said Jerry.

'You know he disabled the gun he gave me?' I said, giving Casey a venomous look. 'He left me defenceless because he was scared I might shoot the Hypersphere before he could get his hands on it. Isn't that right, Casey?'

Jerry shook his head. 'You really are a devious prick, Vishnevsky,' he said, his tone almost admiring.

'What's done is done,' Casey muttered. 'Let's just wait for the others to get here.'

I glared at him. 'If bandaging my arm up with your shirt makes you think I'm happy about the way you—'

'Take it easy,' said Jerry. 'If Nadia and the others really are on their way, we need to be ready.'

I eyed Casey balefully. 'Coming for us, perhaps, but not for *him*.'

'What does it matter?' said Casey. 'I'm damned in all your eyes, whether they come or not.'

'*If* they come,' I said. 'I know they said they would, but once they see all those people and soldiers out there . . .'

'They'll come,' said Jerry.

'Yeah,' said Casey, with no little bitterness. 'One for all, and all for one. Like a bunch of fucking musketeers.'

*

The cell's single barred window gave us a view of the transfer stage and much of the courtyard. We took turns watching out of it as the final preparations for the Tsar's arrival were made. More equipment and supplies arrived, along with a second truck and even a forklift, and several steel trolleys loaded with what looked like medical monitoring equipment of some kind.

I couldn't stop thinking about Pierre's betrayal. I remembered the ease with which Herr Frank had tracked Tomas and me down, and the look that passed between my father and Sevigny when I last mentioned his name in their presence. I wondered if perhaps this was not the first time he had betrayed us. The very idea made me feel as if some part of my soul had been ground to dust.

Daylight came, a pale sun rising over the Crag's battlements. By now, the Pathfinders had surely found both my map and Casey's hastily scribbled notes. They knew where we were, and why.

But where were they?

'Do you think something's gone wrong?' I asked at one point. I didn't need to say who or what I was talking about.

Jerry stood by the window, his forehead pressed against the bars. Casey slept on the bench. 'Nothing's gone wrong,' he said. 'They'll be here.'

'It's just that we've been here since yesterday evening and—'

'Do you know when the hell to shut up, Katya?' he muttered.

I shut up.

And then, finally, someone came. But it wasn't Nadia, or any of the Pathfinders.

Casey shook me roughly awake where I had curled up in a corner. I coughed and sat up, my head throbbing almost as badly as my shoulder.

'Hey,' he whispered. 'Someone's coming.'

The cell door swung open to reveal two imperial guards armed with machine guns.

'You're coming with us,' one of them said to me.

'What about them?' I asked, indicating Jerry and Casey.

'Just you,' the guard grunted.

I struggled upright, swaying slightly. My head throbbed with a strange fever. One of the guards took hold of me by my arm and I let out a cry of pain, but he showed no reaction as he pulled me out into the corridor.

'This way,' he said, gesturing with his weapon.

'Hey!' Casey shouted. 'What the hell is going on? I—'

The second guard slammed the door shut, and I heard Casey's muffled curses as I was led along the corridor.

We stopped at another door and they pushed it open. When I saw what lay on the other side, I turned and tried to run. They caught me easily and dragged me inside.

It was the interrogation room where I had seen Jerry strapped into a chair. They lifted me, kicking and squirming, into the same chair. It took both of them to hold me down.

Then I saw Borodin standing in a corner, Monsieur Sauveterre by his side. He leaned towards Sauveterre and muttered something. Sauveterre nodded, then stepped towards me, selecting a pair of scissors from a trolley.

I swore at him and struggled futilely.

Borodin made an exasperated noise. 'He just wants to take a look at your shoulder.'

I jerked my head around to look at him, then back at Sauveterre.

'Well, look at that,' muttered Sauveterre, stepping around to one side of me and examining Casey's crude bandages. He used the scissors to cut them away, and I hissed with pain as he peeled them from my skin.

'A clean shot through muscle,' he said to Borodin, after studying the exposed wound. 'It just missed the subclavian artery. No permanent damage done, it seems.'

I just gaped at him in utter stupefaction.

'As long as she can stand upright and think clearly, that's all I care about,' muttered Borodin, eyeing me balefully.

'What is this about?' I demanded.

Borodin sighed. 'I suppose I don't need to ask *why* you came back.'

I leaned forward, not resisting as Sauveterre swabbed the wound. I clenched my fists and hissed through my teeth as he applied iodine.

'Almost done,' said Sauveterre, selecting a syringe from the tray. 'Antibiotics,' he explained, before pushing the needle into my arm.

'Tell me,' asked Borodin, as Sauveterre wrapped my shoulder in clean bandages, 'has anything you've said or done made a single bit of difference?' He lit a cigarette and blew smoke into the air, and I noticed the hand holding it was shaking. 'Unfortunately, Pierre insists we have urgent need of you. He says he cannot be sure of success without your help.'

I started to laugh, and it turned into a hacking cough. 'Things not working out as smoothly as you'd hoped, Mikhail?'

His expression darkened. 'Damn you, and especially damn your father.'

'You seriously expect me to help you?'

'The Tsar is coming to the Hypersphere, rather than the other way around,' he said. 'We expect him to arrive here within minutes. Surely that would make you more amenable to lending us your vast intellect?'

'So you *did* believe me when I warned you.'

He sighed and took a final drag on his cigarette, then ground the stub beneath his boot. 'Help me finish this, Katya. If anything goes wrong, it'll go wrong a long, long way from any of the Republics, I swear.'

'And then what?' I sneered. 'We'll all live happily ever after?'

He came closer, gripping the arms of the chair as he leaned over me, nostrils flaring. 'I have family too, Katya; so does Herr Frank, and nearly everyone connected to this project. Dmitri will kill them all, including you and your friends in that cell back there, but only if we let him take the throne from his father. I swear to you that if you help me finish this, I *will* let you go.'

'The last time I saw you,' I said disdainfully, 'you were going to have me shot.'

I saw him fighting down his anger. 'I swear to you, help me finish this and you can live any damn place you want. In the heart of First Republic Moscow, if it takes your fancy – you and all the rest of the exiles. I have heard word Nicholas intends to declare a general amnesty once his place on the throne is secure.' He stabbed a finger at me. 'But I guarantee you this – if we fail here, we die. *All* of us.'

'We'll die anyway,' I said.

He moved away from the chair and rubbed at his face with both hands. There were dark shadows under his eyes, I saw. He lit another cigarette, even though the first one was barely finished.

'We've played this game before,' he said. 'You can either work with Pierre, or watch while Monsieur Sauveterre relieves your friends back in that cell of their fingers and toes.'

I said nothing and he nodded after several moments. 'I'll take that as a yes,' he said, then stepped over to a chair on which some clothing had been piled untidily. He picked out a shirt I recognized as one of my own and threw it at me. 'Get dressed and I'll take you to Pierre.'

I pulled the shirt on and let a guard lead me back outside and past the interrogation block. I looked over my shoulder and saw Casey watching me from inside the cell. Then I was led around the side of the stage to where Pierre stood peering over the shoulder of the technician manning the control rig. The Hypersphere sat in its cradle just metres away.

'Ah!' cried Pierre, glancing round to see me, his face flushed with excitement. 'You're just in time. If only your father could have been here to see this!'

If I'd had a knife at that moment, I believe I could have killed him without compunction. 'Borodin said you needed my help,' I replied through clenched teeth.

'Here,' he said, gesturing to a bank of screens mounted above the rig. Various readings scrolled across them, and there were several error messages. 'There appears to be a misalignment . . .'

'Move,' I said to the technician.

The technician glanced at Pierre, who gave him a small nod. He vacated his seat and I took his place. I tapped at the keyboard for several minutes, and one by one the error readings vanished.

'I knew having you help would be as good as having Josef here,' he said.

'Don't ever mention his name again,' I said quietly, without looking around.

'Then I won't,' he said. 'I know you can never forgive me

for what I did. But you deserve to see the culmination of everything we've been working towards all these years.'

I gave the seat back to the technician. An alarm sounded to clear the stage, and seconds later it filled with light. Once it had faded, I saw that a large crowd of people had materialized on the stage. Amongst them I counted half a dozen imperial guards, plus a gaggle of civilians, most of them expensively – if conservatively – dressed. The majority were elderly, and several were in wheelchairs.

The imperial guards worked to move the crowd apart, and from their midst a motorized wheelchair larger than all the others emerged, rolling down the ramp and trailed by half a dozen men and women wearing surgical smocks and masks.

The wheelchair's occupant was barely visible beneath a dense swathe of heavy blankets laid over his legs and chest. He was tiny and wrinkled, his wizened head completely hairless. His hands shook where they rested in his lap. His eyes were rheumy and unfocused, his complexion sallow and far from healthy. An oxygen mask was strapped over his nose and mouth.

'That can't be . . .'

'Tsar Nicholas the Third,' said Pierre. 'Hard as it is to believe.'

I gaped. Every official photograph or portrait I had ever seen of Nicholas showed a man in robust health, with broad shoulders and a thick, dark beard, his chest rippling with medals. But the figure before me was barely more than an ambulatory corpse.

A doctor helped guide the wheelchair down the ramp. The newly arrived imperial guards followed behind, their machine guns at the ready as they scanned the workers and technicians standing around the stage. The rest of the Tsar's entourage were the last down the ramp. A priest, dressed in black vestments and with a beard to match that of any imperial guard, remained on the stage, walking around and swinging a metal censer that trailed smoke as he made a blessing.

Borodin appeared, stepping towards the Tsar and bowing low. He gestured to the Hypersphere. I was too far away to make out what he was saying but, given the circumstances, I could only assume he was explaining its operation.

'What about the rest of them?' I asked Pierre. 'Those old people. Who are they?'

'Members of Nicholas' inner circle, I suspect,' said Pierre. 'Advisers, perhaps, or hangers-on. Isn't that General Yakov amongst them?'

I looked around until I saw a man in military uniform. The sight of him chilled me. General Yakov was in charge of suppressing the Twelfth Republic's rebellion.

'Yakov?' I asked. 'What's he doing here?'

'Well,' said Pierre, 'he looks as if he could do with a spot of rejuvenation himself.'

'That *must* be why they're all here. This isn't just about keeping Nicholas alive – he's buying their loyalty as well!'

Borodin stepped towards the Hypersphere, and the Tsar was brought closer to it. I watched as Borodin took out the slip of blue paper that had once belonged to Herr Frank, and entered the code into the Hypersphere's cage.

The cage opened, revealing the Hypersphere like a pearl in a shell. The imperial guard moved out of the way, and the upper part of the Tsar's wheelchair began to rise on hydraulics, tilting forward until its wizened occupant was able simply to reach out and place one claw-like hand directly on the Hypersphere's naked surface.

The breath caught in my throat as the surface of the artefact ceased its constant swirling motion. It transformed into a flat cobalt blue. I glanced up at the bank of monitors, seeing data flood across them at ever-increasing speed.

The technician leaned towards his microphone. 'Lock on coordinates,' he said, then repeated the message.

Borodin shouted something to the imperial guards standing next to the Hypersphere. They took hold of the wheelchair and eased it back, breaking the Tsar's contact. The wheelchair sank back down on its hydraulics, and within seconds the Hypersphere had returned to its usual resting state.

'Send the drones through,' said Pierre, leaning on his stick. 'Let's see what's on the other side of those coordinates.'

The technician's voice boomed across the courtyard. Workers moved the exploration drones onto the stage, then stepped back quickly before the light swallowed the machines.

'Fifteen minutes should give us enough data for an initial assessment,' said Pierre.

I glanced towards the interrogation block. A truck blocked my view of much of it, but I knew Jerry and Casey must be watching the proceedings.

Fifteen minutes later the drones transferred back over. Immediately, video and other data appeared on our monitor bank, and Borodin and others crowded around to see. The screens showed a dark and forbidding landscape, with titanic structures scattered across a moonlit plain.

'Remarkable!' said Pierre, with a tone of reverence.

Borodin stepped up to Pierre. 'Make your way to the stage with the others,' he told the old man. 'And you too,' he said, glowering at me. 'I'm not leaving you anywhere I can't keep an eye on you.'

He turned on his heel and followed the Tsar as his wheelchair was guided back onto the stage, trailed by the rest of his entourage.

'Come along,' said Pierre, and I followed him up the ramp, filled with numb despair. Borodin had won, and I had lost. Whether we lived or died was out of my hands.

I glanced towards the Tsar, seeing how he struggled to draw breath, how his body shook from uncontrollable tremors. That he still lived seemed a miracle.

Pierre's technician spoke once more over the tannoy, and moments later we were somewhere else.

TWENTY-FIVE

We materialized on a vast and perfectly flat expanse of obsidian that came to a sudden end just metres from where we stood, sloping down to meet dark-veined rock. There was no sign of vegetation or life of any kind.

The air felt dry and warm. Grey clouds scudded across the face of a moon that loomed so large and close that I felt I could reach up and touch it. Beyond lay a great whorled nebula, lit from within by the light of birthing stars.

I turned the other way, seeing a pale ivory structure rising seamlessly from the expanse of obsidian. It rose up and up, reaching perhaps half a kilometre into the sky. It was thirty or forty metres broad at the base, but narrowed, so far as I could tell, almost to a point at its tip. I tilted my head back, seeing that the top part of the structure curved inwards over the obsidian plain.

I looked around; there were more, identical, structures arranged around the edge of the obsidian plain. They formed a circle perhaps five or six kilometres across. And then it hit me: we were standing on the edge of a transfer stage big enough to transport a small city.

Farther off, in the distance, were more, equally gargantuan transfer stages. I could see nothing else, no matter which direction I turned. Stages of an identical scale marched off beyond the horizon.

'There's something old about this place,' said Pierre from beside me, 'isn't there? It feels abandoned, somehow, like the machines back at the Crag.'

'Over there!' someone yelled.

People gasped and shouted to each other, pointing towards what had at first appeared to me to be another, much smaller stage immediately adjacent to our own, albeit one that lacked any field-pillars. Then I saw that its edges were irregular, and that while at first glance its surface had appeared perfectly flat and black, closer inspection revealed a gelatinous ripple racing across its surface. It suddenly resolved into a hundred-metre wide lake of some oily black liquid.

'Is that it?' I asked. 'The healing pool?' I had told Jerry of its supposed rejuvenating properties during our journey across Delta Twenty-Five, and of the Tsar's desire to be young again.

'I cannot imagine what else it might be,' Pierre replied, a quiver in his voice. 'It certainly matches the Syllogikos' description.'

'But how can we be sure that's really it?'

'Because the Hypersphere brought us to this precise spot,' said Pierre, a peculiar hunger in his voice. 'And there is, after all, only one way to find out.'

Pierre made his way towards Borodin, leaning heavily on his stick every step of the way, and spoke quietly to him. Borodin nodded and took the old man's arm, guiding him towards a member of the Tsar's medical staff. The doctor then led Pierre next to a trolley loaded with monitoring equipment.

I watched, befuddled, as the old man removed his shirt, revealing a hollow chest and sunken shoulders. The doctors glued monitoring patches to his chest and scalp before leading him down off the stage and over to the shore of the black lake.

I stepped towards Borodin while the crowd chattered in excitement. 'Is that his reward? To be your guinea pig?'

'He volunteered, Katya. Who wouldn't?'

The doctors held Pierre steady by the edge of the lake while he undid his trousers, letting them fall to reveal a pair of naked buttocks. Another took his walking stick, and he took a hesitant step forward, sinking up to his shins in the tarry black liquid.

To my horror, the liquid formed feathery tendrils that slithered up to his knees. Suddenly he pitched forwards, quickly sinking beneath the surface.

He was gone, with scarcely a ripple. I put my hand to my mouth, barely able to breathe. A fearful gasping and muttering rose up all around us.

'Is he transmitting?' Borodin called out to one of the medical staff.

'All his life signs are normal,' the doctor replied. 'Heart rate, brain function and breathing are as expected.'

'Breathing?' Borodin stepped towards him. 'How can he be *breathing*?'

'I don't know,' the doctor replied, pointing at a screen. 'But that's what his readings say.'

I saw the Tsar raise a feeble finger to one of the imperial guards, who leaned over his wheelchair and spoke with him. The guard nodded, then approached Borodin. 'His Imperial Majesty wishes to know how long he has to wait.'

'Only a short while, I'm sure,' Borodin replied, sounding anything but certain. 'Please assure the Tsar everything is in hand.'

*

It became a waiting game.

Fifteen minutes passed, then thirty. Borodin asked again and again for the details of Pierre's vital signs, but nothing changed. It was as if Pierre were merely sleeping. More messages were shuttled between Borodin and the Tsar, and I could see his nerves were fraying even more the longer we waited.

An hour passed, and still no sign of Pierre.

Then, at last, a little after the two-hour mark, I heard a cry and saw hands pointing towards the black lake. Someone had emerged from it, spluttering and naked and shivering.

I say *someone*. It was far from immediately clear it was Pierre; it might have been Pierre's son, perhaps, or a young nephew. Gone were the drooping shoulders and sunken chest; instead the figure that came staggering up onto the shore was that of a dazed but clearly vital young man, staring around at the people watching him in blank confusion. The only clue that this really was Pierre lay in the medical patches still glued to his transformed flesh.

The doctors rushed forward, helping him up onto the stage and seating him on a stool next to an equipment trolley. He followed without protest or question, blinking at everything around him.

There was a sudden commotion as the Tsar struggled feebly to lift himself out of his wheelchair.

'I will not wait!' I heard him shout feebly, his arms trembling as he attempted to rise. 'Take me there. Now!'

One of the doctors made the mistake of trying to get the old man to lie back down. An imperial guard struck the doctor hard across the back of the head with his machine gun, and he sprawled on the ground next to the wheelchair, bleeding from a gash above one ear.

A second imperial guard quickly pushed the wheelchair

down to the edge of the pool, while others came hurrying forward to help. They rapidly stripped the blankets from the Tsar's lap, one of them lifting him up in his arms as if he were cradling a wizened baby. A long coat fell from the Tsar's shoulders, and I saw that beneath it he wore little more than a paper hospital gown.

The guard took one or two tentative steps into the tarry black water, then carefully lowered the Tsar down. The ruler of the Novaya Empire clutched weakly at the guard's arms for a moment, then let go, sinking immediately from sight. The guard stepped quickly back before he, too, could succumb to the waters.

I struggled to believe everything I had witnessed. To one side of me, Pierre was being interrogated on the details of his life by a doctor, presumably to check if his mind was functioning normally. I tried to reconcile this youthful stranger with the old man I had known for so many years.

Pierre saw me looking his way. 'Katya,' he said with a grin. 'Look at me! It's a miracle, isn't it?'

I didn't know what to say, so I turned away. I watched with growing incredulity as several bottles of champagne were produced from a trolley. Glasses were filled and handed out.

It was like being at a party in Hell. I wandered over to the nearest field-pillar and, out of sight of the Tsar's entourage, slumped against it, staring out towards the horizon. The sight and sound of those old men and women drinking and chattering as if they were at some third-rate reception in the First Republic Kremlin made me sick. The sun rose, its light making the field-pillars look like the bleached bones of fallen gods.

Finally, long after the champagne had run dry, the Tsar emerged.

Like Pierre, he had been wholly transformed. It was like

seeing one of his old photographs come to life: his back was strong and straight, his shoulders broad and muscular, his scalp and cheeks already darkened by stubble. His gaze, however, was unfocused, his jaw slack as if in shock. He stumbled and fell to his knees once he reached the shore, vomiting up black water as his imperial guards rushed to help him.

I stood and came back around the pillar, watching as they guided the Tsar back up onto the stage, where he blinked and stared around himself in much the same way as Pierre had.

Then a great shout went up, and several of the oldest amongst the royal entourage dashed towards the lake, throwing off their clothes once they reached the shore. Those in wheelchairs negotiated their way down to the lake with the aid of the imperial guards.

The Tsar, who had stopped to stare at his own wheelchair in apparent wonder, turned to observe them. A grin spread across his handsome face, and he laughed in delight as a doctor guided him to a stool next to one of the equipment trolleys. He sat while a blood pressure cuff was fitted around his upper arm.

Borodin walked towards the edge of the stage, where it dipped down to meet rock. He watched the old men and women sink deep into the black waters. Then he stepped out of his shoes and started to make his way down to join them, his cheeks damp with tears.

'Mikhail, wait.'

I saw General Yakov approach him. 'The Tsar gives you his thanks,' he said to Borodin. 'He says he never doubted you for a moment. But there is something we must discuss first.'

I thought I saw a flicker of uncertainty on Borodin's face as Yakov led him closer to where I stood, half-hidden around one side of a field-pillar. I ducked back a little and heard them come to a stop close by. They hadn't seen me.

'What's going on?' Borodin demanded. 'Why can't he thank me in person?'

'I'm sorry, Mikhail. His Majesty informs me that you do not have permission to enter the pool. Mikhail – wait!'

I moved back around the pillar until I could see them. They were looking away from me. Yakov had grabbed Borodin by the arm.

'Don't make a fool of yourself,' Yakov hissed.

'I refuse to believe this!'

Yakov stepped closer to him. 'Let me be clear, Mikhail. These are politically delicate times, and there are certain matters that . . . well, if your role in them ever came to light, it would reflect *extremely* badly on the Tsar. Do you see?'

'Everything I have done has been on his direct orders!' Borodin exploded, loudly enough that his voice carried far across the stage. I saw the Tsar dart a look towards him before resuming chatting with one of the doctors.

Yakov made a hushing motion, and pushed Borodin back towards the field-pillar. I quickly moved out of sight again.

'Of course,' said Yakov. 'But some things never stay hidden forever. You *know* that, Mikhail. And when they come to light, as they must, someone must be held accountable.'

'You don't understand,' said Borodin, his voice thick with emotion. 'I am . . . not a well man, General.'

'I know, Mikhail. The Tsar informed me himself. Tell me – how long do you have?'

'A few months, perhaps,' said Borodin, his voice full of bitter despair.

Thunderstruck, I remembered Borodin's handkerchief spotted with blood, his violent coughing fits . . .

'It's better this way, don't you see?' said Yakov. 'Just let nature take its course. Better that than living long enough to see your name dragged through the mud, or wasting your newfound youth in some imperial prison.'

'That sounds like a threat,' said Borodin.

'For God's sake, Mikhail, you knew what you were getting into. Just take my advice and – *Mikhail*!'

I again stepped back out from the pillar. Borodin had pushed past General Yakov and was striding briskly towards the Tsar.

Imperial guards blocked his path, pushing him back. 'Your Majesty,' Borodin shouted past them. 'I just want to speak with you!'

The doctor removed the pressure cuff from the Tsar's arm. The Tsar stood and turned the other way, gesturing to one of his entourage to follow him.

'Your Majesty!' Borodin shouted again, his voice growing hoarse as the Tsar moved farther away.

One of the guards came nose to nose with Borodin and said something I couldn't hear. Borodin's face turned to ash while everyone else around them did their level best to pretend they had seen and heard nothing.

I should have felt vindicated to see Mikhail Borodin fall so far, and so very quickly. To my surprise, however, I felt nothing.

We returned to the Crag shortly after, leaving behind most of the medical staff and several guards to wait for those still immersed in the healing pool. I was escorted back through early morning light to the interrogation block, where Casey and Jerry confronted me with a thousand questions: where had I been, what happened, what did I see?

'We're going to die in here,' I said, after I gave them my answers. 'Your friends aren't coming for us.'

'They'll come,' said Jerry obstinately, slumping back down against a wall. Casey, seated on the bench, stared into a corner with a hopeless expression.

'It's been too long,' I said, peering out at the stage, which was as busy as ever. 'Either something went wrong, or they realized it was pointless.'

Neither of them said anything in reply.

The rest of the day passed with interminable slowness. One of the Crag's guards brought us what looked like scraps and left-overs from the canteen. Doubt dug its roots deeper into my thoughts with every passing hour. Perhaps I had been wrong about the Portal-Monoliths after all, and my father's death had been meaningless. If so, every one of my sacrifices had led to nothing.

I watched as workers brought machinery and furniture up from other parts of the Crag, stacking it all in great piles to one side of the stage before either crating it up or burning it. A forklift moved the crates onto the stage, where they soon vanished in a rush of light.

There was no sign of Borodin. Yakov appeared to be in charge now; I watched him marching around and giving orders. Whenever I saw Pierre, my hands would tighten on the window bars, imagining my fingers were closing around his throat.

Later, in the early evening, the Tsar climbed onto the stage and vanished in a rush of light, presumably on his way back to the First Republic.

'The Hypersphere's still here,' said Jerry, when he came to

stand by my side soon after the Tsar departed. He nodded at where it still sat in its cradle, farther around the transfer stage. 'How come he's not taking it back with him?'

'Your guess,' I said, 'is as good as mine.'

We watched in silence for another minute.

'He's not going to risk taking it back yet,' said Casey. He lay on his back on the floor, one arm thrown over his eyes. 'Too dangerous.'

Jerry looked back at him. 'How do you figure that?'

Casey moved his arm and looked at him. 'You saw him. He's thirty, forty years younger than he was. Soon as they see him back home, there'll be people saying he's an impostor.' He sat up and hooked his arms over his knees. 'All those other people who went over with him, I figure, are meant to be witnesses that he's the real deal. He won't risk taking the Hypersphere back home until the political situation is much more settled. In the meantime, he's got it tucked up nice and safe here.'

'As long as it stays here,' I said, pressing my forehead against the bars, 'everyone back home is safe.'

'Nothing's happened yet, though,' said Jerry. 'No sign of anything falling out of the sky, or anything like that.'

'Not yet, no,' I said.

A few hours later, after night had fallen, an armoured truck materialized on the stage. It drove down the ramp and parked across the courtyard from the stage. My heart sank as I watched imperial guards, under Yakov's watchful gaze, load the Hypersphere into the rear of the truck. Casey, it appeared, had guessed wrong.

I thought they would send it back immediately, but they did not. I could see the artefact's faint glow illuminating the inside of the truck. I wanted more than anything to close my eyes and sleep, but I was afraid to wake up and find it gone.

I could only stay awake for so long, however, and I hadn't slept since I had lain on the cot in Nadia's tiny shack. The moment I finally sat down with my back against a wall and tucked my forehead against my knees, I fell into a deep and dreamless sleep.

It felt as if only an instant had passed before I woke again to the sound of gunfire.

TWENTY-SIX

I heard a brief, staccato burst of noise, like hail pounding on a tin roof. It echoed across the courtyard, coming from somewhere farther down the mountain.

Casey and Jerry were already up and standing on either side of the window, peering out at a gloomy dawn. My tongue felt furry and thick, and there was an unpleasant, throbbing dampness beneath the bandages on my shoulder.

A sudden vibration rolled through the floor.

Jerry glanced at me. 'Get much in the way of earthquakes here?'

I shook my head and swallowed. 'Never.'

'That's the second tremor in just the past few minutes.' He stepped over and helped me to my feet. 'I think maybe you should see this.'

I squeezed past him and peered out of the window. The stage was crammed with dozens of people all shouting and yelling at once, their eyes wide with panic. I saw that nearly all of the Crag's guards were amongst them.

A trickle of dread worked its way into my belly when I saw several of them looking and pointing upwards at something only they could see. I pulled my face up close against the bars, hoping to catch sight of whatever it was that had caught their attention, but all I could make out was a single thin sliver of sky above the roof of the building on the far side of the court-yard.

Several imperial guards ran towards the bottom of the ramp, waving their machine guns at the mass of people on the stage and shouting at them. Another rushed to the open door of the truck into which the Hypersphere had been loaded. He climbed into the cabin, then leaned back out, yelling at the crowd and waving at them to show he wanted them to get clear.

Then, to my astonishment, one of the imperial guards near the bottom of the ramp slipped his weapon from his shoulder and opened fire on the crowd gathered on the stage. My heart clenched at the sudden eruption of noise, and I saw several people, including one of the Crag's own guards, crumple and fall.

A terrible wail went up, and I thought the crowd might scatter, leaving room for the imperial guards to drive the truck onto the stage as they clearly intended. Instead, the surviving members of the Crag's guards – who, it appeared, were attempting to desert *en masse* – unshouldered their own rifles and returned fire.

'They're fighting amongst themselves,' Casey muttered from beside me. 'What the hell's going on out there?'

The imperial guard who had commandeered the truck was the first to die. I saw him struggle to climb back down from the cabin before falling under a volley of shots. His compatriots meanwhile moved to defend themselves, but too late: Herr Frank's men were quick to take the advantage, and within seconds the remaining imperial guards had fallen to the cobble-stones.

'Hey!' Casey pushed a hand between the bars and hammered at the thick glass. 'What about us? We're in here! Hey!'

Light formed above the crowd. I glanced towards the control rig and saw that Pierre was manning it. In the last instant before the light swallowed them all, he ran forward, leaping onto the stage just in time.

The light faded, and I stared out at the suddenly deserted courtyard. The only sound I could hear was the quiet grumbling of the truck's engine.

There was, I realized, no one left to guard it – or the Hypersphere mounted in its rear.

'Jesus, did all of that really just happen?' shouted Casey. 'What the hell spooked them so badly?'

'Guess,' I said.

But I needed to see with my own eyes.

More gunfire echoed through the air, coming, perhaps, from the lower terraces.

'Sounds as if we're not alone after all,' muttered Jerry.

'Hey,' said Casey in a loud whisper, pointing to the cell door. 'Someone's coming.'

I listened, and heard the scuff of boots coming down the corridor.

'Could be someone coming to rescue us,' said Jerry, hopefully.

Casey shook his head hard. 'Or kill us.' He snatched up the stamped-tin tray our food had been brought on.

'There's no point in killing us,' I said, albeit a touch uncertainly.

'Yeah?' snapped Casey. 'You already said they're getting rid of all the evidence. What if that includes us?'

Jerry gaped at him in disbelief. 'What the hell are you going to do, Casey, *tray* whoever it is to death?'

'You got any better ideas?' he hissed, pressing himself against the wall on one side of the door. 'We don't know who's out there.'

Jerry shook his head. 'You've got a tray. The people running this place have machine guns and rifles.'

My nerves got the better of me, and I pressed myself against the wall on the opposite side of the door from Casey. 'If it's guards,' I said to him, 'we try and grab their guns.'

Not that I really believed I had it in me to do any such thing – especially not with a festering gunshot wound in one shoulder. But it was either that, or just stand there and do nothing.

Jerry muttered something obscene under his breath and pressed himself next to me. I felt the blood pounding in my skull, and reached out, taking a tight grip on his hand.

'Jerry!' a voice shouted from the other side of the door. 'Where the *fuck* are you?'

'Randall!' shouted Jerry, jerking back from the wall. 'Goddammit, is that you?'

Casey leaned his head back and laughed from sheer relief while Jerry battered the door with his bare hands. 'In here, you goddam redneck!' he bellowed. 'Get us out of here!'

'Sweet fucking hallelujah,' said a woman's voice: Nadia. 'We found him!'

'Hey! Get back from the door,' Randall shouted. 'I'm gonna try and shoot out the lock.'

'Shoot what?' said Nadia scornfully. 'That crap only ever happens in mov—'

Randall fired three times. The noise was deafening in the confined space. I let out a shriek and clapped my hands over my ears. The door jerked under the impact, and the lock mechanism shattered.

'You see, huh?' I heard Randall say, his voice full of scorn. 'Maybe you've been watching the *wrong* movies.' He shoved the door, but it still wouldn't open wide enough to let him through.

'Hang on,' he shouted. The door jerked hard, and then again, and on the third try it flew open. Randall had his hands braced against the door frame, one boot raised to kick at the door. Nadia and Chloe stood behind him, clutching rifles.

Nadia's eyes nearly popped out when she saw me and Casey along with Jerry. 'Jesus Christ on a pogo stick,' she said slowly. 'I hope you sons of bitches have been having fun.'

Chloe pushed past me and grabbed hold of Jerry in a tight embrace. I looked away from them, a sudden tightness in my throat.

'Nadia,' said Casey, stepping towards her, 'I—'

Nadia pulled back her fist and punched Casey hard in the jaw. The big man took a step backwards, his head twisting round from the impact. I held my breath, but he made no move to retaliate.

'That wasn't called for,' he said thickly, rubbing at his jaw from beneath hooded eyes.

'Fuck you, it wasn't called for,' she shouted. 'Five minutes you were on the island – *five minutes* – and that's all it took for you to start screwing us about!'

I stepped between them, facing Nadia. 'For God's sake, stop this! We need to get *out* of here.'

Nadia's expression became more sober. 'Do you even know what's out there?' she asked me.

'I think I have a pretty good idea.'

We made our way outside. It was a shock actually seeing a Portal-Monolith with my own two eyes. Nothing could have prepared me for it: not even a dead man's memories.

It hovered motionless in the air a few kilometres above us. That surprised me: I had assumed it would simply keep falling until it hit the ground. Not so, evidently. It was high enough still that clouds obscured the upper part of its bulk. I raised my eyes yet higher and caught glimpses of a ragged hole in the sky through occasional breaks in the cloud cover.

One thing was different, however: the Portal-Monolith's leading edge was coming apart like so much wind-blown ash, apparently dissolving from the bottom up. Instead of being carried away by the wind, uncountable thousands of black specks swarmed around the enormous craft with what was clearly intelligent purpose.

Even as we watched, a number of these specks spiralled down towards the Crag.

I looked past the battlements at the edge of the terrace and saw more Portal-Monoliths, far off in the distance, falling through more tears in reality.

'I have seen some crazy shit,' said Casey in a half-whisper, 'but this really beats it all.'

'That's nothing compared to what we saw on the way up here,' said Randall. 'We ran into people a couple of times, but they were in such a panic it was like they didn't even see us.' He nodded upwards. 'Those things flying around it seem to come in waves. Some of them came down and sort of . . . flowed over people, and they just disappeared. If we hadn't managed to find somewhere to hide, we might not have made it this far.'

'There's a big-ass stage around the other side of this building,' said Nadia. 'Any reason we can't use it to get back home?'

'I thought of that too,' said Chloe. 'It's got to be better than trying to go all the way back down to the forest with those things flying about.'

311

'Sounds like a great idea to me,' said Jerry.

Casey nodded. 'I figure there's a good chance we're the only ones left by now, so we're not likely to get interrupted. Or at least if there is anyone left, they're probably hiding from those things.'

'Chloe, use your radio, call Oskar,' said Nadia. 'Tell him to head home and wait for us.'

'Where is he right now?' asked Jerry.

'Down in the forest, waiting at the transfer point,' said Chloe, pulling out a walkie-talkie. She switched it on and relayed the message.

Just as she put the radio away, voices came from the direction of the transfer stage, around the other side of the interrogation block.

'Spoke too soon,' said Nadia, glaring at Casey.

She moved quickly and quietly to the nearest corner and peered around it towards the stage, then hustled back over. 'There's two of them,' she said, her voice low and urgent. 'Long dark coats, machine guns. They're wandering all around that stage. *Fuck!*'

'Imperial guards,' I said.

'We can't take on machine guns,' said Randall.

'Should I tell Oskar to wait for us?' asked Chloe.

Nadia shook her head. 'Not yet. But it's an option.' She looked at me. 'Katya? Is there a faster way back down to the forest?'

'Not really,' I admitted. 'There are the elevators, but that would leave you very exposed.'

'Yeah, and I don't want to have to go all the way back down there with those things flying around,' said Randall.

'What choice do we have?' Nadia hissed, then put a hand up to silence him before he could say anything more. 'We'll head back around the other side of this building and hit the same stairs that brought us here,' she said, nodding towards the opposite corner of the interrogation block. Then she glanced up, and I did too, seeing black shapes spiralling down towards us.

'Okay, let's go,' she said, grabbing my arm.

I pulled myself free.

'What the fuck?' she exclaimed.

'You have Jerry,' I said. 'Those guards are going to try and take the Hypersphere back home to the Empire. I can't allow that.'

Nadia unslung her rifle and aimed it at me. 'We don't have time for this bullshit,' she hissed. 'You're coming with us.'

'Pull that trigger,' I said, 'and they'll come running.' I put out my hand. 'At least give me a rifle so I have a fighting chance.'

'Goddamn you,' said Nadia, 'don't do this! We need you back on the islan—'

'*Stoy*!'

A third imperial guard appeared from the direction of the stairs, his machine gun levelled. 'Sergei! Ensel! Over here!' he shouted in Russian.

I heard a response from the direction of the stage. The other two guards appeared around the other corner moments later.

'Drop your weapons!' the first guard shouted in Russian at the Pathfinders. 'Drop them now!'

I turned to Nadia. 'He's saying—'

'I can guess.' She let her rifle clatter to the cobblestones with a sour expression. 'Thanks a fucking bundle,' she added, as the others followed suit.

Casey was staring hard at the three guards. 'Look at them,'

he muttered. 'They're scared shitless. We could take them if we play it right.'

'Don't do one damn fool thing,' Nadia muttered, 'or I swear if I'm still alive afterwards I'll put a bullet in you myself.'

'Those things are getting closer,' muttered Randall, glancing up at the black specks overhead.

The first guard, who had flecks of grey in his beard, was clearly in charge. 'Who the hell are you people?' he demanded.

'We're technicians,' I replied.

'Technicians with guns?' one of the other guards sneered, kicking our rifles out of reach before pointing his gun at Casey. '*He* doesn't look like any kind of scientist to me.'

'Who killed those guards next to the stage?' Greybeard demanded. He stepped up close to me, eyes bright with anger. 'Which of you murdering bastards is responsible?'

'There was panic,' I said. 'A lot of people crowded onto the stage to try and get away. Your men tried to chase them off, but some of Herr Frank's guards shot them before escaping with the rest.'

'And you just stood and watched all this, did you?' said Greybeard.

'Yes,' I said, then flexed my shoulder. 'I got hit in the crossfire. You see?'

His eyes studied my wounded shoulder for a moment, then he gave me a narrow-eyed stare before moving his attention to Casey. 'What's your name?' he asked, still speaking in Russian.

Casey stared down at him and said nothing. My lungs felt as if they had turned to stone.

'And you?' the guard repeated, addressing Jerry this time. 'Are you mute or something?'

'I told you,' I said, 'we're technicians. These people only just arrived from the Twelfth Republic – that's why they don't speak any Russian.'

'Wait a minute!' shouted one of the other men. 'Sergeant, they're prisoners, or some of them are, anyway. They were locked up in there.' He gestured at the interrogation block. 'This woman was helping operate the stage. I don't know who the hell the rest of them are, though.'

'All I care about,' said Greybeard, looking around all of us, 'is if one of you people knows how to program a stage so we can get the hell back home. Well? Anyone?'

I held my tongue, afraid to say anything. I did not want them to take us back to the Novaya Empire. I especially did not want them to take the Hypersphere back.

'Those things are getting very close,' said one of the other guards, looking up.

A black shape swooped low over the terrace's rooftops, close enough that I could see it resembled nothing so much as an airborne manta ray. Its skin was jet black.

'Tell your friends to keep together,' Greybeard said to me. 'If any of them try and run away, we'll shoot them down. Sergei, Ensel, take up the rear and keep an eye on them. We'll head for the admin building past the stage. *Move!*'

I relayed the message to the Pathfinders. Greybeard took the lead, and we dashed around the corner of the interrogation block, past the stage and in through the open door of a building.

Inside was an office space that looked as if it had been hit by a whirlwind. Paper was scattered everywhere, and chairs lay toppled on their sides. Desks had been pushed up against walls, and ancient-looking computers had been dumped in a haphazard pile in one corner. Shift schedules were still pinned to a notice board beside the door.

One of the guards slammed the door shut, then peered through the window beside it. Greybeard kept his machine gun trained on us as we backed into the rear of the office.

Just that short run across the courtyard had taken its toll on me: my skin felt slick and hot, and my bandaged shoulder had transformed into a mass of burning and itching. I wanted little more than to lie down and rest for just a few minutes; but unless I could persuade these men we were on their side, all was lost.

An idea was forming in my mind.

I pushed the sickness down, even as it clawed at my senses. I composed myself as best I could and stepped back up to Greybeard.

'Your friend was right,' I said. 'Yes, I was a prisoner. But I am also a member of the science staff here on the Crag. I was there with the Tsar and his entourage when they transferred over to that new alternate.'

'That's true,' said one of the other guards. 'She came with us.'

'Shut up, Sergei,' said Greybeard, glowering at me. 'If you're part of the science staff, why were you locked up with those others?'

'For acts of insubordination,' I lied. 'Look, you said you wanted someone to program that stage – I can do it.'

Greybeard's eyes narrowed. 'You're lying,' he said. 'Not about operating the stage, but the rest of it. There's something here I don't like.'

'For God's sake, Sergeant!' shouted Ensel. 'You saw what happened to Yakov – we need to get out of here!'

'What happened to Yakov?' I asked.

'Taken,' said Ensel, 'by one of those things. It swooped

down and he just . . . vanished.' His hands holding the machine gun shook. 'Others, too.'

'Ensel, *shut up*,' bellowed Greybeard.

'Katya,' Nadia said in a very low voice from just behind my shoulder, 'I don't know what the hell you're all saying, but I sure as shit hope you know what you're doing.'

Greybeard turned back to me. 'You can get us back home?'

'Believe me, I'm quite expert with transfer stages.'

He studied my eyes, then nodded with approval. That much he believed. 'We have orders to get that truck out there back to the First Republic at any cost. If we go home without it, we might as well have just stayed here. Do you understand?'

'I understand,' I said.

'All right. Sergei here will take you to the control rig once we're sure it's safe to go back out there. Ensel, you'll head for the truck at the same time. Get it up the ramp and onto the stage.'

Ensel nodded.

'Your name?' Greybeard asked me.

'Katya Orlova.'

'Tell your friends as soon as you've initiated the transfer and I give the signal, they're to come out and join us on the stage. Will you have time to run over and join us?'

I nodded. 'You don't need to have your man escort me to the control rig. There's no need to risk anyone else's life.'

'I wasn't asking for your opinion,' he snapped. 'Sergei? You have the coordinates?'

Sergei nodded and handed Greybeard a piece of folded paper. He opened it up and I saw a set of coordinates neatly printed on it.

'You'll enter these coordinates,' said Greybeard, showing it to me before passing it back to Sergei. 'I don't know just what your game is, but he'll be keeping a close eye on you. Is that understood?'

I nodded, my heart sinking. My plan had been to program the stage with a null sequence – a set of random coordinates – and send the Hypersphere into oblivion. I was at a loss for what to do if I had an imperial guard looking over my shoulder while I did my work.

Greybeard pushed the door open and ducked his head out for a moment before just as quickly pulling it back in. 'There are a few of those things circling up above the courtyard, but they're pretty high up. It's risky, but we can't stay in here forever. Sergei, soon as I say, get Miss Orlova to the control rig.'

'Tell me right now what the hell is going on,' muttered Nadia from behind me.

I summarized everything Greybeard had told me. 'That's going to leave just this old guy guarding all of us,' Casey said quietly.

'There's no way we're going back to that fucking Empire of yours,' said Nadia. 'I hate to say it, but Casey might have a point.'

'Yeah,' said Chloe, 'and he'd mow most of us down before we got anywhere near him. You need to think of something better.'

'All you need to do,' I said, 'is when he tells you to join them on the stage – don't.'

Which of course left the more immediate problem of how to keep them from transporting the Hypersphere back to the Empire. I thought furiously, but nothing would come to mind.

'But if we stay put,' Chloe insisted, 'they're going to know we're up to something for sure.'

'Doesn't matter,' said Randall. 'They'll still be gone.'

Sweat trickled down the small of my back. Was there any way

I could persuade them *not* to take the Hypersphere back? However I ran it through my mind, I felt certain it would only make the imperial guard even more suspicious of us.

'What the fuck are you saying to them?' Greybeard shouted, staring at the Pathfinders, who all gazed sullenly back.

'You said to tell them what to do when we're ready to leave. I did.'

Greybeard cast a contemptuous glance at us, his lip curled. I had the feeling he was wondering whether it might just be easier to kill them all.

'You ready, Ensel?' asked Greybeard, still staring hard at the Pathfinders. 'Don't take any chances. Check the sky before you make for the truck.'

Ensel – who was clearly in a state of barely controlled panic – eased the door open and leaned out to take a look. 'Coast is cl—' He stopped, then began to wave frantically. 'Hey!' he shouted. 'Over here!'

'Who is it?' said Greybeard, grabbing his shoulder.

'There's someone else still alive!' Ensel shouted in glee, moving aside so that Mikhail Borodin could enter.

TWENTY-SEVEN

Borodin was breathing heavily, as if he'd run a long way. There was a wild look in his eyes, and his breath, even from a distance, stank of alcohol. He stared speechlessly at me and at the Pathfinders gathered around and behind me.

'Sir,' said Greybeard, 'these are—'

'I know who they are,' he said, clumsily wiping a hand across his mouth. 'Yakov. Where is he?'

'Dead, sir,' said Greybeard. 'One of those . . . things took him, and some others.'

'What's been going on here? Who killed your men outside?'

He pointed at me. 'This woman says they were killed by the Crag's own guards.'

Borodin turned bloodshot eyes on Greybeard and examined him closely. 'And where were *you*, Sergeant, when all this was going on?'

'Down on the lower terraces, sir, helping to clear them out under General Yakov's supervision. When those things appeared in the sky, we started to make our way up here. Out of more than a dozen of us, it's just me and my two men left.' He nodded at me. 'This woman says she can program the stage to get us home.'

'She does, does she?' His gaze, when it fell on me, was hard and unblinking. 'Back to the Empire?' he asked me in Russian.

'Or did you have somewhere else in mind?' he added, switching to English.

'Sir?' said Greybeard, 'the Tsar's artefact is still out there. General Yakov's last orders were to get it back home at any cost. Ensel here can drive the truck onto the stage while the girl sets the coordinates under Sergei's supervision.'

'I'll decide what we do here, Sergeant.'

'But General Yakov—'

'Is dead,' Borodin finished, glaring at him. 'I believe you mentioned that already. As the senior officer present, I am taking command.'

Greybeard, however, persisted. 'I'm aware, *sir*, that you were relieved of your command by the General. And frankly, sir, I can smell your breath and don't believe that you're fit for duty.'

'Do you want to get out of here or not?' Borodin screamed at him. 'If Yakov is dead, you imbecile, authority automatically reverts back to the next most senior officer present, does it not?'

Greybeard's face coloured. 'Sir, I—'

'Shut up,' Borodin seethed, 'until I need you.'

Greybeard fell silent and ducked his head down.

'Mikhail,' I said to him in English, 'listen to me. You've seen those things out there. You know we can't let them take the Hypersphere back to the Empire.'

He glared at me sullenly, swaying slightly. He must have been sitting alone for hours, I thought, steadily drinking himself into a stupor. 'Damn you,' he said, his voice low. 'Don't tell me what to do.'

My temper started to get the better of me. 'You idiot,' I jeered at him. 'None of this would have happened if you'd damn well just listened to me in the first place.'

'Easy, Katya,' said Nadia. She turned to Borodin. 'Mikhail, we need your help.'

'I cannot prevent them taking the Hypersphere back,' he said to her. 'They will kill all of us, me included, if we try and stop them.'

'No,' I said, thinking harder than I ever had in my whole life, 'there is a way.'

They all looked at me.

'You can end this, Mikhail,' I said, 'and save yourself in the process.'

Borodin stared at me. 'What the hell are you talking about?'

Something inside me recoiled from the idea of helping save the life of the man I hated more than any other, but I could see no other way. 'Maybe you can't stop them trying to take the Hypersphere back,' I explained, 'but you might be able to persuade them to let you into the back of the truck where it is. Then all you need to do is open its cage and take the Hypersphere for yourself.'

'No!' Casey shouted. 'You can't—'

'Shut up,' said Chloe from beside him. 'Not one more damn word from you, or we'll leave you here to rot.'

Borodin stared at me with a perplexed expression. 'Are you insane? Steal the Hypersphere? And go where?'

'Back to the healing pool, where else? You did everything Nicholas asked of you, and he threw you away like a used tissue. You can cure yourself, then use the Hypersphere to get away to some remote and preferably unpopulated alternate, before the Portal-Monoliths can come looking for you. But you can't ever use it to return to the Empire, or billions will die.'

'They'd shoot me before they'd let me anywhere near the

Hypersphere,' he said in a hoarse whisper. 'There's only so far they'll follow my orders, believe me.'

'Then we need to think of something,' I said. 'Do you still have the code for the Hypersphere's cage?'

He nodded. 'I do.'

'I need some answers,' said Greybeard, his tone increasingly belligerent. 'Are you just going to stand there bickering with each other all day?'

Borodin squared his shoulders and gave me a look before turning to face the imperial guard.

'Don't question me, Sergeant,' he shouted in Russian. 'Take your men back down to the main comms room on the next terrace down from this one. You should be able to contact every other part of the Crag from there. Look for other survivors. I'll take the truck onto the stage while Miss Orlova programs the control rig.'

'Three of us aren't needed for that, sir. Ensel is good with trucks, and Sergei can reconnoitre the comms room on his own – as per your orders.' I saw his finger tighten just very slightly around the trigger of his machine gun. 'I'll remain here to render whatever support you require.'

He knows, I thought, feeling a sudden uprush of panic. Or at least suspects.

'Very well, then,' said Borodin without missing a beat. 'I'll escort Miss Orlova to the stage controls and watch out for danger while she programs them.'

Greybeard stared hard into Borodin's eyes for several long moments before finally giving his men their orders. 'And radio in when you get to the comms room,' he told Sergei.

Ensel went first, tensing in the moment before he dashed towards the truck. Sergei first gave the coordinates for the First Republic to Greybeard, who in turn handed them to Borodin.

Sergei ducked out of the door, his pale face drenched with sweat.

Then only Greybeard was left, standing between us and the exit with his machine gun.

Borodin glanced at me. 'This won't be easy,' he said in English. 'We're going to have to improvise once we're out there.'

'Just do your best,' I said.

'Your name, Sergeant?' he asked Greybeard.

'Podolski, sir.'

Through the window, I could see Ensel inside the front cabin of the truck. Its headlights came on, and the engine roared into life. My skin prickled as he drove it up the ramp, then came to a halt in the middle of the transfer stage.

Podolski pulled out a walkie-talkie. 'Ensel?'

'Here, sir,' came a crackly voice. 'Ready to go.'

'Good work, Ensel.' He switched to another channel. 'Sergei, report in. Are you at the comms room yet?' He waited several seconds and tried again. 'Sergei? Call in.'

'There might just be the two of them left,' I said quietly to Borodin as Podolski tried yet again to make contact.

He nodded minutely, then moved past Podolski and towards the door. 'Miss Orlova,' he said in Russian. 'We'll make our move now. Sergeant, perhaps you should go and wait with your man in the truck.'

Podolski shook his head. 'Ensel can handle himself, sir. I think it's best that I stay here and keep an eye on these others. You should hurry.'

I stepped up beside Borodin. He seemed to have sobered up entirely.

He opened the door and looked outside. 'Now, Katya.'

We ran, skirting the stage and heading for the control rig. I made the mistake of looking up, and faltered when I saw that the sky was now almost entirely black with winged shapes. There must have been tens of thousands of them – perhaps even millions. There were so many that they spread from one horizon to another, like a great cloud of locusts blackening the sky. The Portal-Monoliths were still coming apart, like a black tide threatening to swallow the whole world.

All my strength fled. How could we possibly fight against such things? Then Borodin came back and grabbed hold of me, tugging me towards the control rig. We dropped down next to it in a low crouch.

'We'll die out here,' I said, overwhelmed by panic. We were entirely exposed. If one of those things saw us and dived for us . . .

'We'll die for certain if you don't program this stage,' he said. 'Not for the Empire – set it for the Authority.'

'But what about the Hypersphere?'

'I'll make a run for the back of the truck,' he said. 'That guard in the front cabin won't see me coming unless he happens to look in the rear-view mirror.'

'But Podolski . . . !'

'There's nothing I can do about him,' he said. 'But he can't watch me *and* your friends all at the same time now, can he?'

A shadow passed just above the stage. I shrieked, pressing myself flat against the cobblestones. Borodin crouched over me, staring upwards.

'Get in the seat,' he snapped, pulling me back upright. 'Now, Katya – hurry!'

I pulled myself into the seat facing the rig console. It lit up automatically as I sat before it. Borodin reached past me and tapped at its keyboard, bringing up a list of stored coordinates. He selected one, and the screen blinked in response.

'The coordinates for Alpha Zero are already stored here,' he explained. 'Just remember – even if I get away with the Hyper-sphere, you're on your own with at least two imperial guards.'

I nodded, then glanced back the way we had come. I saw Podolski with his back to the window. He looked to be keeping a careful eye on the Pathfinders. He turned to glance briefly towards us, then looked away again.

Borodin took a final glance upwards at the sky, then ran forward and onto the stage, throwing himself into the back of the truck. I saw him lean over the caged Hypersphere, the slip of blue paper gripped in one hand.

Any second now, and Podolski would look back out the window and see Borodin wasn't beside me any more.

I got to work powering up the stage, and then had a sudden, sobering thought: there was nothing to prevent me sending Borodin, the truck, and the Hypersphere to a null sequence. No need to wait until he had his hands on the Hypersphere – in one stroke, I could send Tomas' murderer into oblivion, and eliminate any threat to the Empire.

I reached for the keyboard, and quickly input a set of random coordinates. The stage was primed: all I had to do was hit the activation button, and seconds later they would be gone.

My hand hovered over the button, but for some reason I could not bring myself to press it.

I heard angry shouting, and looked around to see Sergei standing at the open door of an elevator across the courtyard, staring towards the truck.

'Stop!' he shouted at Borodin, and ran towards the stage with his machine gun at the ready.

Borodin had not yet finished entering the code. He glanced over at Sergei, running towards him, then continued working.

Sergei fired a burst into the air above the truck, afraid, I assumed, of hitting the Hypersphere. 'Sergeant! Ensel!' he bellowed. 'For God's sake, stop him!'

Podolski emerged from the doorway, shouting angrily. Casey rushed up behind him and the two men began to grapple. I heard a brief rattle of fire as Podolski managed to twist free, pieces of cobblestone kicking up around his feet.

Casey ran back inside, and slammed the door shut.

I ducked down low, so Podolski couldn't see me. He ran towards the stage, shouting Ensel's name.

Now, I thought. Borodin was still leaning over the Hypersphere in the rear of the truck. *End it now.*

I still couldn't do it. No matter how many times I had imagined killing him in the past, I simply could not act.

Ensel, finally hearing the Sergeant's shouts, jumped down from the front cabin and ran around to the back of the truck. At first, he didn't see Borodin, instead staring towards Sergei.

'Sergei!' he screamed, pointing into the air. 'For pity's sake, look out!'

Too late, Sergei looked up as one of the black-winged shapes swooped down over him. He yelled with horror, the broad wings obscuring him momentarily from sight.

Then it flew back upwards, sailing lazily into the air above the stage. There was no sign of Sergei, as if he had simply been erased from existence.

Ensel gaped for a moment, then did a double-take when he realized Borodin was in the back of the truck. He got in and fought with Borodin, trying to pull him back from the Hypersphere just as its cage finally hissed open.

Borodin fought hard, but Ensel was younger and, I suspected, a lot stronger. Podolski, who had come to a halt when Sergei was swept away, ran forward again, slinging his gun back over his shoulder before also climbing into the back of the truck.

I knew, then, that I had no choice but to act or it would be too late. I somehow found the strength to bring my hand slamming down, triggering the null sequence.

The truck was enveloped by light, making it hard to see the men fighting in the back. Podolski and Ensel were still grappling with Borodin, but in the last instant before the truck vanished, I thought I saw Borodin lunge towards the exposed Hypersphere, throwing himself on top of it.

A second light joined that of the transfer stage: I closed my eyes from the overwhelming brilliance and looked away, dark spots dancing before my eyes.

When I was next able to look, the light had faded and the stage was empty.

The Pathfinders came running out of the doorway towards me. 'Katya!' Nadia shouted. 'What happened? Where did they go?'

'I'm not sure.' I had stood back up without realizing it. Had Borodin got away? He might have, but I didn't know. Nor, most likely, would I ever find out.

'Get up on the stage,' I shouted over at them. 'I'll set it to take us back to the Authority.'

'Then hurry up,' Chloe shouted back, pointing upwards. 'There are more of those things on the way.'

I nodded and worked quickly as the others gathered on the stage. I glanced up, feeling a freezing moment of terror as a black-winged shape dropped towards me.

'Katya!' someone shouted. 'Get up on the stage!'

I hit the activation switch and ran towards the platform. The others shouted to me to move, their faces making it quite evident just what was closing on me from behind. I narrowed my eyes against the growing brightness as I hurled myself up onto the platform.

Nadia gaped, her eyes wide with terror as she pointed right behind me. I didn't think: I threw myself down flat on the platform just as a great black shadow seemed to flow over me . . .

. . . And was gone.

Hands pulled me up, and I staggered upright, gasping for air. We were in the main hangar back on the island, back on Alternate Alpha Zero.

My legs gave out from under me and Randall caught me. 'She's hurt,' he shouted. 'She needs help. Hey! Get someone!'

I heard voices shouting, saw people come running in from outside to stare at us. A technician stood open-mouthed by the control rig, while soldiers shouted to each other.

Nadia helped Randall guide me down the ramp. 'Did you see it?' she exclaimed. 'I swear, Katya, I thought you were a goner for sure. Whoosh! Right overhead! Just one more second . . .'

'Did he make it?' asked Randall, as he helped me to sit on the ramp. 'Borodin. Do you think he got away?'

I shook my head tiredly. 'Maybe. I don't know. I saw him reach out for the Hypersphere, but – there was so much light . . .'

'Where did you send them to, Katya?' asked Nadia. 'You never told me.'

I just looked at her and she nodded slowly. 'Null sequence, right?'

'It seemed the only way to be sure.'

'Maybe he got what he deserved,' she said.

I saw Jerry being led down the ramp by Chloe, where he was greeted by medical orderlies from the compound hospital. Two more came towards me with a stretcher.

'What happens now?' I asked Nadia, as I was lifted onto the stretcher.

'I don't know, Katya. I'm guessing you're stuck with us after all. I don't think they'd welcome you back wherever you call home.'

A tremendous weight seemed to pull my head down against the stretcher. I realized I was still alive, which seemed tremendously unlikely. But then, in an infinite universe, all things, no matter how improbable, may occur at least once . . .

The last thing I saw before they carried me outside and across the compound was Casey, still standing on the stage, staring out past me through the open doors with a faraway expression.

TWENTY-EIGHT

Easter Island Forward Base, Alternate Alpha Zero
Three Weeks Later

The sky above the island was grey: winter was coming, and with it, damp, cool winds. I watched as the excavator's driver worked his twin joysticks so that the blade slid deep into the grassy soil. He drove forward, operating the machine with expert ease. The blade lifted up a crumbling slice of topsoil, widening the hole already dug. The excavator rolled back, its cabin rotating to deposit the soil on a growing mound of dirt.

A line of pegs marked out the dimensions of what would soon be one of several new buildings next to the island's crumbling runway. The blade dipped again, lifting more soil. I found it strangely calming to watch.

I turned at the sound of an approaching jeep. It pulled up next to one of the temporary buildings I had asked to be erected until the permanent facilities were finished. Jerry and Nadia climbed out, and for a moment they watched as soldiers unloaded furniture and lab equipment from a truck, before carrying it inside the nearest building.

Jerry turned to see me as I stepped towards them. 'I'm impressed,' he said with a grin. 'Hardly a month since we got back, and already you've got them running around doing all this for you.' He looked around, taking in the whole building site. 'And it's going to be *big*. No wonder we've hardly seen sight or sound of you.'

I nodded. 'They're giving me everything I asked for. All the equipment, the resources . . . even the staff I wanted.'

'Who are you getting?' asked Nadia.

'The Soviets.' They both looked at me in surprise. 'I couldn't ask for better people,' I explained, 'and most of them are happy to come back here and work with me. Although it's going to take a little explaining about who I really am.'

'And Blodel's . . . okay with them coming back here?' asked Jerry.

I gave him a crooked smile. 'He's anything *but* "okay" with it. Senator Bramnik didn't give him any choice, however.'

I had received confirmation that same morning, delivered to me at my new home on the island by one of Major Howes' men. Nor did the Soviet authorities have much of a say in the matter: they had initially demanded my repatriation, perhaps not quite understanding that, although Russian, I was nonetheless the citizen of a quite *different* Russia from the one they knew. They were soon persuaded to back down once it was explained to them just how much I had to contribute.

'I can't even guess what half this stuff is,' said Nadia, looking around. She nodded towards the half-finished transfer stage, its pillars already towering over the prefabricated buildings surrounding it. 'Is that thing functional?'

I nodded. 'It is. Come on and I'll give you the tour.'

I showed them where the permanent research lab would be built, and the containment facility where exotic forms of matter, essential to powering the transfer stages, would be stored in special magnetic containment devices. Another building would house the computer systems responsible for generating the coordinates of viable alternates.

'Really,' I explained, 'my work is twofold. On the one hand, the Authority want me to find alternates suitable for them to colonize. On the other, their transfer stages are too small and too few in number for a mass global evacuation.'

I stopped next to a building for which the foundations were still being laid. 'Once this is finished,' I explained, 'it'll function as a training centre. First, I will train the Soviets as well as the Authority's own scientists in the construction, maintenance and operation of transfer stages, and they in turn will train others to do the same. Before long, they'll be able to begin the mass construction of new stages in preparation for a staged evacuation.'

'Got some news for you,' said Jerry, once I had finished. 'They finally called off the search for Casey. We found the EV truck he stole about two hundred kilometres south-east of Site A. But he's long gone. We'll never find him.'

'So he *did* go back to Delta Twenty-Five,' I said. I still had nightmares about being chased by invisible monsters through that alternate's forests. 'How can he even survive in such a place for long?'

'You'd be surprised.' Jerry toed a pebble into a pit recently dug by one of the excavators. 'He stole enough supplies to keep him alive for a good long time. He must have packed that truck with water filtration systems, sampling and testing kits, long-life protein packs – you name it. They found some of it cached in a hole in the ground not far from where they discovered the truck. By now the rest of it's squirreled away in all kinds of corners.'

'If he's on Delta Twenty-Five,' I said, 'the only possible reason is that he's looking for another Hypersphere.'

Nadia, standing next to Jerry, pushed her hands in her pockets and shrugged. 'Well, it doesn't matter now. Whether he finds one or not, he's out of our hair for good. Even Blodel's not dumb enough to try and retrieve another Casey.'

A light rain began to fall, and I pulled the collar of my jacket up close around my neck, seeing something in both their faces. 'You didn't both come all the way out here just to tell me this, did you?'

They exchanged a look. 'Well . . . now that you mention it,' said Nadia, 'I've been wanting to apologize for a while. Not just on my behalf – for all of us. You came back here from the Crag looking for our help, and we tried to stop you. It was . . .' She shook her head. 'I don't know what it was, but the more I think about it, the more I think that what we did wasn't right.'

I reached out and touched her forearm. 'We were all trying to save people that mattered to us, Nadia. It's all in the past now.'

The rain started to fall with more intensity and the two of them shared another, conspiratorial look.

'What is it?' I said. 'Is there something else?'

'I have an umbrella back in my jeep,' said Nadia, casting a significant glance at some workers pouring concrete nearby. 'And maybe we can talk in private,' she added, lowering her voice.

I took the hint and followed them back over to their jeep. The truck had departed, and we were alone for the moment.

Nadia lifted a particoloured golf umbrella out of the rear of the vehicle and put it up. 'We thought you ought to know that the Authority are discussing whether or not to send more ex-peditions back to Delta Twenty-Five.'

'For what? To look for Casey? I thought you said . . .'

Jerry shook his head tightly. 'Not Casey.'

I swallowed. 'Please tell me they're not going looking for another Hypersphere.'

'Katya . . .'

I leaned against the side of the jeep, suddenly dizzy, and put a hand over my mouth.

'They're calling it a contingency plan,' said Jerry. 'In case your search for viable alternates doesn't work out.'

'Of all the stupid, ignorant . . . !' I shouted. 'How could they even *consider* such a plan of action? *Contingency plan?* Contingency against what? Do you support this madness?'

'No,' Jerry said heatedly. 'Of course we don't – none of us does.' He meant the Pathfinders, of course. 'And I've been in touch with Senator Bramnik as well. He says it's unlikely to happen, but . . .'

'But there's only so much he can do,' Nadia finished. 'Besides, you won't fail – we all know that. As soon as they realized how much you could do for them, you became the Big Kahuna around here, remember?'

'Or perhaps,' I ranted, 'they'll set a time limit. Give us a viable alternate within six months, they might say, Or we'll go looking for another Hypersphere. Or perhaps they won't wait that long,' I continued, feeling my anger grow. 'Perhaps they'll go looking for a Hypersphere right now! And perhaps if they find one, they'll run their *own* secret research programme to figure out how it works . . . just as a *contingency*, of course.'

I slid down against the side of the jeep until I was sitting on damp soil. I felt drained, exhausted.

'I should have known better,' I continued, clasping my hands over my knees. 'Once people know such a thing exists, they will do everything in their power to acquire it, even if they end up cutting their own throats. And I . . . I will be right back where I was, in the service of madmen.'

Jerry stared towards the horizon, and I had the sense he was choosing his next words carefully. 'We never did tell you *why* we had that secret stage hidden offshore, did we?' he said at last.

I looked between them. 'No, you didn't.'

It hadn't taken long for the Authority to realize that the Pathfinders had access to a stage of their own. There had already been questions after the disappearance of Borodin, myself, and Jerry, but within hours of our appearing on the main stage they had finally managed to locate and confiscate it.

'That stage they built for you,' said Nadia, nodding back the way we had come. 'You said it's operational?'

I nodded.

'Then there's something we'd like to show you,' she continued. 'But we're going to have to use your stage to get to it. And we're also going to have to ask you to keep the coordinates of our destination a secret.'

I stood back up, feeling a faint tingle in my spine. 'What are you up to?'

'You'll see,' said Nadia, then turned and walked towards the stage.

I stared after her, then gave Jerry a questioning look.

'After you,' he said.

I stepped over churned soil and around piles of bricks waiting to be laid as I followed the Pathfinder, knowing that in that same moment I had slipped back into subterfuge and secrets. Perhaps, I thought, it would always be this way.

The control rig for the new stage was unmanned for the moment. Nadia pulled out her own notebook, and read out a sequence of letters and numbers, which I dutifully entered into the machine.

I followed the two Pathfinders onto the stage just as it began to fill with light, and a moment later we were somewhere new.

I looked around, seeing a deserted street. A circle of field-pillars surrounded us. Towering buildings rose up on one side of me, while trees grew behind a rusted iron fence on the other. Beyond the fence I saw what might once have been a park, half-gone to wilderness. Along the street lay the ruined shells of cars, clearly abandoned for decades, while a faded advertisement hoarding read *Welcome to New York*. Here and there, wildflowers and saplings pushed through the broken tarmac.

'Which alternate is this?' I asked.

'Nowhere special,' said Jerry, stepping out of the circle. 'It's a fairly standard post-apocalyptic. We bagged and tagged this reality a long time ago.'

I looked up at the empty windows of the buildings. 'How safe is it?'

'Perfectly safe, as long as it's daylight,' said Nadia. She nodded up at the midday sun, reduced to a silvery disc behind grey clouds. 'That gives us a good seven hours – not that we'll be here that long.'

'You said there was something you wanted to show me?'

'This way,' said Jerry, setting off down the street. I followed after him, Nadia walking by my side. 'But remember it's a secret,' he added over his shoulder.

'At some point soon,' explained Nadia as we walked, 'we – by which I mean, the Pathfinders – are going to become excess to requirements. The moment the Authority can build and program their own stages, they won't need us any more. We've been offered no clear plan for what happens to us when that time comes, and that doesn't strike us as fair. So we decided to make our own preparations in advance.'

We had arrived outside an enormous complex facing out from the park. A sign outside read METROPOLITAN MUSEUM OF ART. The two Pathfinders led me inside, crossing a marbled hall with tall Grecian pillars, the air thick with the scent of animal droppings and decay.

We climbed a flight of stone steps before coming to a halt outside a service door. Jerry produced a key and unlocked it, pushing it inwards.

Increasingly mystified, I followed them up a narrow stairway and into a corridor lined with open doors. They led me through one of the doors, and I found myself inside a high-ceilinged room, its walls stacked with paintings, their canvases scarred by moss and fungus.

The centre of the room, however, was taken up by piles of mostly new-looking equipment. Just at first glance I saw a dozen field-pillars, several control rigs, engine parts, the dismantled chassis of a jeep, desalinization units, crates of medical supplies, and much more.

Nor was the room unoccupied: Yuichi was there, standing next to an open crate, sorting through its contents with one hand while consulting a clipboard held in the other. His face widened into a grin when he saw me.

'Hey,' he said, bounding over to shake my hand. 'You made it.'

'Will someone,' I said, '*please* tell me what the hell is going on?'

'You're here,' said Jerry, 'because we decided we can trust you enough to show you all this.'

'We're just as worried as you are,' said Nadia, 'about the chances of the Authority going looking for any more Hyper-spheres.' She nodded at the stockpiled contraband. 'If that's their contingency plan, then this is ours.'

'Our missions have pretty much dried up since we brought you back,' said Yuichi. 'Everyone's spending so much time hanging out at the bar they've pretty much drunk my entire stock of beer dry.'

'And whenever we're there,' said Jerry, 'we mostly talk about what we're going to do next.' He stepped over to the jeep chassis and patted it. 'We started stealing bits and pieces just after we got back from the Crag.'

'But why?'

'I know we turned away from you when you needed us,' said Nadia, 'and I know we have no right to ask this, but we're hoping we can persuade you to find us some other alternate we can someday make into our own permanent base of operations. Preferably one that's deserted like this is, but safe to occupy.'

'You want me to find you your own alternate universe?' I asked faintly.

'We weren't sure if you'd want to help us or not,' said Jerry, 'otherwise we'd have asked sooner. But when it comes down to it, we can't do a thing without you. Until they found it and took it away, that secret stage we were keeping hidden offshore was our one and only escape route in case things ever got bad between the Pathfinders and the Authority – and now that they know about that stage, things are about as bad as they've ever been between us.'

'But surely whatever alternate I find for the Authority,' I

said, 'would be big enough that you'd have plenty of room to hide from them if you wanted?'

'*Unless* they bring back another of those Hyperspheres,' Nadia reminded me. 'No, we want to find some place far away from whichever alternate you find for them.'

'And I don't want to stop exploring,' said Yuichi. 'Neither do most of the rest of us, frankly, not when we've got the whole of infinity out there waiting to be discovered. Believe me, once you've lived this life long enough, just the one universe starts to feel a little cramped.'

'All we ask,' said Nadia, 'is that at the same time you're hunting for viable coordinates for the Authority, you look for coordinates for us as well.'

I gaped at her. 'You can't be serious.'

'Why not?' asked Jerry. 'You said yourself you're going to train other people how to build and operate the stages, even search for other alternates. Once they have all that, they won't need you any more. You'll be just as surplus to requirements as we already are. So why stick around?'

'You're . . . asking me to come with you?'

'Nobody's going anywhere just yet,' said Yuichi, putting up his hands. 'We still need a lot more in the way of supplies and material if we're going to set up properly on some other alternate. But now you've got yourself that shiny new transfer stage back on the island, it'll be a lot easier to move things around without fear of being caught – if you let us use it.'

'But . . . what if the Authority find out?'

'They won't,' said Nadia, gazing at me levelly, 'unless someone tells them.'

'It's not as simple as just going some place and setting up,' I said. 'You'd be starting from scratch. The difficulties would be enormous – and you'd have only each other to rely on.'

'Believe me,' said Jerry, 'we know. We're hoping that having you along for the ride might help us overcome those difficulties a little sooner. We could really use you, Katya.'

'So?' asked Nadia. 'The question is, are you in?'

Yuichi shook his head. 'She'll need time to think before she—'

'No,' I interrupted. I had the vertiginous sense of teetering on some threshold, much as when I had first escaped the Crag with Tomas. 'I already know. When the time comes, I'll go with you.'

Jerry walked back with me through the deserted streets, while Nadia remained behind to help Yuichi with his work. 'A post-apocalyptic similar to this one is our best option,' he explained as he walked, 'because it has the advantage of a nearly intact infrastructure. Unfortunately, the things that come out at night here make it uninhabitable even in the short term. The best option is to find an alternate that closely resembles this one, but where the threat – the thing that triggered the extinction event – is long gone.'

'And what would I do there?' I asked him.

We came to a halt by the circle of field-pillars. 'Build more stages for us, I guess. Help us to find other alternates to explore.'

'Forgive me if I'm being paranoid,' I said, 'but I can't help but sense there's something else behind all these grand plans. I've become very skilled at working out when somebody isn't being wholly truthful with me.'

He opened his mouth, then closed it again. 'Well . . . maybe there is.'

'I think now would be a good time to tell me,' I said.

He sighed. 'I think the Stage-Builders are still out there somewhere – and that they've been watching us all this time.'

It took me a moment to absorb this information. 'That's not possible,' I said. 'They were wiped out. It was all in the beads—'

'No.' He put a finger up. 'What Lars Ulven *witnessed* was in the beads. Maybe there were other survivors that he didn't know about.'

'Maybe,' I said. 'But anything else is just speculation, surely?'

He shook his head. 'I met one of them. Or at least I'm damn sure I did.'

My jaw dropped. 'You *met* one?'

'There was a Pathfinder named Haden Brooks, long before you and the rest of those Russians ever turned up. He saved my life one time. Just appeared out of nowhere on an alternate he couldn't possibly have known I'd be on, and he did it without using a transfer stage.' He shook his head as if he didn't quite believe his own words. 'Okay, he didn't actually *say* he was one of them, but in the few brief moments I got to talk to him, it seemed to me to be pretty heavily implied. Then he disappeared – and by disappeared, I mean literally vanished into thin air, right before my eyes – and none of us ever saw sight or sound of him again.'

I listened to him continue as he powered up the transfer stage. 'And to me,' he explained, 'that means they're still out there somewhere, or their descendants are, at any rate. Maybe there's only a few of them – or maybe there's a whole lot. Or maybe it's just Haden, all on his own.' He shook his head. 'But I don't think so. I think he was sent to keep an eye on us, and I'd really like to know why.'

'You want me to help you find him, then. That's your grand purpose behind all this?'

He nodded towards the transfer stage, now fully powered up, and I followed him inside the circle of field-pillars. 'Life's more interesting when you've got a goal in mind, don't you think?'

'I couldn't agree more,' I said as the light swallowed us up. For the first time in what felt like a very long time, I realized, I neither knew what the future held, nor did I fear it.

And in the next moment, we were somewhere else.